GODDESS GIRLS

ARTEMIS THE BRAVE

CREATED BY
JOAN HOLUB &
SUZANNE WILLIAMS
ADAPTED BY **DAVID CAMPITI**

ILLUSTRATED BY **MARTINA DI GIOVANNI**
· AT GLASS HOUSE GRAPHICS ·

Aladdin
New York   London   Toronto   Sydney   New Delhi

ALADDIN
AN IMPRINT OF SIMON & SCHUSTER CHILDREN'S PUBLISHING DIVISION
1230 AVENUE OF THE AMERICAS, NEW YORK, NEW YORK 10020
FIRST ALADDIN EDITION FEBRUARY 2023
TEXT COPYRIGHT © 2023 BY JOAN HOLUB AND SUZANNE WILLIAMS
ILLUSTRATIONS COPYRIGHT © 2023 BY GLASS HOUSE GRAPHICS
COVER ILLUSTRATION BY MANUEL PREITANO
LAYOUTS BY DAVE SANTANA
INTERIORS ILLUSTRATED BY MARTINA DI GIOVANNI AT GLASS HOUSE GRAPHICS.
ASSISTANTS ON PENCILS ONOFRIO ORLANDO AND MARTINA RITANO.
COLORS BY NATALIYA TORRETTA, VANESSA COSTANZO, GAETANO INGALISO, FRANCESCA INGRASSIA,
CHIARA SPINOSO AND MARZIA MIGLIORI.
SUPERVISION BY SALVATORE DI MARCO/GRAFIMATED CARTOON.
LETTERING AND ADDITIONAL ART BY MEMY MEDIA.
ALL RIGHTS RESERVED, INCLUDING THE RIGHT OF REPRODUCTION IN WHOLE OR IN PART IN ANY
FORM. ALADDIN AND RELATED LOGO ARE REGISTERED TRADEMARKS OF SIMON & SCHUSTER, INC.
FOR INFORMATION ABOUT SPECIAL DISCOUNTS FOR BULK PURCHASES, PLEASE CONTACT
SIMON & SCHUSTER SPECIAL SALES AT 1-866-506-1949 OR BUSINESS@SIMONANDSCHUSTER.COM.
THE SIMON & SCHUSTER SPEAKERS BUREAU CAN BRING AUTHORS TO YOUR LIVE EVENT. FOR MORE
INFORMATION OR TO BOOK AN EVENT CONTACT THE SIMON & SCHUSTER SPEAKERS BUREAU AT
1-866-248-3049 OR VISIT OUR WEBSITE AT WWW.SIMONSPEAKERS.COM.
THE ILLUSTRATIONS FOR THIS BOOK WERE RENDERED DIGITALLY.
THE TEXT THIS BOOK WAS SET IN ANIME ACE 2.0 AND STEINANTIK.
MANUFACTURED IN CHINA 1022 SCP
2 4 6 8 10 9 7 5 3 1
THIS BOOK HAS BEEN CATALOGED BY THE LIBRARY OF CONGRESS.
ISBN 9781534473966 (HC)
ISBN 9781534473959 (PBK)
ISBN 9781534473973 (EBOOK)

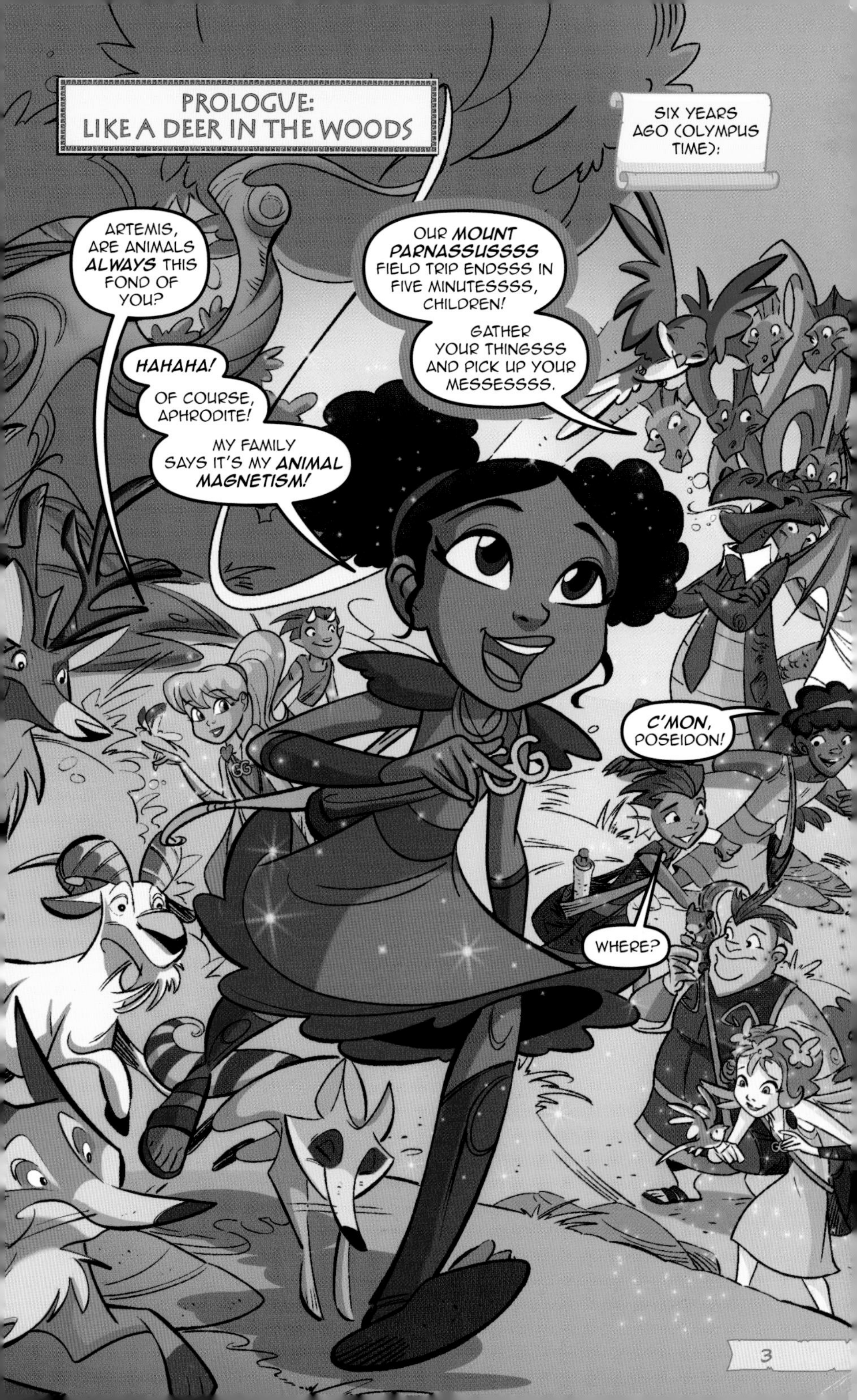
PROLOGUE:
LIKE A DEER IN THE WOODS
SIX YEARS AGO (OLYMPUS TIME):
ARTEMIS, ARE ANIMALS ALWAYS THIS FOND OF YOU?
OUR MOUNT PARNASSUSSSS FIELD TRIP ENDSSS IN FIVE MINUTESSSS, CHILDREN!
GATHER YOUR THINGSSS AND PICK UP YOUR MESSESSSS.
HAHAHA!
OF COURSE, APHRODITE!
MY FAMILY SAYS IT'S MY ANIMAL MAGNETISM!
C'MON, POSEIDON!
WHERE?

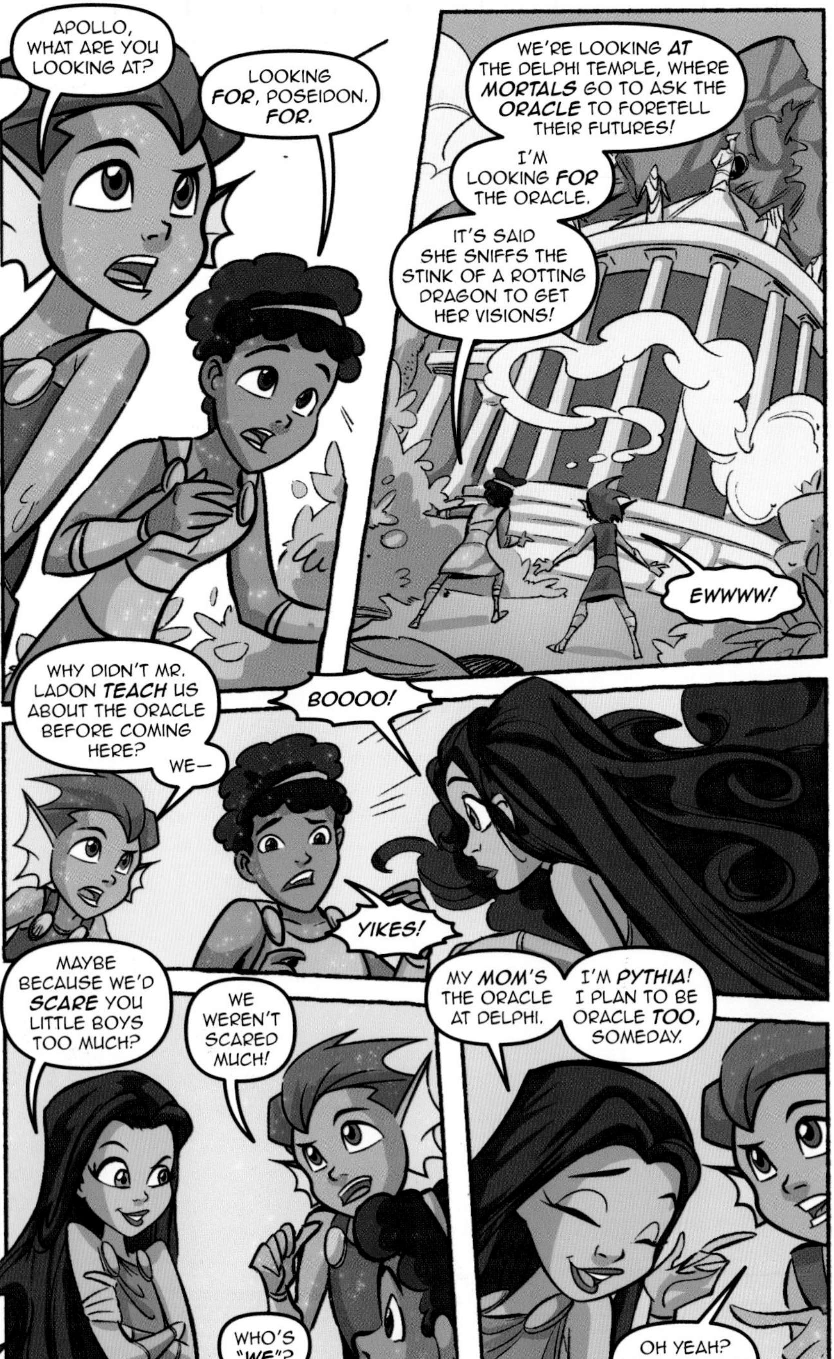
APOLLO, WHAT ARE YOU LOOKING AT?
LOOKING FOR, POSEIDON. FOR.
WE'RE LOOKING AT THE DELPHI TEMPLE, WHERE MORTALS GO TO ASK THE ORACLE TO FORETELL THEIR FUTURES!
I'M LOOKING FOR THE ORACLE.
IT'S SAID SHE SNIFFS THE STINK OF A ROTTING DRAGON TO GET HER VISIONS!
EWWWW!
WHY DIDN'T MR. LADON TEACH US ABOUT THE ORACLE BEFORE COMING HERE?
WE—
BOOOO!
YIKES!
MAYBE BECAUSE WE'D SCARE YOU LITTLE BOYS TOO MUCH?
WE WEREN'T SCARED MUCH!
WHO'S "WE"?
MY MOM'S THE ORACLE AT DELPHI.
I'M PYTHIA! I PLAN TO BE ORACLE TOO, SOMEDAY.
OH YEAH? YOU GOT ANY POWERS?

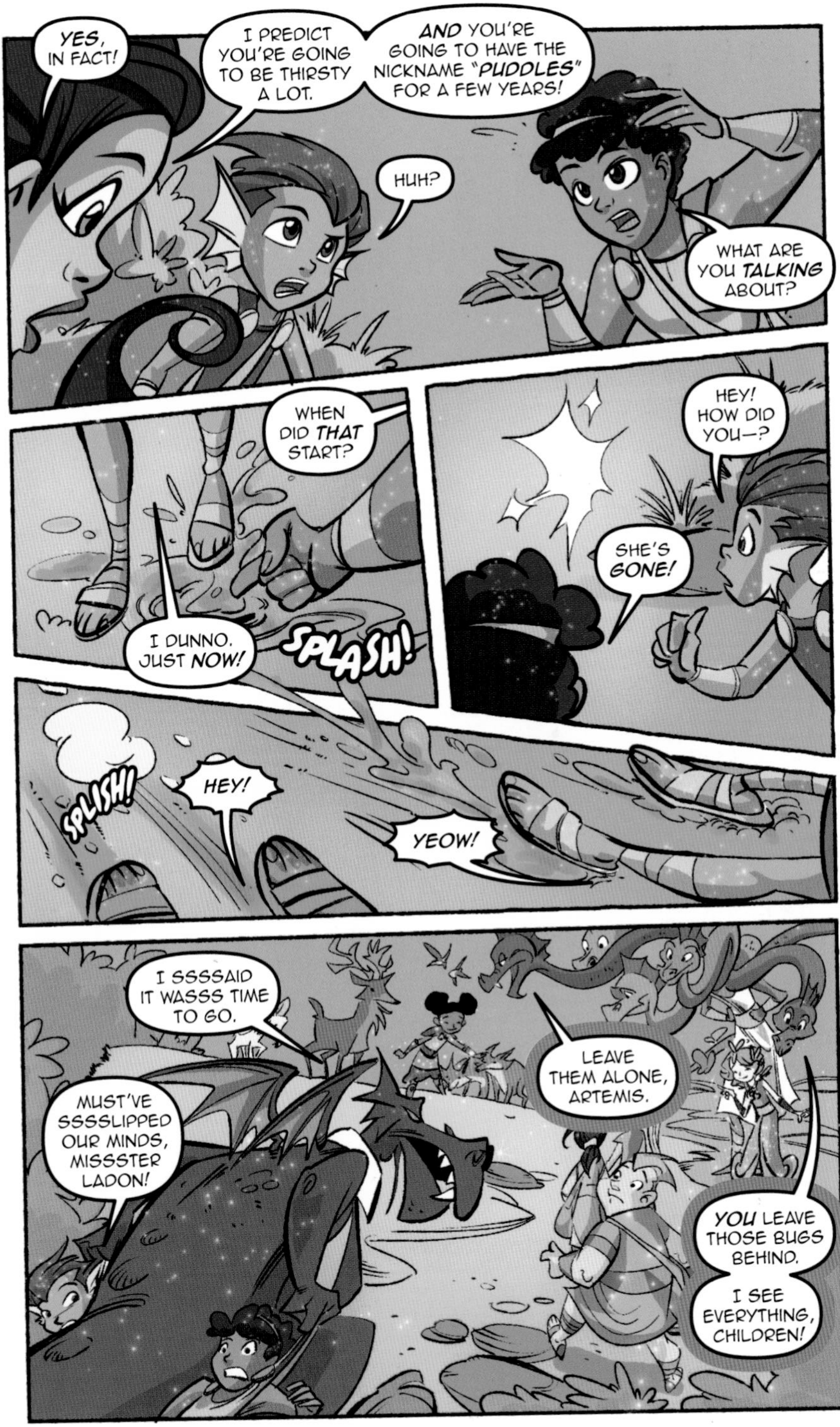
YES, IN FACT!
I PREDICT YOU'RE GOING TO BE THIRSTY A LOT.
AND YOU'RE GOING TO HAVE THE NICKNAME "PUDDLES" FOR A FEW YEARS!
HUH?
WHAT ARE YOU TALKING ABOUT?
WHEN DID THAT START?
I DUNNO. JUST NOW!
SPLASH!
HEY! HOW DID YOU—?
SHE'S GONE!
SPLISH!
HEY!
YEOW!
I SSSSAID IT WASSS TIME TO GO.
MUST'VE SSSSLIPPED OUR MINDS, MISSSTER LADON!
LEAVE THEM ALONE, ARTEMIS.
YOU LEAVE THOSE BUGS BEHIND.
I SEE EVERYTHING, CHILDREN!

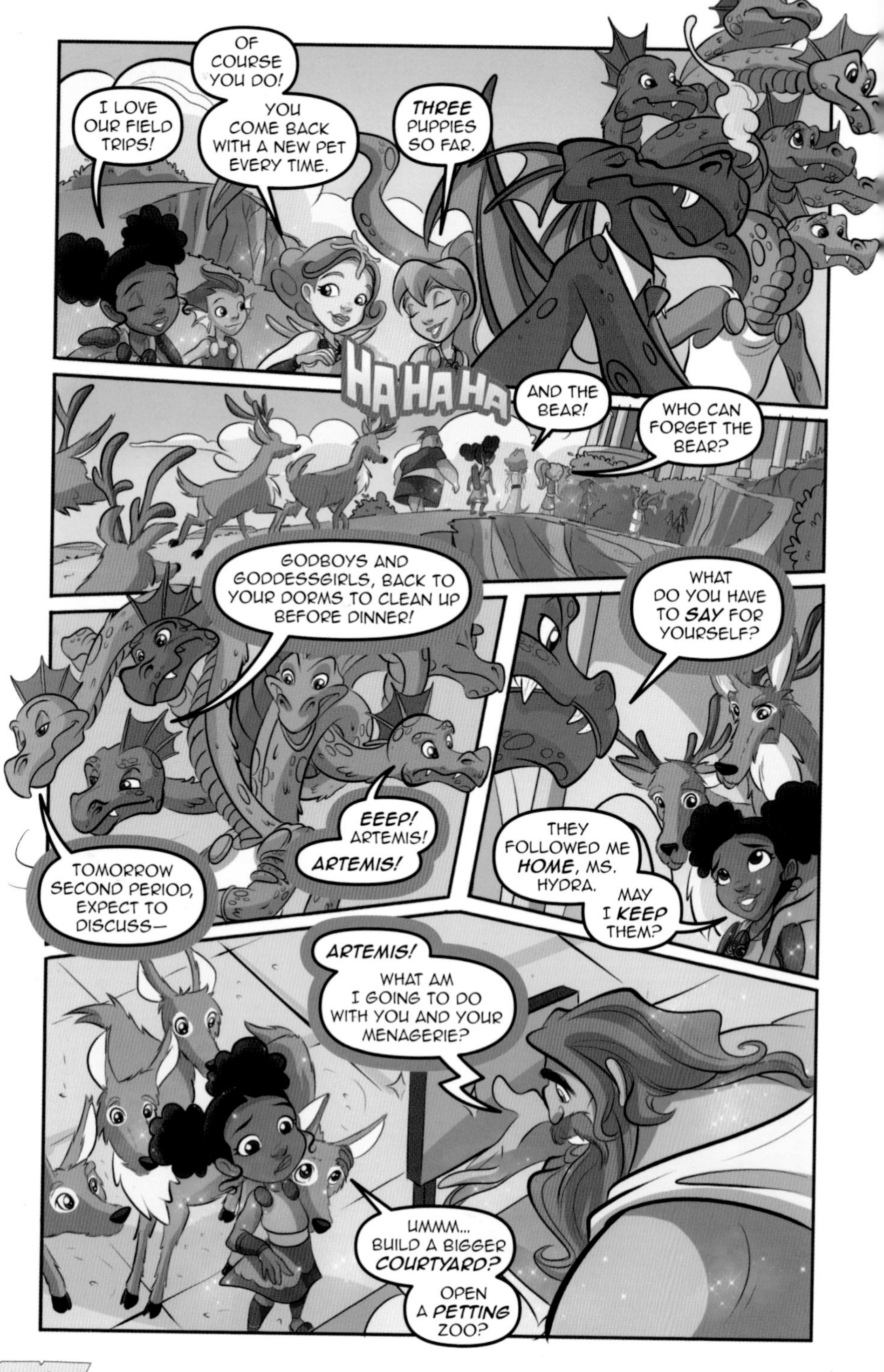
I LOVE OUR FIELD TRIPS!
OF COURSE YOU DO!
YOU COME BACK WITH A NEW PET EVERY TIME.
THREE PUPPIES SO FAR.
HA HA HA
AND THE BEAR!
WHO CAN FORGET THE BEAR?
GODBOYS AND GODDESSGIRLS, BACK TO YOUR DORMS TO CLEAN UP BEFORE DINNER!
EEEP! ARTEMIS! ARTEMIS!
TOMORROW SECOND PERIOD, EXPECT TO DISCUSS—
WHAT DO YOU HAVE TO SAY FOR YOURSELF?
THEY FOLLOWED ME HOME, MS. HYDRA.
MAY I KEEP THEM?
ARTEMIS!
WHAT AM I GOING TO DO WITH YOU AND YOUR MENAGERIE?
UMMM... BUILD A BIGGER COURTYARD?
OPEN A PETTING ZOO?

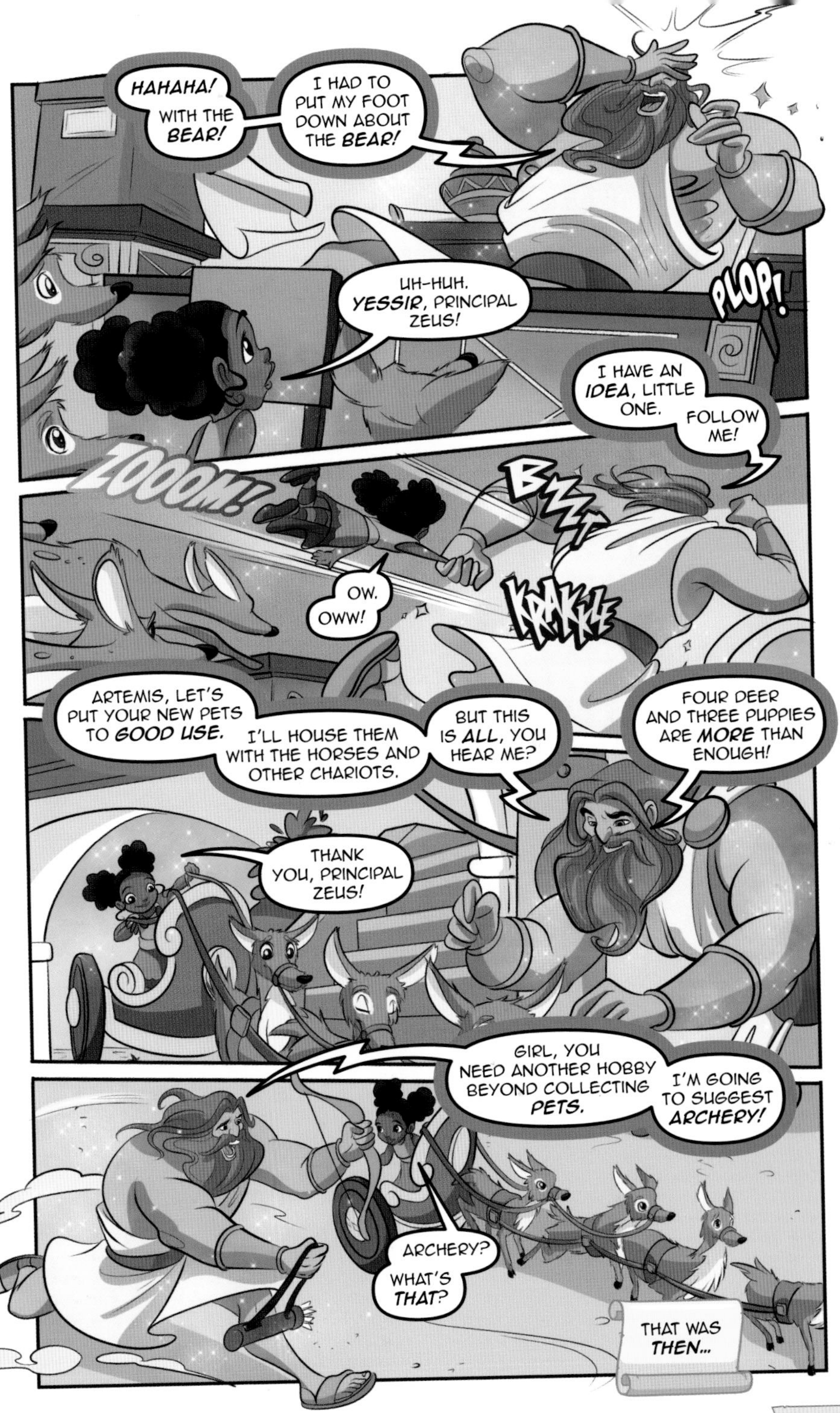
HAHAHA! WITH THE BEAR!
I HAD TO PUT MY FOOT DOWN ABOUT THE BEAR!
UH-HUH. YESSIR, PRINCIPAL ZEUS!
PLOP!
I HAVE AN IDEA, LITTLE ONE.
FOLLOW ME!
ZOOOM!
BZZT
OW. OWW!
KRAKKLE
ARTEMIS, LET'S PUT YOUR NEW PETS TO GOOD USE.
I'LL HOUSE THEM WITH THE HORSES AND OTHER CHARIOTS.
BUT THIS IS ALL, YOU HEAR ME?
FOUR DEER AND THREE PUPPIES ARE MORE THAN ENOUGH!
THANK YOU, PRINCIPAL ZEUS!
GIRL, YOU NEED ANOTHER HOBBY BEYOND COLLECTING PETS.
I'M GOING TO SUGGEST ARCHERY!
ARCHERY? WHAT'S THAT?
THAT WAS THEN...

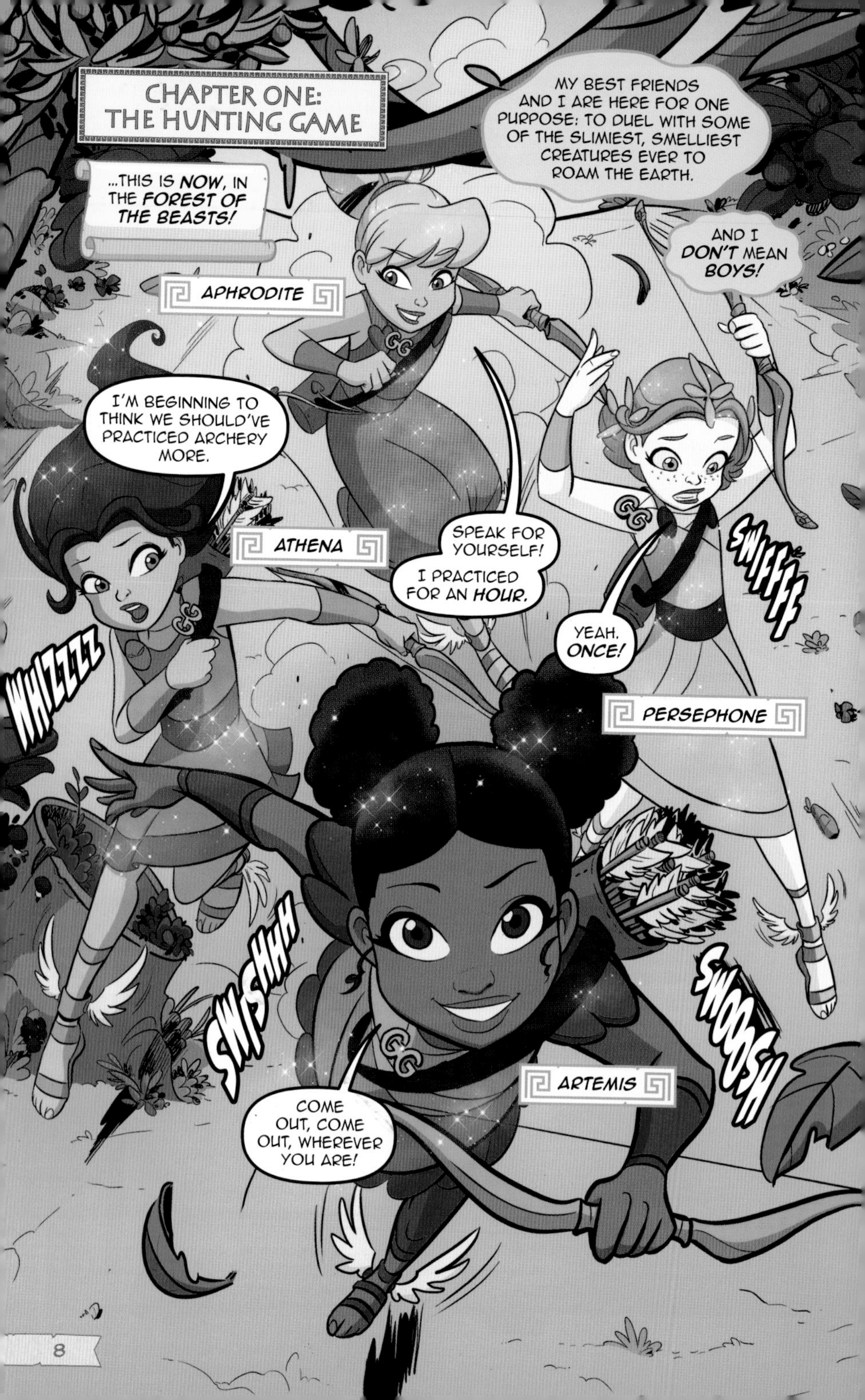
CHAPTER ONE: THE HUNTING GAME
...THIS IS NOW, IN THE FOREST OF THE BEASTS!
MY BEST FRIENDS AND I ARE HERE FOR ONE PURPOSE: TO DUEL WITH SOME OF THE SLIMIEST, SMELLIEST CREATURES EVER TO ROAM THE EARTH.
AND I DON'T MEAN BOYS!
APHRODITE
I'M BEGINNING TO THINK WE SHOULD'VE PRACTICED ARCHERY MORE.
ATHENA
SPEAK FOR YOURSELF!
I PRACTICED FOR AN HOUR.
YEAH. ONCE!
SWIFFFF
WHIZZZZZ
PERSEPHONE
SWISHHH
SWOOOSH
ARTEMIS
COME OUT, COME OUT, WHEREVER YOU ARE!

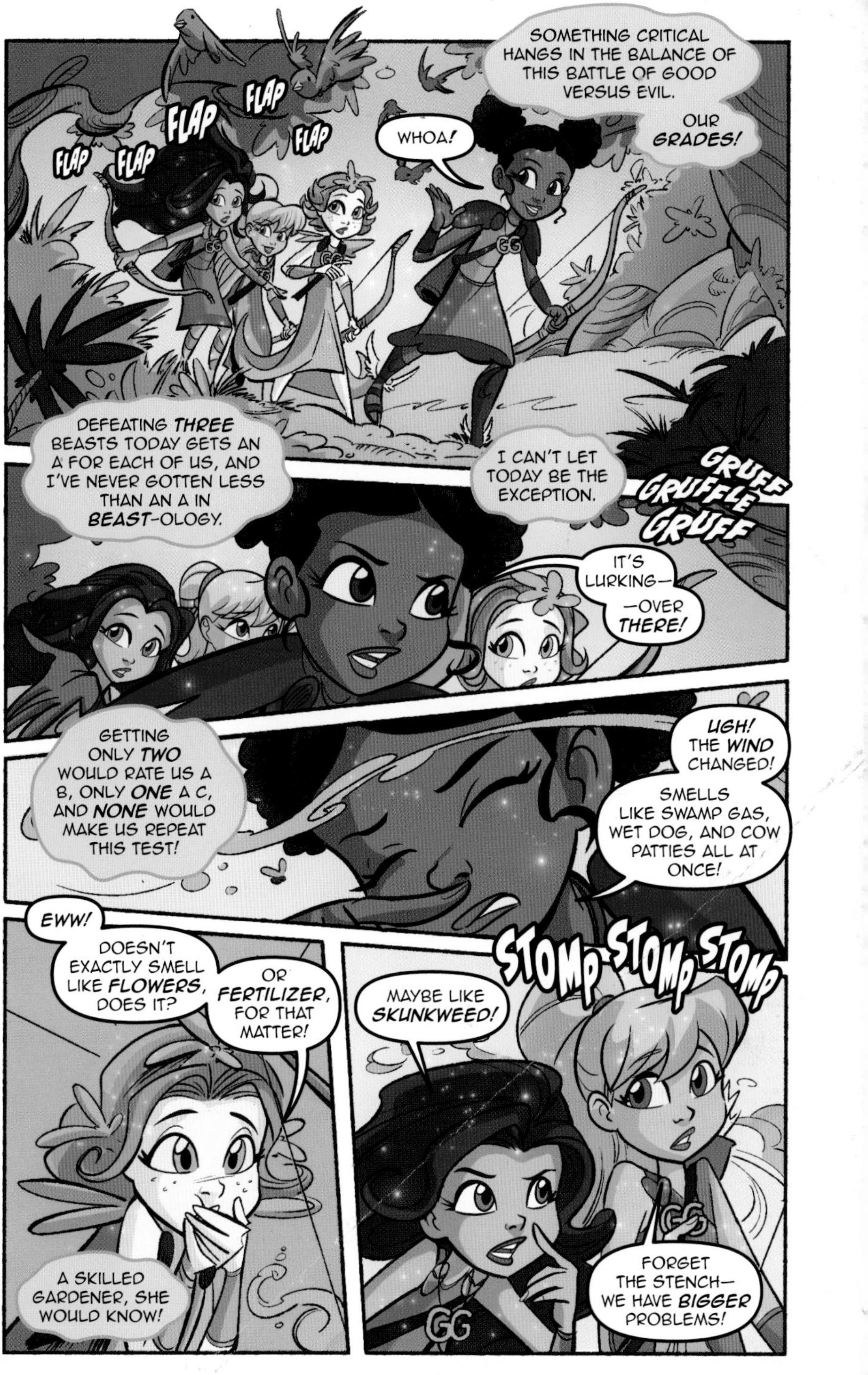
FLAP
FLAP
FLAP
FLAP
FLAP
SOMETHING CRITICAL HANGS IN THE BALANCE OF THIS BATTLE OF GOOD VERSUS EVIL.
WHOA!
OUR GRADES!
DEFEATING THREE BEASTS TODAY GETS AN A FOR EACH OF US, AND I'VE NEVER GOTTEN LESS THAN AN A IN BEAST-OLOGY.
I CAN'T LET TODAY BE THE EXCEPTION.
GRUFF GRUFFLE GRUFF
IT'S LURKING—
—OVER THERE!
GETTING ONLY TWO WOULD RATE US A B, ONLY ONE A C, AND NONE WOULD MAKE US REPEAT THIS TEST!
UGH! THE WIND CHANGED!
SMELLS LIKE SWAMP GAS, WET DOG, AND COW PATTIES ALL AT ONCE!
EWW!
DOESN'T EXACTLY SMELL LIKE FLOWERS, DOES IT?
OR FERTILIZER, FOR THAT MATTER!
A SKILLED GARDENER, SHE WOULD KNOW!
STOMP STOMP STOMP
MAYBE LIKE SKUNKWEED!
FORGET THE STENCH— WE HAVE BIGGER PROBLEMS!

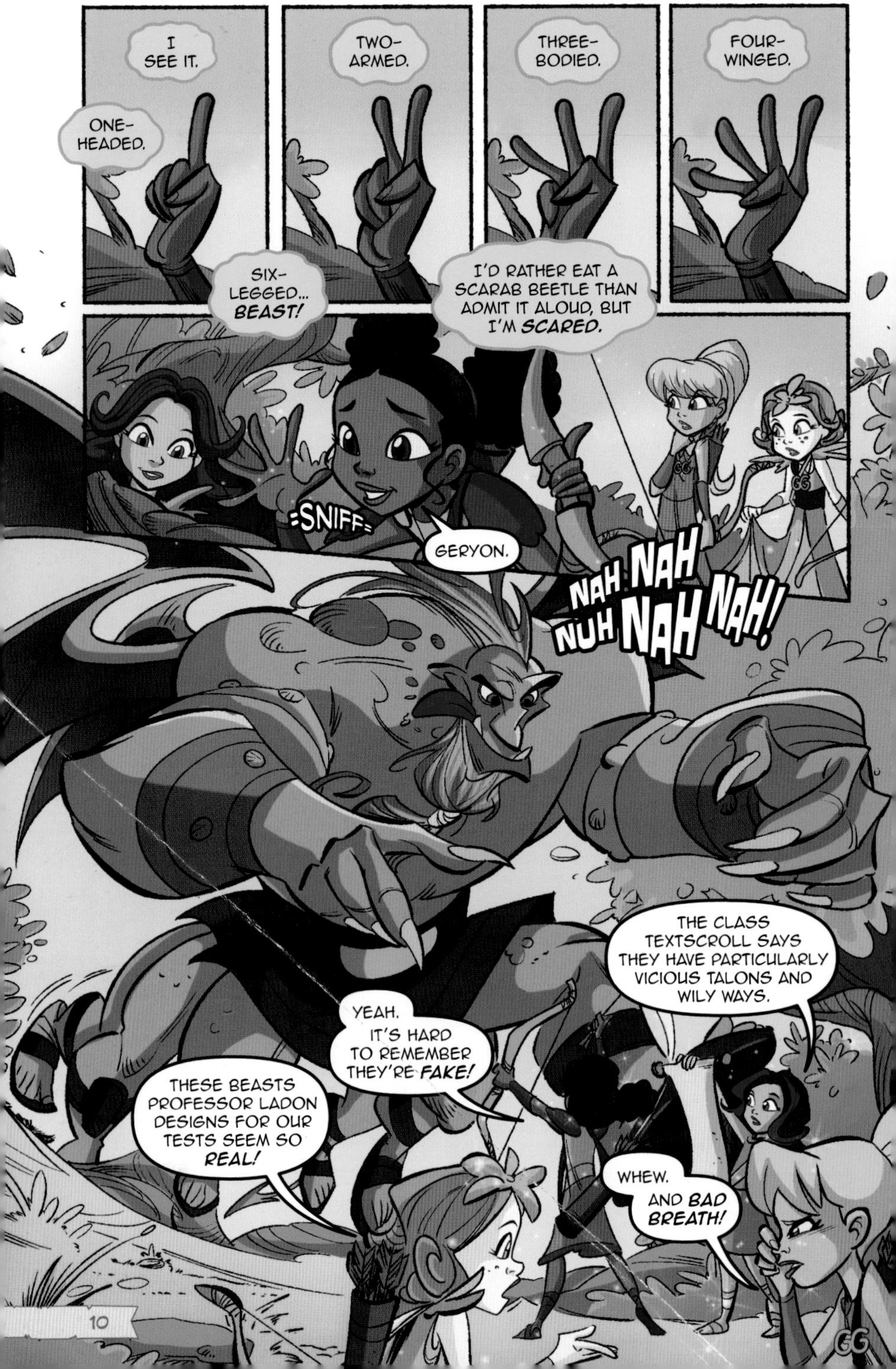
I SEE IT.
ONE-HEADED.
TWO-ARMED.
THREE-BODIED.
FOUR-WINGED.
SIX-LEGGED... **BEAST!**
I'D RATHER EAT A SCARAB BEETLE THAN ADMIT IT ALOUD, BUT I'M **SCARED.**
=SNIFF=
GERYON.
NAH NAH NUH NAH NAH!
THE CLASS TEXTSCROLL SAYS THEY HAVE PARTICULARLY VICIOUS TALONS AND WILY WAYS.
YEAH.
IT'S HARD TO REMEMBER THEY'RE **FAKE!**
THESE BEASTS PROFESSOR LADON DESIGNS FOR OUR TESTS SEEM SO **REAL!**
WHEW.
AND **BAD BREATH!**
GG

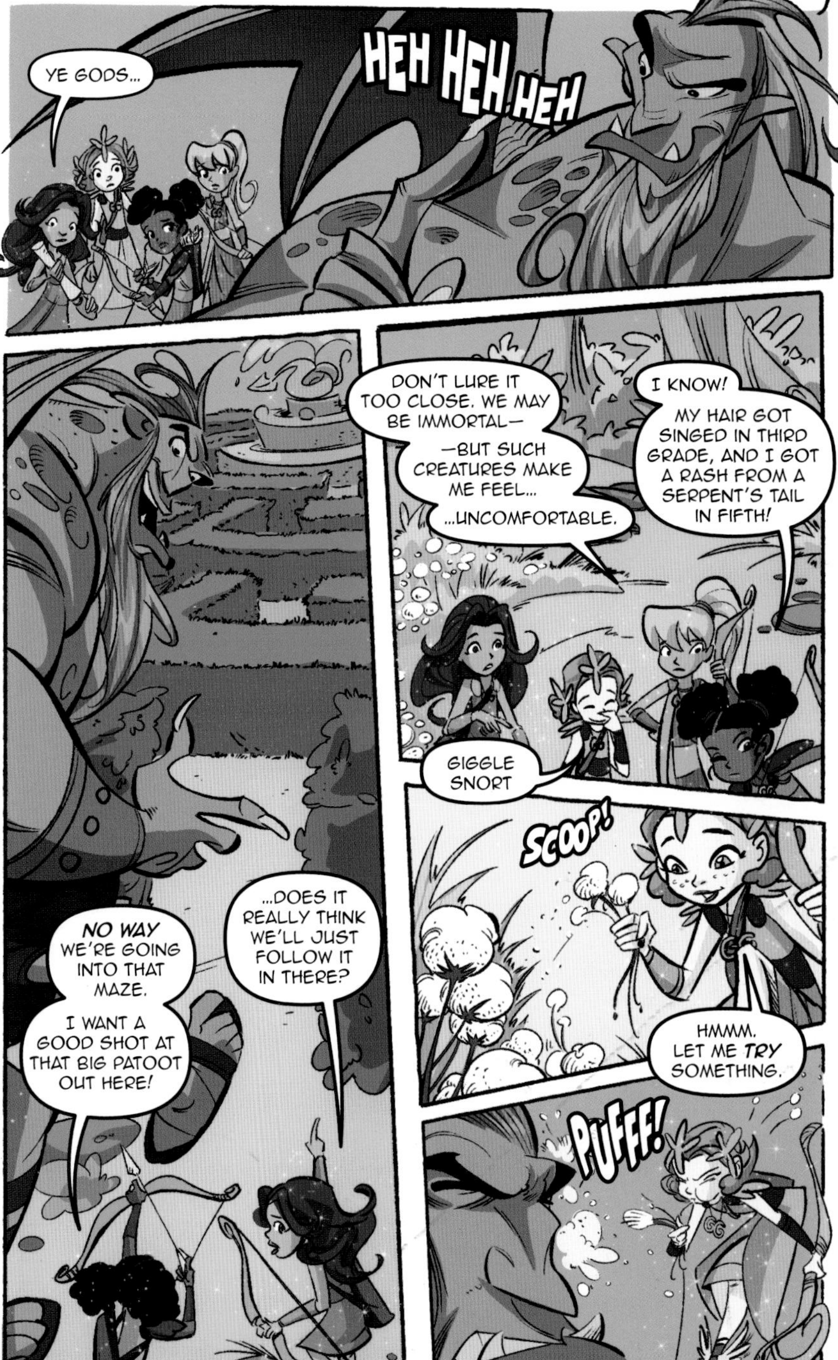
YE GODS...
HEH HEH HEH
NO WAY WE'RE GOING INTO THAT MAZE.
I WANT A GOOD SHOT AT THAT BIG PATOOT OUT HERE!
...DOES IT REALLY THINK WE'LL JUST FOLLOW IT IN THERE?
DON'T LURE IT TOO CLOSE. WE MAY BE IMMORTAL—
—BUT SUCH CREATURES MAKE ME FEEL...
...UNCOMFORTABLE.
I KNOW!
MY HAIR GOT SINGED IN THIRD GRADE, AND I GOT A RASH FROM A SERPENT'S TAIL IN FIFTH!
GIGGLE SNORT
SCOOP!
HMMM. LET ME TRY SOMETHING.
PUFFF!

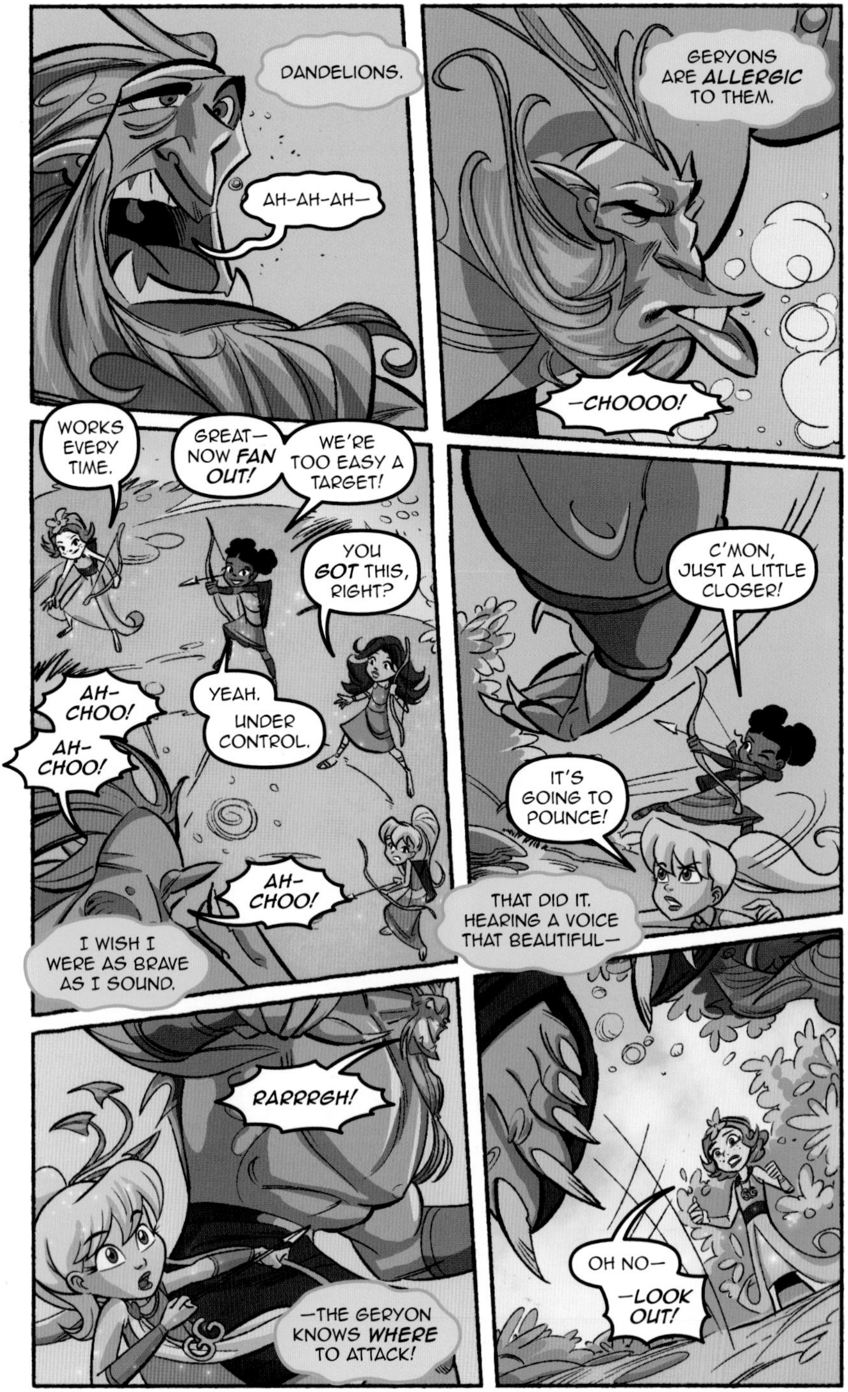
DANDELIONS.
AH-AH-AH—
GERYONS ARE **ALLERGIC** TO THEM.
—CHOOOO!
WORKS EVERY TIME.
GREAT— NOW **FAN OUT!**
WE'RE TOO EASY A TARGET!
YOU **GOT** THIS, RIGHT?
YEAH.
UNDER CONTROL.
AH-CHOO!
AH-CHOO!
AH-CHOO!
I WISH I WERE AS BRAVE AS I SOUND.
C'MON, JUST A LITTLE CLOSER!
IT'S GOING TO POUNCE!
THAT DID IT. HEARING A VOICE THAT BEAUTIFUL—
RARRRGH!
—THE GERYON KNOWS **WHERE** TO ATTACK!
OH NO—
—**LOOK OUT!**

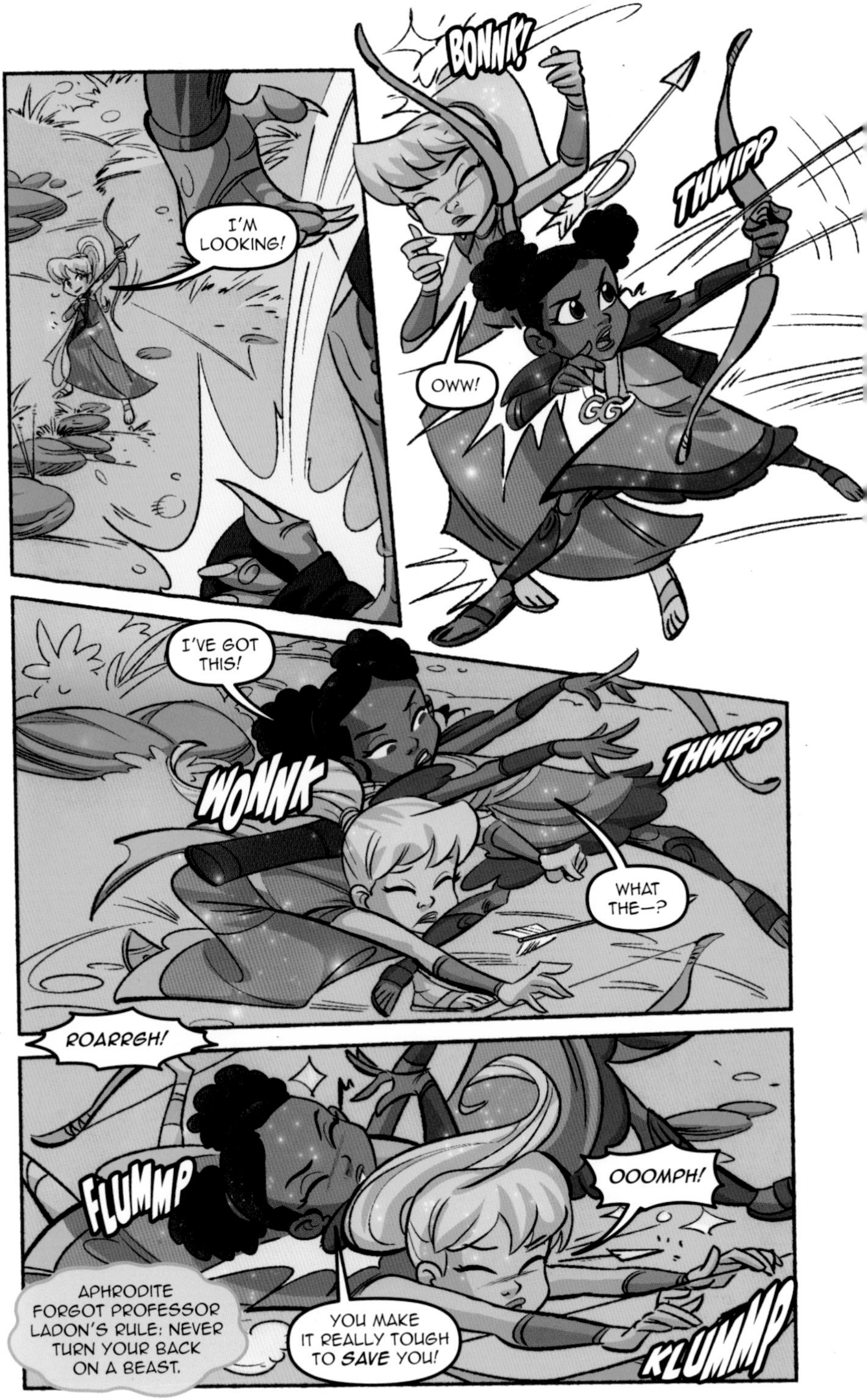
BONNK!
I'M LOOKING!
THWIPP
OWW!
I'VE GOT THIS!
WONNK
THWIPP
WHAT THE—?
ROARRGH!
FLUMMP
OOOMPH!
APHRODITE FORGOT PROFESSOR LADON'S RULE: NEVER TURN YOUR BACK ON A BEAST.
YOU MAKE IT REALLY TOUGH TO *SAVE* YOU!
KLUMMP

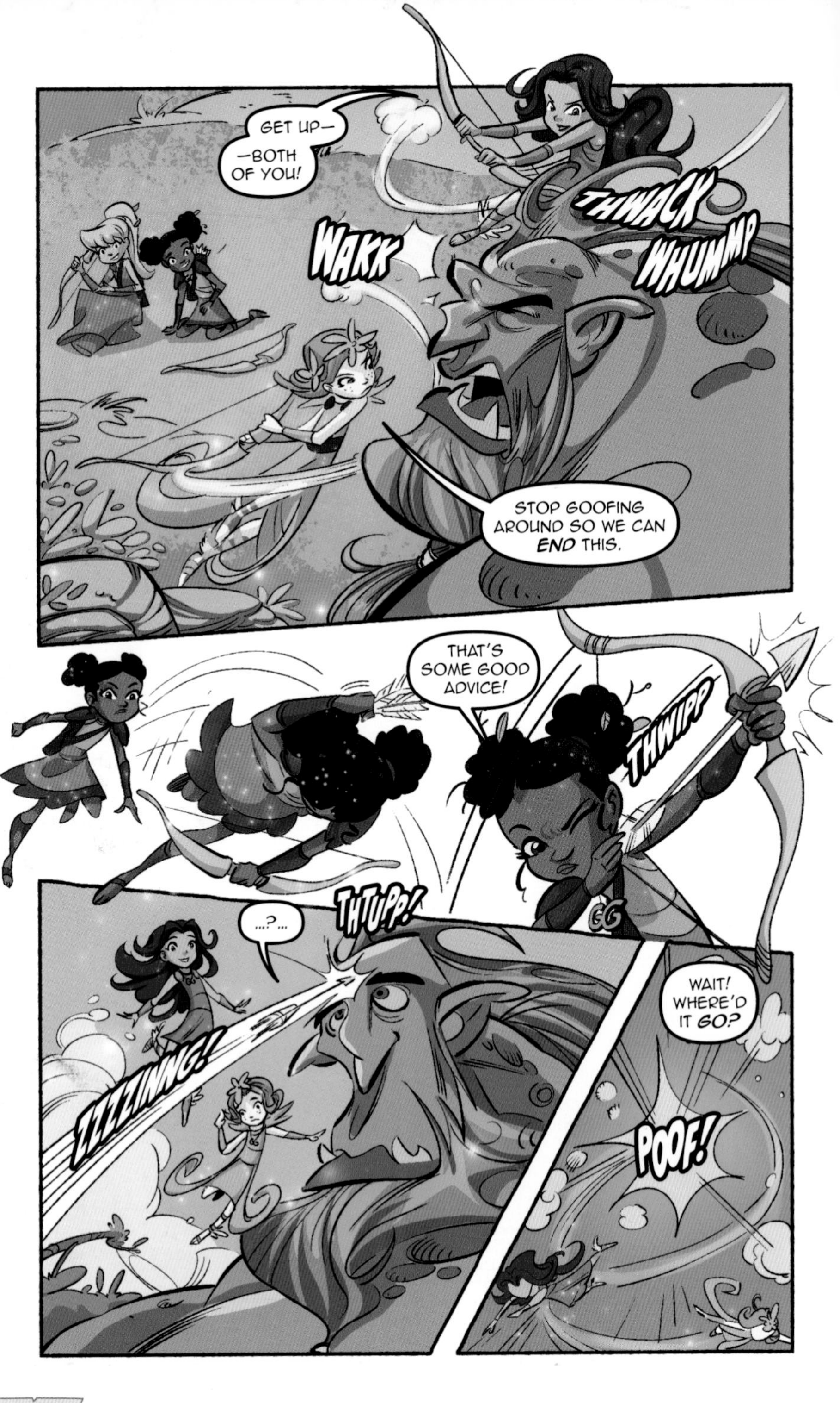
GET UP—
—BOTH OF YOU!
THWACK
WAKK
WHUMMP
STOP GOOFING AROUND SO WE CAN END THIS.
THAT'S SOME GOOD ADVICE!
THWIPP
THTUPP!
...?...
ZZZZING!
WAIT! WHERE'D IT GO?
POOF!

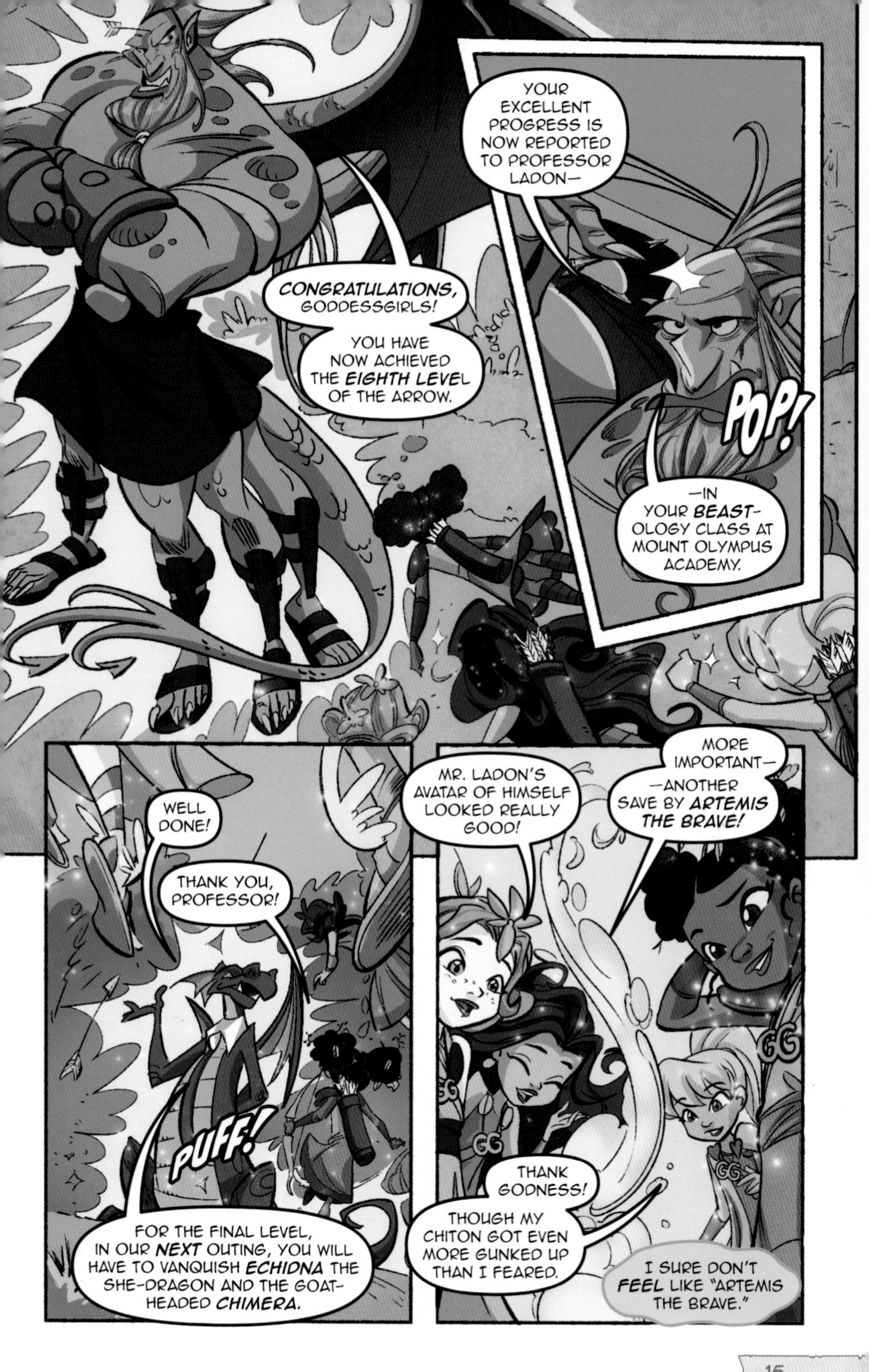
CONGRATULATIONS, GODDESSGIRLS!
YOU HAVE NOW ACHIEVED THE EIGHTH LEVEL OF THE ARROW.
YOUR EXCELLENT PROGRESS IS NOW REPORTED TO PROFESSOR LADON—
POP!
—IN YOUR BEAST-OLOGY CLASS AT MOUNT OLYMPUS ACADEMY.
WELL DONE!
THANK YOU, PROFESSOR!
PUFF!
FOR THE FINAL LEVEL, IN OUR NEXT OUTING, YOU WILL HAVE TO VANQUISH ECHIDNA THE SHE-DRAGON AND THE GOAT-HEADED CHIMERA.
MR. LADON'S AVATAR OF HIMSELF LOOKED REALLY GOOD!
MORE IMPORTANT—
—ANOTHER SAVE BY ARTEMIS THE BRAVE!
THANK GODNESS!
THOUGH MY CHITON GOT EVEN MORE GUNKED UP THAN I FEARED.
I SURE DON'T FEEL LIKE "ARTEMIS THE BRAVE."

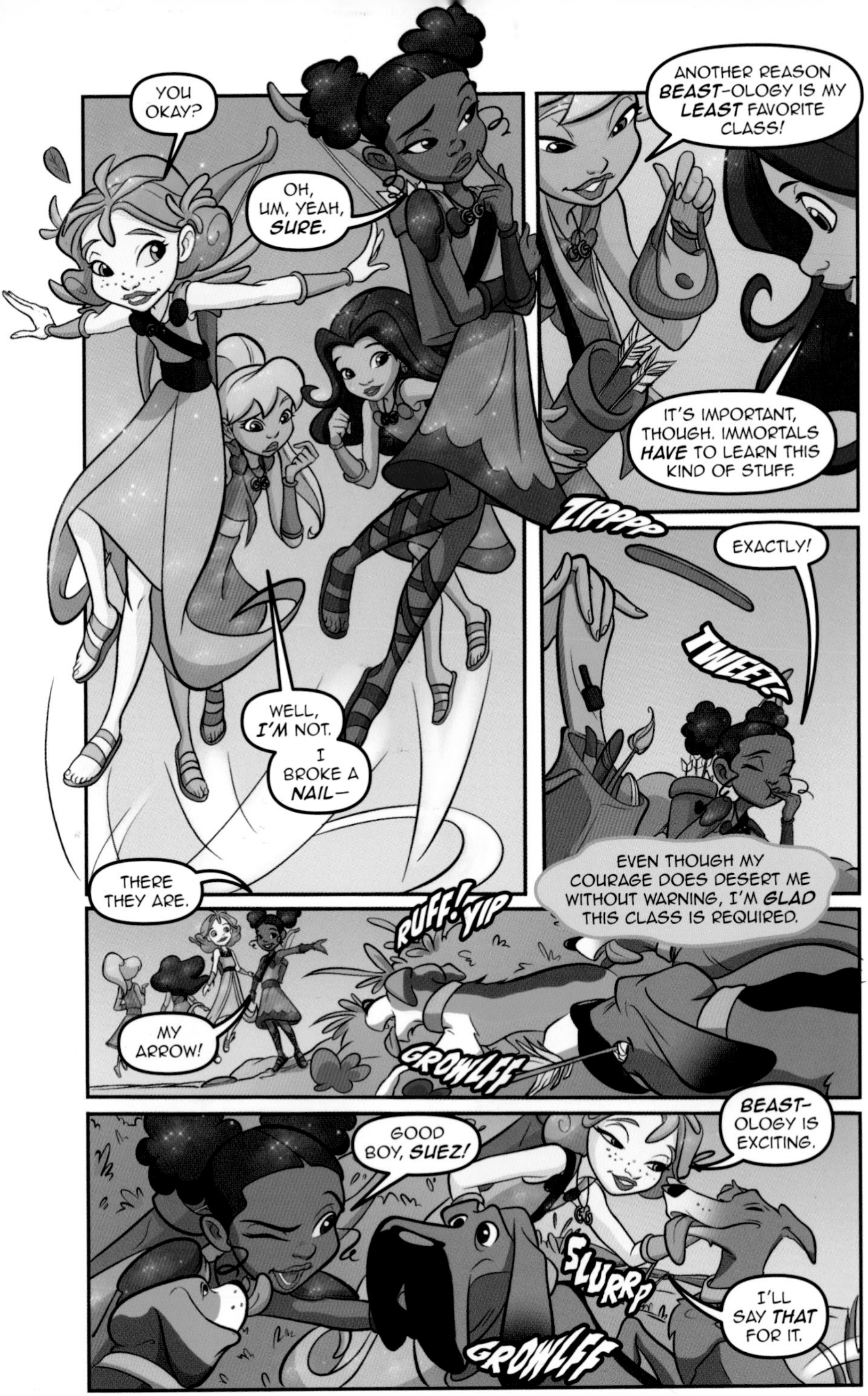
YOU OKAY?
OH, UM, YEAH, SURE.
WELL, I'M NOT.
I BROKE A NAIL—
ANOTHER REASON BEAST-OLOGY IS MY LEAST FAVORITE CLASS!
IT'S IMPORTANT, THOUGH. IMMORTALS HAVE TO LEARN THIS KIND OF STUFF.
ZIPPPP
EXACTLY!
TWEET!
EVEN THOUGH MY COURAGE DOES DESERT ME WITHOUT WARNING, I'M GLAD THIS CLASS IS REQUIRED.
THERE THEY ARE.
RUFF! YIP
MY ARROW!
GROWLFF
GOOD BOY, SUEZ!
BEAST-OLOGY IS EXCITING.
SLURRP
I'LL SAY THAT FOR IT.
GROWLFF

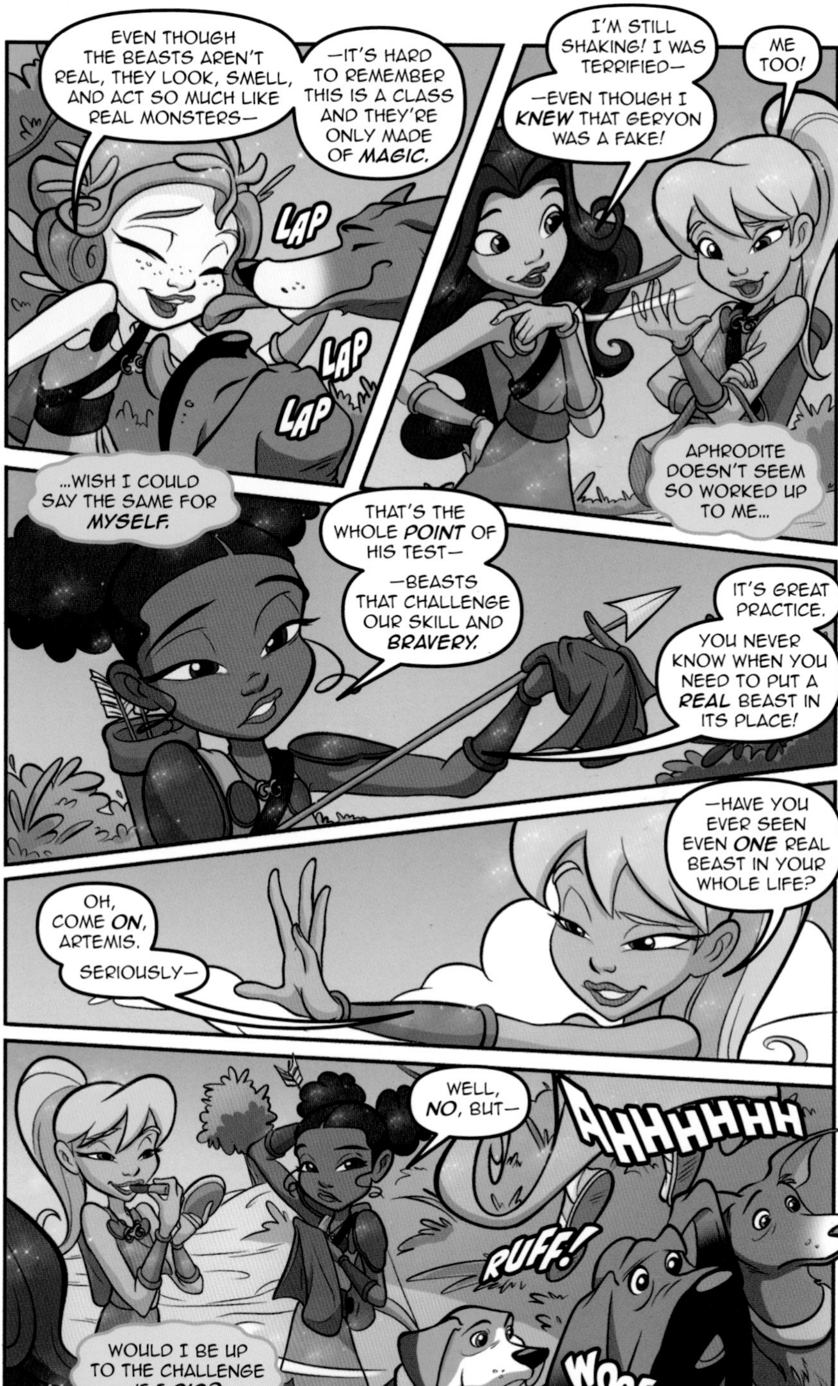
EVEN THOUGH THE BEASTS AREN'T REAL, THEY LOOK, SMELL, AND ACT SO MUCH LIKE REAL MONSTERS—
—IT'S HARD TO REMEMBER THIS IS A CLASS AND THEY'RE ONLY MADE OF MAGIC.
LAP
LAP
LAP
I'M STILL SHAKING! I WAS TERRIFIED—
—EVEN THOUGH I KNEW THAT GERYON WAS A FAKE!
ME TOO!
APHRODITE DOESN'T SEEM SO WORKED UP TO ME...
...WISH I COULD SAY THE SAME FOR MYSELF.
THAT'S THE WHOLE POINT OF HIS TEST—
—BEASTS THAT CHALLENGE OUR SKILL AND BRAVERY.
IT'S GREAT PRACTICE.
YOU NEVER KNOW WHEN YOU NEED TO PUT A REAL BEAST IN ITS PLACE!
OH, COME ON, ARTEMIS.
SERIOUSLY—
—HAVE YOU EVER SEEN EVEN ONE REAL BEAST IN YOUR WHOLE LIFE?
WELL, NO, BUT—
AHHHHHH
RUFF!
WOULD I BE UP TO THE CHALLENGE IF I DID?
WOOF

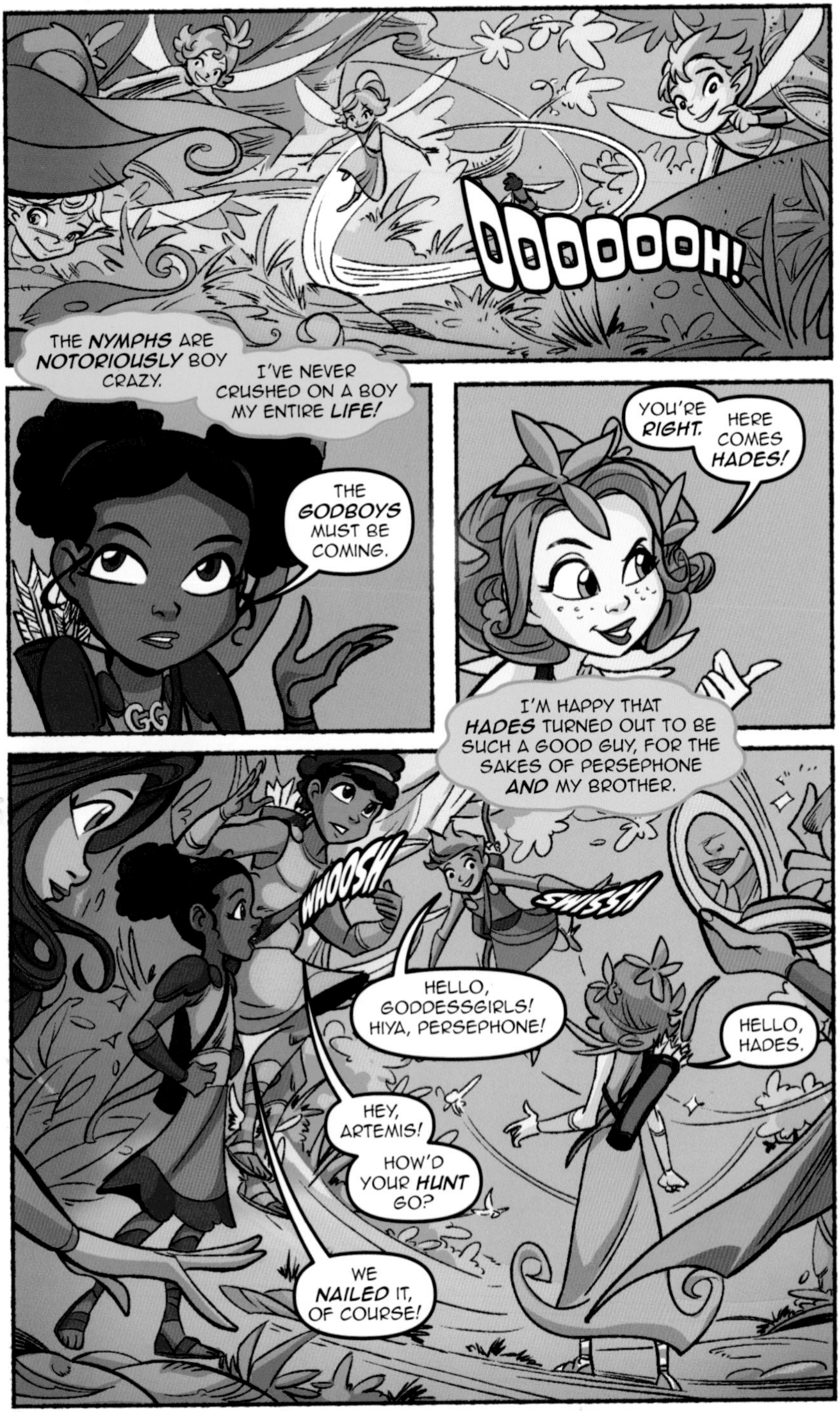
OOOOOOOH!
THE NYMPHS ARE NOTORIOUSLY BOY CRAZY.
I'VE NEVER CRUSHED ON A BOY MY ENTIRE LIFE!
THE GODBOYS MUST BE COMING.
YOU'RE RIGHT.
HERE COMES HADES!
I'M HAPPY THAT HADES TURNED OUT TO BE SUCH A GOOD GUY, FOR THE SAKES OF PERSEPHONE AND MY BROTHER.
WHOOSH
SWISSH
HELLO, GODDESSGIRLS! HIYA, PERSEPHONE!
HELLO, HADES.
HEY, ARTEMIS!
HOW'D YOUR HUNT GO?
WE NAILED IT, OF COURSE!

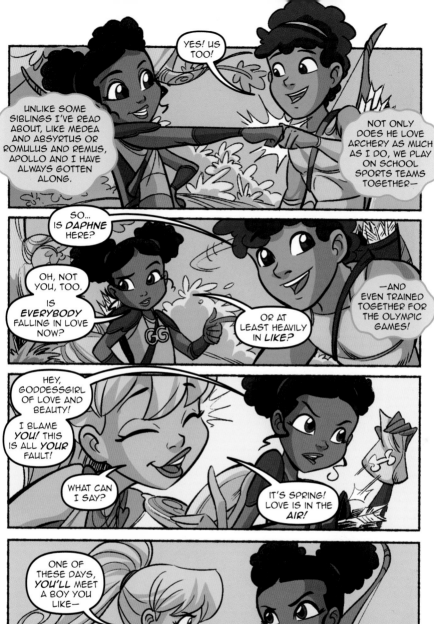

YES! US TOO!

UNLIKE SOME SIBLINGS I'VE READ ABOUT, LIKE MEDEA AND ABSYRTUS OR ROMULUS AND REMUS, APOLLO AND I HAVE ALWAYS GOTTEN ALONG.

NOT ONLY DOES HE LOVE ARCHERY AS MUCH AS I DO, WE PLAY ON SCHOOL SPORTS TEAMS TOGETHER—

SO... IS *DAPHNE* HERE?

OH, NOT YOU, TOO.

IS *EVERYBODY* FALLING IN LOVE NOW?

OR AT LEAST HEAVILY IN *LIKE*?

—AND EVEN TRAINED TOGETHER FOR THE OLYMPIC GAMES!

HEY, GODDESSGIRL OF LOVE AND BEAUTY!

I BLAME *YOU!* THIS IS ALL *YOUR* FAULT!

WHAT CAN I SAY?

IT'S SPRING! LOVE IS IN THE *AIR*!

ONE OF THESE DAYS, *YOU'LL* MEET A BOY YOU LIKE—

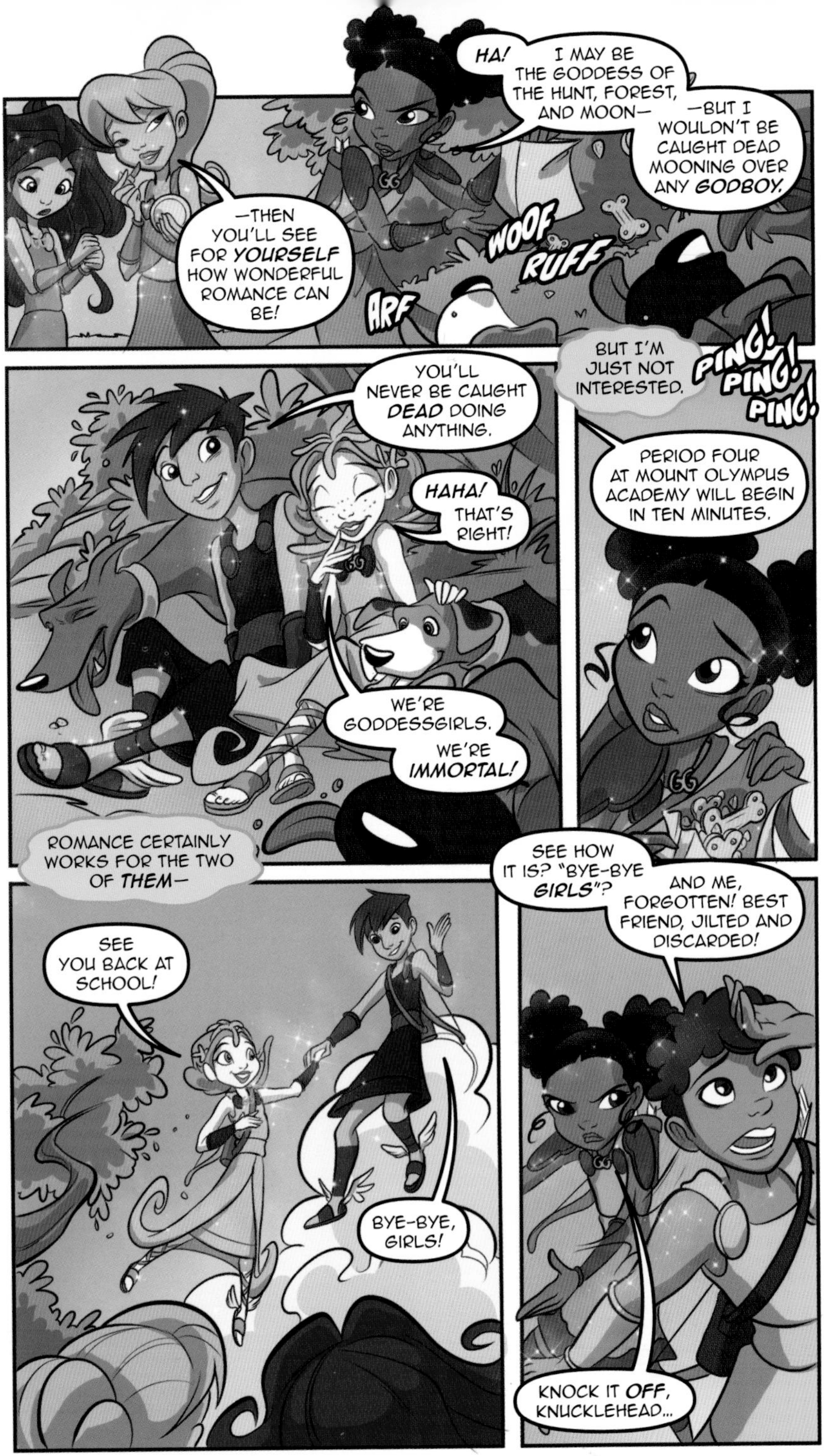

HA!
I MAY BE THE GODDESS OF THE HUNT, FOREST, AND MOON—
—BUT I WOULDN'T BE CAUGHT DEAD MOONING OVER ANY GODBOY.
—THEN YOU'LL SEE FOR YOURSELF HOW WONDERFUL ROMANCE CAN BE!
WOOF
RUFF
ARF
YOU'LL NEVER BE CAUGHT DEAD DOING ANYTHING.
HAHA! THAT'S RIGHT!
WE'RE GODDESSGIRLS.
WE'RE IMMORTAL!
BUT I'M JUST NOT INTERESTED.
PING! PING! PING!
PERIOD FOUR AT MOUNT OLYMPUS ACADEMY WILL BEGIN IN TEN MINUTES.
ROMANCE CERTAINLY WORKS FOR THE TWO OF THEM—
SEE YOU BACK AT SCHOOL!
BYE-BYE, GIRLS!
SEE HOW IT IS? "BYE-BYE GIRLS"?
AND ME, FORGOTTEN! BEST FRIEND, JILTED AND DISCARDED!
KNOCK IT OFF, KNUCKLEHEAD...

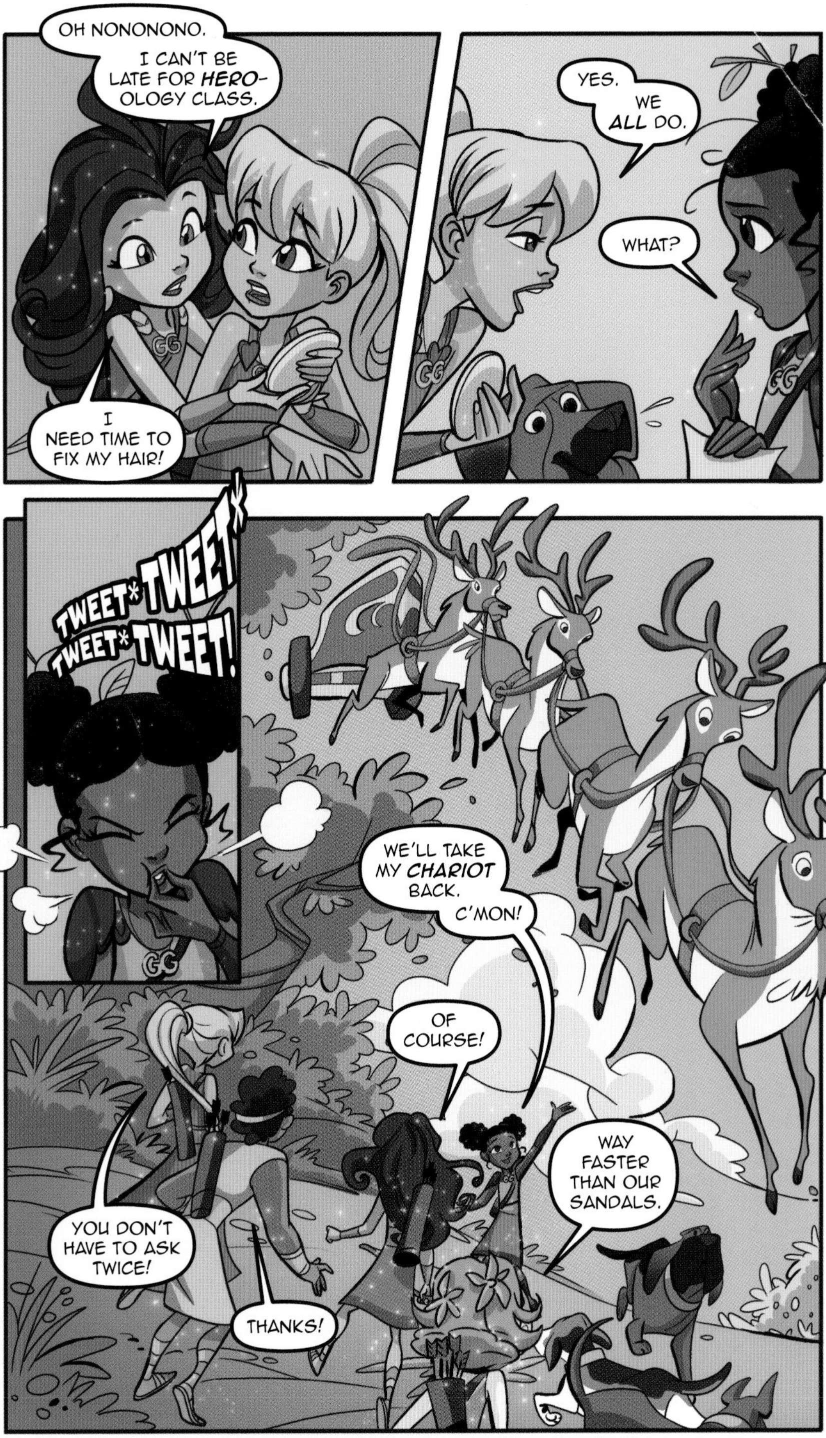
OH NONONONO.
I CAN'T BE LATE FOR HERO-OLOGY CLASS.
I NEED TIME TO FIX MY HAIR!
YES.
WE ALL DO.
WHAT?
TWEET* TWEET! TWEET* TWEET!
WE'LL TAKE MY CHARIOT BACK.
C'MON!
OF COURSE!
WAY FASTER THAN OUR SANDALS.
YOU DON'T HAVE TO ASK TWICE!
THANKS!

CHAPTER TWO: THE NEW BOY

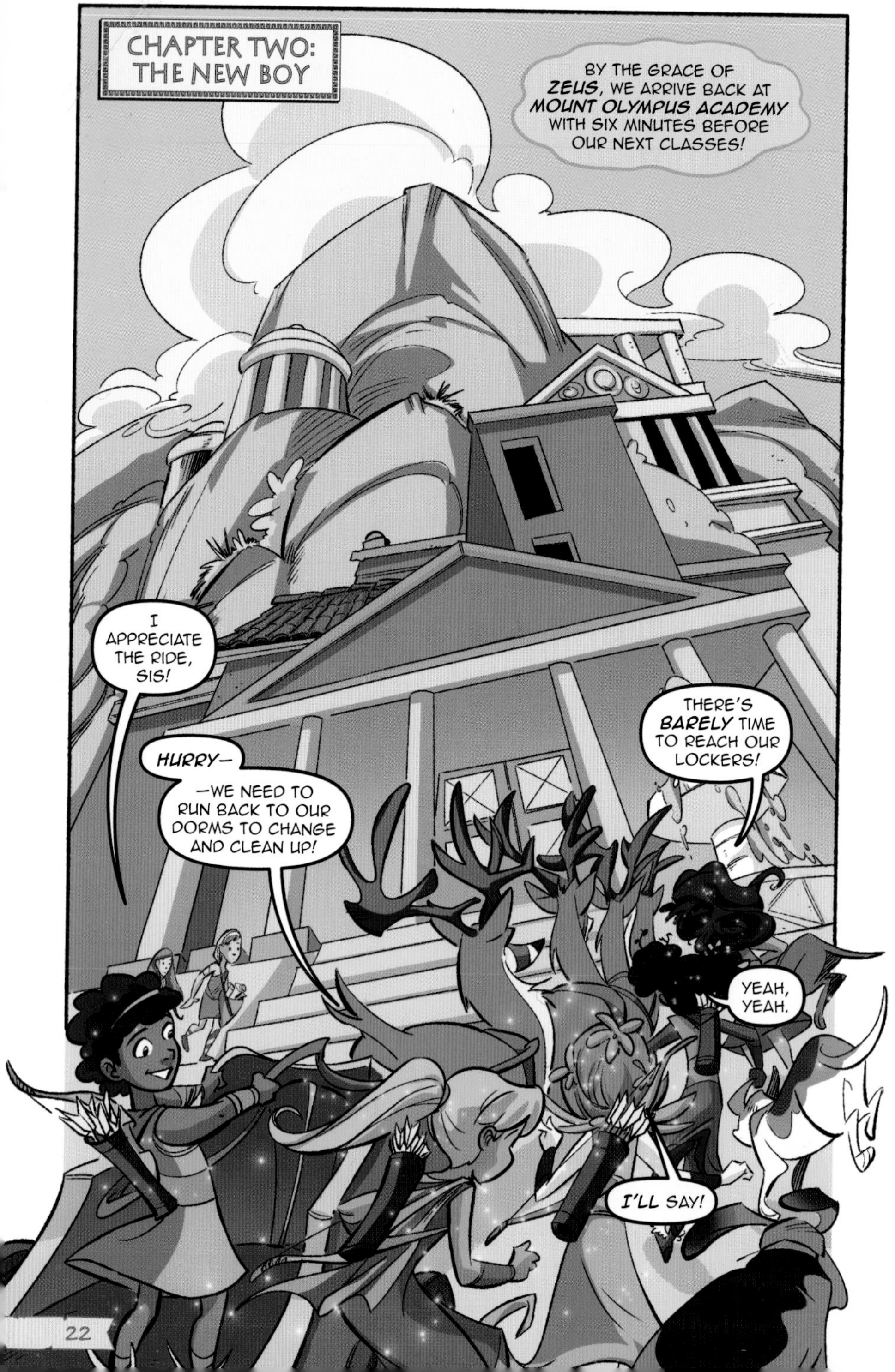
BY THE GRACE OF ZEUS, WE ARRIVE BACK AT MOUNT OLYMPUS ACADEMY WITH SIX MINUTES BEFORE OUR NEXT CLASSES!
I APPRECIATE THE RIDE, SIS!
HURRY—
—WE NEED TO RUN BACK TO OUR DORMS TO CHANGE AND CLEAN UP!
THERE'S BARELY TIME TO REACH OUR LOCKERS!
YEAH, YEAH.
I'LL SAY!

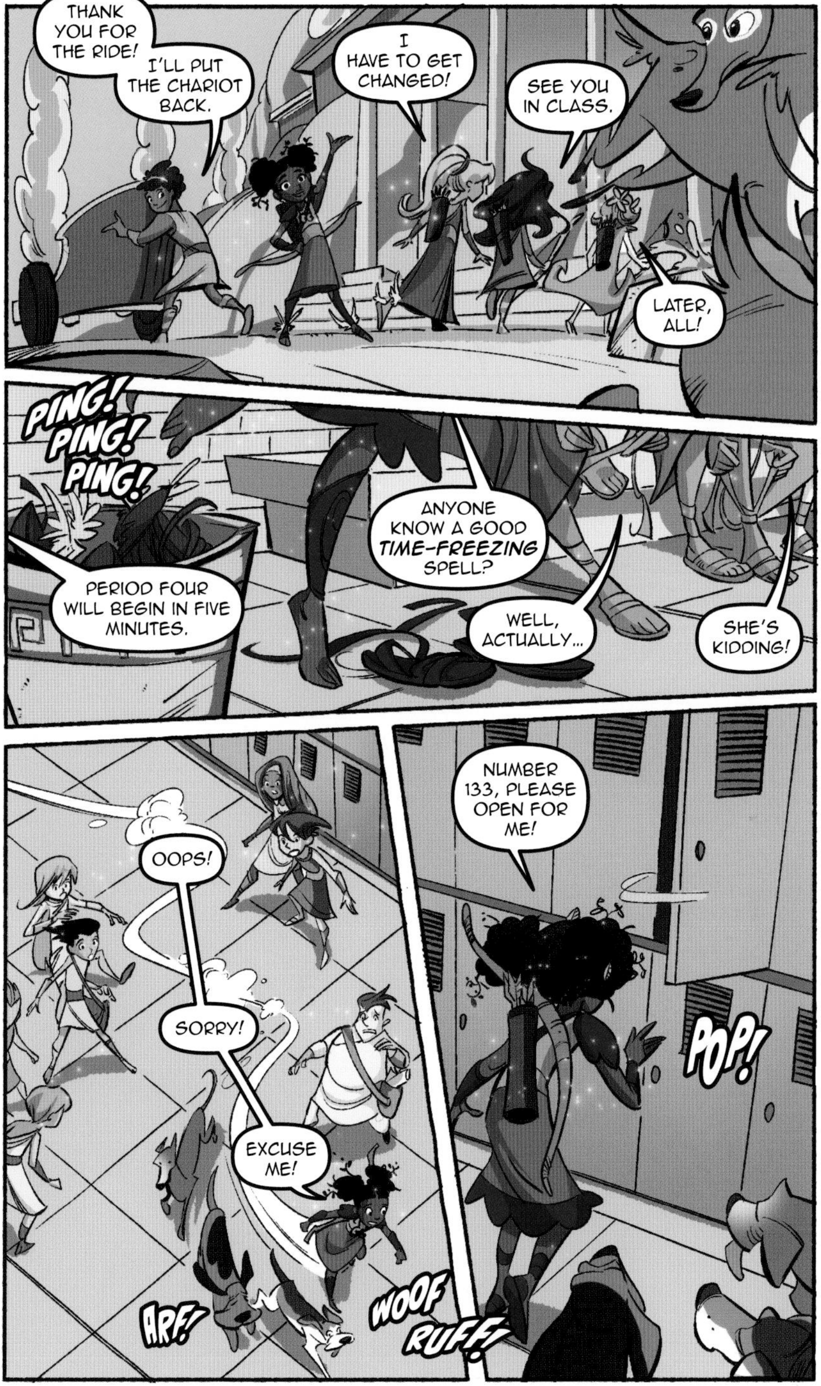
THANK YOU FOR THE RIDE!
I'LL PUT THE CHARIOT BACK.
I HAVE TO GET CHANGED!
SEE YOU IN CLASS.
LATER, ALL!
PING! PING! PING!
PERIOD FOUR WILL BEGIN IN FIVE MINUTES.
ANYONE KNOW A GOOD *TIME-FREEZING* SPELL?
WELL, ACTUALLY...
SHE'S KIDDING!
OOPS!
SORRY!
EXCUSE ME!
ARF!
WOOF
RUFF!
NUMBER 133, PLEASE OPEN FOR ME!
POP!

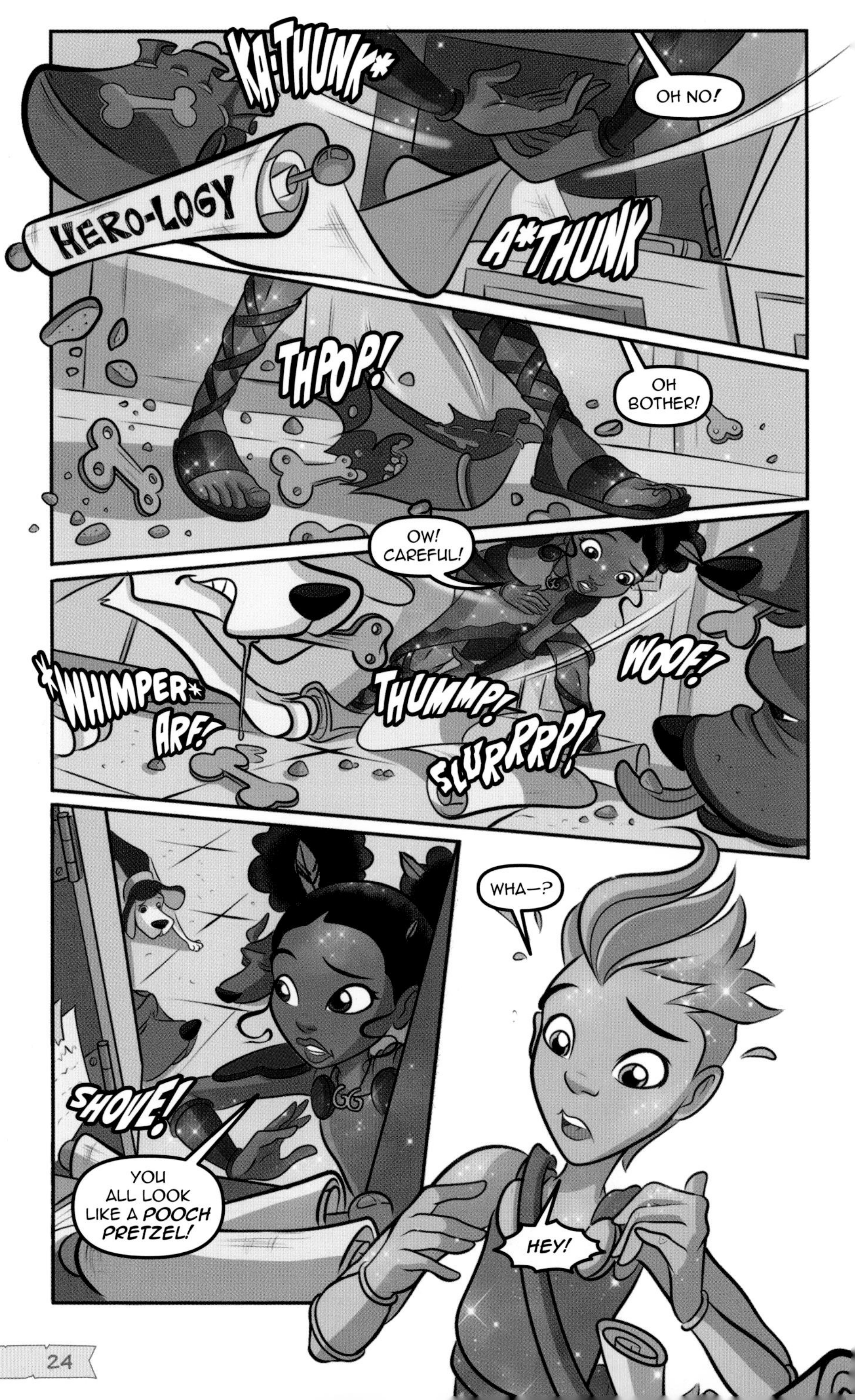
KA-THUNK*
OH NO!
HERO-LOGY
A*THUNK
THPOP!
OH BOTHER!
OW! CAREFUL!
WHIMPER
ARF!
THUMMP!
WOOF!
SLURRRP!
WHA—?
SHOVE!
YOU ALL LOOK LIKE A *POOCH PRETZEL!*
HEY!

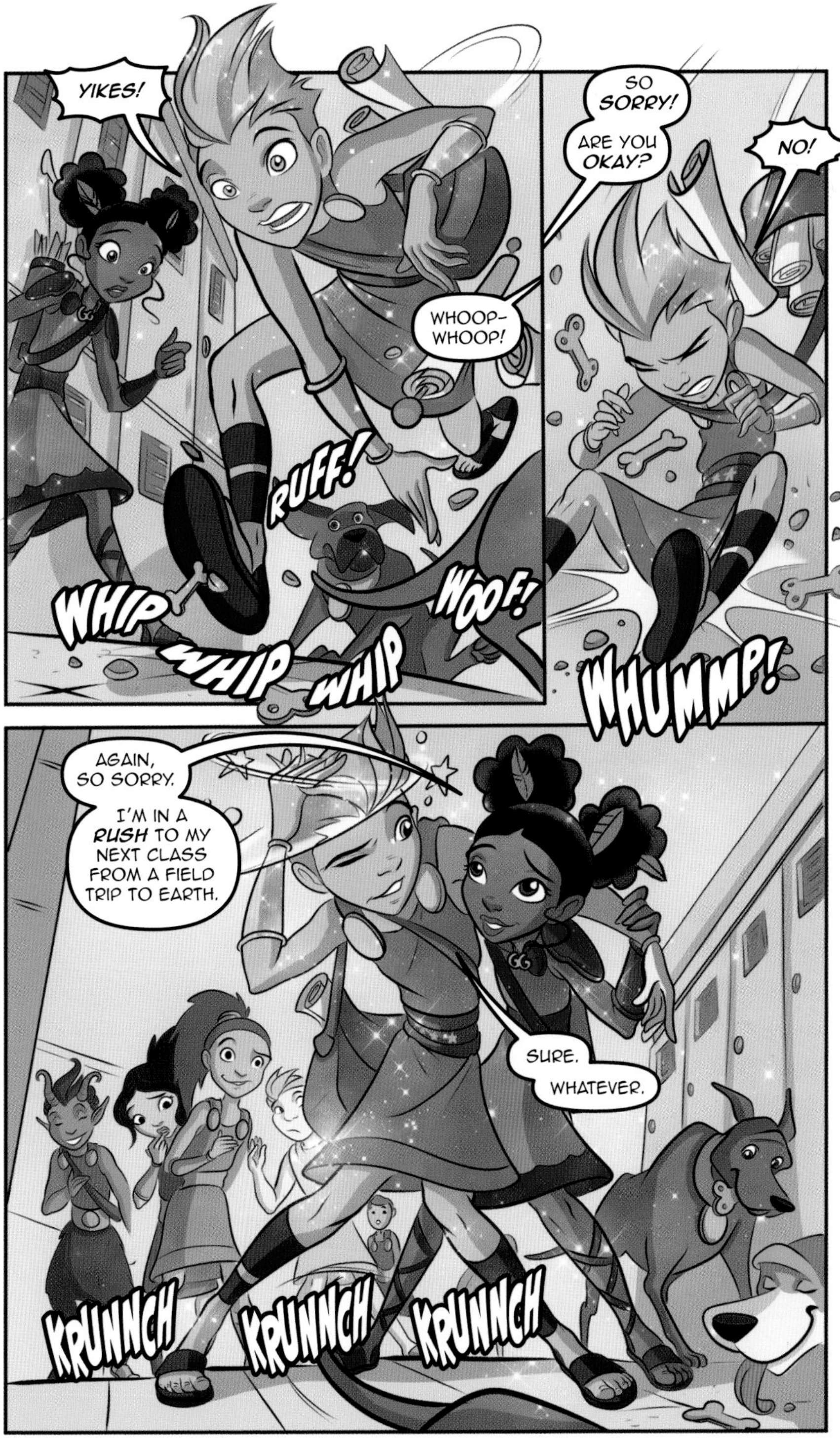
YIKES!
WHOOP-WHOOP!
RUFF!
WHIP
WHIP
WHIP
WOOF!
SO SORRY!
ARE YOU OKAY?
NO!
WHUMMP!
AGAIN, SO SORRY.
I'M IN A RUSH TO MY NEXT CLASS FROM A FIELD TRIP TO EARTH.
SURE.
WHATEVER.
KRUNNCH
KRUNNCH
KRUNNCH

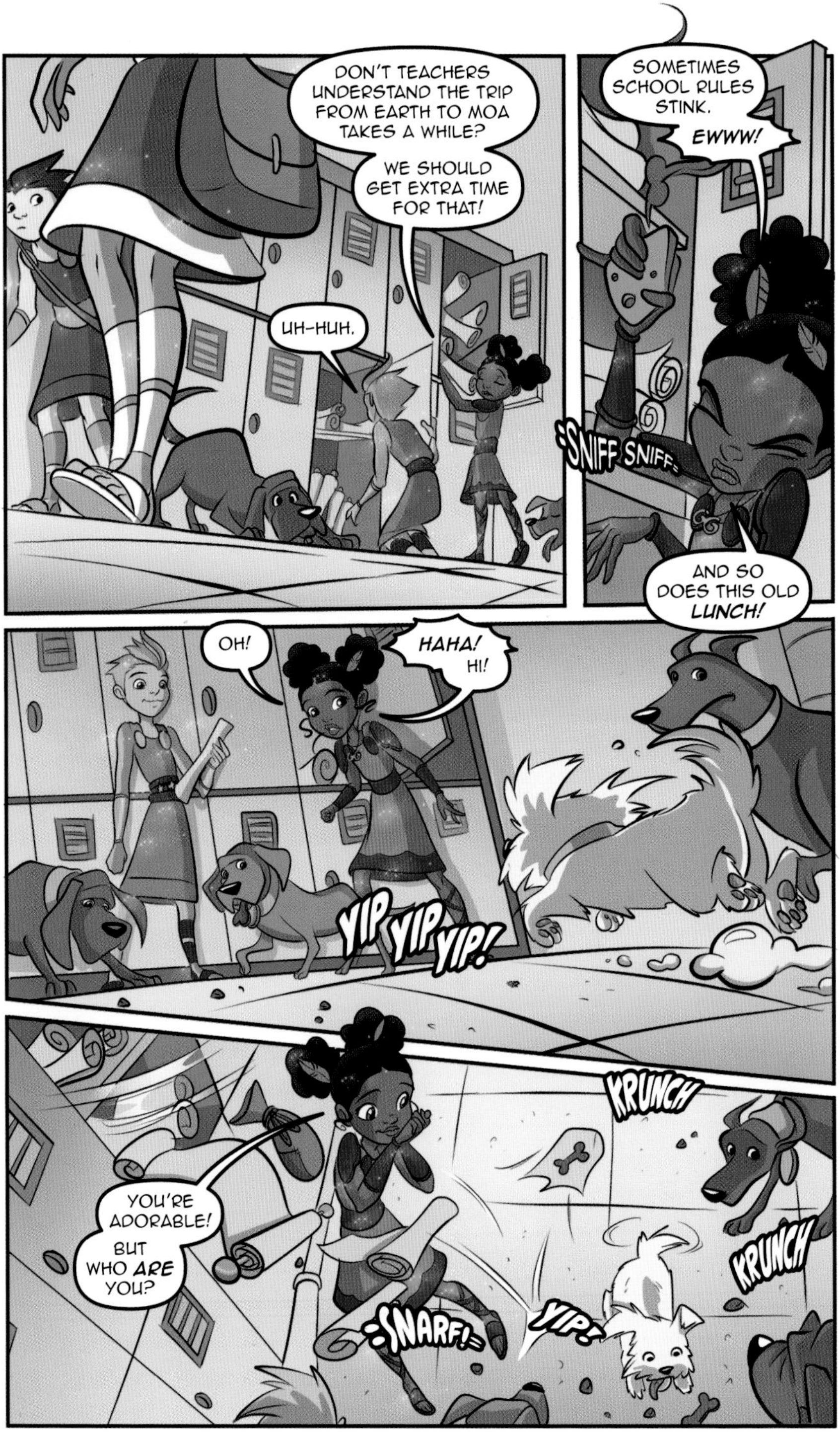

DON'T TEACHERS UNDERSTAND THE TRIP FROM EARTH TO MOA TAKES A WHILE?
WE SHOULD GET EXTRA TIME FOR THAT!
UH-HUH.
SOMETIMES SCHOOL RULES STINK.
EWWW!
SNIFF SNIFF
AND SO DOES THIS OLD LUNCH!
OH!
HAHA! HI!
YIP YIP YIP!
KRUNCH
YOU'RE ADORABLE!
BUT WHO ARE YOU?
KRUNCH
SNARF!
YIP!

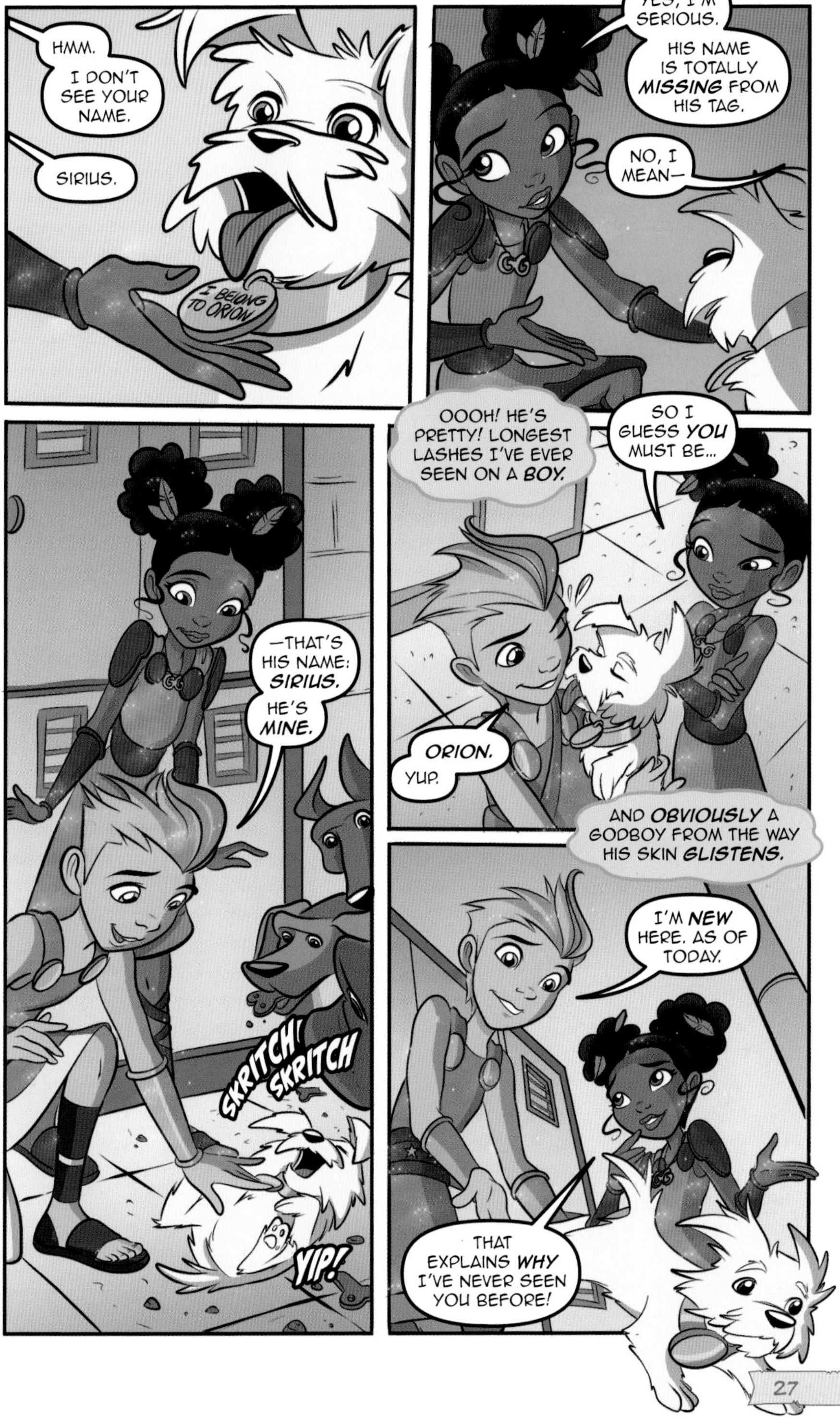
HMM.
I DON'T SEE YOUR NAME.
SIRIUS.
I BELONG TO ORION
YES, I'M SERIOUS.
HIS NAME IS TOTALLY MISSING FROM HIS TAG.
NO, I MEAN—
—THAT'S HIS NAME: SIRIUS.
HE'S MINE.
SKRITCH SKRITCH
YIP!
OOOH! HE'S PRETTY! LONGEST LASHES I'VE EVER SEEN ON A BOY.
SO I GUESS YOU MUST BE...
ORION.
YUP.
AND OBVIOUSLY A GODBOY FROM THE WAY HIS SKIN GLISTENS.
I'M NEW HERE. AS OF TODAY.
THAT EXPLAINS WHY I'VE NEVER SEEN YOU BEFORE!

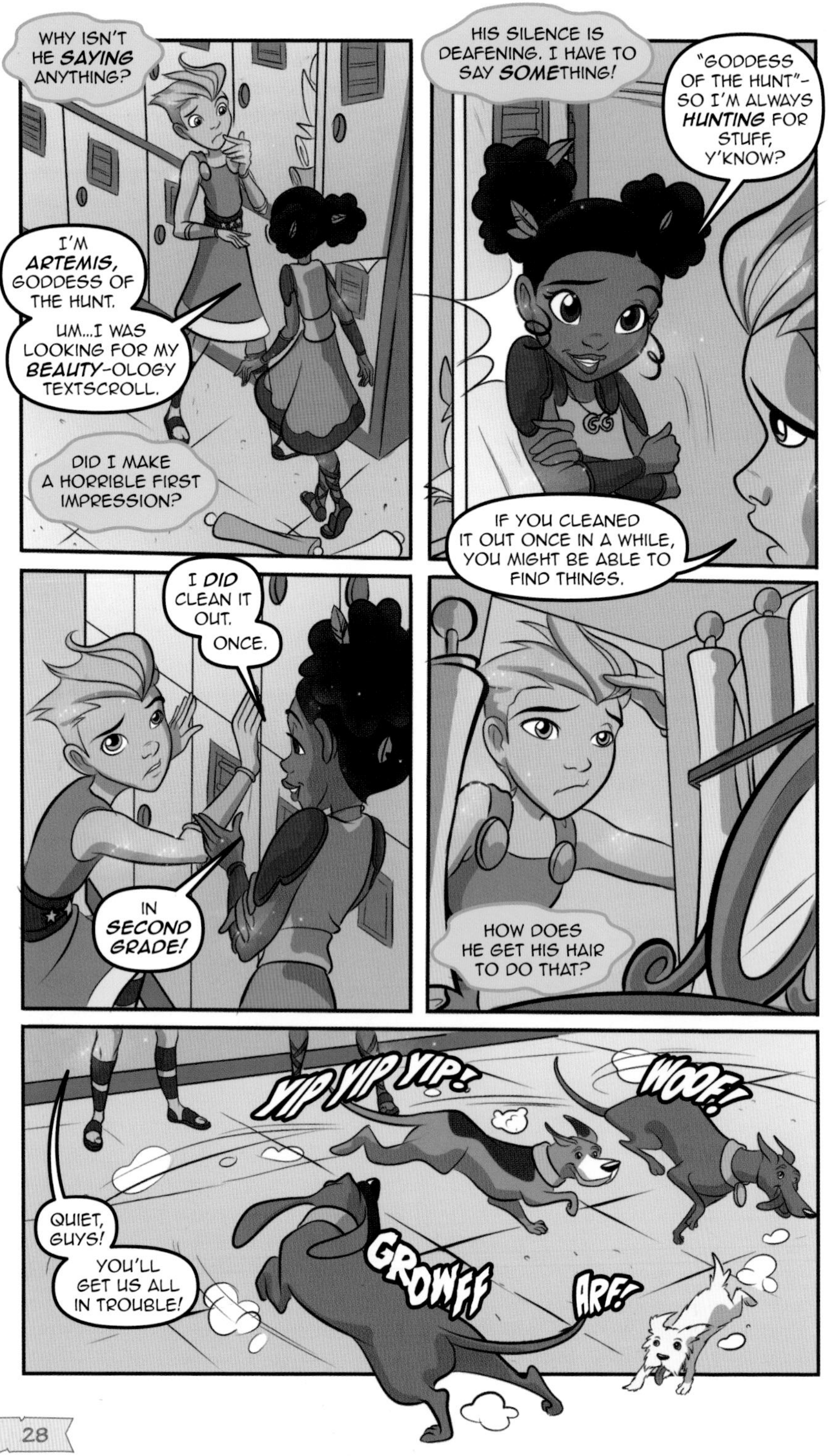
WHY ISN'T HE SAYING ANYTHING?
I'M ARTEMIS, GODDESS OF THE HUNT.
UM...I WAS LOOKING FOR MY BEAUTY-OLOGY TEXTSCROLL.
DID I MAKE A HORRIBLE FIRST IMPRESSION?
HIS SILENCE IS DEAFENING. I HAVE TO SAY SOMETHING!
"GODDESS OF THE HUNT"– SO I'M ALWAYS HUNTING FOR STUFF, Y'KNOW?
IF YOU CLEANED IT OUT ONCE IN A WHILE, YOU MIGHT BE ABLE TO FIND THINGS.
I DID CLEAN IT OUT.
ONCE.
IN SECOND GRADE!
HOW DOES HE GET HIS HAIR TO DO THAT?
YIP YIP YIP!
WOOF!
QUIET, GUYS!
YOU'LL GET US ALL IN TROUBLE!
GROWFF
ARF!

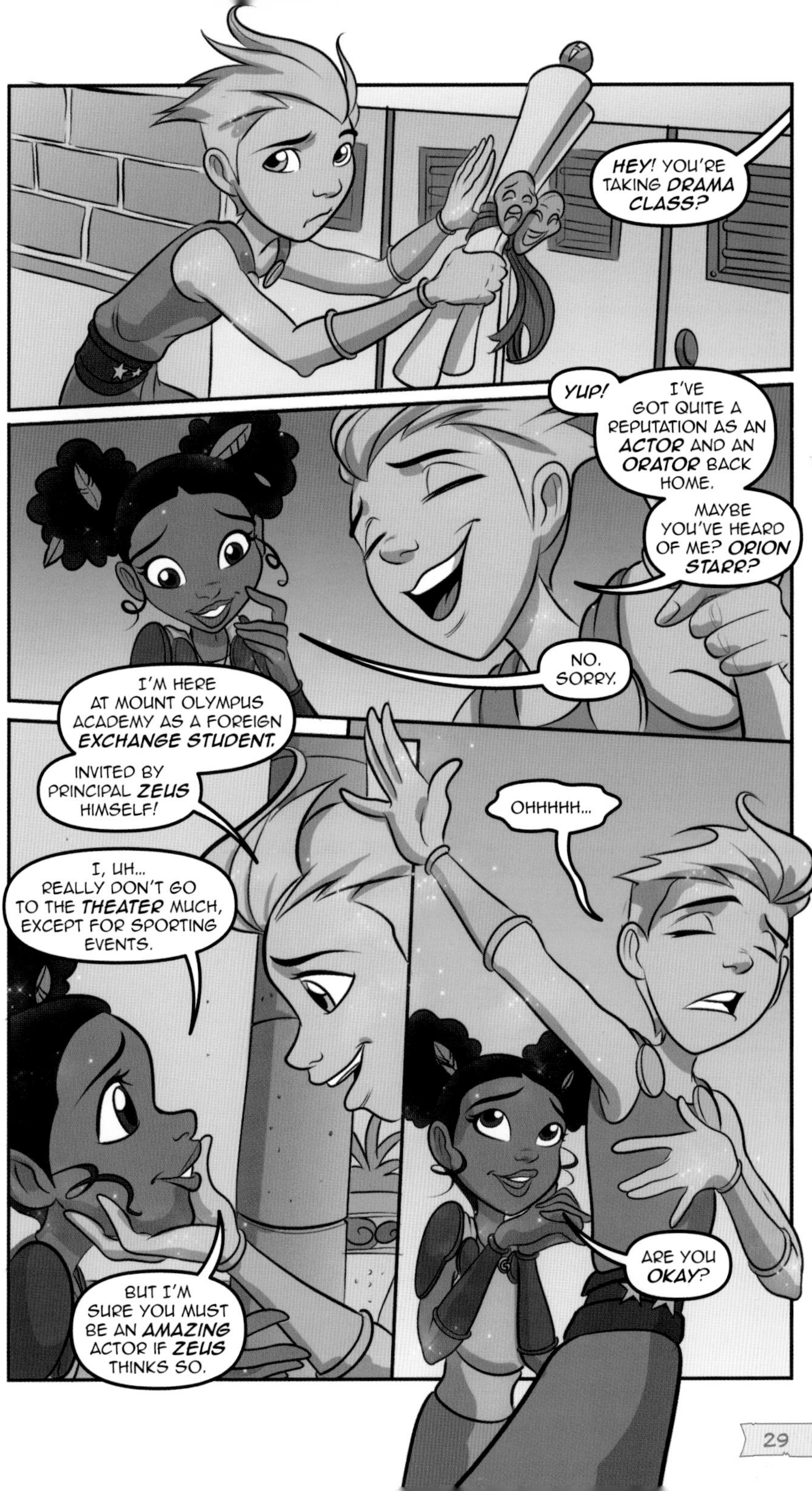
HEY! YOU'RE TAKING DRAMA CLASS?
YUP!
I'VE GOT QUITE A REPUTATION AS AN ACTOR AND AN ORATOR BACK HOME.
MAYBE YOU'VE HEARD OF ME? ORION STARR?
NO. SORRY.
I'M HERE AT MOUNT OLYMPUS ACADEMY AS A FOREIGN EXCHANGE STUDENT.
INVITED BY PRINCIPAL ZEUS HIMSELF!
I, UH... REALLY DON'T GO TO THE THEATER MUCH, EXCEPT FOR SPORTING EVENTS.
BUT I'M SURE YOU MUST BE AN AMAZING ACTOR IF ZEUS THINKS SO.
OHHHHH...
ARE YOU OKAY?

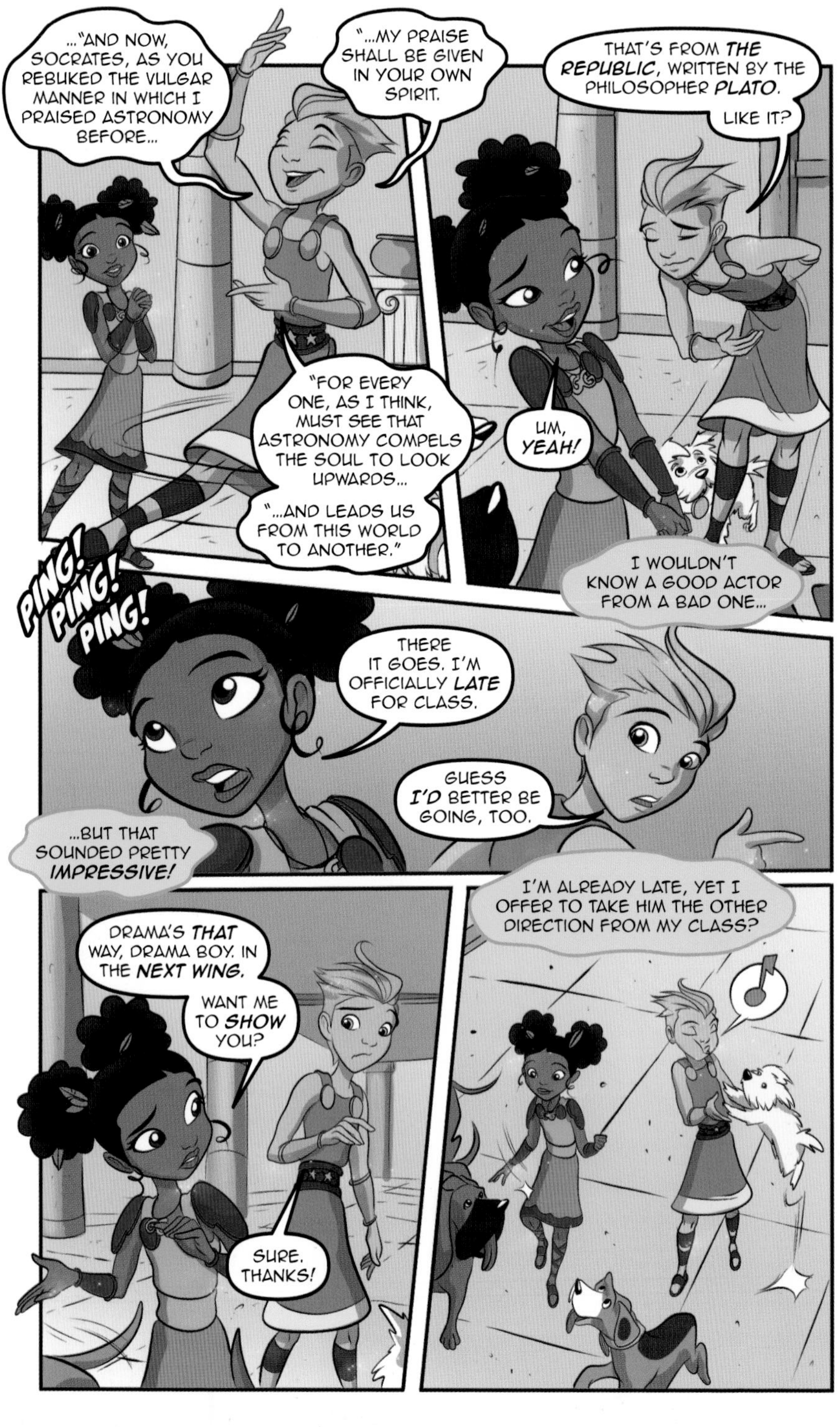
..."AND NOW, SOCRATES, AS YOU REBUKED THE VULGAR MANNER IN WHICH I PRAISED ASTRONOMY BEFORE...
"...MY PRAISE SHALL BE GIVEN IN YOUR OWN SPIRIT.
"FOR EVERY ONE, AS I THINK, MUST SEE THAT ASTRONOMY COMPELS THE SOUL TO LOOK UPWARDS...
"...AND LEADS US FROM THIS WORLD TO ANOTHER."
THAT'S FROM THE REPUBLIC, WRITTEN BY THE PHILOSOPHER PLATO.
LIKE IT?
UM, YEAH!
I WOULDN'T KNOW A GOOD ACTOR FROM A BAD ONE...
PING! PING! PING!
THERE IT GOES. I'M OFFICIALLY LATE FOR CLASS.
GUESS I'D BETTER BE GOING, TOO.
...BUT THAT SOUNDED PRETTY IMPRESSIVE!
DRAMA'S THAT WAY, DRAMA BOY. IN THE NEXT WING.
WANT ME TO SHOW YOU?
SURE. THANKS!
I'M ALREADY LATE, YET I OFFER TO TAKE HIM THE OTHER DIRECTION FROM MY CLASS?

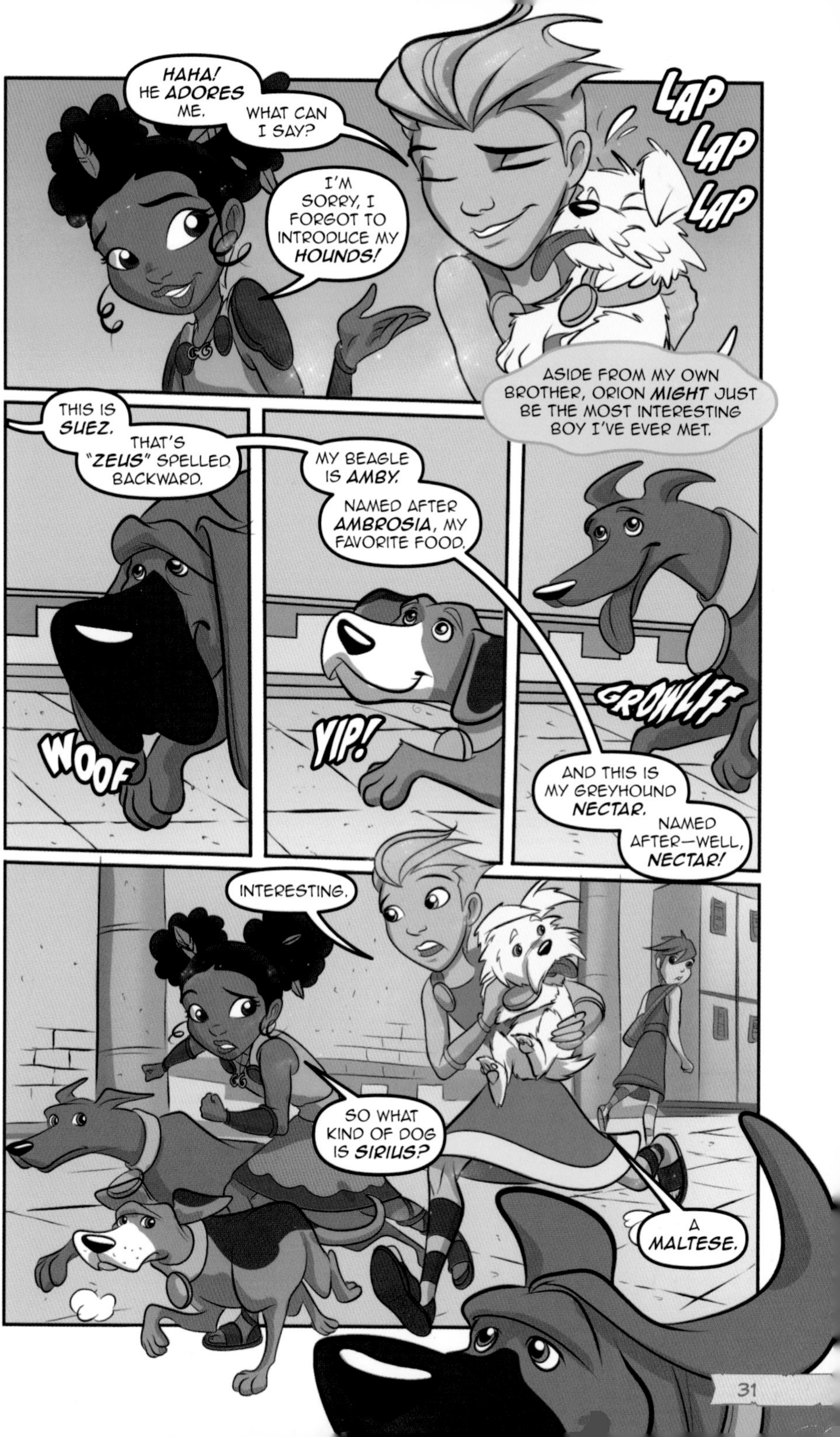
HAHA! HE ADORES ME.
WHAT CAN I SAY?
LAP LAP LAP
I'M SORRY, I FORGOT TO INTRODUCE MY HOUNDS!
ASIDE FROM MY OWN BROTHER, ORION MIGHT JUST BE THE MOST INTERESTING BOY I'VE EVER MET.
THIS IS SUEZ.
THAT'S "ZEUS" SPELLED BACKWARD.
WOOF
MY BEAGLE IS AMBY.
NAMED AFTER AMBROSIA, MY FAVORITE FOOD.
YIP!
GROWLFF
AND THIS IS MY GREYHOUND NECTAR.
NAMED AFTER—WELL, NECTAR!
INTERESTING.
SO WHAT KIND OF DOG IS SIRIUS?
A MALTESE.

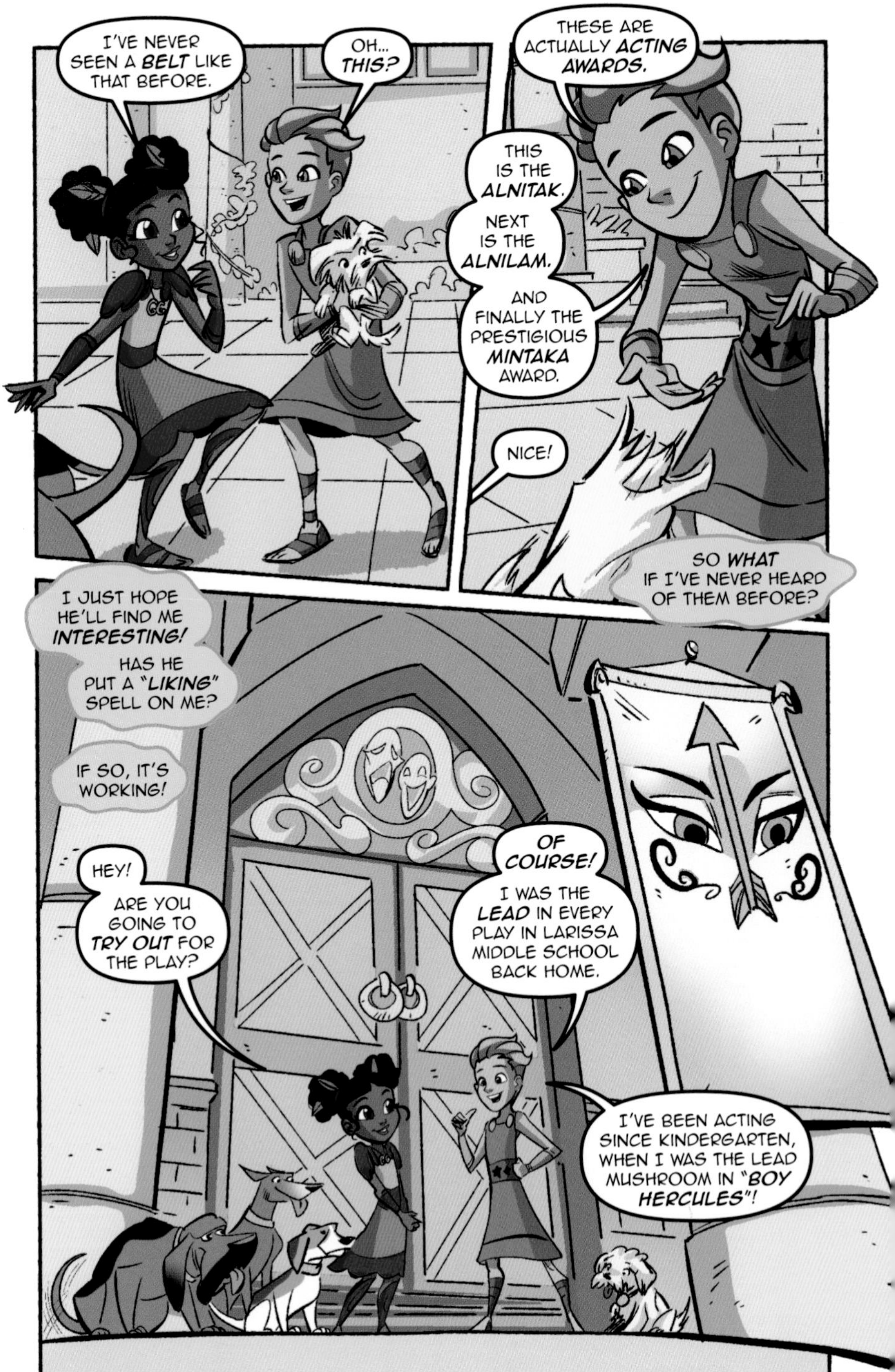
I'VE NEVER SEEN A BELT LIKE THAT BEFORE.
OH... THIS?
THESE ARE ACTUALLY ACTING AWARDS.
THIS IS THE ALNITAK.
NEXT IS THE ALNILAM.
AND FINALLY THE PRESTIGIOUS MINTAKA AWARD.
NICE!
SO WHAT IF I'VE NEVER HEARD OF THEM BEFORE?
I JUST HOPE HE'LL FIND ME INTERESTING!
HAS HE PUT A "LIKING" SPELL ON ME?
IF SO, IT'S WORKING!
HEY!
ARE YOU GOING TO TRY OUT FOR THE PLAY?
OF COURSE!
I WAS THE LEAD IN EVERY PLAY IN LARISSA MIDDLE SCHOOL BACK HOME.
I'VE BEEN ACTING SINCE KINDERGARTEN, WHEN I WAS THE LEAD MUSHROOM IN "BOY HERCULES"!

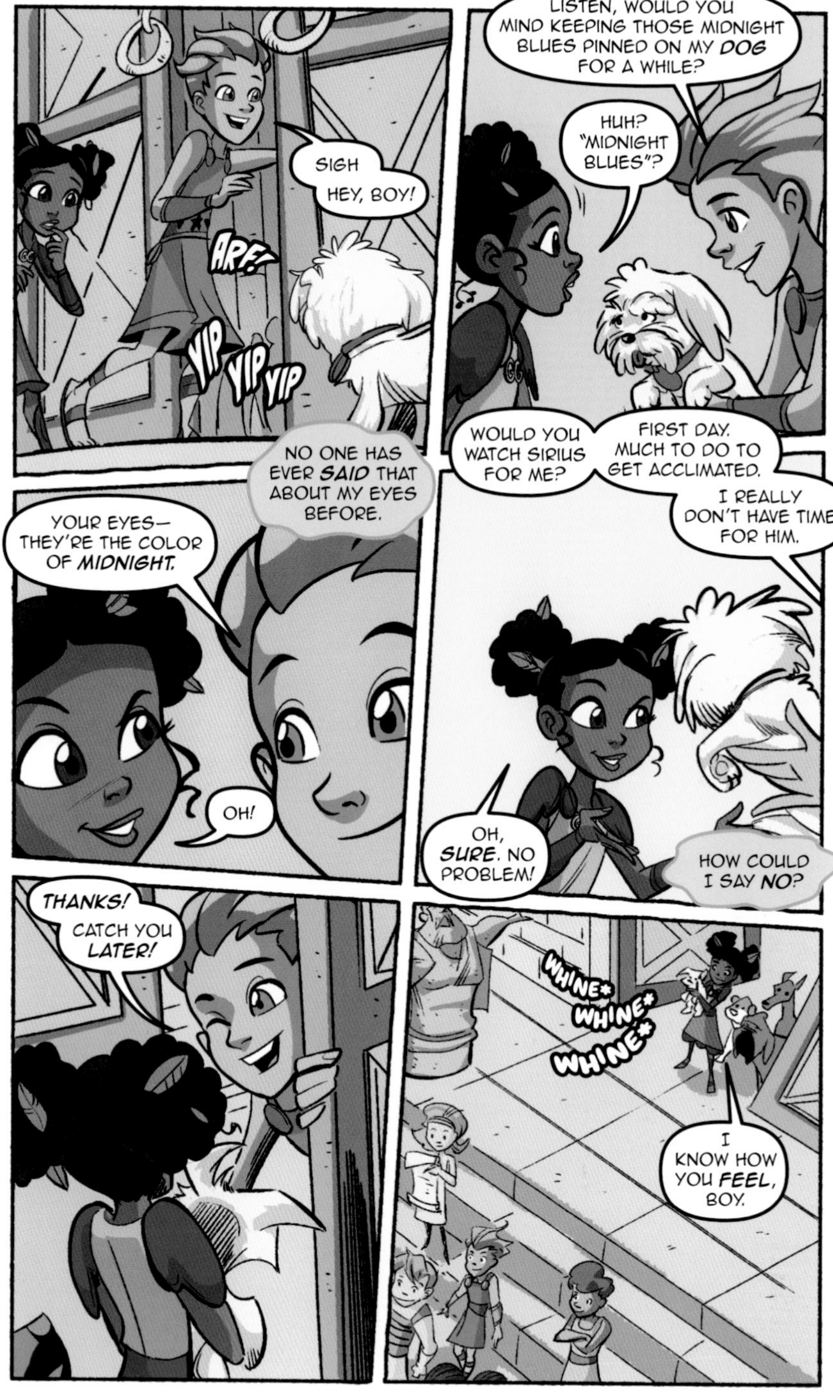
SIGH
HEY, BOY!
ARF!
YIP YIP YIP
LISTEN, WOULD YOU MIND KEEPING THOSE MIDNIGHT BLUES PINNED ON MY DOG FOR A WHILE?
HUH? "MIDNIGHT BLUES"?
YOUR EYES— THEY'RE THE COLOR OF MIDNIGHT.
NO ONE HAS EVER SAID THAT ABOUT MY EYES BEFORE.
OH!
WOULD YOU WATCH SIRIUS FOR ME?
FIRST DAY. MUCH TO DO TO GET ACCLIMATED.
I REALLY DON'T HAVE TIME FOR HIM.
OH, SURE. NO PROBLEM!
HOW COULD I SAY NO?
THANKS!
CATCH YOU LATER!
WHINE*
WHINE*
WHINE*
I KNOW HOW YOU FEEL, BOY.

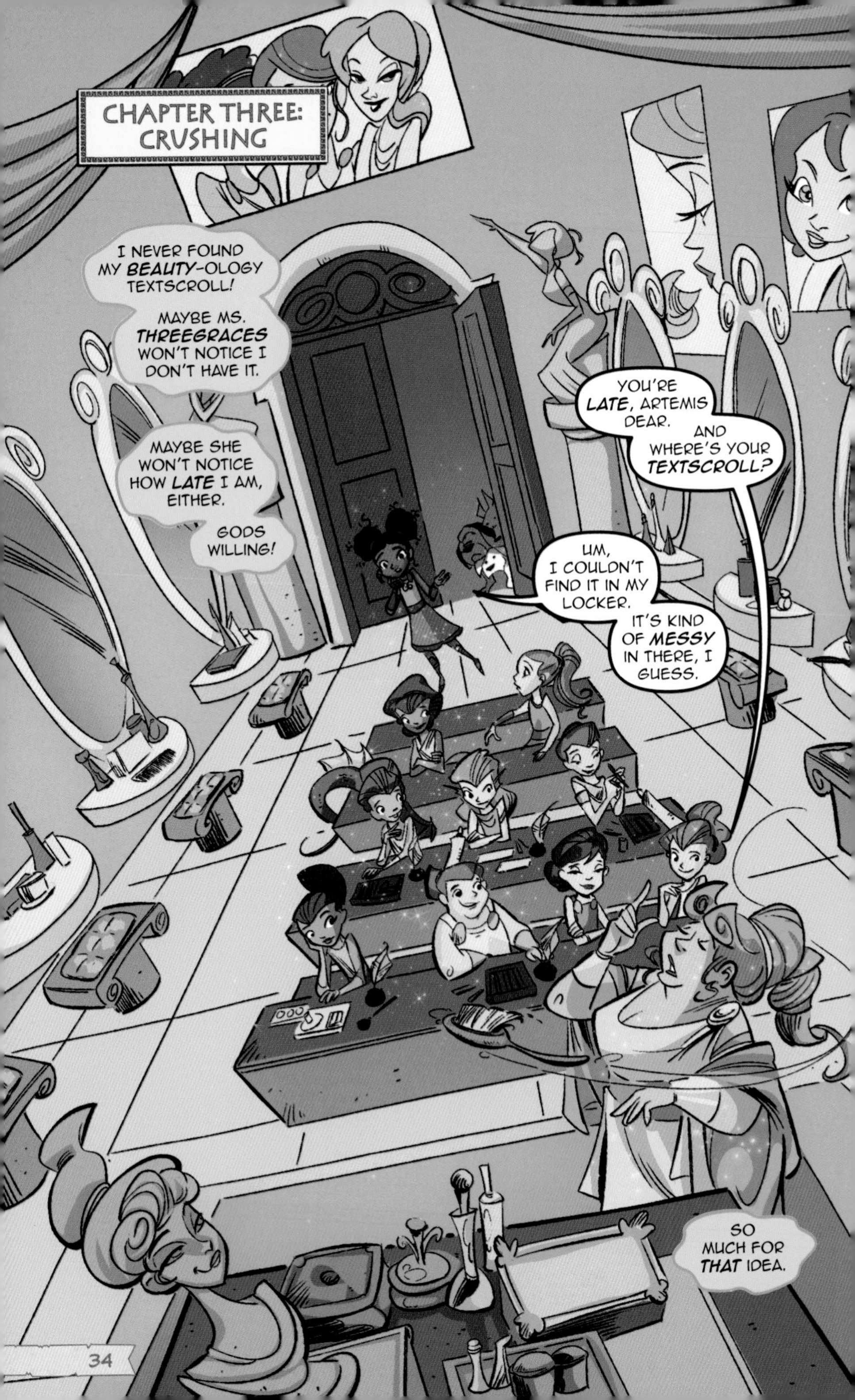
CHAPTER THREE: CRUSHING
I NEVER FOUND MY BEAUTY-OLOGY TEXTSCROLL!
MAYBE MS. THREEGRACES WON'T NOTICE I DON'T HAVE IT.
MAYBE SHE WON'T NOTICE HOW LATE I AM, EITHER.
GODS WILLING!
YOU'RE LATE, ARTEMIS DEAR.
AND WHERE'S YOUR TEXTSCROLL?
UM, I COULDN'T FIND IT IN MY LOCKER.
IT'S KIND OF MESSY IN THERE, I GUESS.
SO MUCH FOR THAT IDEA.

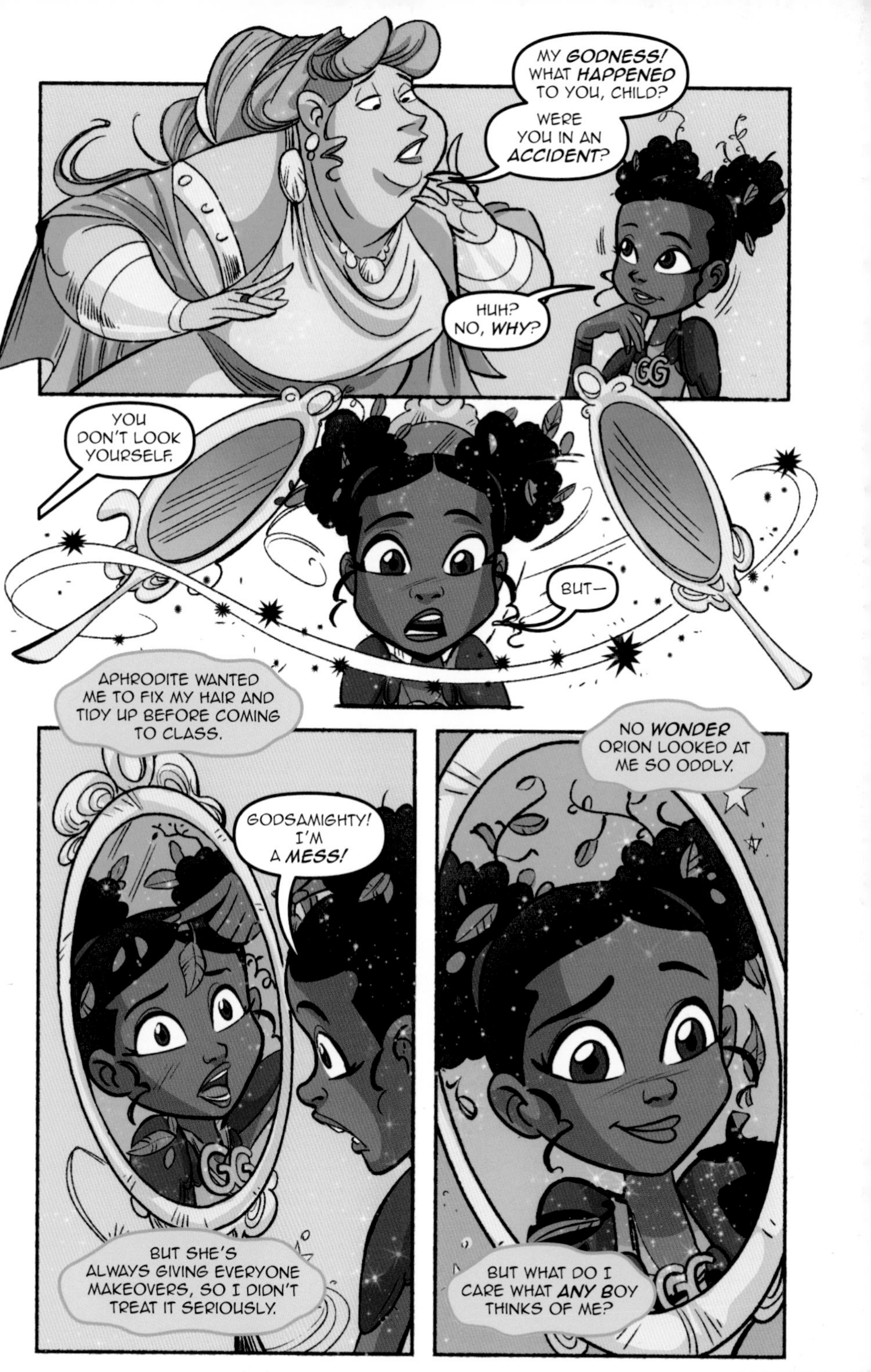
MY GODNESS! WHAT HAPPENED TO YOU, CHILD?
WERE YOU IN AN ACCIDENT?
HUH? NO, WHY?
YOU DON'T LOOK YOURSELF.
BUT—
APHRODITE WANTED ME TO FIX MY HAIR AND TIDY UP BEFORE COMING TO CLASS.
GODSAMIGHTY! I'M A MESS!
BUT SHE'S ALWAYS GIVING EVERYONE MAKEOVERS, SO I DIDN'T TREAT IT SERIOUSLY.
NO WONDER ORION LOOKED AT ME SO ODDLY.
BUT WHAT DO I CARE WHAT ANY BOY THINKS OF ME?

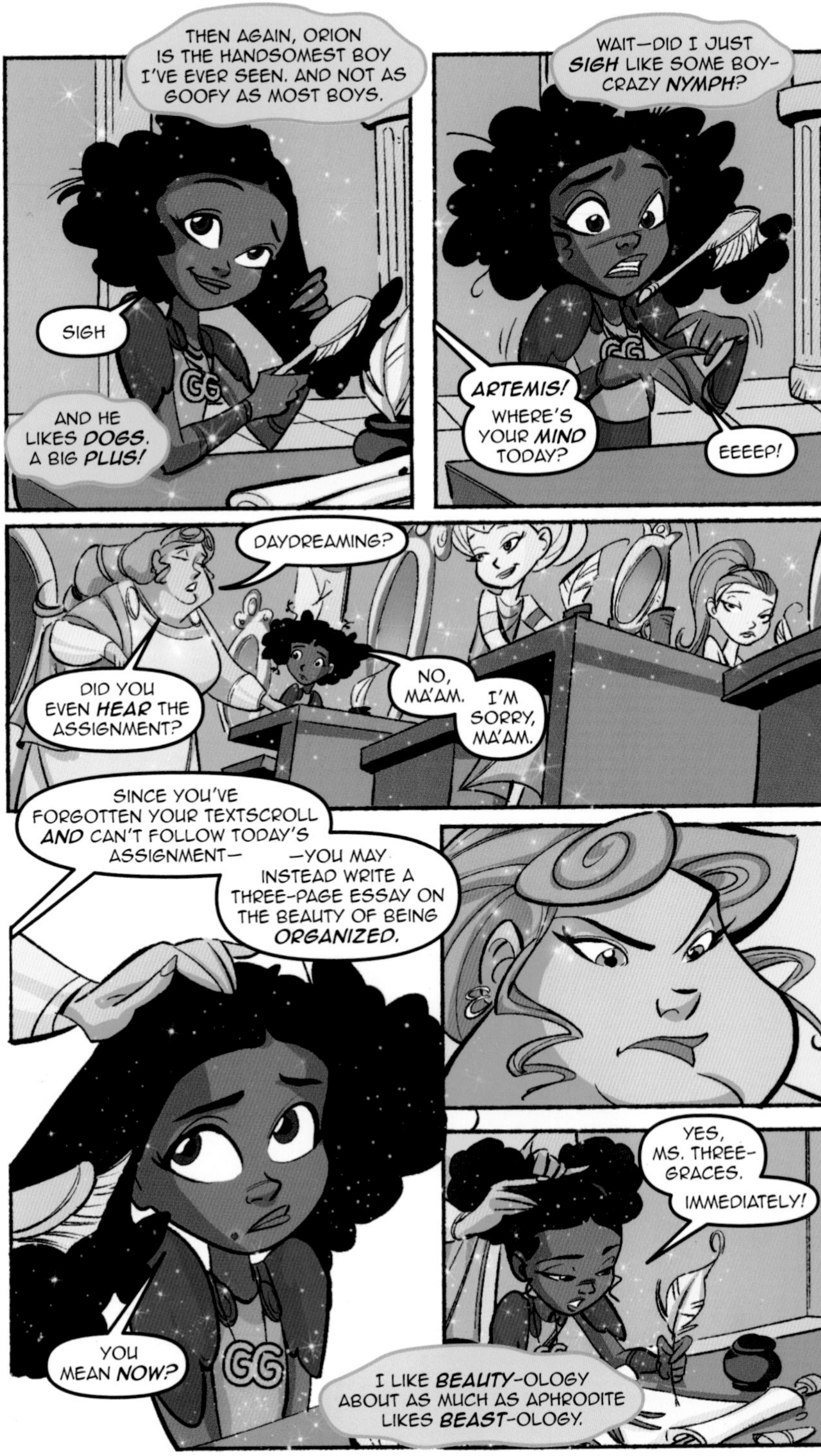
THEN AGAIN, ORION IS THE HANDSOMEST BOY I'VE EVER SEEN. AND NOT AS GOOFY AS MOST BOYS.
SIGH
AND HE LIKES DOGS. A BIG PLUS!
WAIT—DID I JUST SIGH LIKE SOME BOY-CRAZY NYMPH?
ARTEMIS! WHERE'S YOUR MIND TODAY?
EEEEP!
DAYDREAMING?
DID YOU EVEN HEAR THE ASSIGNMENT?
NO, MA'AM.
I'M SORRY, MA'AM.
SINCE YOU'VE FORGOTTEN YOUR TEXTSCROLL AND CAN'T FOLLOW TODAY'S ASSIGNMENT—
—YOU MAY INSTEAD WRITE A THREE-PAGE ESSAY ON THE BEAUTY OF BEING ORGANIZED.
YOU MEAN NOW?
YES, MS. THREE-GRACES.
IMMEDIATELY!
I LIKE BEAUTY-OLOGY ABOUT AS MUCH AS APHRODITE LIKES BEAST-OLOGY.

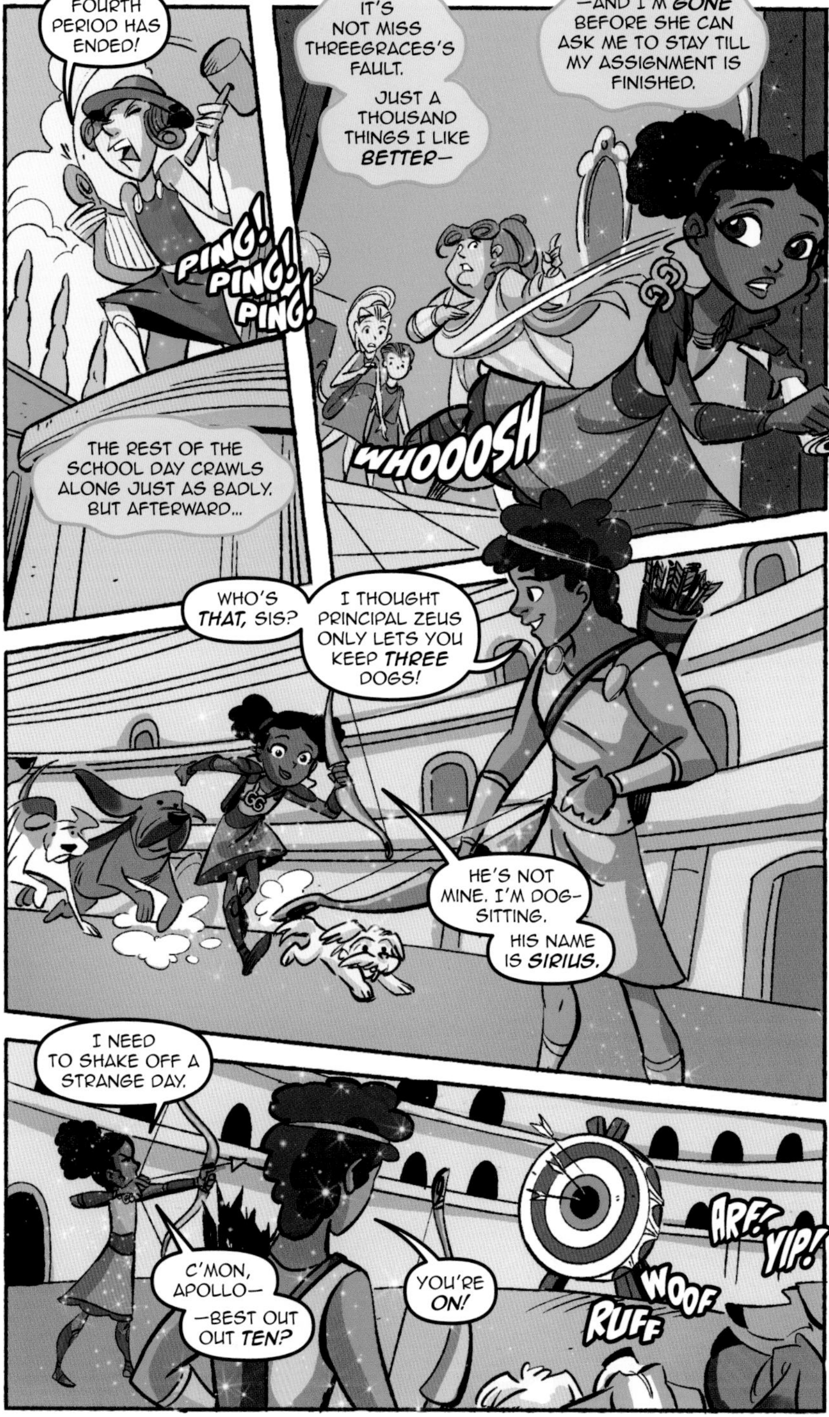
FOURTH PERIOD HAS ENDED!
PING! PING! PING!
IT'S NOT MISS THREEGRACES'S FAULT.
JUST A THOUSAND THINGS I LIKE BETTER—
—AND I'M GONE BEFORE SHE CAN ASK ME TO STAY TILL MY ASSIGNMENT IS FINISHED.
WHOOOOSH
THE REST OF THE SCHOOL DAY CRAWLS ALONG JUST AS BADLY. BUT AFTERWARD...
WHO'S THAT, SIS?
I THOUGHT PRINCIPAL ZEUS ONLY LETS YOU KEEP THREE DOGS!
HE'S NOT MINE. I'M DOG-SITTING.
HIS NAME IS SIRIUS.
I NEED TO SHAKE OFF A STRANGE DAY.
C'MON, APOLLO—
—BEST OUT OUT TEN?
YOU'RE ON!
ARF! YIP!
WOOF
RUFF

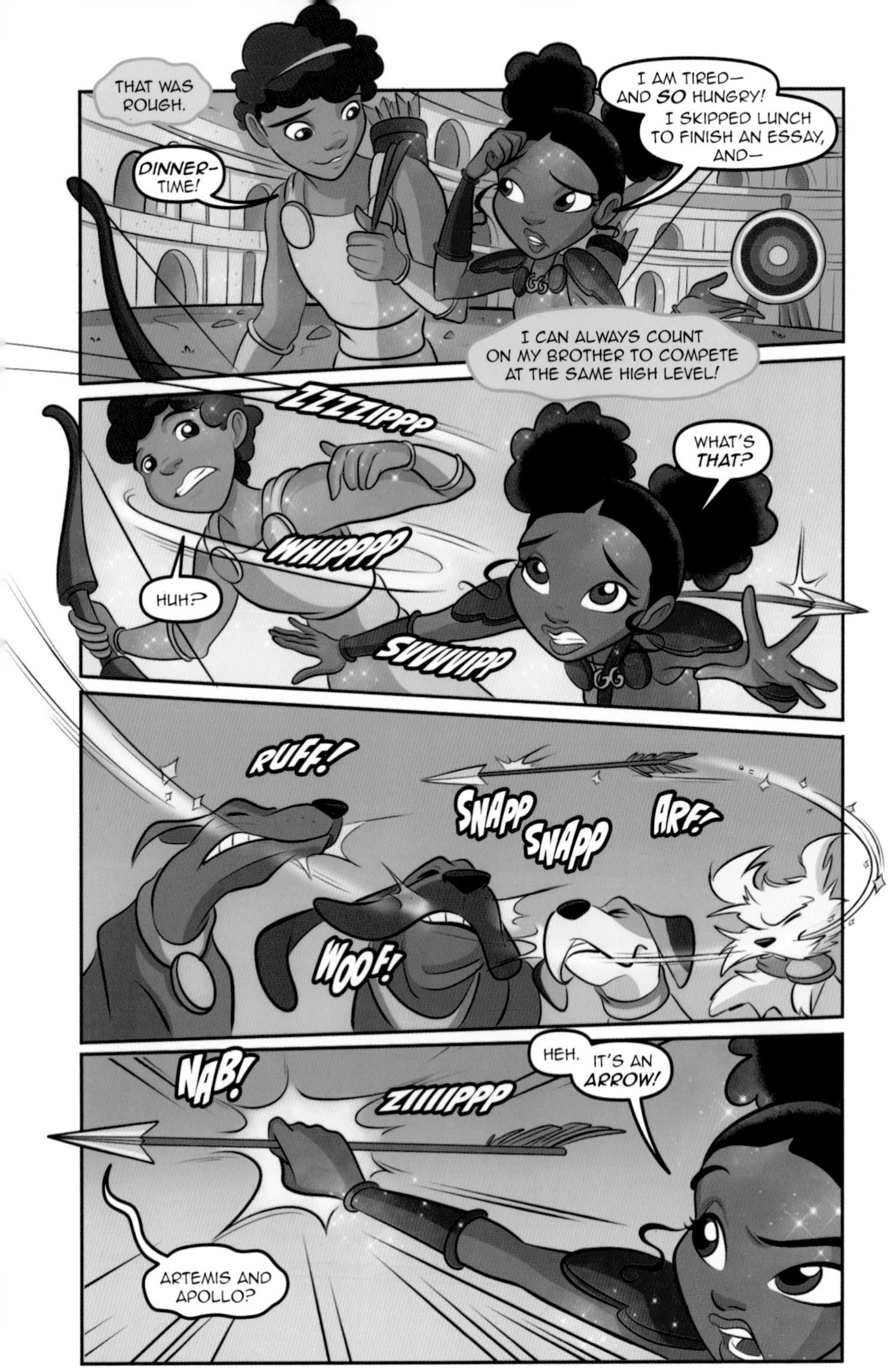
THAT WAS ROUGH.
I AM TIRED— AND SO HUNGRY! I SKIPPED LUNCH TO FINISH AN ESSAY, AND—
DINNER-TIME!
I CAN ALWAYS COUNT ON MY BROTHER TO COMPETE AT THE SAME HIGH LEVEL!
ZZZZZIPPP
WHAT'S THAT?
WHIPPPP
HUH?
SVVVVIPP
RUFF!
SNAPP
SNAPP
ARF!
WOOF!
NAB!
HEH.
IT'S AN ARROW!
ZIIIIPPP
ARTEMIS AND APOLLO?

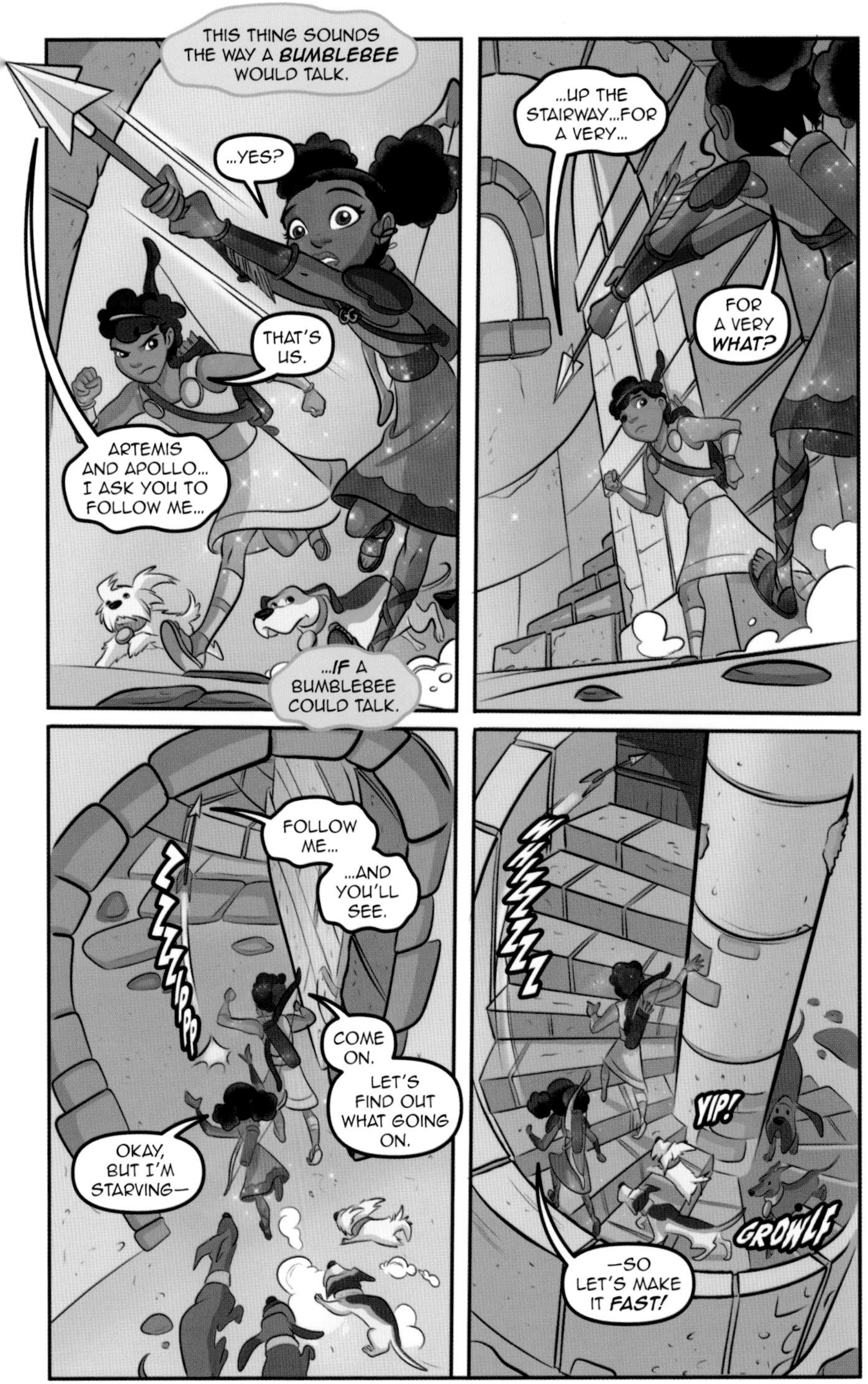
THIS THING SOUNDS THE WAY A ***BUMBLEBEE*** WOULD TALK.
...YES?
THAT'S US.
ARTEMIS AND APOLLO... I ASK YOU TO FOLLOW ME...
...***IF*** A BUMBLEBEE COULD TALK.
...UP THE STAIRWAY...FOR A VERY...
FOR A VERY ***WHAT?***
FOLLOW ME...
...AND YOU'LL SEE.
ZZZZZIPPP
COME ON.
LET'S FIND OUT WHAT GOING ON.
OKAY, BUT I'M STARVING—
WHZZZZZZZ
YIP!
GROWLF
—SO LET'S MAKE IT ***FAST!***

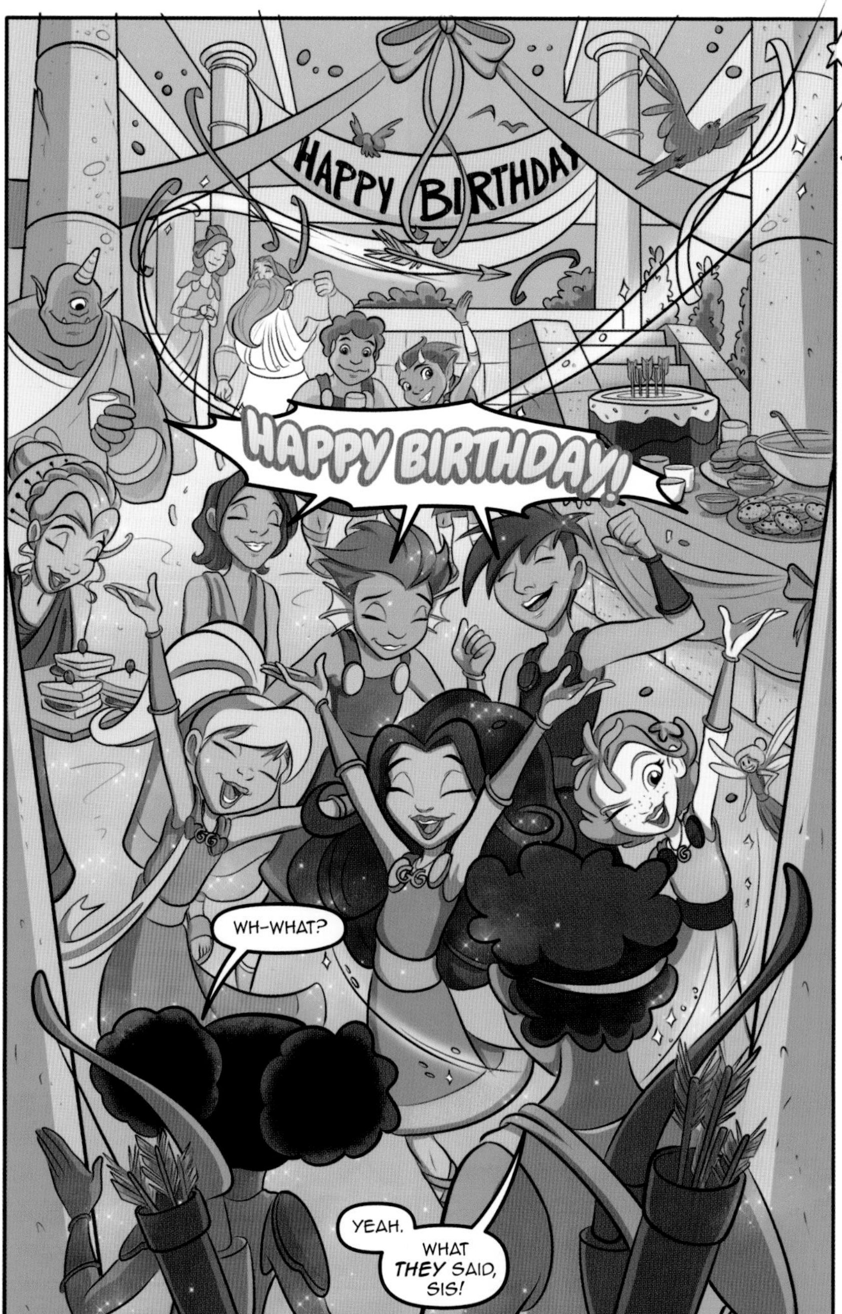
HAPPY BIRTHDAY
HAPPY BIRTHDAY!
WH-WHAT?
YEAH. WHAT THEY SAID, SIS!

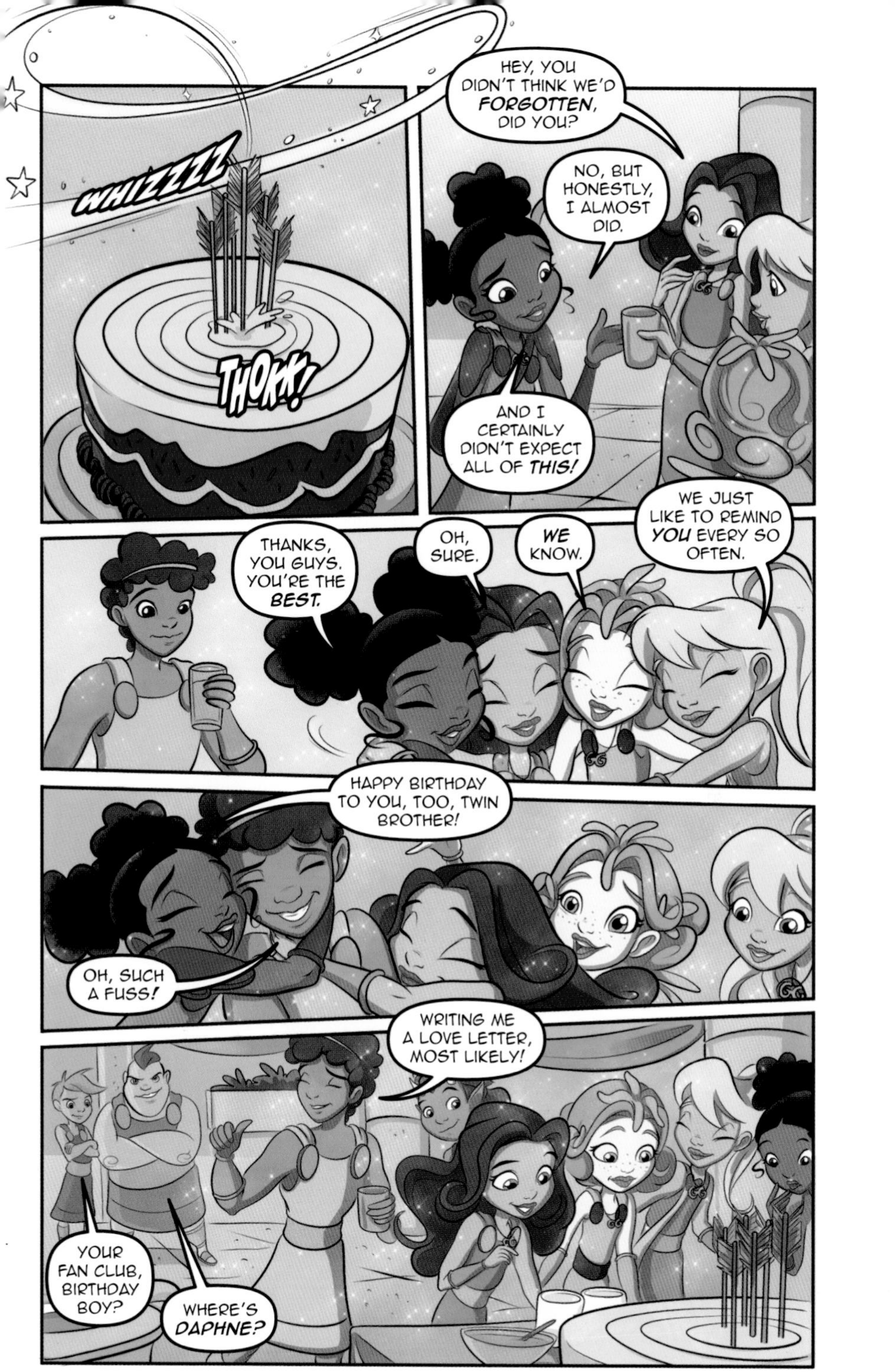
WHIZZZZZ
THOKK!
HEY, YOU DIDN'T THINK WE'D FORGOTTEN, DID YOU?
NO, BUT HONESTLY, I ALMOST DID.
AND I CERTAINLY DIDN'T EXPECT ALL OF THIS!
THANKS, YOU GUYS. YOU'RE THE BEST.
OH, SURE.
WE KNOW.
WE JUST LIKE TO REMIND YOU EVERY SO OFTEN.
HAPPY BIRTHDAY TO YOU, TOO, TWIN BROTHER!
OH, SUCH A FUSS!
WRITING ME A LOVE LETTER, MOST LIKELY!
YOUR FAN CLUB, BIRTHDAY BOY?
WHERE'S DAPHNE?

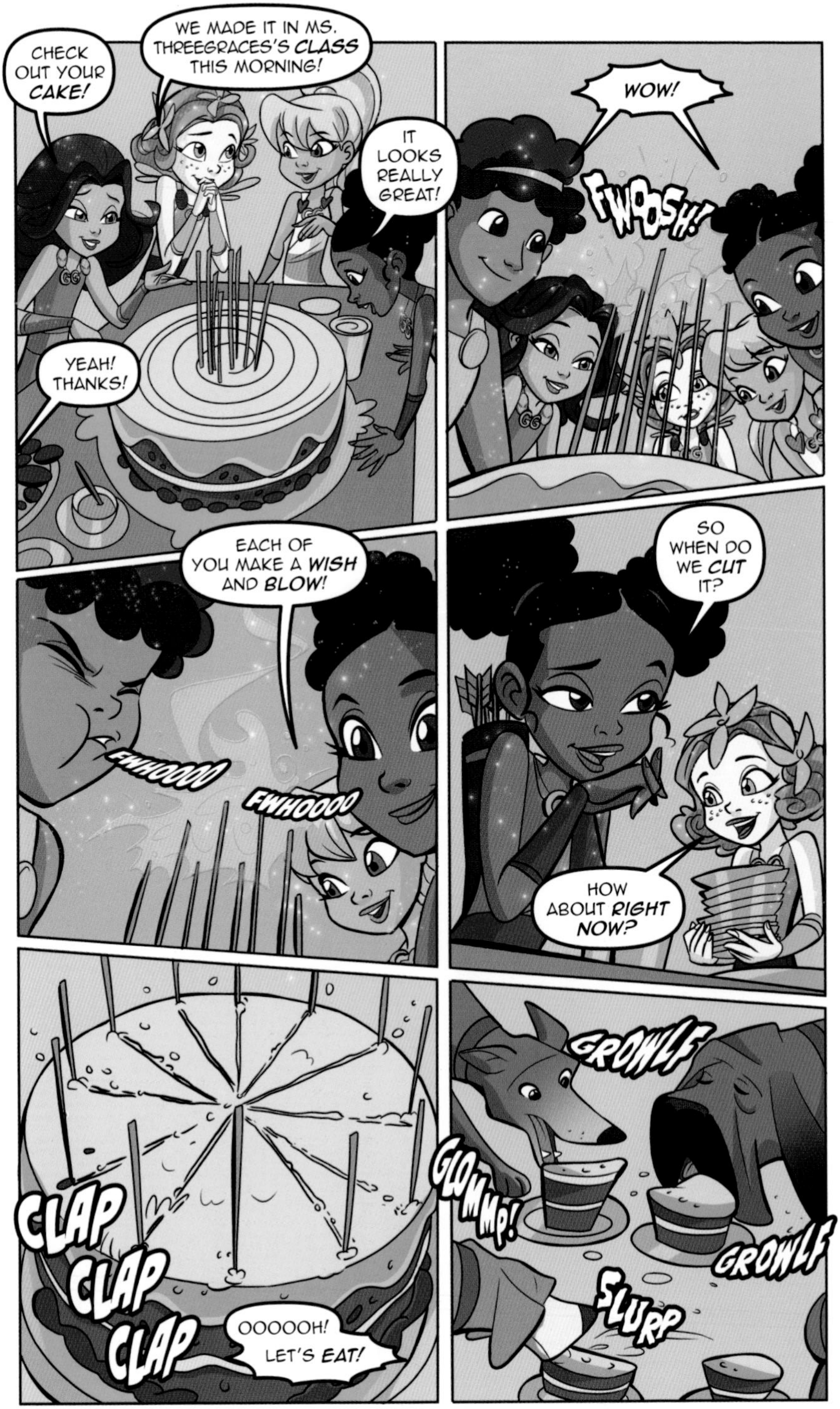

CHECK OUT YOUR CAKE!
WE MADE IT IN MS. THREEGRACES'S CLASS THIS MORNING!
IT LOOKS REALLY GREAT!
YEAH! THANKS!
WOW!
FWOOSH!
EACH OF YOU MAKE A WISH AND BLOW!
FWHOOOO
FWHOOOO
SO WHEN DO WE CUT IT?
HOW ABOUT RIGHT NOW?
CLAP
CLAP
CLAP
OOOOOH!
LET'S EAT!
GROWLF
GLOMMP!
GROWLF
SLURP

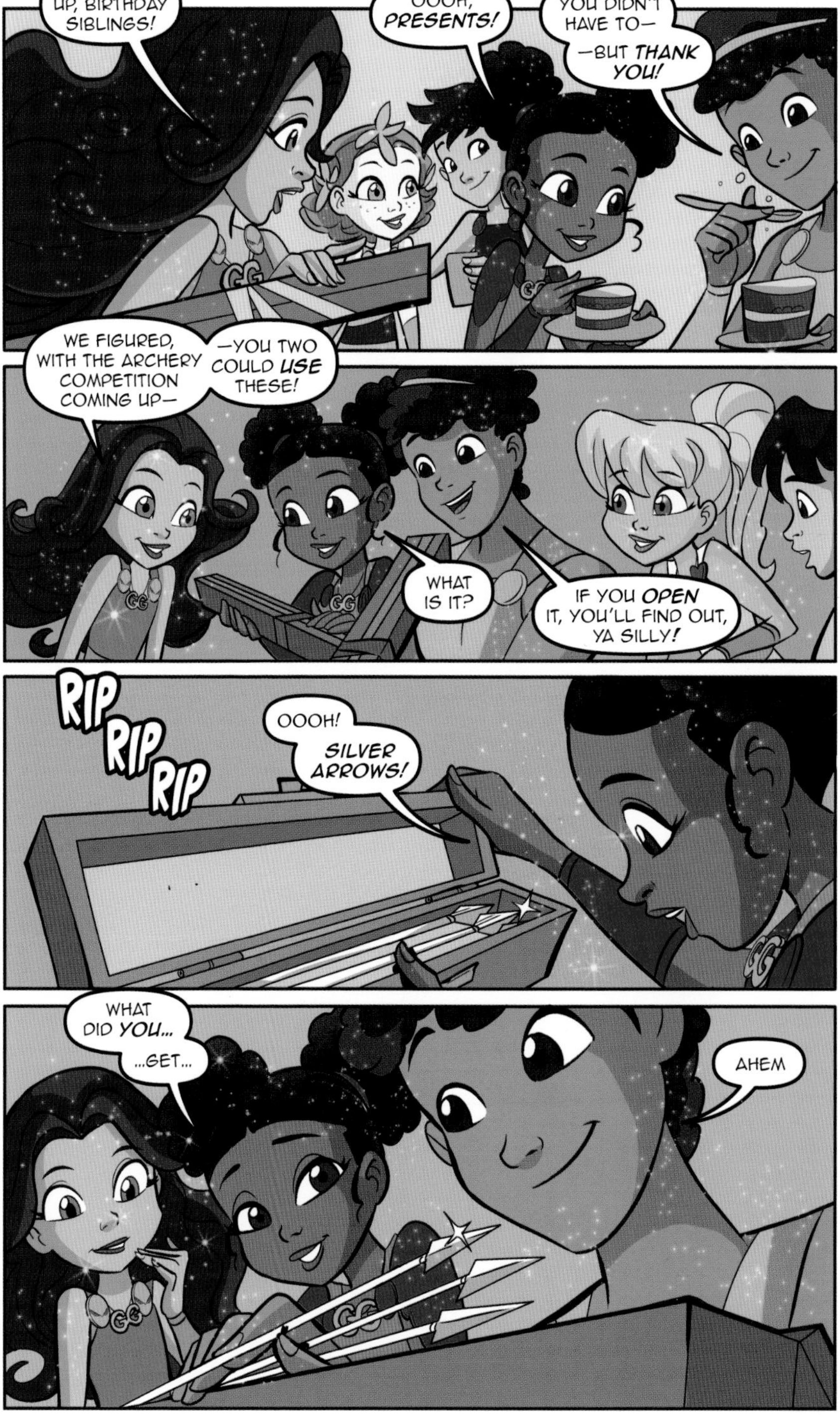
HEADS-UP, BIRTHDAY SIBLINGS!
OOOH, PRESENTS!
YOU DIDN'T HAVE TO—
—BUT THANK YOU!
WE FIGURED, WITH THE ARCHERY COMPETITION COMING UP—
—YOU TWO COULD USE THESE!
WHAT IS IT?
IF YOU OPEN IT, YOU'LL FIND OUT, YA SILLY!
RIP RIP RIP
OOOH!
SILVER ARROWS!
WHAT DID YOU...
...GET...
AHEM

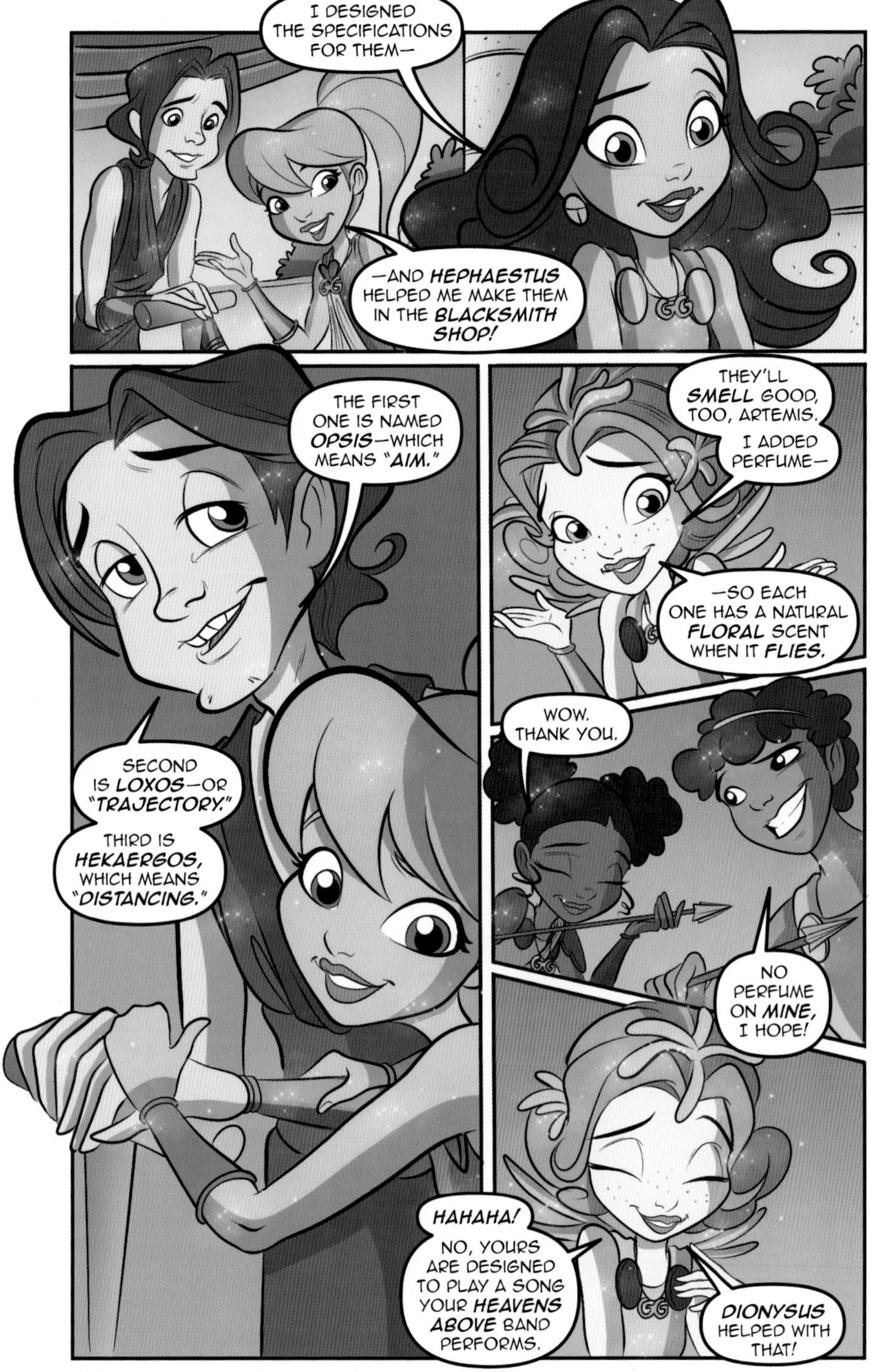
I DESIGNED THE SPECIFICATIONS FOR THEM—
—AND HEPHAESTUS HELPED ME MAKE THEM IN THE BLACKSMITH SHOP!
THE FIRST ONE IS NAMED OPSIS—WHICH MEANS "AIM."
SECOND IS LOXOS—OR "TRAJECTORY."
THIRD IS HEKAERGOS, WHICH MEANS "DISTANCING."
THEY'LL SMELL GOOD, TOO, ARTEMIS.
I ADDED PERFUME—
—SO EACH ONE HAS A NATURAL FLORAL SCENT WHEN IT FLIES.
WOW. THANK YOU.
NO PERFUME ON MINE, I HOPE!
HAHAHA!
NO, YOURS ARE DESIGNED TO PLAY A SONG YOUR HEAVENS ABOVE BAND PERFORMS.
DIONYSUS HELPED WITH THAT!

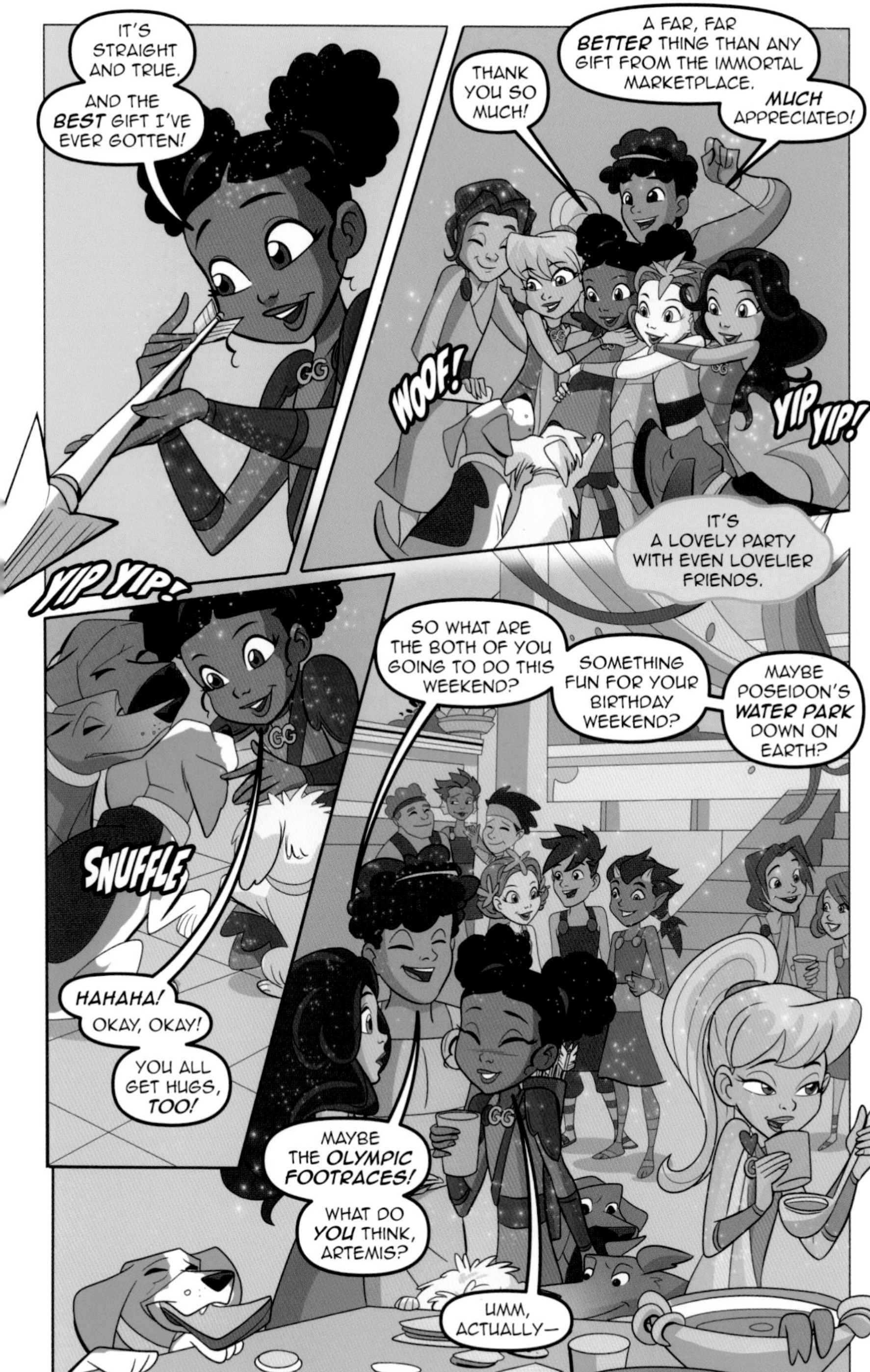
IT'S STRAIGHT AND TRUE.
AND THE BEST GIFT I'VE EVER GOTTEN!
THANK YOU SO MUCH!
A FAR, FAR BETTER THING THAN ANY GIFT FROM THE IMMORTAL MARKETPLACE.
MUCH APPRECIATED!
WOOF!
YIP YIP!
YIP YIP!
SNUFFLE
HAHAHA!
OKAY, OKAY!
YOU ALL GET HUGS, TOO!
IT'S A LOVELY PARTY WITH EVEN LOVELIER FRIENDS.
SO WHAT ARE THE BOTH OF YOU GOING TO DO THIS WEEKEND?
SOMETHING FUN FOR YOUR BIRTHDAY WEEKEND?
MAYBE POSEIDON'S WATER PARK DOWN ON EARTH?
MAYBE THE OLYMPIC FOOTRACES!
WHAT DO YOU THINK, ARTEMIS?
UMM, ACTUALLY—

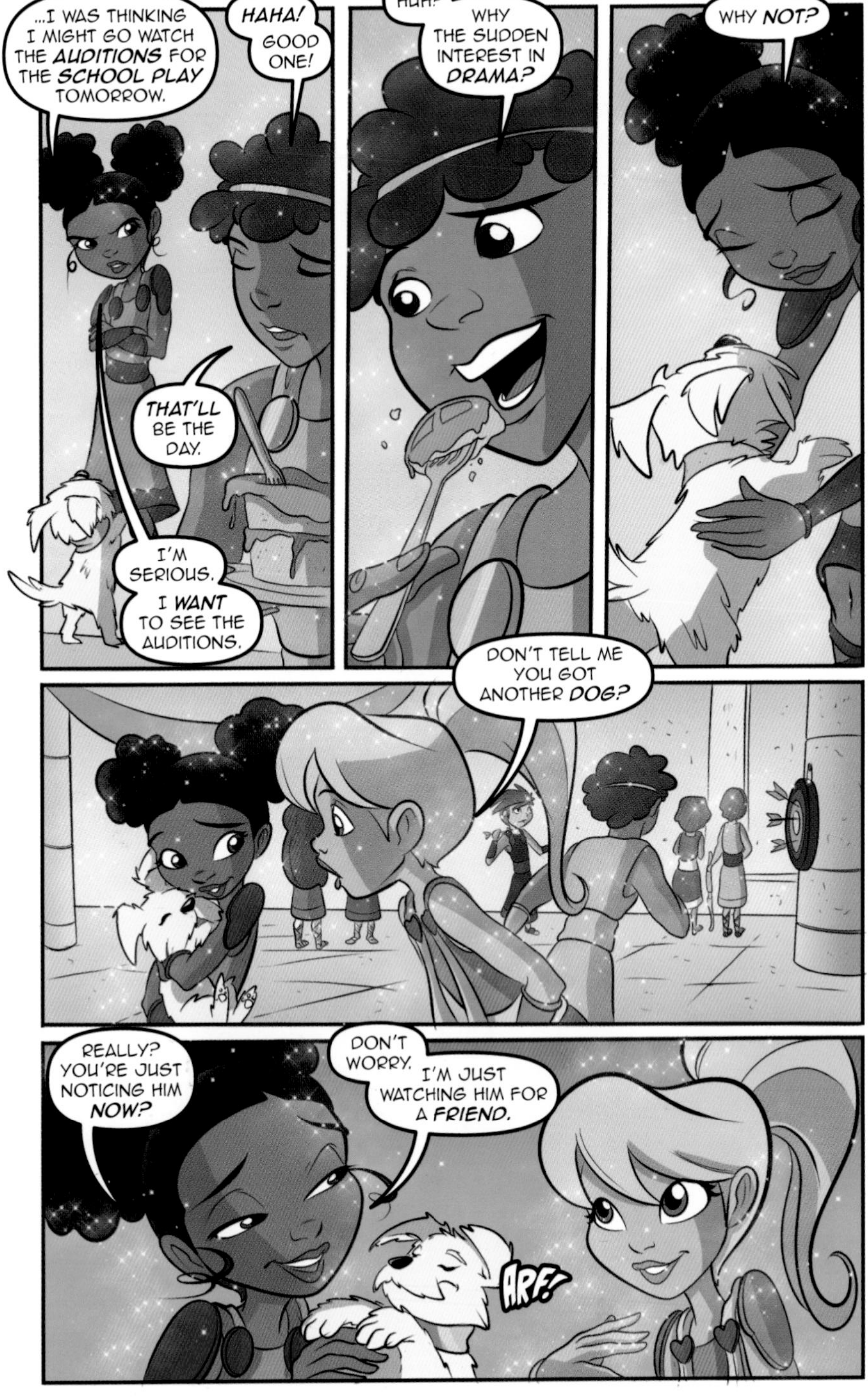
...I WAS THINKING I MIGHT GO WATCH THE AUDITIONS FOR THE SCHOOL PLAY TOMORROW.
HAHA! GOOD ONE!
THAT'LL BE THE DAY.
I'M SERIOUS.
I WANT TO SEE THE AUDITIONS.
HUH?
WHY THE SUDDEN INTEREST IN DRAMA?
WHY NOT?
DON'T TELL ME YOU GOT ANOTHER DOG?
REALLY? YOU'RE JUST NOTICING HIM NOW?
DON'T WORRY.
I'M JUST WATCHING HIM FOR A FRIEND.
ARF!

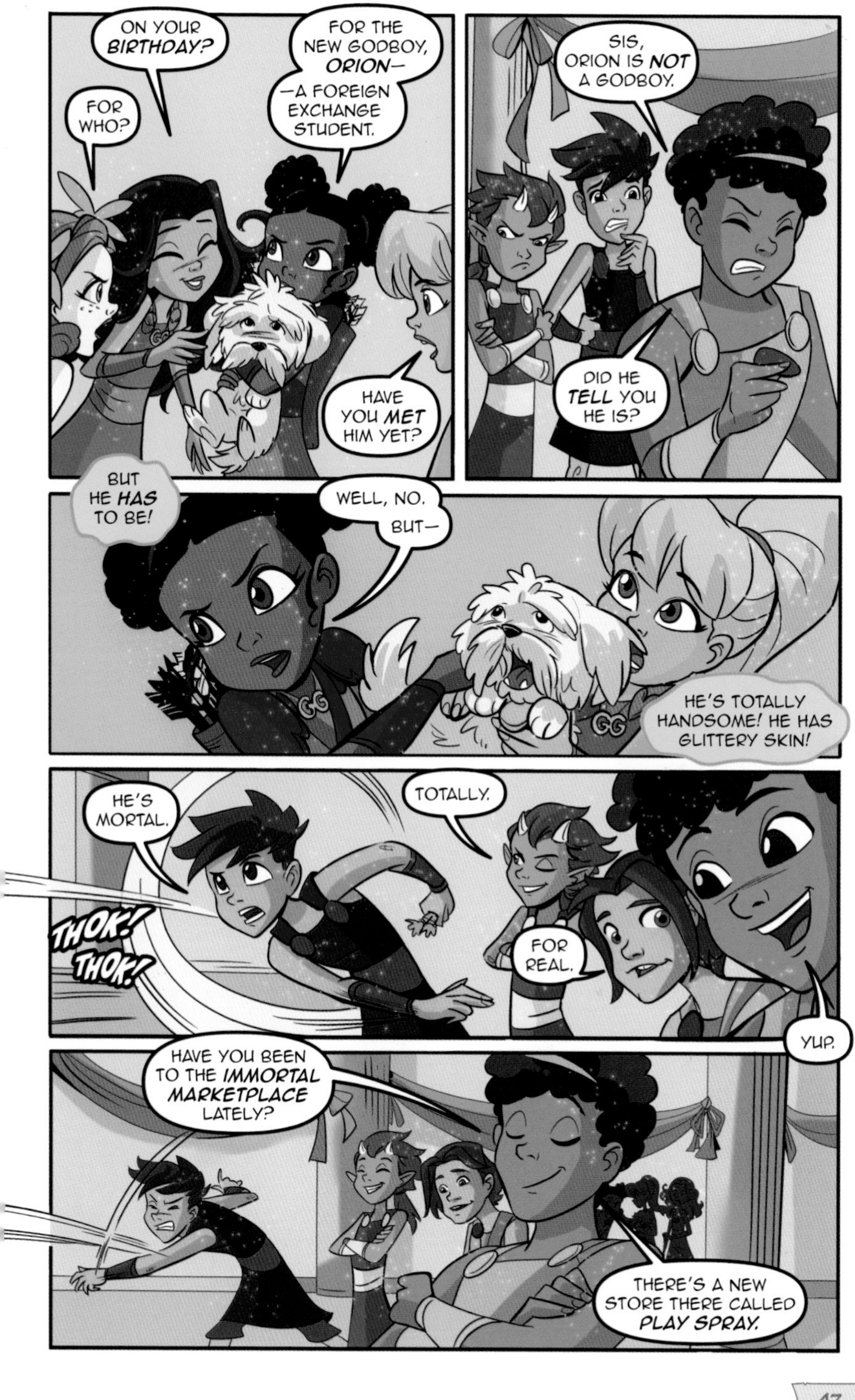

FOR WHO?
ON YOUR BIRTHDAY?
FOR THE NEW GODBOY, ORION—
—A FOREIGN EXCHANGE STUDENT.
HAVE YOU MET HIM YET?
SIS, ORION IS NOT A GODBOY.
DID HE TELL YOU HE IS?
WELL, NO. BUT—
BUT HE HAS TO BE!
HE'S TOTALLY HANDSOME! HE HAS GLITTERY SKIN!
HE'S MORTAL.
TOTALLY.
FOR REAL.
THOK! THOK!
YUP.
HAVE YOU BEEN TO THE IMMORTAL MARKETPLACE LATELY?
THERE'S A NEW STORE THERE CALLED PLAY SPRAY.

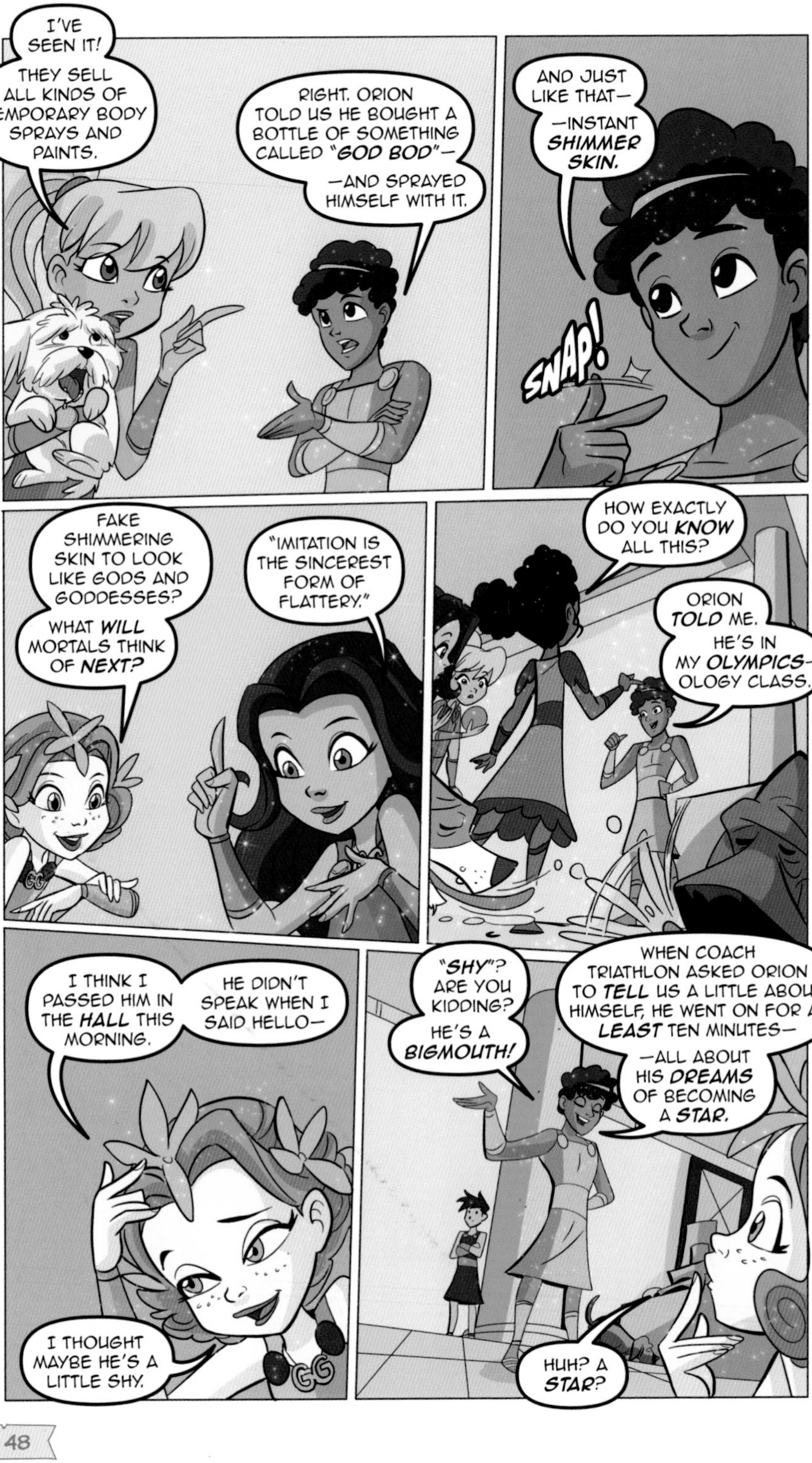
I'VE SEEN IT!
THEY SELL ALL KINDS OF TEMPORARY BODY SPRAYS AND PAINTS.
RIGHT. ORION TOLD US HE BOUGHT A BOTTLE OF SOMETHING CALLED "GOD BOD"—
—AND SPRAYED HIMSELF WITH IT.
AND JUST LIKE THAT—
—INSTANT SHIMMER SKIN.
SNAP!
FAKE SHIMMERING SKIN TO LOOK LIKE GODS AND GODDESSES?
WHAT WILL MORTALS THINK OF NEXT?
"IMITATION IS THE SINCEREST FORM OF FLATTERY."
HOW EXACTLY DO YOU KNOW ALL THIS?
ORION TOLD ME.
HE'S IN MY OLYMPICS-OLOGY CLASS.
I THINK I PASSED HIM IN THE HALL THIS MORNING.
HE DIDN'T SPEAK WHEN I SAID HELLO—
I THOUGHT MAYBE HE'S A LITTLE SHY.
"SHY"? ARE YOU KIDDING?
HE'S A BIGMOUTH!
WHEN COACH TRIATHLON ASKED ORION TO TELL US A LITTLE ABOUT HIMSELF, HE WENT ON FOR AT LEAST TEN MINUTES—
—ALL ABOUT HIS DREAMS OF BECOMING A STAR.
HUH? A STAR?

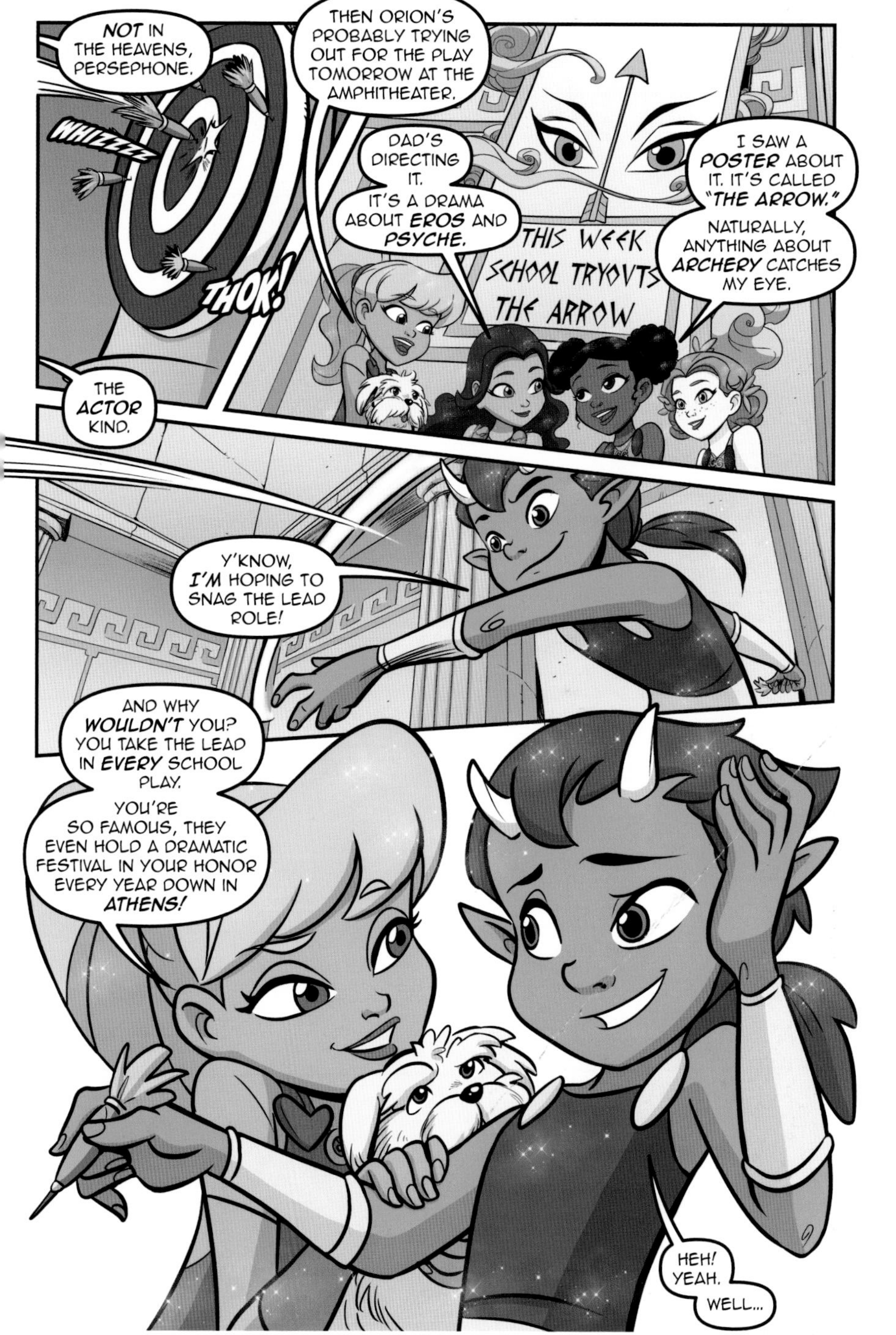
NOT IN THE HEAVENS, PERSEPHONE.
THEN ORION'S PROBABLY TRYING OUT FOR THE PLAY TOMORROW AT THE AMPHITHEATER.
WHIZZZZZ
DAD'S DIRECTING IT.
IT'S A DRAMA ABOUT EROS AND PSYCHE.
I SAW A POSTER ABOUT IT. IT'S CALLED "THE ARROW."
NATURALLY, ANYTHING ABOUT ARCHERY CATCHES MY EYE.
THIS WEEK SCHOOL TRYOUTS THE ARROW
THOK!
THE ACTOR KIND.
Y'KNOW, I'M HOPING TO SNAG THE LEAD ROLE!
AND WHY WOULDN'T YOU? YOU TAKE THE LEAD IN EVERY SCHOOL PLAY.
YOU'RE SO FAMOUS, THEY EVEN HOLD A DRAMATIC FESTIVAL IN YOUR HONOR EVERY YEAR DOWN IN ATHENS!
HEH! YEAH.
WELL...

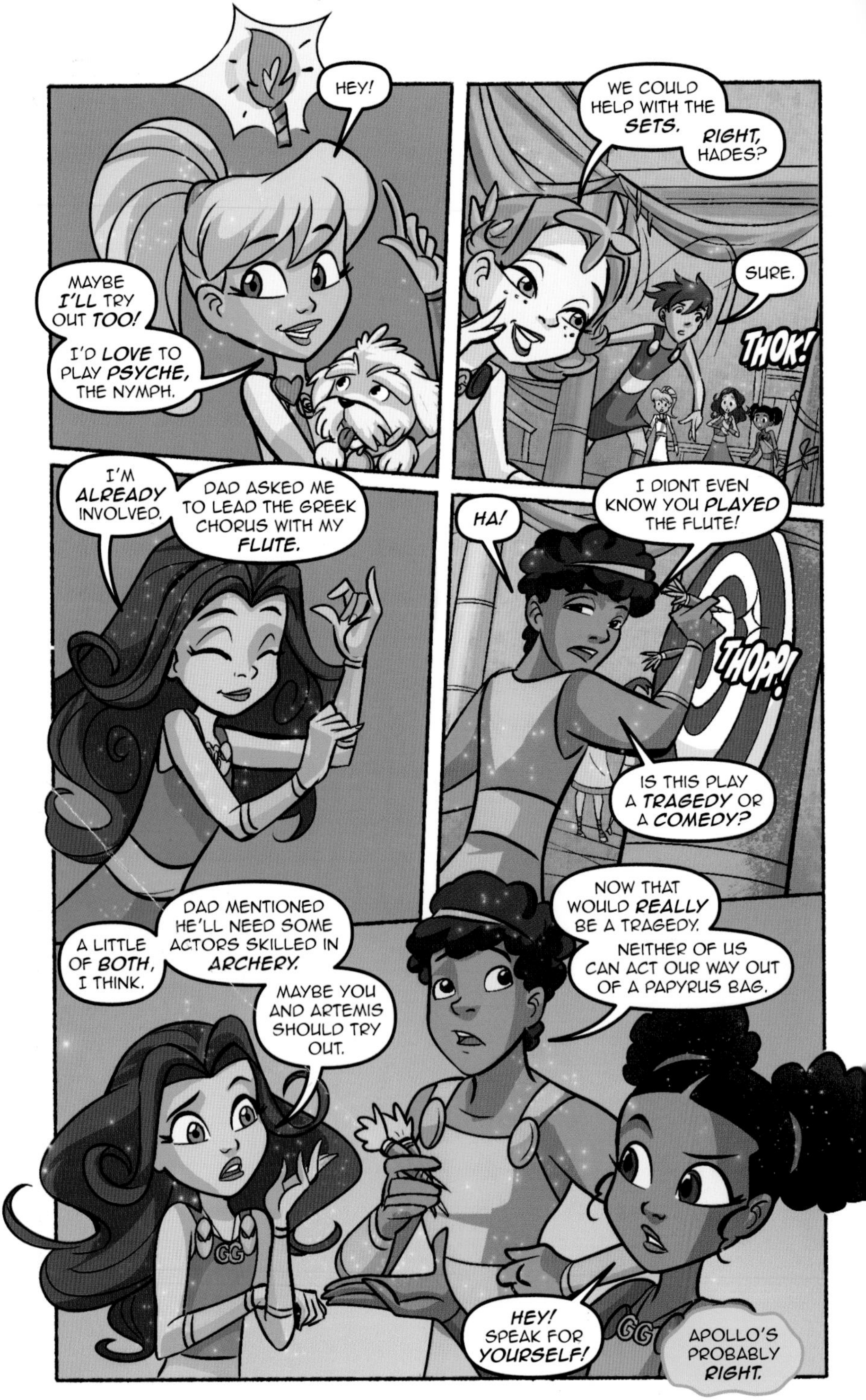
HEY!
MAYBE I'LL TRY OUT TOO!
I'D LOVE TO PLAY PSYCHE, THE NYMPH.
WE COULD HELP WITH THE SETS.
RIGHT, HADES?
SURE.
THOK!
I'M ALREADY INVOLVED.
DAD ASKED ME TO LEAD THE GREEK CHORUS WITH MY FLUTE.
HA!
I DIDNT EVEN KNOW YOU PLAYED THE FLUTE!
THOPP!
IS THIS PLAY A TRAGEDY OR A COMEDY?
A LITTLE OF BOTH, I THINK.
DAD MENTIONED HE'LL NEED SOME ACTORS SKILLED IN ARCHERY.
MAYBE YOU AND ARTEMIS SHOULD TRY OUT.
NOW THAT WOULD REALLY BE A TRAGEDY.
NEITHER OF US CAN ACT OUR WAY OUT OF A PAPYRUS BAG.
HEY! SPEAK FOR YOURSELF!
APOLLO'S PROBABLY RIGHT.

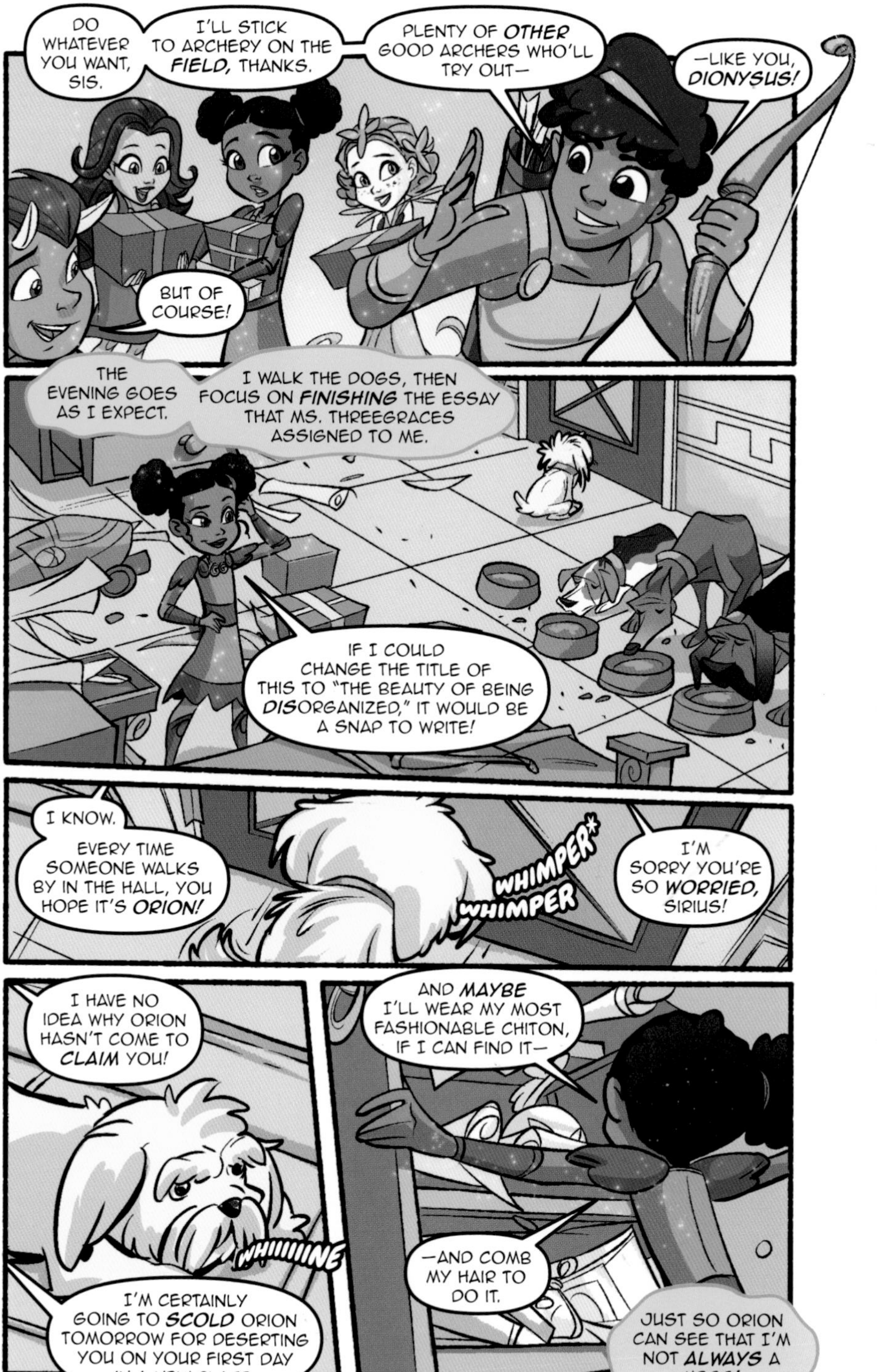
DO WHATEVER YOU WANT, SIS.
I'LL STICK TO ARCHERY ON THE *FIELD*, THANKS.
PLENTY OF *OTHER* GOOD ARCHERS WHO'LL TRY OUT—
—LIKE YOU, *DIONYSUS!*
BUT OF COURSE!
THE EVENING GOES AS I EXPECT.
I WALK THE DOGS, THEN FOCUS ON *FINISHING* THE ESSAY THAT MS. THREEGRACES ASSIGNED TO ME.
IF I COULD CHANGE THE TITLE OF THIS TO "THE BEAUTY OF BEING *DIS*ORGANIZED," IT WOULD BE A SNAP TO WRITE!
I KNOW.
EVERY TIME SOMEONE WALKS BY IN THE HALL, YOU HOPE IT'S *ORION!*
WHIMPER*
WHIMPER
I'M SORRY YOU'RE SO *WORRIED*, SIRIUS!
I HAVE NO IDEA WHY ORION HASN'T COME TO *CLAIM* YOU!
WHIIIIIINE
I'M CERTAINLY GOING TO *SCOLD* ORION TOMORROW FOR DESERTING YOU ON YOUR FIRST DAY IN A NEW PLACE.
AND *MAYBE* I'LL WEAR MY MOST FASHIONABLE CHITON, IF I CAN FIND IT—
—AND COMB MY HAIR TO DO IT.
JUST SO ORION CAN SEE THAT I'M NOT *ALWAYS* A MESS!

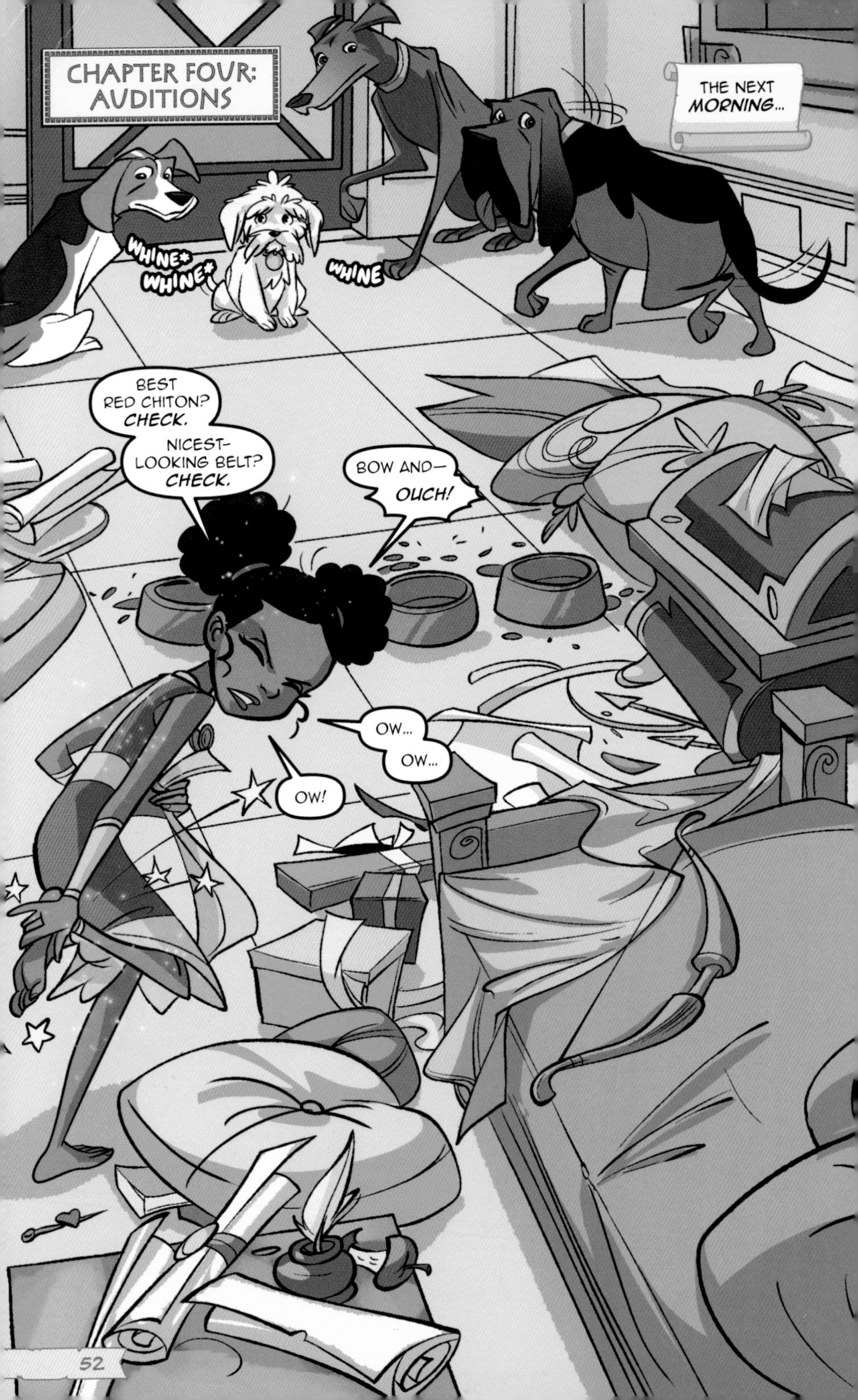

CHAPTER FOUR: AUDITIONS
THE NEXT MORNING...
WHINE* WHINE*
WHINE
BEST RED CHITON? CHECK.
NICEST-LOOKING BELT? CHECK.
BOW AND— OUCH!
OW... OW...
OW!

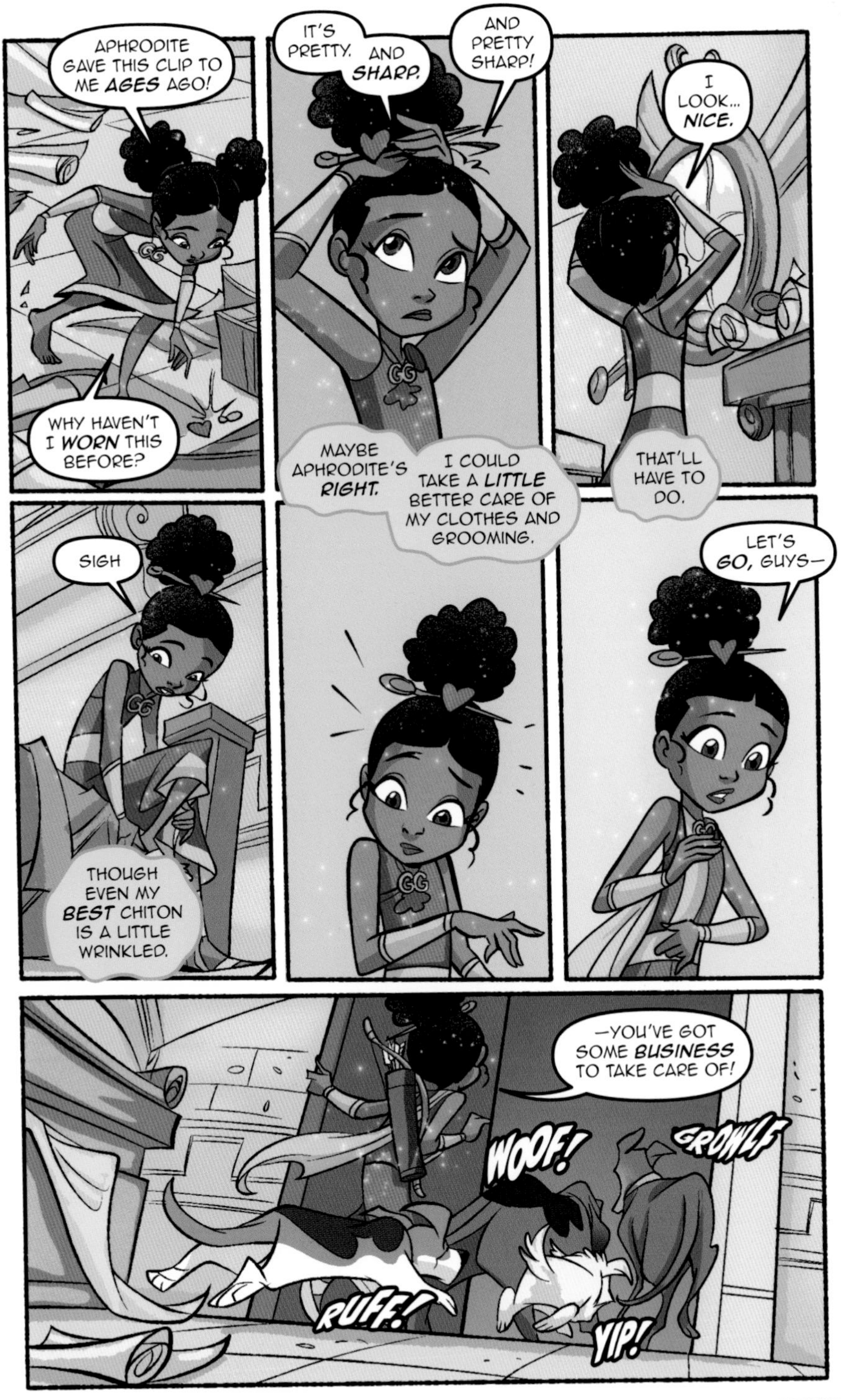
APHRODITE GAVE THIS CLIP TO ME AGES AGO!
WHY HAVEN'T I WORN THIS BEFORE?
IT'S PRETTY.
AND SHARP.
AND PRETTY SHARP!
MAYBE APHRODITE'S RIGHT.
I COULD TAKE A LITTLE BETTER CARE OF MY CLOTHES AND GROOMING.
I LOOK... NICE.
THAT'LL HAVE TO DO.
SIGH
THOUGH EVEN MY BEST CHITON IS A LITTLE WRINKLED.
LET'S GO, GUYS—
—YOU'VE GOT SOME BUSINESS TO TAKE CARE OF!
WOOF!
GROWLF
RUFF!
YIP!

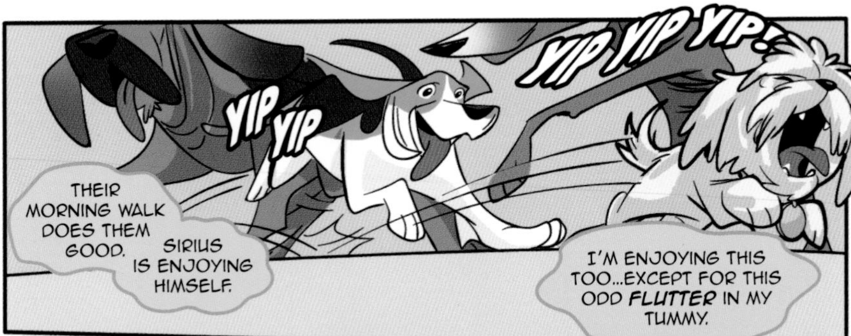
YIP YIP YIP!
YIP YIP
THEIR MORNING WALK DOES THEM GOOD.
SIRIUS IS ENJOYING HIMSELF.
I'M ENJOYING THIS TOO...EXCEPT FOR THIS ODD FLUTTER IN MY TUMMY.

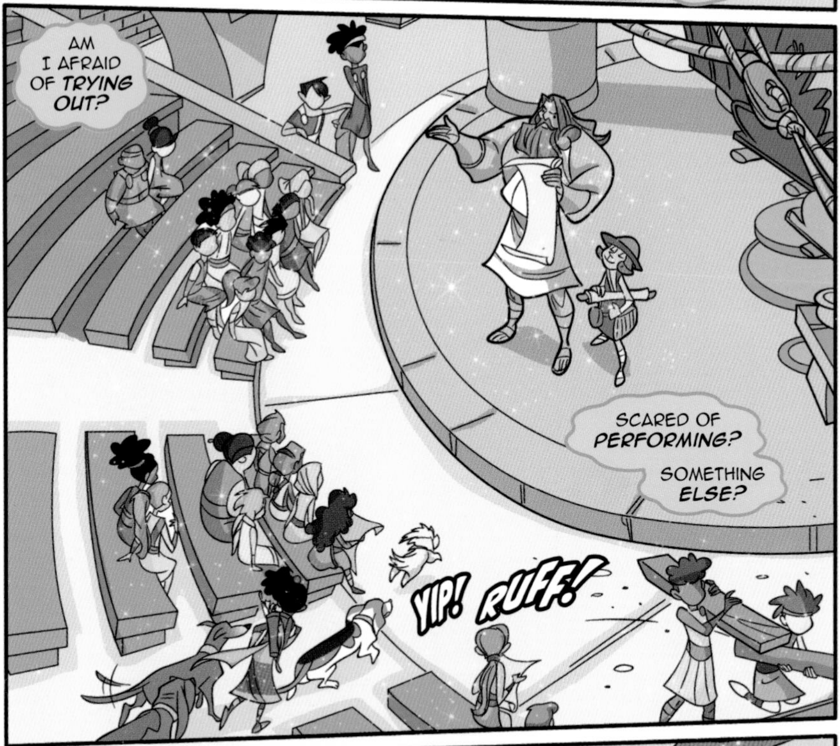
AM I AFRAID OF TRYING OUT?
SCARED OF PERFORMING?
SOMETHING ELSE?
YIP! RUFF!

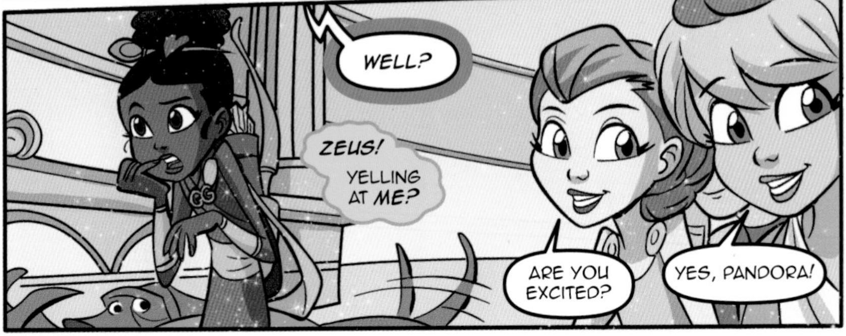
WELL?
ZEUS!
YELLING AT ME?
ARE YOU EXCITED?
YES, PANDORA!

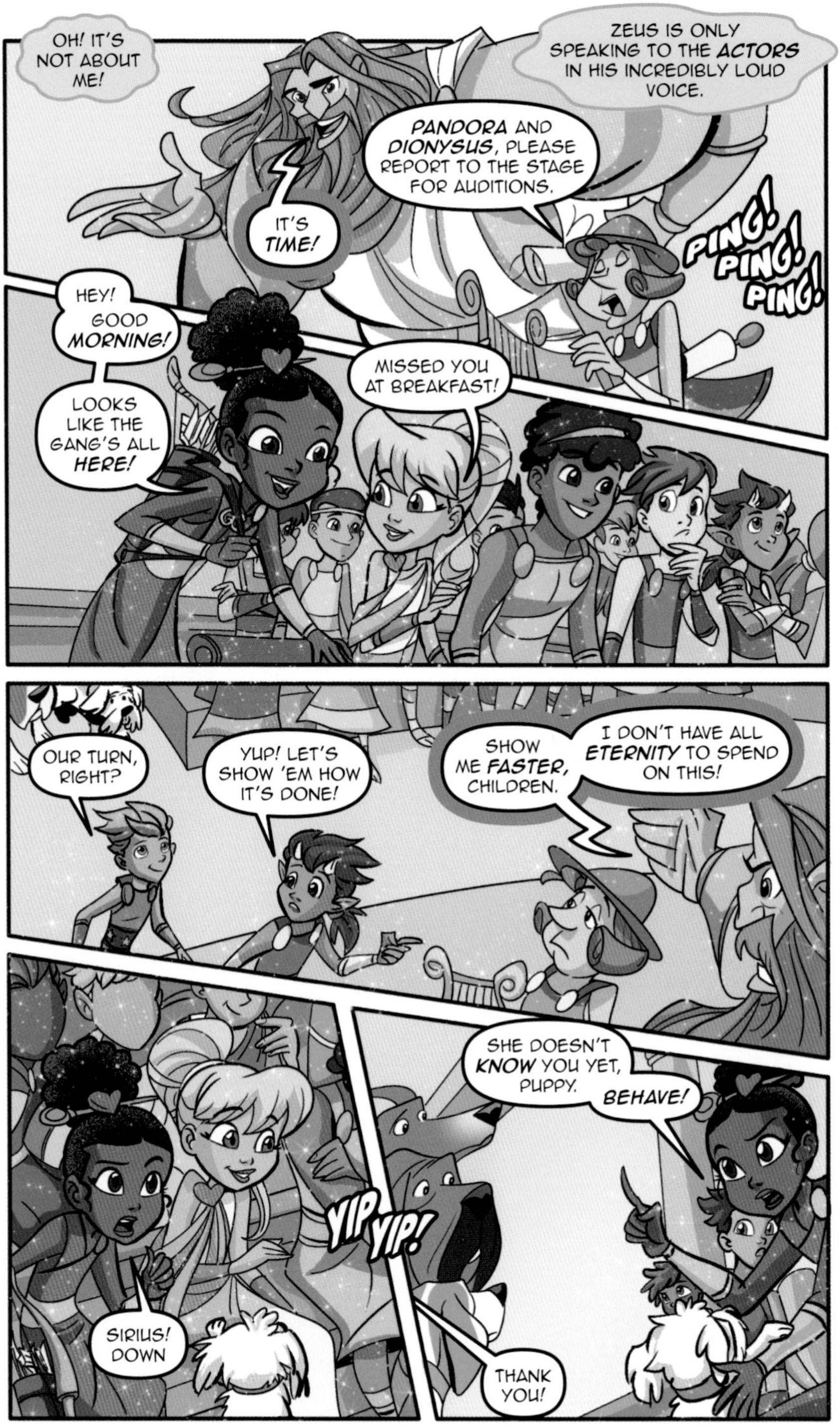
OH! IT'S NOT ABOUT ME!
ZEUS IS ONLY SPEAKING TO THE ACTORS IN HIS INCREDIBLY LOUD VOICE.
PANDORA AND DIONYSUS, PLEASE REPORT TO THE STAGE FOR AUDITIONS.
IT'S TIME!
PING! PING! PING!
HEY! GOOD MORNING!
LOOKS LIKE THE GANG'S ALL HERE!
MISSED YOU AT BREAKFAST!
OUR TURN, RIGHT?
YUP! LET'S SHOW 'EM HOW IT'S DONE!
SHOW ME FASTER, CHILDREN.
I DON'T HAVE ALL ETERNITY TO SPEND ON THIS!
YIP YIP!
SIRIUS! DOWN
SHE DOESN'T KNOW YOU YET, PUPPY.
BEHAVE!
THANK YOU!

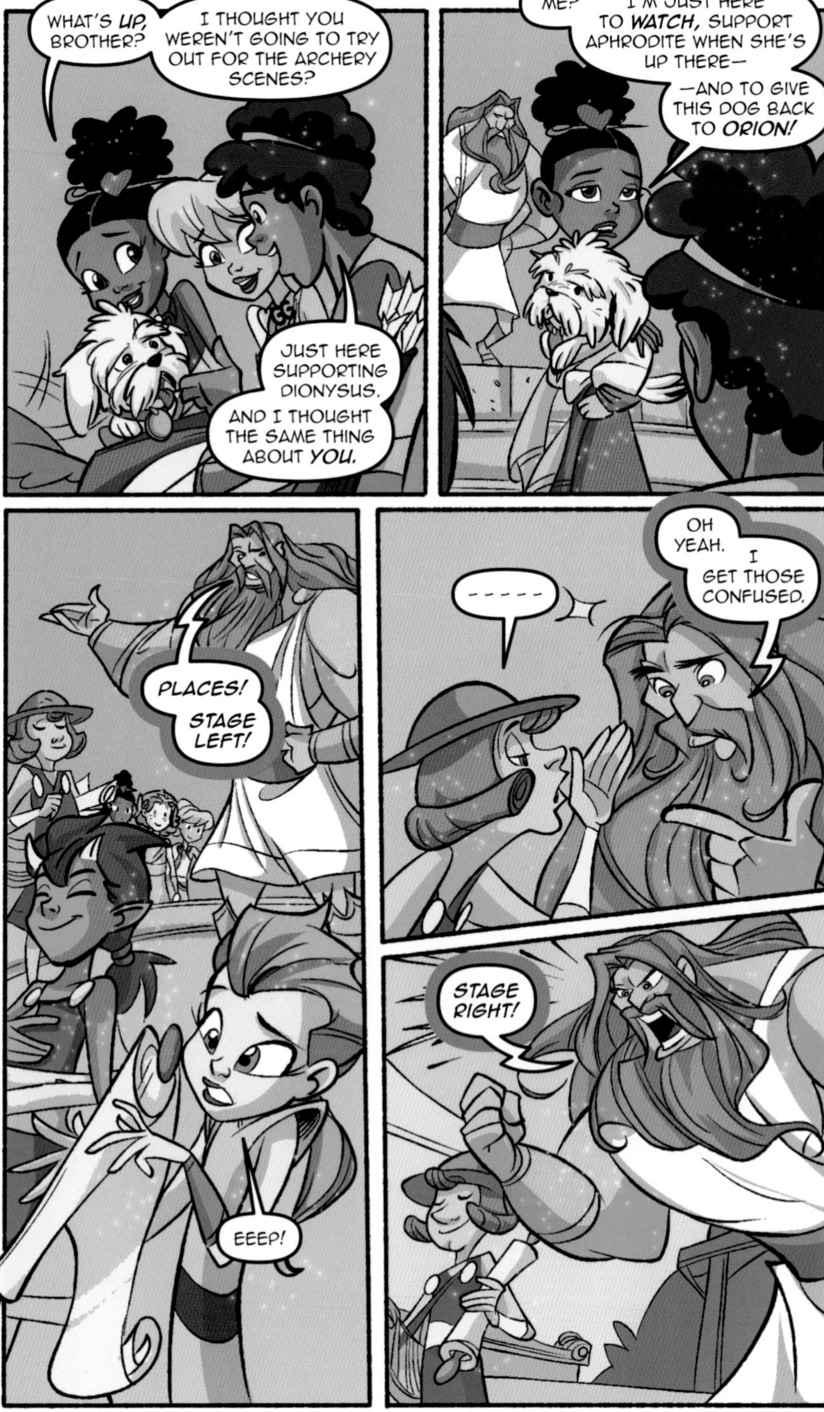
WHAT'S UP, BROTHER?
I THOUGHT YOU WEREN'T GOING TO TRY OUT FOR THE ARCHERY SCENES?
JUST HERE SUPPORTING DIONYSUS.
AND I THOUGHT THE SAME THING ABOUT YOU.
ME?
I'M JUST HERE TO WATCH, SUPPORT APHRODITE WHEN SHE'S UP THERE—
—AND TO GIVE THIS DOG BACK TO ORION!
PLACES! STAGE LEFT!
EEEP!

OH YEAH.
I GET THOSE CONFUSED.
STAGE RIGHT!

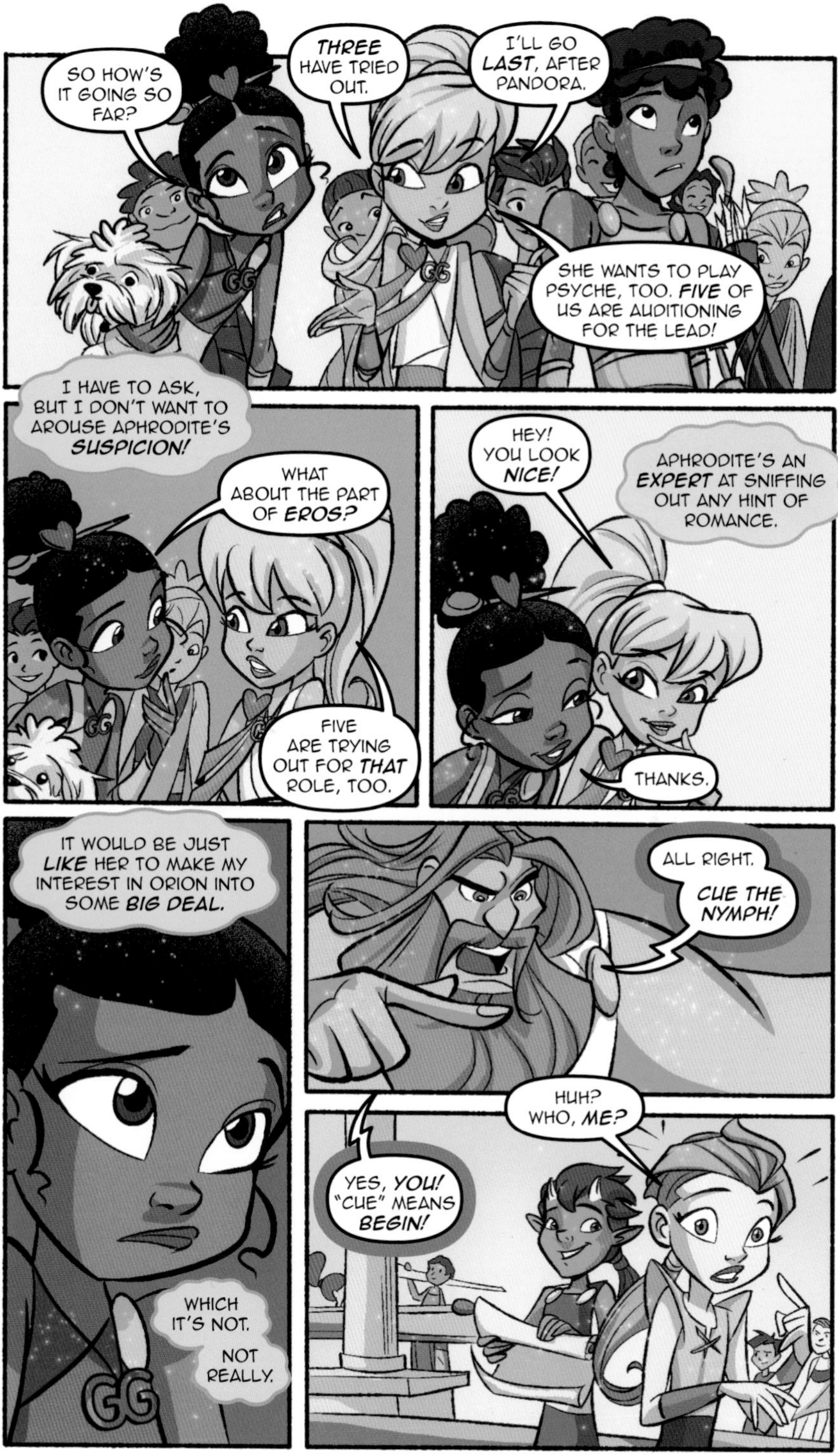
SO HOW'S IT GOING SO FAR?
THREE HAVE TRIED OUT.
I'LL GO LAST, AFTER PANDORA.
SHE WANTS TO PLAY PSYCHE, TOO. FIVE OF US ARE AUDITIONING FOR THE LEAD!
I HAVE TO ASK, BUT I DON'T WANT TO AROUSE APHRODITE'S SUSPICION!
WHAT ABOUT THE PART OF EROS?
FIVE ARE TRYING OUT FOR THAT ROLE, TOO.
HEY! YOU LOOK NICE!
APHRODITE'S AN EXPERT AT SNIFFING OUT ANY HINT OF ROMANCE.
THANKS.
IT WOULD BE JUST LIKE HER TO MAKE MY INTEREST IN ORION INTO SOME BIG DEAL.
WHICH IT'S NOT.
NOT REALLY.
ALL RIGHT.
CUE THE NYMPH!
HUH? WHO, ME?
YES, YOU! "CUE" MEANS BEGIN!

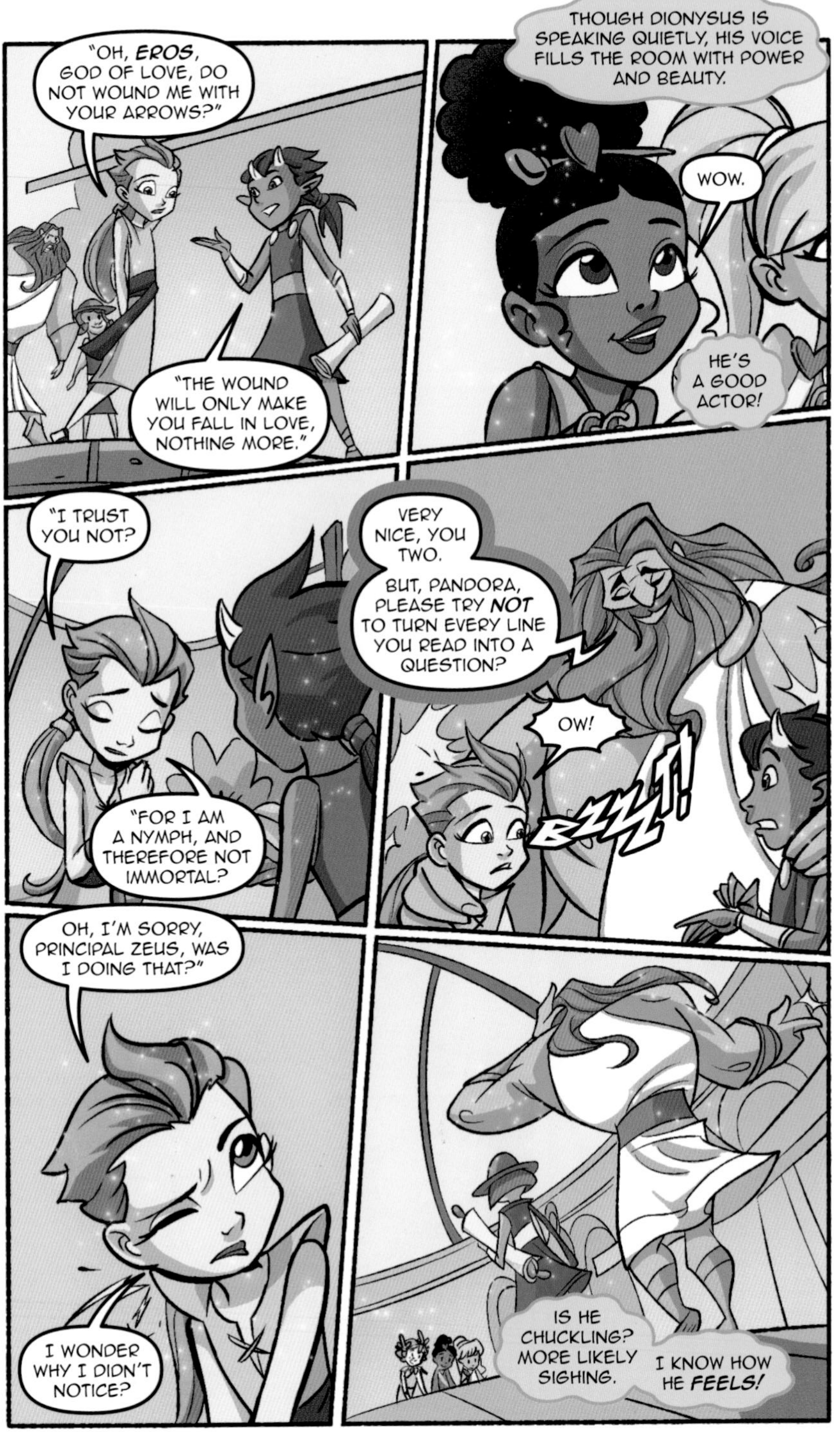
"OH, EROS, GOD OF LOVE, DO NOT WOUND ME WITH YOUR ARROWS?"
"THE WOUND WILL ONLY MAKE YOU FALL IN LOVE, NOTHING MORE."
THOUGH DIONYSUS IS SPEAKING QUIETLY, HIS VOICE FILLS THE ROOM WITH POWER AND BEAUTY.
WOW.
HE'S A GOOD ACTOR!
"I TRUST YOU NOT?
"FOR I AM A NYMPH, AND THEREFORE NOT IMMORTAL?
VERY NICE, YOU TWO.
BUT, PANDORA, PLEASE TRY NOT TO TURN EVERY LINE YOU READ INTO A QUESTION?
OW!
BZZZT!
OH, I'M SORRY, PRINCIPAL ZEUS, WAS I DOING THAT?"
I WONDER WHY I DIDN'T NOTICE?
IS HE CHUCKLING? MORE LIKELY SIGHING.
I KNOW HOW HE FEELS!

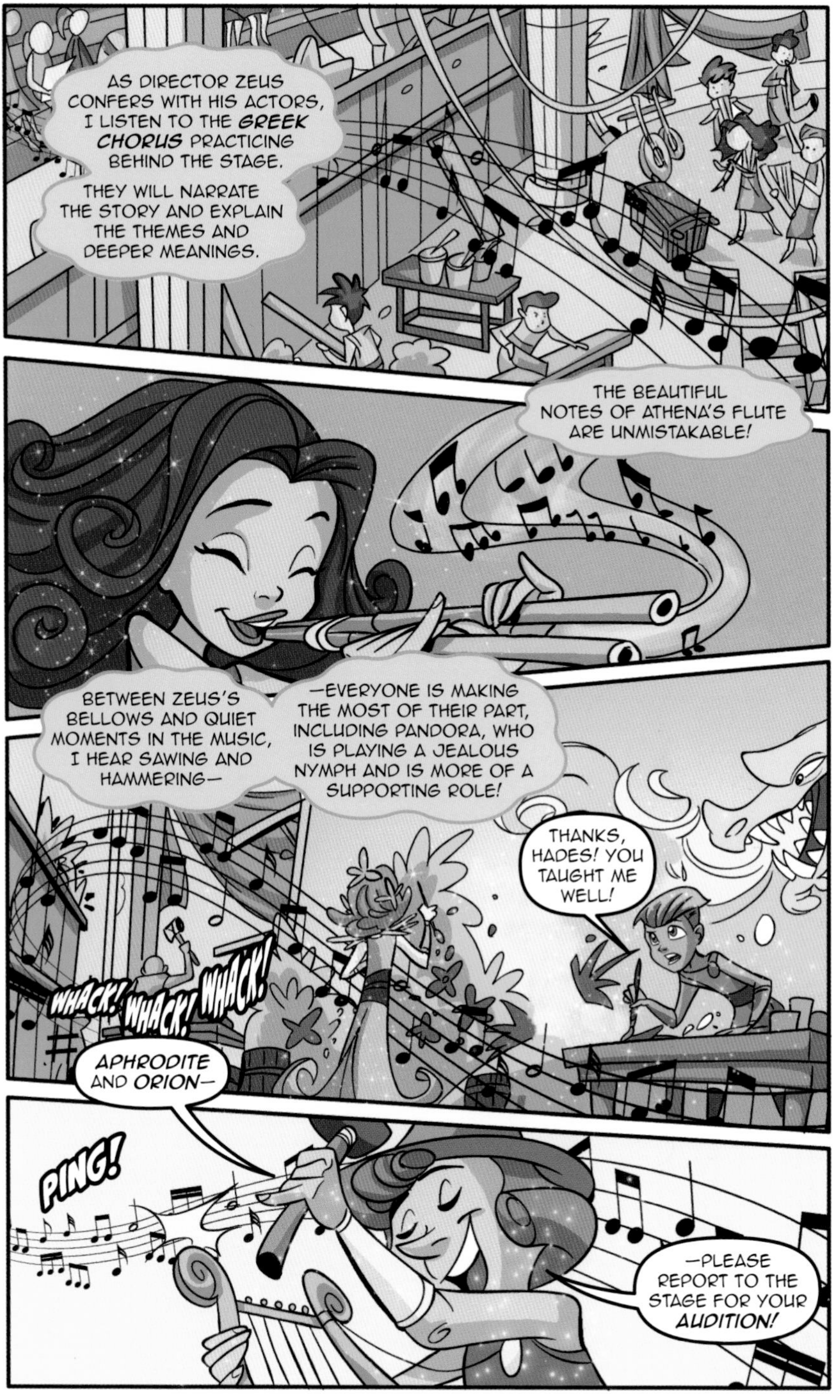
AS DIRECTOR ZEUS CONFERS WITH HIS ACTORS, I LISTEN TO THE *GREEK CHORUS* PRACTICING BEHIND THE STAGE.
THEY WILL NARRATE THE STORY AND EXPLAIN THE THEMES AND DEEPER MEANINGS.
THE BEAUTIFUL NOTES OF ATHENA'S FLUTE ARE UNMISTAKABLE!
BETWEEN ZEUS'S BELLOWS AND QUIET MOMENTS IN THE MUSIC, I HEAR SAWING AND HAMMERING—
—EVERYONE IS MAKING THE MOST OF THEIR PART, INCLUDING PANDORA, WHO IS PLAYING A JEALOUS NYMPH AND IS MORE OF A SUPPORTING ROLE!
THANKS, HADES! YOU TAUGHT ME WELL!
WHACK! WHACK! WHACK!
APHRODITE AND *ORION*—
PING!
—PLEASE REPORT TO THE STAGE FOR YOUR *AUDITION!*

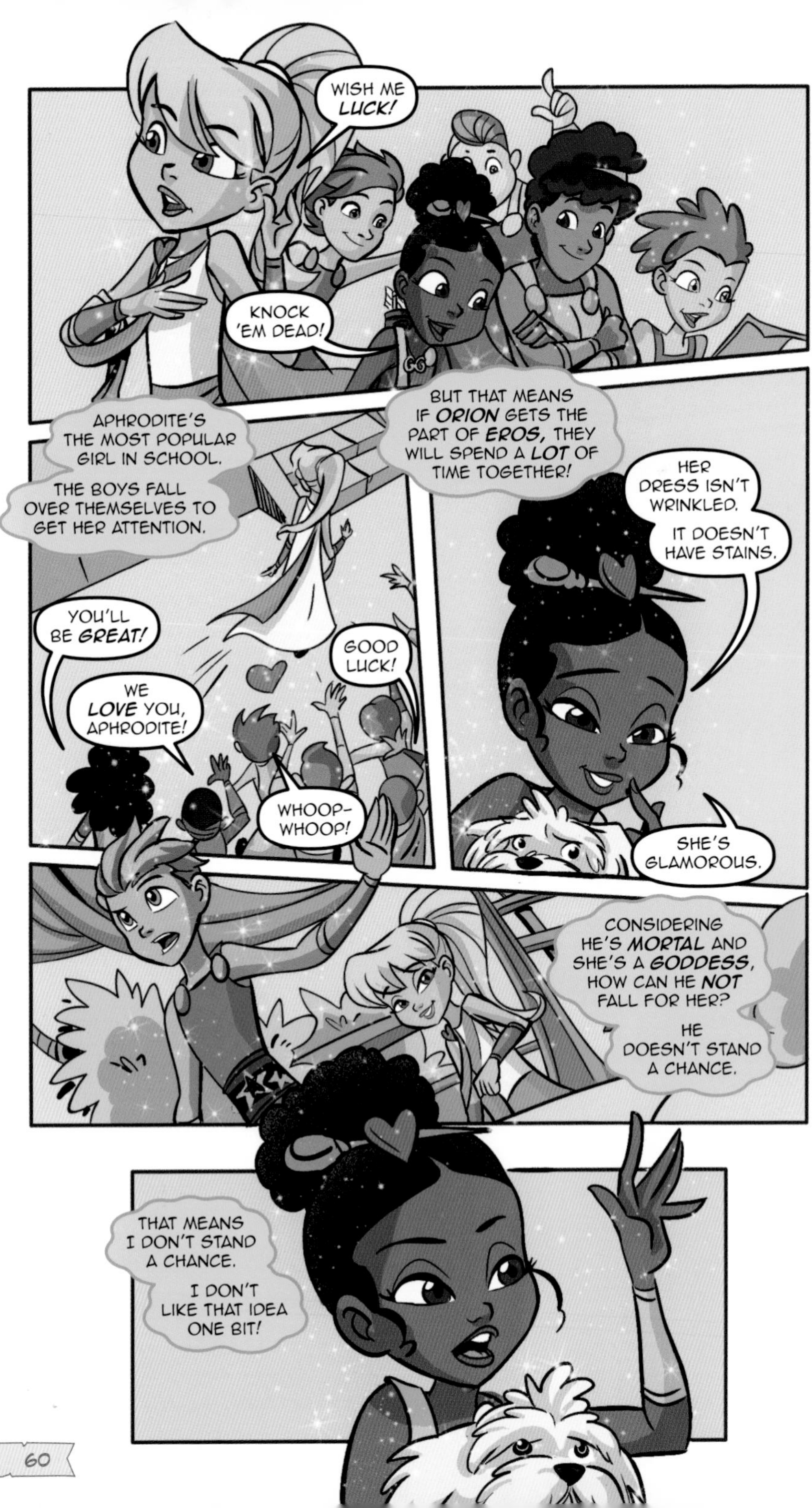
WISH ME LUCK!
KNOCK 'EM DEAD!
APHRODITE'S THE MOST POPULAR GIRL IN SCHOOL.
THE BOYS FALL OVER THEMSELVES TO GET HER ATTENTION.
YOU'LL BE GREAT!
WE LOVE YOU, APHRODITE!
GOOD LUCK!
WHOOP-WHOOP!
BUT THAT MEANS IF ORION GETS THE PART OF EROS, THEY WILL SPEND A LOT OF TIME TOGETHER!
HER DRESS ISN'T WRINKLED.
IT DOESN'T HAVE STAINS.
SHE'S GLAMOROUS.
CONSIDERING HE'S MORTAL AND SHE'S A GODDESS, HOW CAN HE NOT FALL FOR HER?
HE DOESN'T STAND A CHANCE.
THAT MEANS I DON'T STAND A CHANCE.
I DON'T LIKE THAT IDEA ONE BIT!

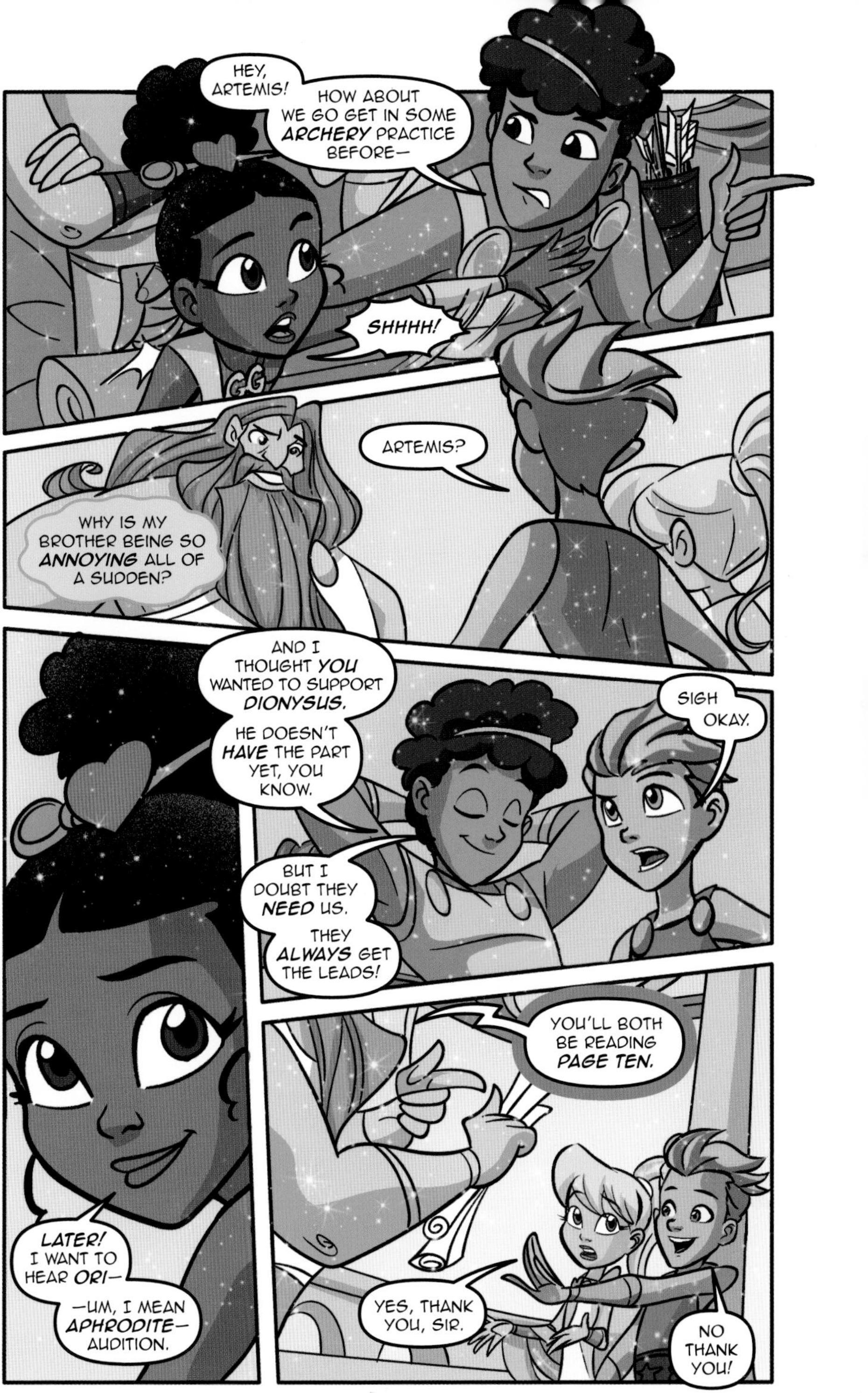

HEY, ARTEMIS!
HOW ABOUT WE GO GET IN SOME ARCHERY PRACTICE BEFORE—
SHHHH!
ARTEMIS?
WHY IS MY BROTHER BEING SO ANNOYING ALL OF A SUDDEN?
AND I THOUGHT YOU WANTED TO SUPPORT DIONYSUS.
HE DOESN'T HAVE THE PART YET, YOU KNOW.
SIGH OKAY.
BUT I DOUBT THEY NEED US.
THEY ALWAYS GET THE LEADS!
LATER! I WANT TO HEAR ORI—
—UM, I MEAN APHRODITE— AUDITION.
YOU'LL BOTH BE READING PAGE TEN.
YES, THANK YOU, SIR.
NO THANK YOU!

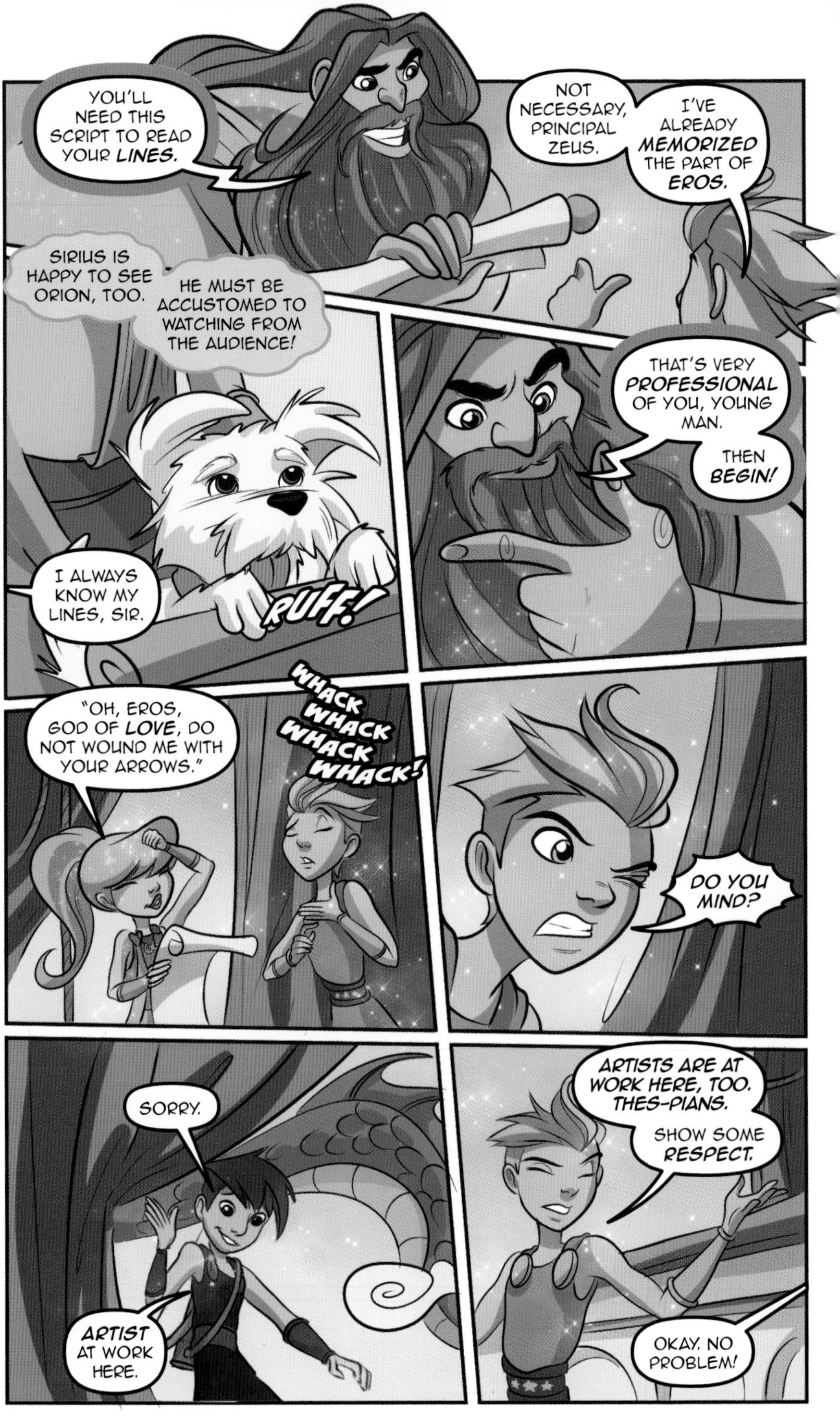
YOU'LL NEED THIS SCRIPT TO READ YOUR LINES.
NOT NECESSARY, PRINCIPAL ZEUS.
I'VE ALREADY MEMORIZED THE PART OF EROS.
SIRIUS IS HAPPY TO SEE ORION, TOO.
HE MUST BE ACCUSTOMED TO WATCHING FROM THE AUDIENCE!
I ALWAYS KNOW MY LINES, SIR.
RUFF!
THAT'S VERY PROFESSIONAL OF YOU, YOUNG MAN.
THEN BEGIN!
"OH, EROS, GOD OF LOVE, DO NOT WOUND ME WITH YOUR ARROWS."
WHACK WHACK WHACK WHACK!
DO YOU MIND?
SORRY.
ARTIST AT WORK HERE.
ARTISTS ARE AT WORK HERE, TOO. THES-PIANS.
SHOW SOME RESPECT.
OKAY. NO PROBLEM!

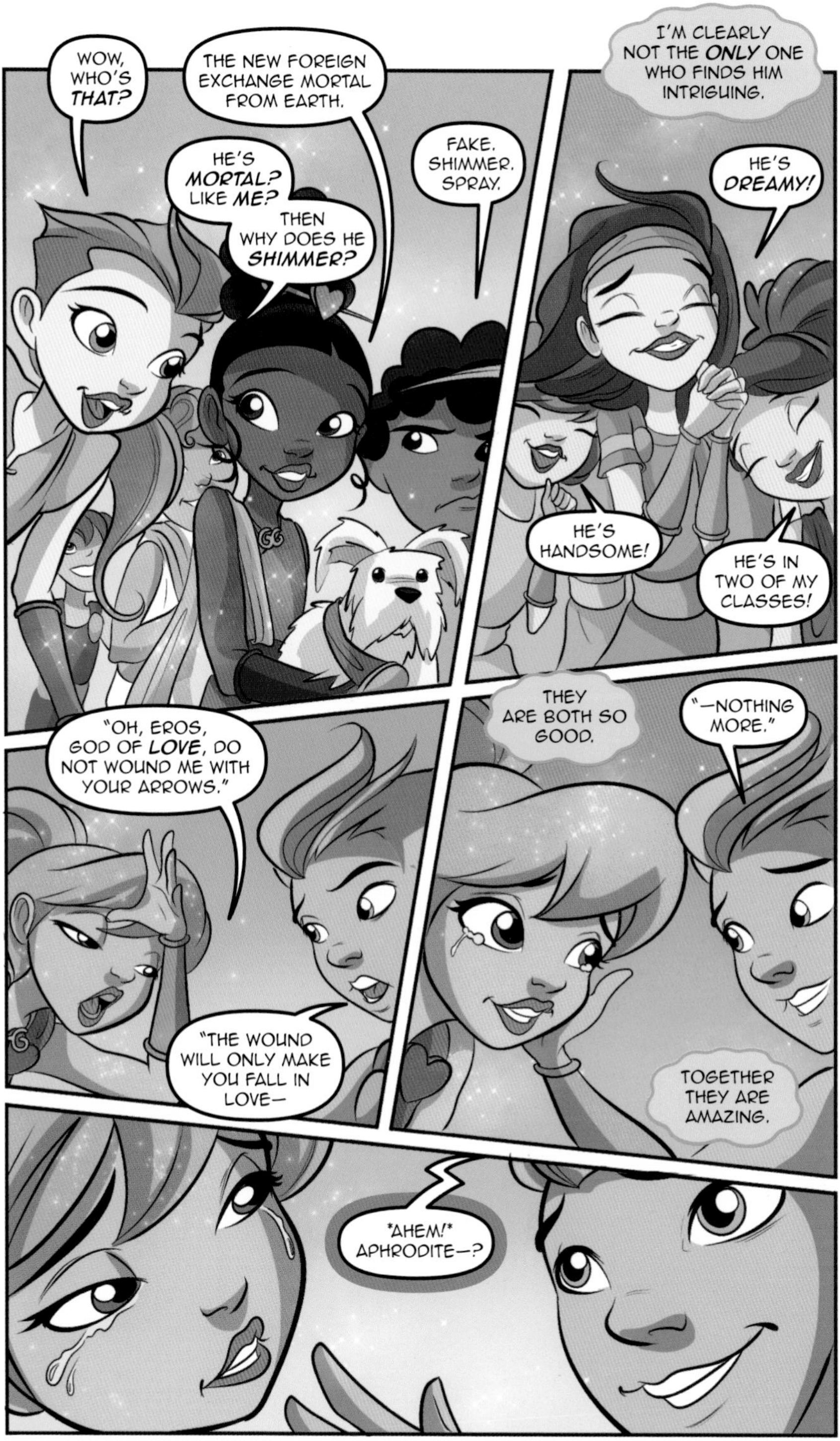

WOW, WHO'S THAT?
THE NEW FOREIGN EXCHANGE MORTAL FROM EARTH.
HE'S MORTAL? LIKE ME?
THEN WHY DOES HE SHIMMER?
FAKE. SHIMMER. SPRAY.
I'M CLEARLY NOT THE ONLY ONE WHO FINDS HIM INTRIGUING.
HE'S DREAMY!
HE'S HANDSOME!
HE'S IN TWO OF MY CLASSES!
"OH, EROS, GOD OF LOVE, DO NOT WOUND ME WITH YOUR ARROWS."
"THE WOUND WILL ONLY MAKE YOU FALL IN LOVE—
THEY ARE BOTH SO GOOD.
"—NOTHING MORE."
TOGETHER THEY ARE AMAZING.
AHEM! APHRODITE—?

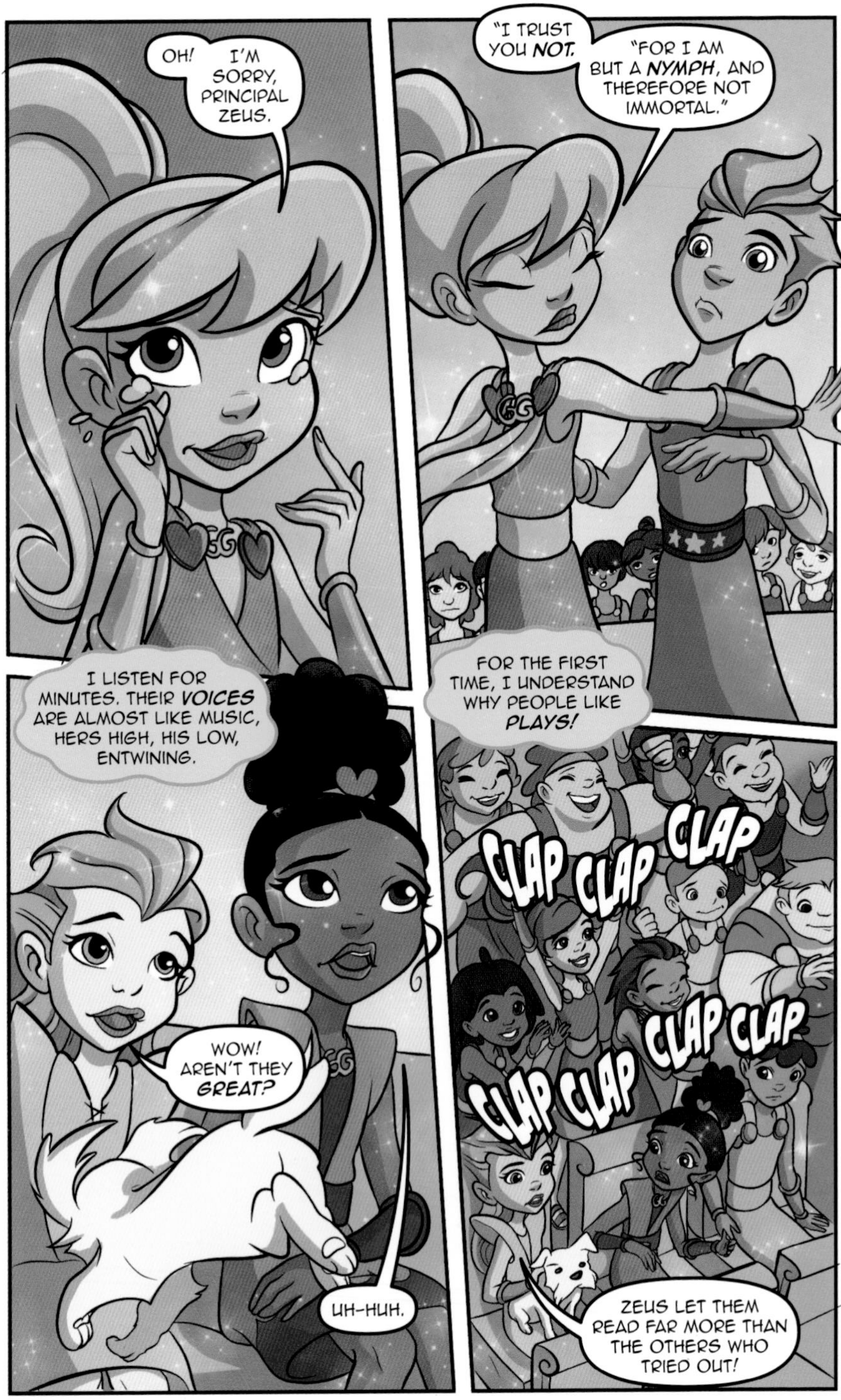
OH!
I'M SORRY, PRINCIPAL ZEUS.
"I TRUST YOU NOT.
"FOR I AM BUT A NYMPH, AND THEREFORE NOT IMMORTAL."
I LISTEN FOR MINUTES. THEIR VOICES ARE ALMOST LIKE MUSIC, HERS HIGH, HIS LOW, ENTWINING.
WOW! AREN'T THEY GREAT?
UH-HUH.
FOR THE FIRST TIME, I UNDERSTAND WHY PEOPLE LIKE PLAYS!
CLAP CLAP CLAP
CLAP CLAP CLAP CLAP
ZEUS LET THEM READ FAR MORE THAN THE OTHERS WHO TRIED OUT!

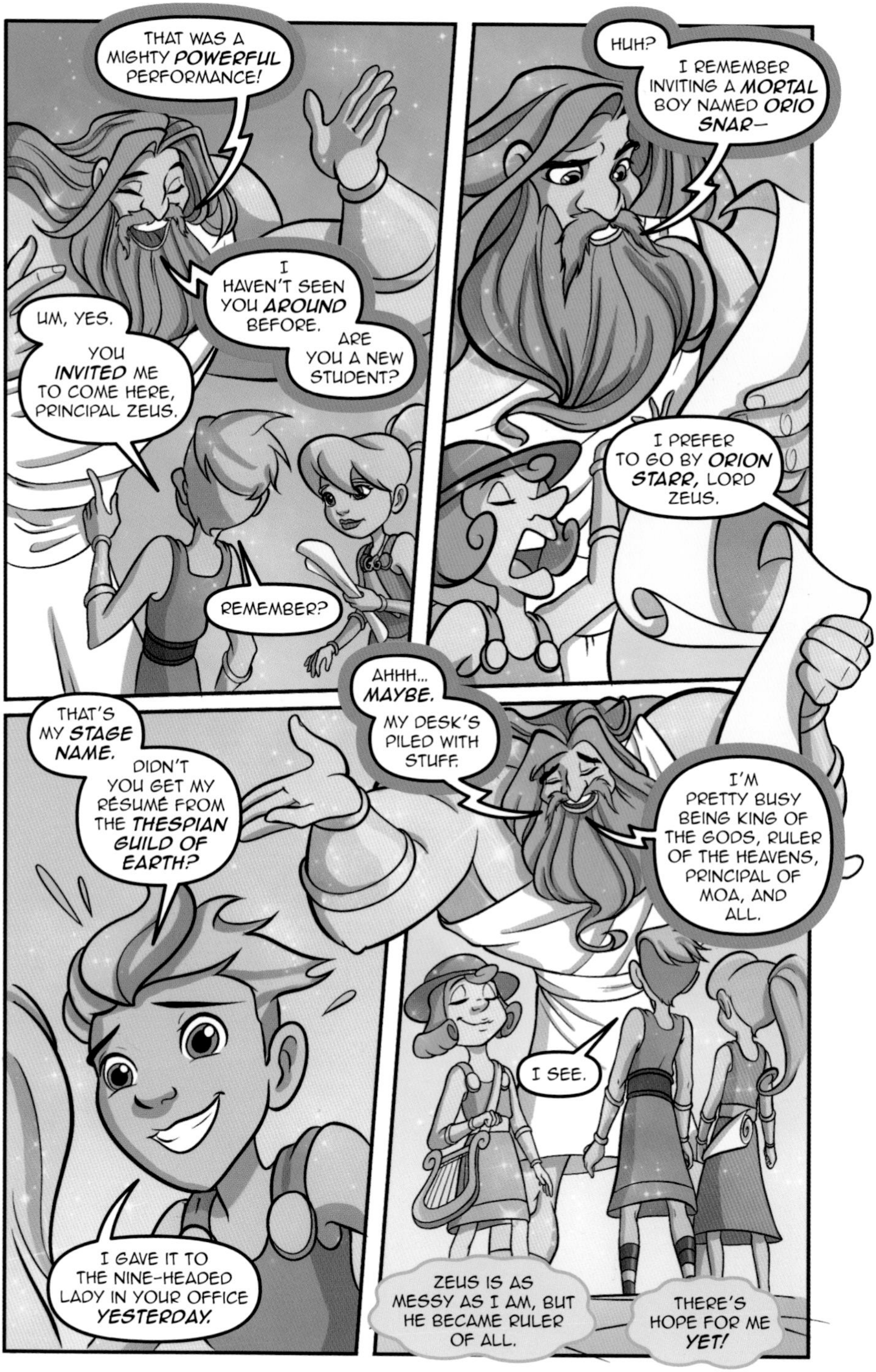
THAT WAS A MIGHTY POWERFUL PERFORMANCE!
I HAVEN'T SEEN YOU AROUND BEFORE.
ARE YOU A NEW STUDENT?
UM, YES.
YOU INVITED ME TO COME HERE, PRINCIPAL ZEUS.
REMEMBER?
HUH?
I REMEMBER INVITING A MORTAL BOY NAMED ORIO SNAR—
I PREFER TO GO BY ORION STARR, LORD ZEUS.
THAT'S MY STAGE NAME.
DIDN'T YOU GET MY RÉSUMÉ FROM THE THESPIAN GUILD OF EARTH?
I GAVE IT TO THE NINE-HEADED LADY IN YOUR OFFICE YESTERDAY.
AHHH... MAYBE.
MY DESK'S PILED WITH STUFF.
I'M PRETTY BUSY BEING KING OF THE GODS, RULER OF THE HEAVENS, PRINCIPAL OF MOA, AND ALL.
I SEE.
ZEUS IS AS MESSY AS I AM, BUT HE BECAME RULER OF ALL.
THERE'S HOPE FOR ME YET!

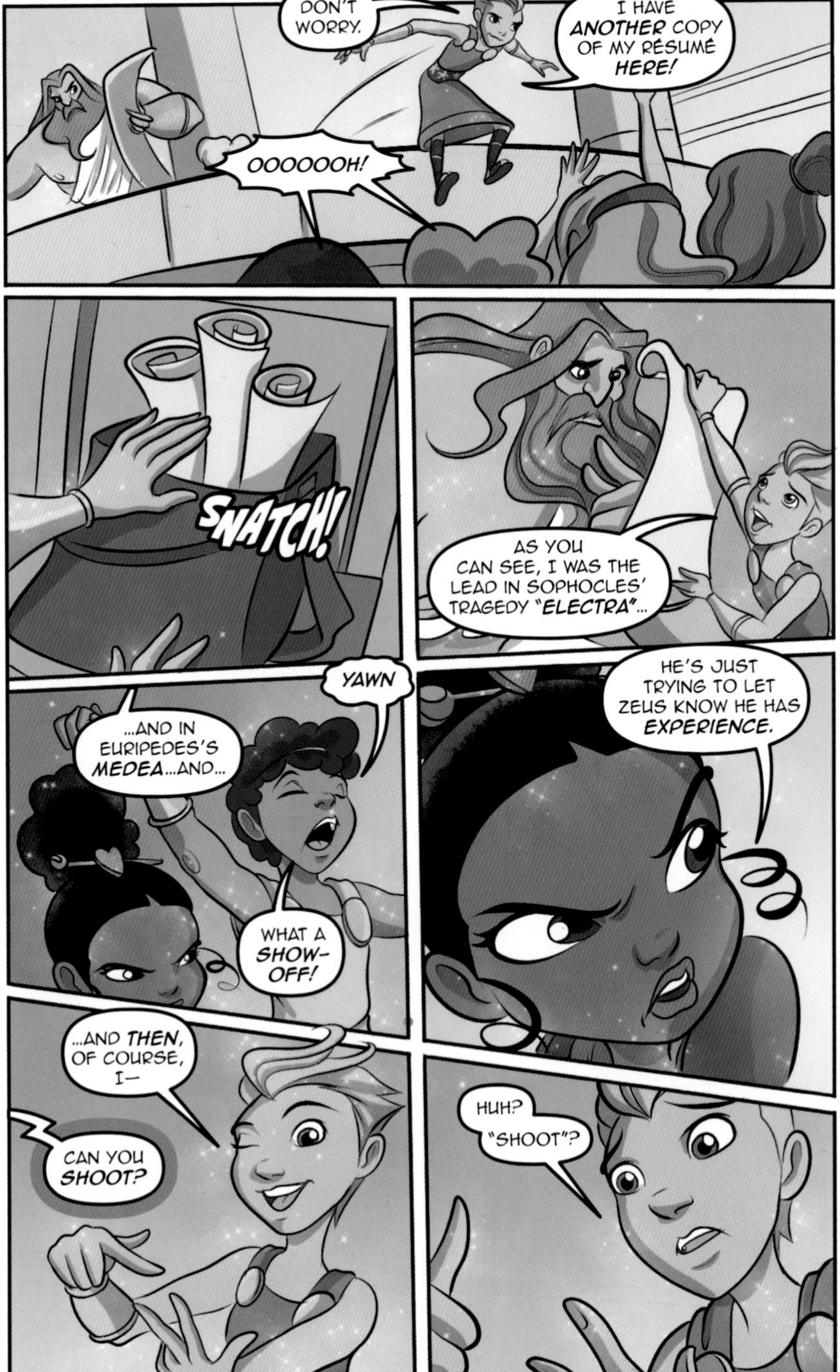
DON'T WORRY.
I HAVE ANOTHER COPY OF MY RÉSUMÉ HERE!
OOOOOOH!
SNATCH!
AS YOU CAN SEE, I WAS THE LEAD IN SOPHOCLES' TRAGEDY "ELECTRA"...
...AND IN EURIPEDES'S MEDEA...AND...
YAWN
WHAT A SHOW-OFF!
HE'S JUST TRYING TO LET ZEUS KNOW HE HAS EXPERIENCE.
...AND THEN, OF COURSE, I—
CAN YOU SHOOT?
HUH? "SHOOT"?

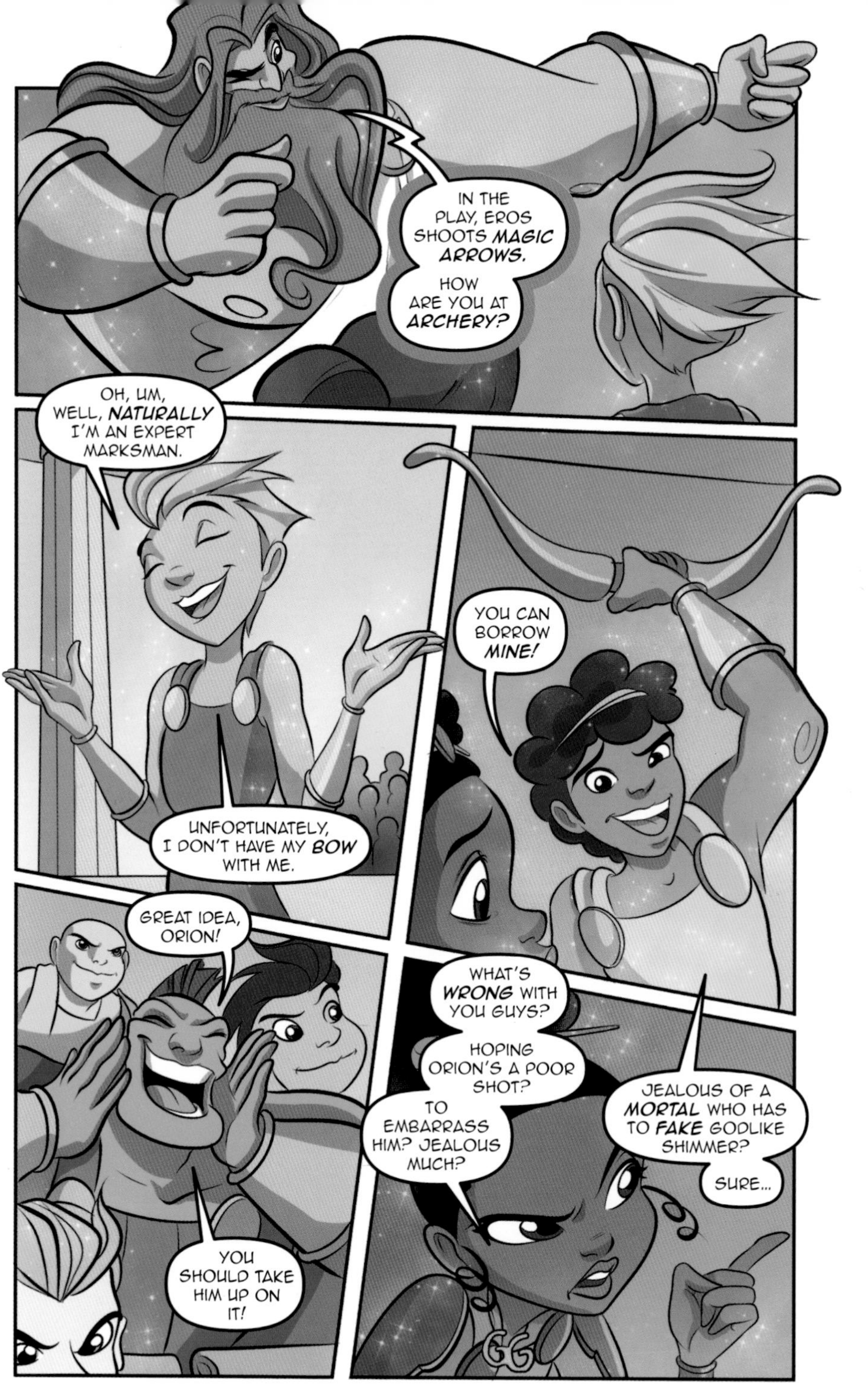
IN THE PLAY, EROS SHOOTS MAGIC ARROWS.
HOW ARE YOU AT ARCHERY?
OH, UM, WELL, NATURALLY I'M AN EXPERT MARKSMAN.
UNFORTUNATELY, I DON'T HAVE MY BOW WITH ME.
YOU CAN BORROW MINE!
GREAT IDEA, ORION!
YOU SHOULD TAKE HIM UP ON IT!
WHAT'S WRONG WITH YOU GUYS?
HOPING ORION'S A POOR SHOT?
TO EMBARRASS HIM? JEALOUS MUCH?
JEALOUS OF A MORTAL WHO HAS TO FAKE GODLIKE SHIMMER?
SURE...

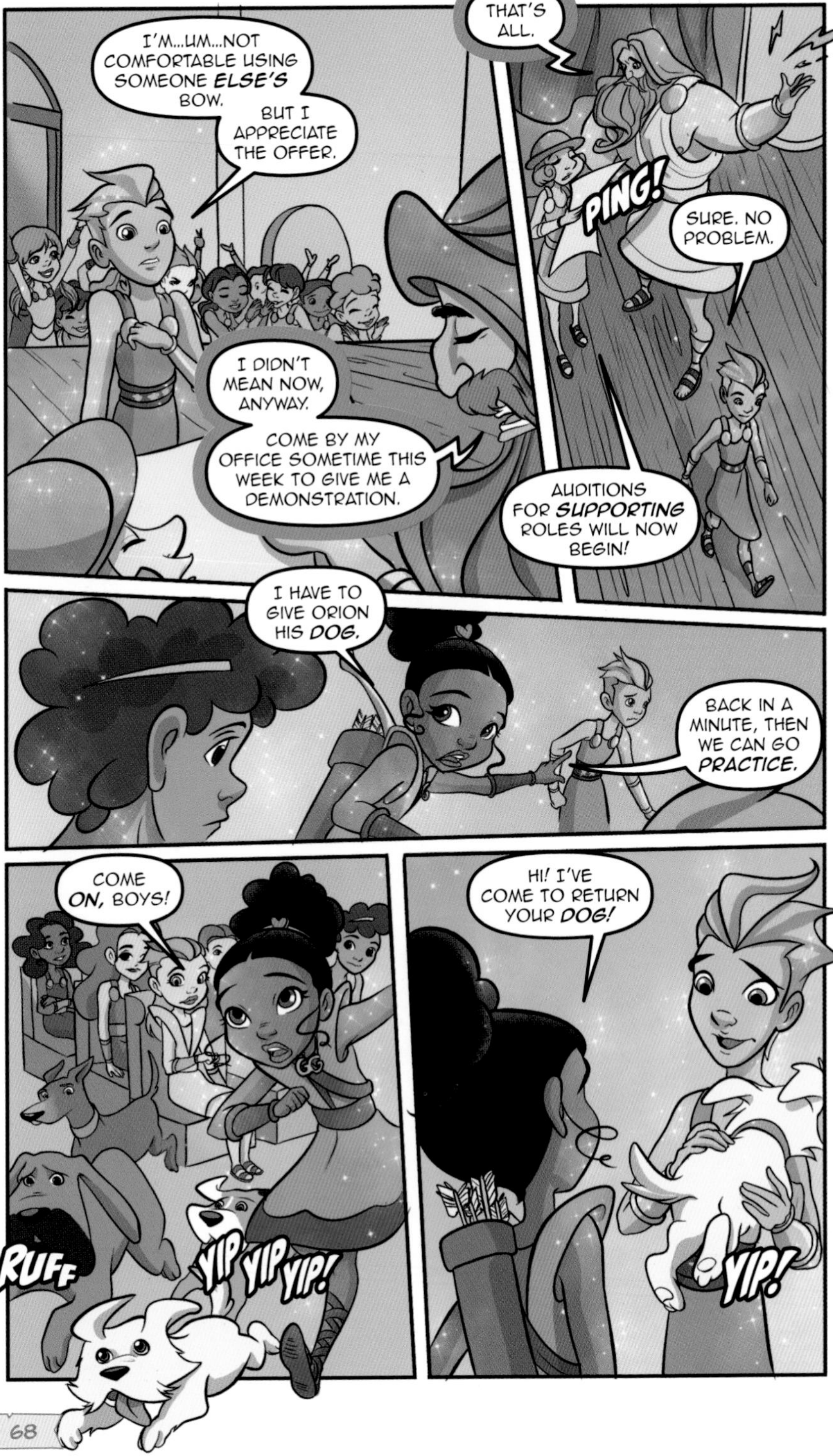
I'M...UM...NOT COMFORTABLE USING SOMEONE ELSE'S BOW.
BUT I APPRECIATE THE OFFER.
I DIDN'T MEAN NOW, ANYWAY.
COME BY MY OFFICE SOMETIME THIS WEEK TO GIVE ME A DEMONSTRATION.
THAT'S ALL.
PING!
SURE. NO PROBLEM.
AUDITIONS FOR SUPPORTING ROLES WILL NOW BEGIN!
I HAVE TO GIVE ORION HIS DOG.
BACK IN A MINUTE, THEN WE CAN GO PRACTICE.
COME ON, BOYS!
RUFF
YIP YIP YIP!
HI! I'VE COME TO RETURN YOUR DOG!
YIP!

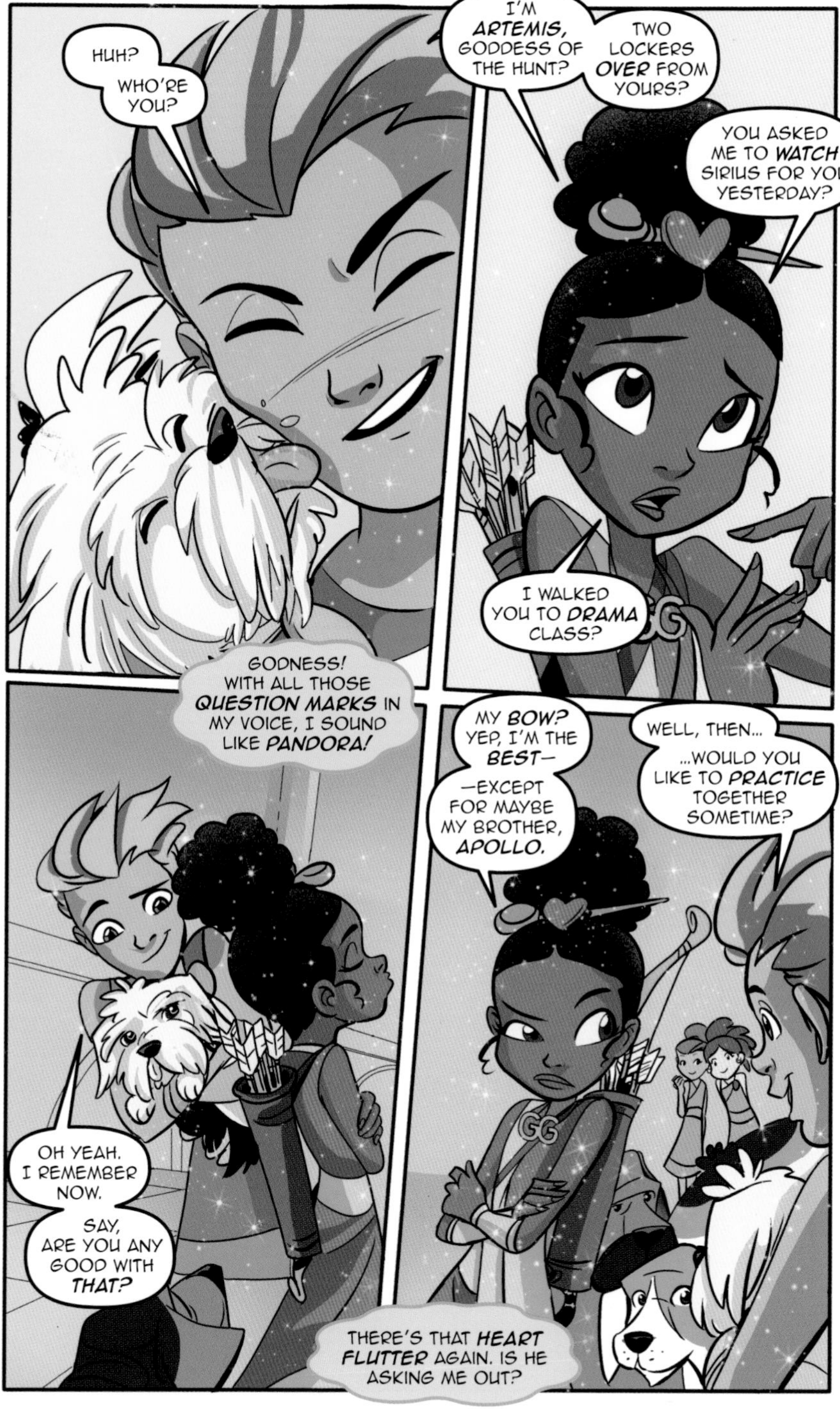
HUH?
WHO'RE YOU?
I'M ARTEMIS, GODDESS OF THE HUNT?
TWO LOCKERS OVER FROM YOURS?
YOU ASKED ME TO WATCH SIRIUS FOR YOU YESTERDAY?
I WALKED YOU TO DRAMA CLASS?
GODNESS! WITH ALL THOSE QUESTION MARKS IN MY VOICE, I SOUND LIKE PANDORA!
OH YEAH. I REMEMBER NOW.
SAY, ARE YOU ANY GOOD WITH THAT?
MY BOW? YEP, I'M THE BEST—
—EXCEPT FOR MAYBE MY BROTHER, APOLLO.
WELL, THEN...
...WOULD YOU LIKE TO PRACTICE TOGETHER SOMETIME?
THERE'S THAT HEART FLUTTER AGAIN. IS HE ASKING ME OUT?

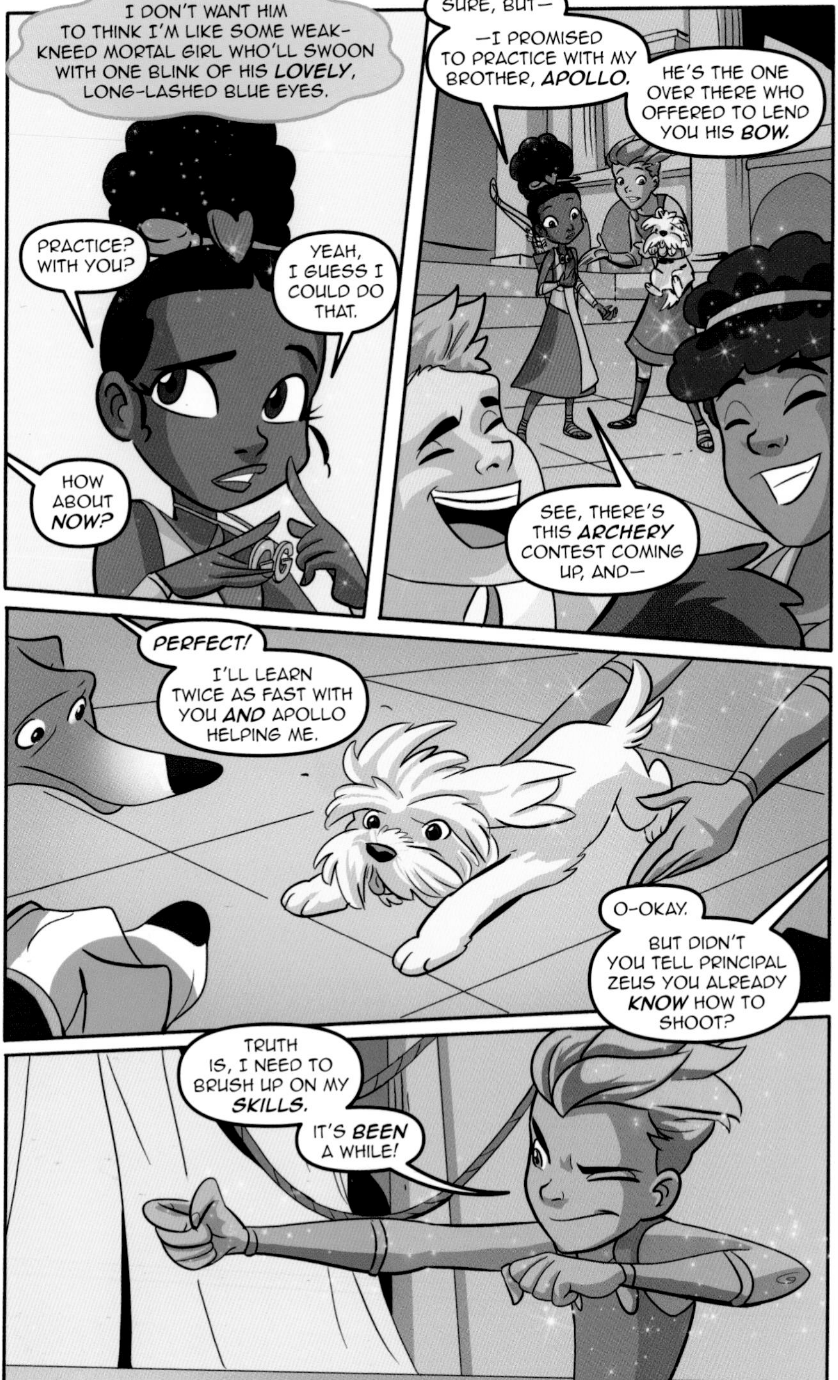
I DON'T WANT HIM TO THINK I'M LIKE SOME WEAK-KNEED MORTAL GIRL WHO'LL SWOON WITH ONE BLINK OF HIS *LOVELY*, LONG-LASHED BLUE EYES.
PRACTICE? WITH YOU?
YEAH, I GUESS I COULD DO THAT.
HOW ABOUT *NOW?*
SURE, BUT—
—I PROMISED TO PRACTICE WITH MY BROTHER, *APOLLO.*
HE'S THE ONE OVER THERE WHO OFFERED TO LEND YOU HIS *BOW.*
SEE, THERE'S THIS *ARCHERY* CONTEST COMING UP, AND—
PERFECT!
I'LL LEARN TWICE AS FAST WITH YOU *AND* APOLLO HELPING ME.
O-OKAY.
BUT DIDN'T YOU TELL PRINCIPAL ZEUS YOU ALREADY *KNOW* HOW TO SHOOT?
TRUTH IS, I NEED TO BRUSH UP ON MY *SKILLS.*
IT'S *BEEN* A WHILE!

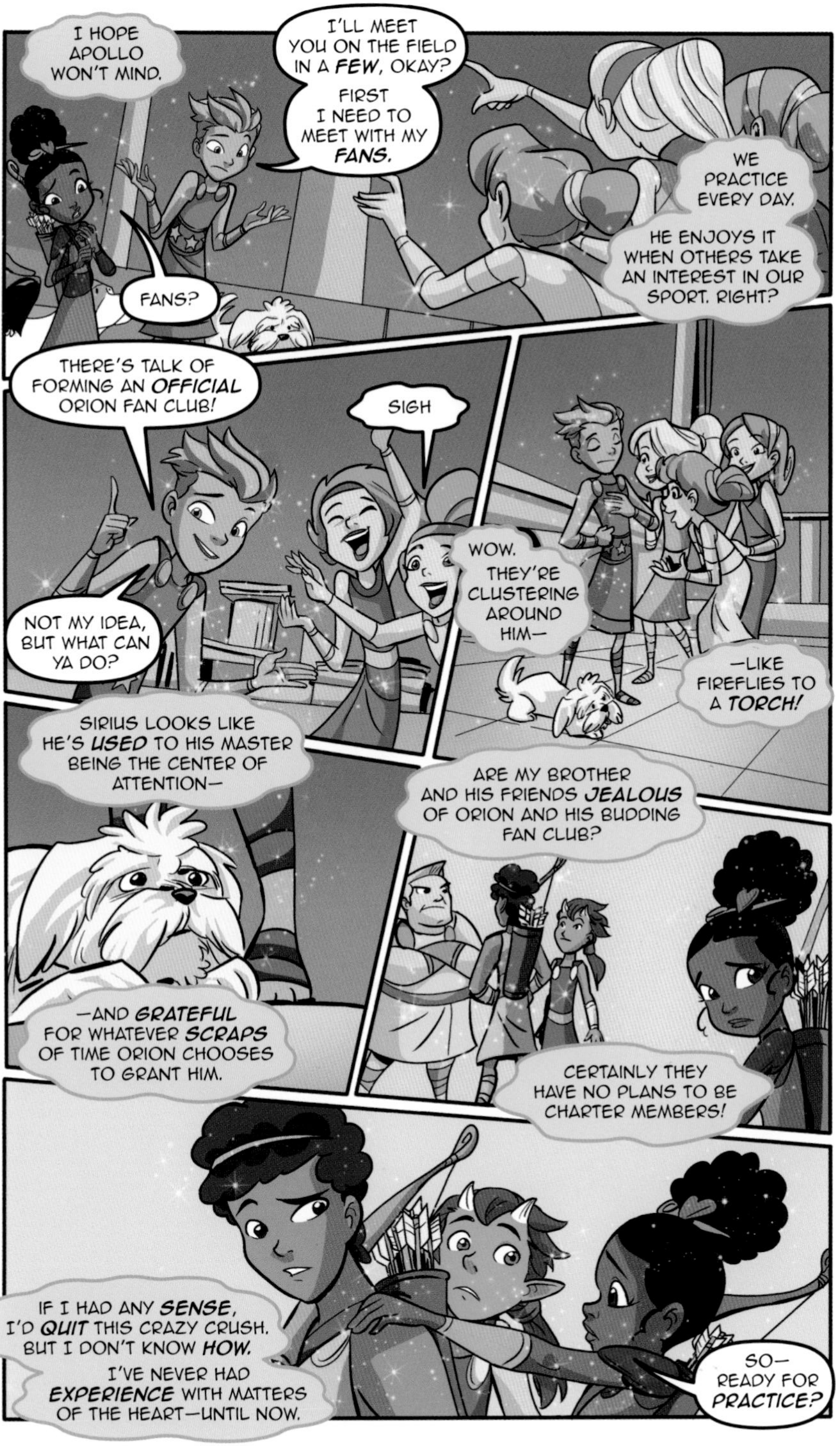
I HOPE APOLLO WON'T MIND.
I'LL MEET YOU ON THE FIELD IN A FEW, OKAY?
FIRST I NEED TO MEET WITH MY FANS.
WE PRACTICE EVERY DAY.
HE ENJOYS IT WHEN OTHERS TAKE AN INTEREST IN OUR SPORT. RIGHT?
FANS?
THERE'S TALK OF FORMING AN OFFICIAL ORION FAN CLUB!
SIGH
NOT MY IDEA, BUT WHAT CAN YA DO?
WOW.
THEY'RE CLUSTERING AROUND HIM—
—LIKE FIREFLIES TO A TORCH!
SIRIUS LOOKS LIKE HE'S USED TO HIS MASTER BEING THE CENTER OF ATTENTION—
—AND GRATEFUL FOR WHATEVER SCRAPS OF TIME ORION CHOOSES TO GRANT HIM.
ARE MY BROTHER AND HIS FRIENDS JEALOUS OF ORION AND HIS BUDDING FAN CLUB?
CERTAINLY THEY HAVE NO PLANS TO BE CHARTER MEMBERS!
IF I HAD ANY SENSE, I'D QUIT THIS CRAZY CRUSH. BUT I DON'T KNOW HOW.
I'VE NEVER HAD EXPERIENCE WITH MATTERS OF THE HEART—UNTIL NOW.
SO— READY FOR PRACTICE?

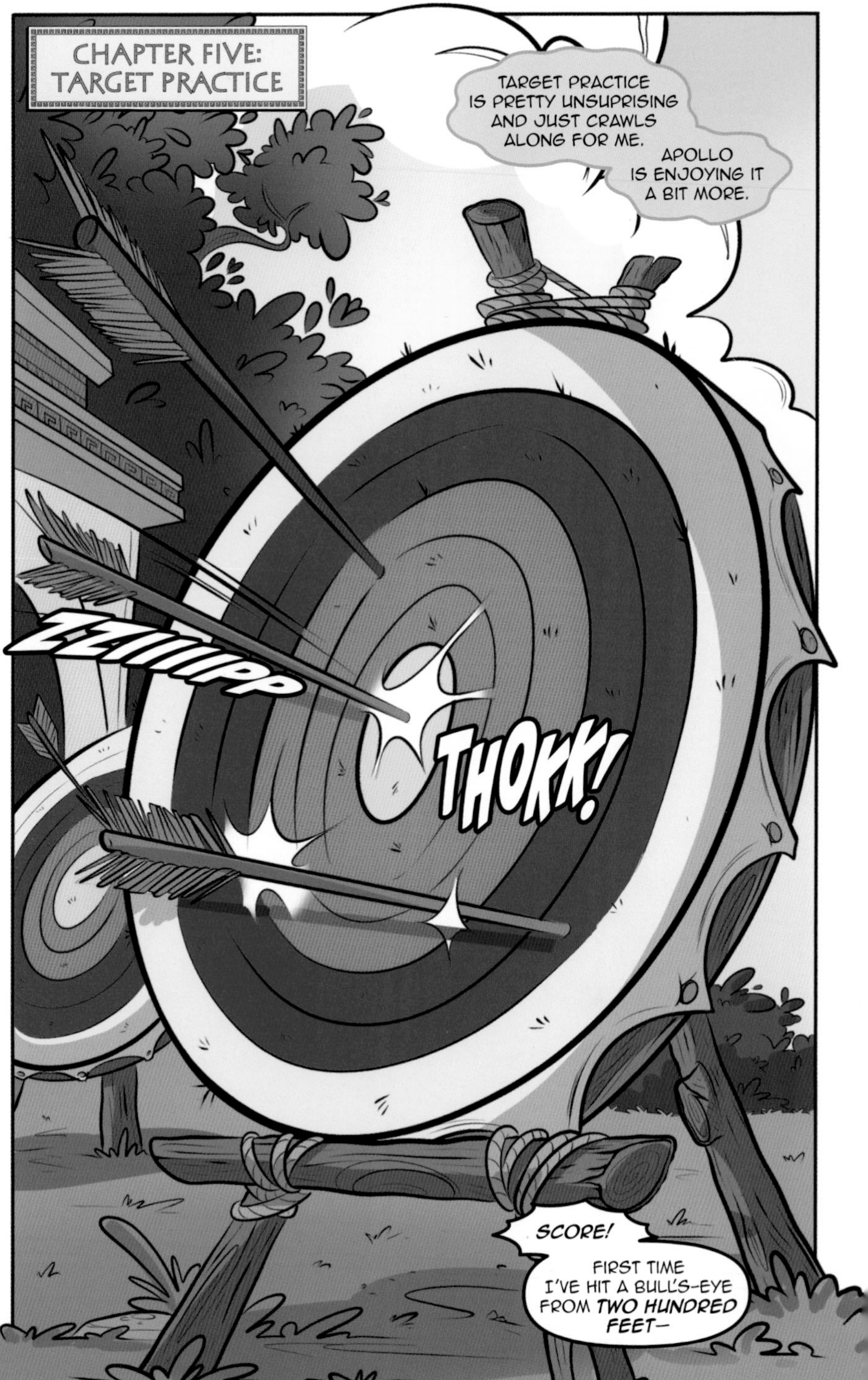
CHAPTER FIVE:
TARGET PRACTICE
TARGET PRACTICE IS PRETTY UNSUPRISING AND JUST CRAWLS ALONG FOR ME.
APOLLO IS ENJOYING IT A BIT MORE.
ZZIIIIPP
THOKK!
SCORE!
FIRST TIME I'VE HIT A BULL'S-EYE FROM *TWO HUNDRED FEET*—

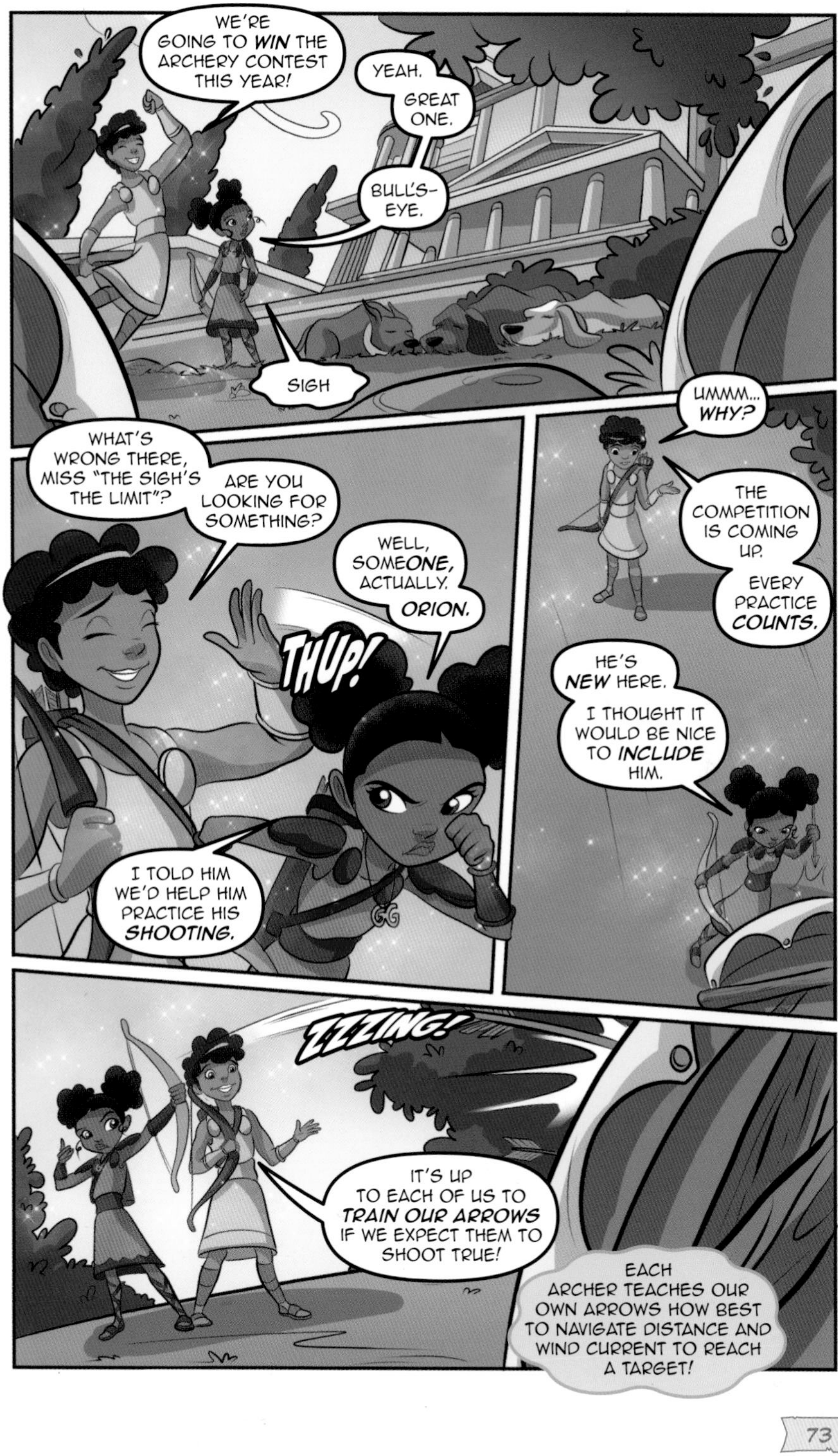
WE'RE GOING TO WIN THE ARCHERY CONTEST THIS YEAR!
YEAH.
GREAT ONE.
BULL'S-EYE.
SIGH
WHAT'S WRONG THERE, MISS "THE SIGH'S THE LIMIT"?
ARE YOU LOOKING FOR SOMETHING?
WELL, SOMEONE, ACTUALLY.
ORION.
THUP!
I TOLD HIM WE'D HELP HIM PRACTICE HIS SHOOTING.
UMMM... WHY?
THE COMPETITION IS COMING UP.
EVERY PRACTICE COUNTS.
HE'S NEW HERE.
I THOUGHT IT WOULD BE NICE TO INCLUDE HIM.
ZZZING!
IT'S UP TO EACH OF US TO TRAIN OUR ARROWS IF WE EXPECT THEM TO SHOOT TRUE!
EACH ARCHER TEACHES OUR OWN ARROWS HOW BEST TO NAVIGATE DISTANCE AND WIND CURRENT TO REACH A TARGET!

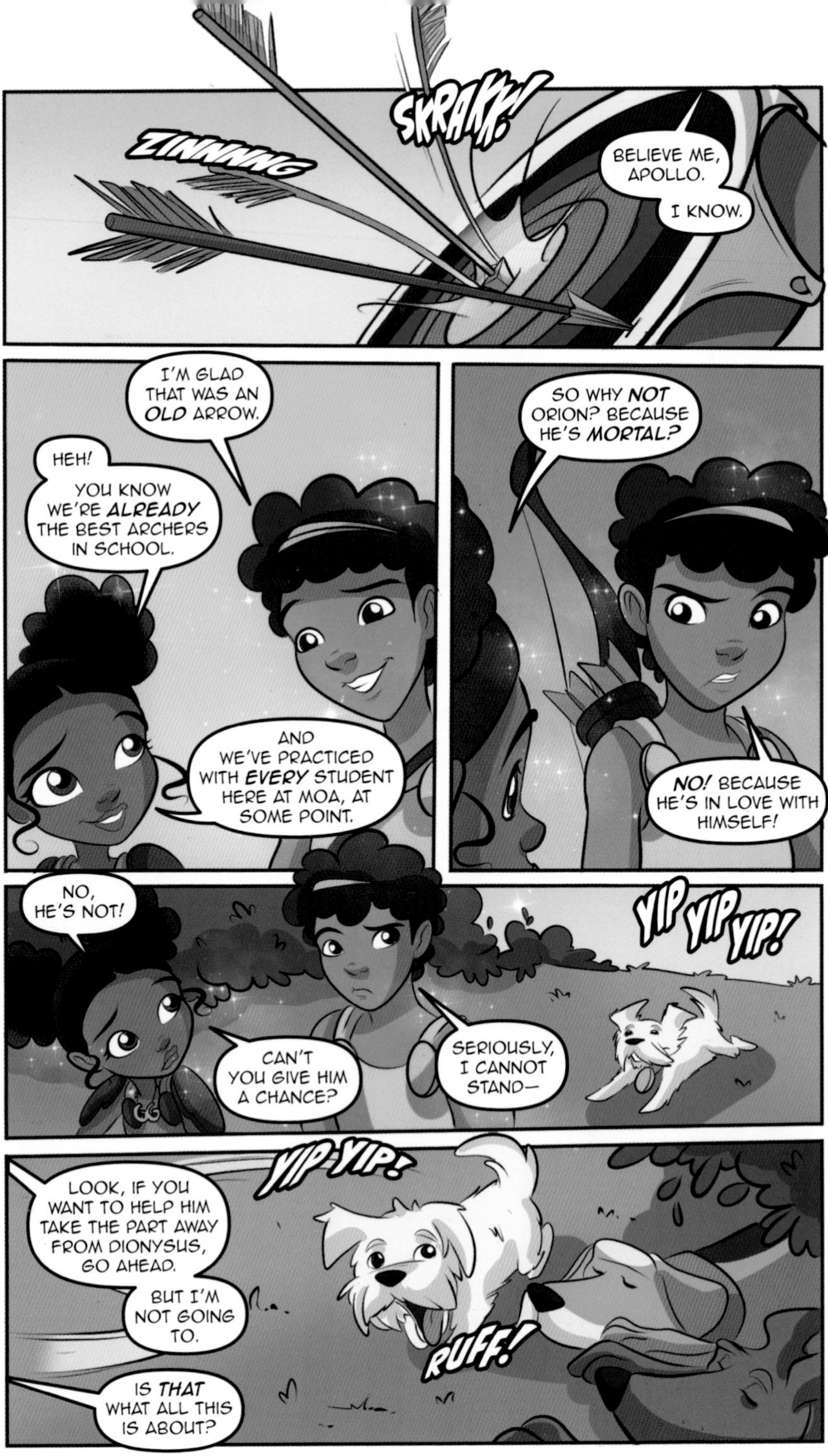
ZINNNNG
SKRAKK!
BELIEVE ME, APOLLO.
I KNOW.
I'M GLAD THAT WAS AN OLD ARROW.
HEH!
YOU KNOW WE'RE ALREADY THE BEST ARCHERS IN SCHOOL.
AND WE'VE PRACTICED WITH EVERY STUDENT HERE AT MOA, AT SOME POINT.
SO WHY NOT ORION? BECAUSE HE'S MORTAL?
NO! BECAUSE HE'S IN LOVE WITH HIMSELF!
NO, HE'S NOT!
YIP YIP YIP!
CAN'T YOU GIVE HIM A CHANCE?
SERIOUSLY, I CANNOT STAND—
YIP-YIP!
LOOK, IF YOU WANT TO HELP HIM TAKE THE PART AWAY FROM DIONYSUS, GO AHEAD.
BUT I'M NOT GOING TO.
RUFF!
IS THAT WHAT ALL THIS IS ABOUT?

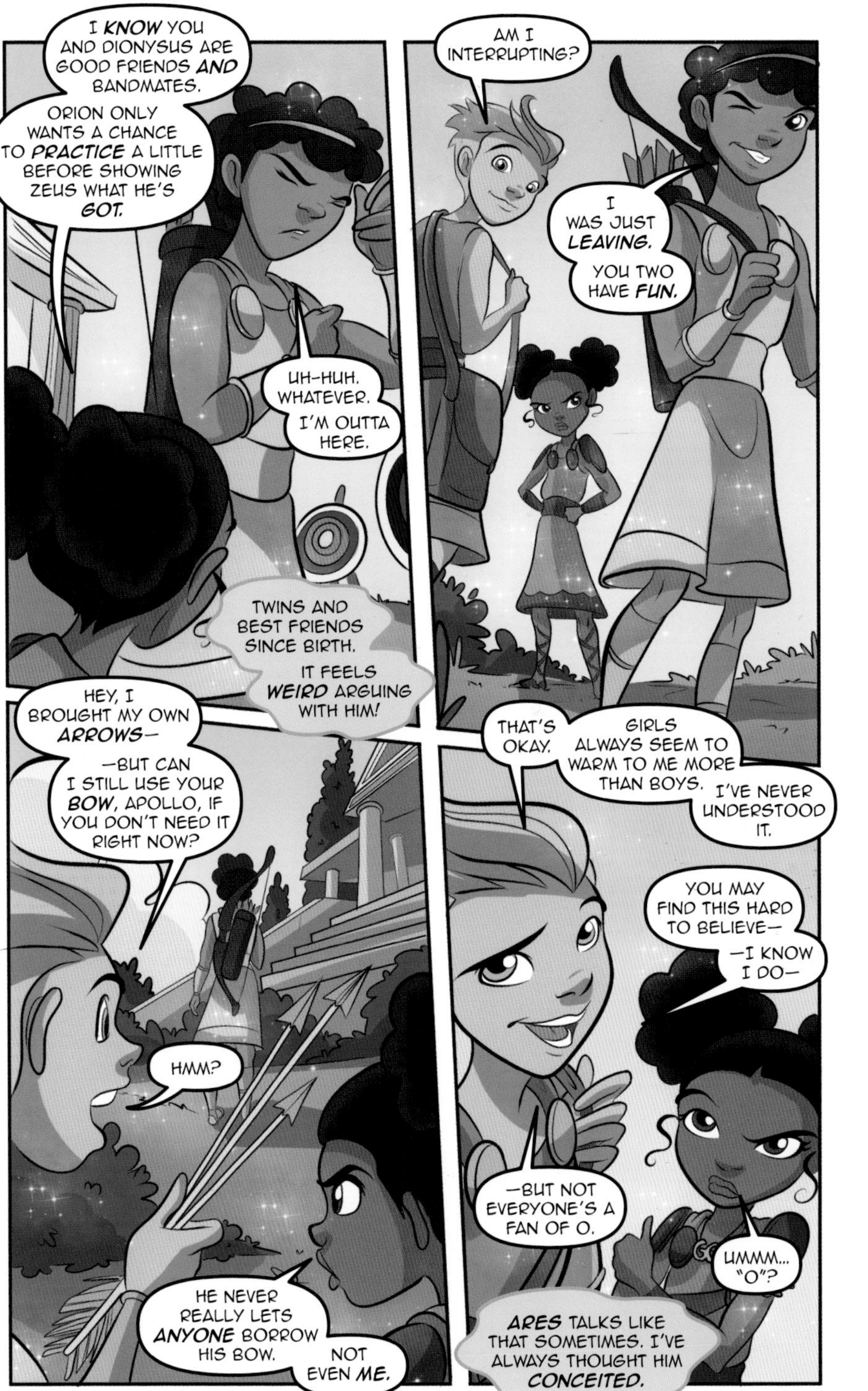
I KNOW YOU AND DIONYSUS ARE GOOD FRIENDS AND BANDMATES.
ORION ONLY WANTS A CHANCE TO PRACTICE A LITTLE BEFORE SHOWING ZEUS WHAT HE'S GOT.
UH-HUH. WHATEVER. I'M OUTTA HERE.
TWINS AND BEST FRIENDS SINCE BIRTH.
IT FEELS WEIRD ARGUING WITH HIM!
AM I INTERRUPTING?
I WAS JUST LEAVING.
YOU TWO HAVE FUN.
HEY, I BROUGHT MY OWN ARROWS—
—BUT CAN I STILL USE YOUR BOW, APOLLO, IF YOU DON'T NEED IT RIGHT NOW?
HMM?
HE NEVER REALLY LETS ANYONE BORROW HIS BOW.
NOT EVEN ME.
THAT'S OKAY.
GIRLS ALWAYS SEEM TO WARM TO ME MORE THAN BOYS.
I'VE NEVER UNDERSTOOD IT.
YOU MAY FIND THIS HARD TO BELIEVE—
—I KNOW I DO—
—BUT NOT EVERYONE'S A FAN OF O.
UMMM... "O"?
ARES TALKS LIKE THAT SOMETIMES. I'VE ALWAYS THOUGHT HIM CONCEITED.

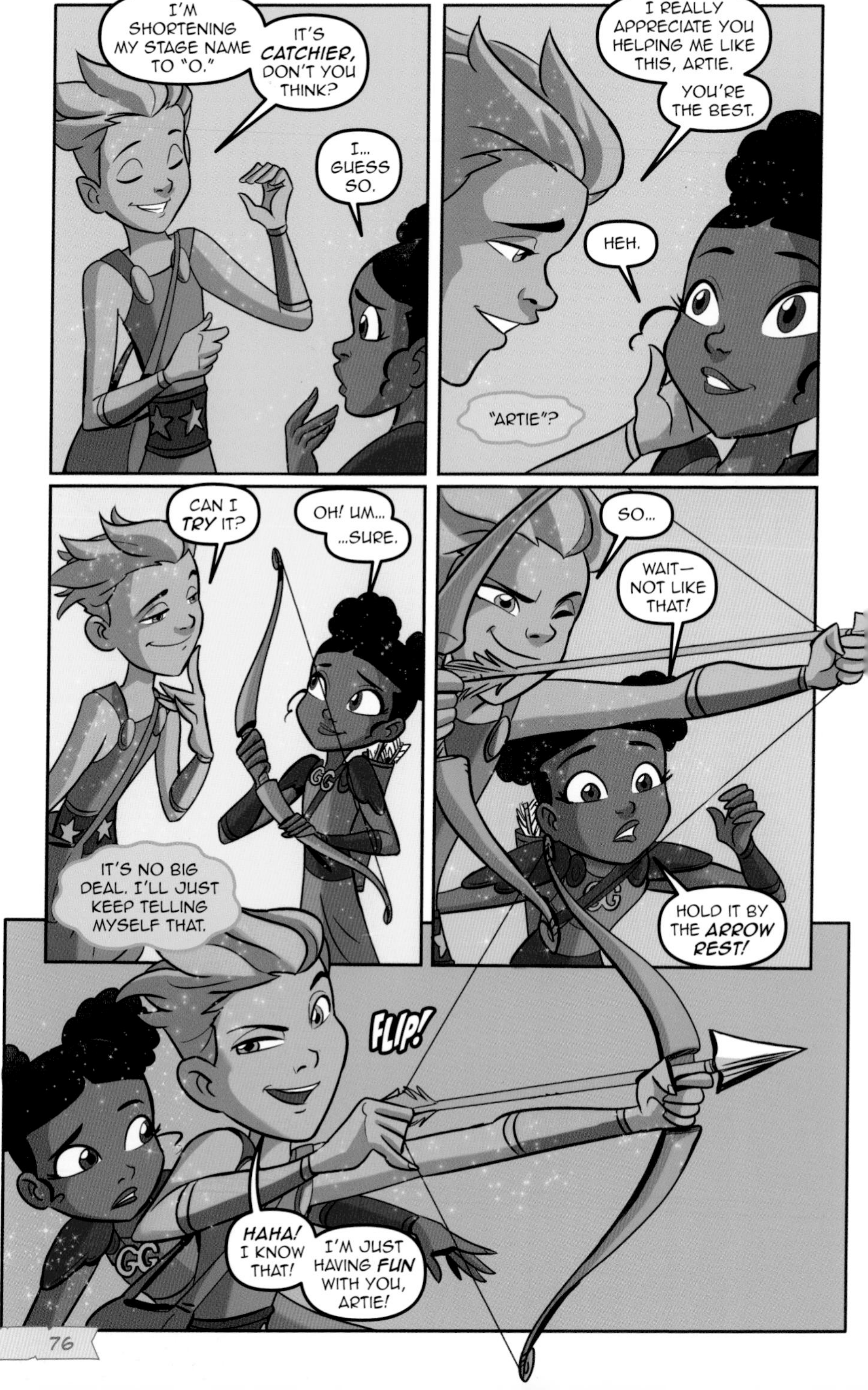
I'M SHORTENING MY STAGE NAME TO "O."
IT'S CATCHIER, DON'T YOU THINK?
I... GUESS SO.
I REALLY APPRECIATE YOU HELPING ME LIKE THIS, ARTIE.
YOU'RE THE BEST.
HEH.
"ARTIE"?
CAN I TRY IT?
OH! UM... ...SURE.
IT'S NO BIG DEAL. I'LL JUST KEEP TELLING MYSELF THAT.
SO...
WAIT— NOT LIKE THAT!
HOLD IT BY THE ARROW REST!
FLIP!
HAHA! I KNOW THAT!
I'M JUST HAVING FUN WITH YOU, ARTIE!

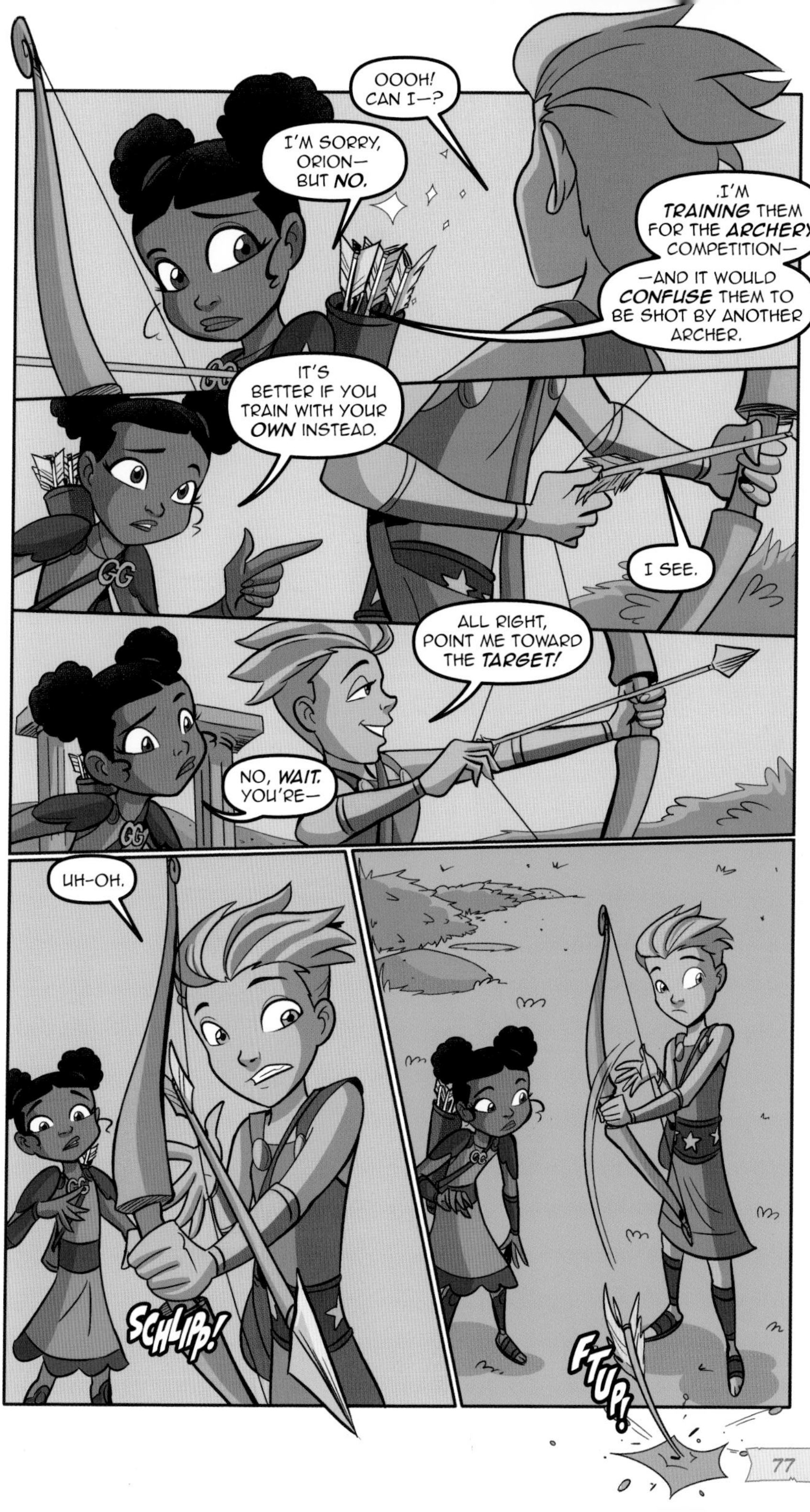

OOOH! CAN I—?
I'M SORRY, ORION— BUT NO.
...I'M TRAINING THEM FOR THE ARCHERY COMPETITION—
—AND IT WOULD CONFUSE THEM TO BE SHOT BY ANOTHER ARCHER.
IT'S BETTER IF YOU TRAIN WITH YOUR OWN INSTEAD.
I SEE.
ALL RIGHT, POINT ME TOWARD THE TARGET!
NO, WAIT. YOU'RE—
UH-OH.
SCHLIPP!
FTUP!

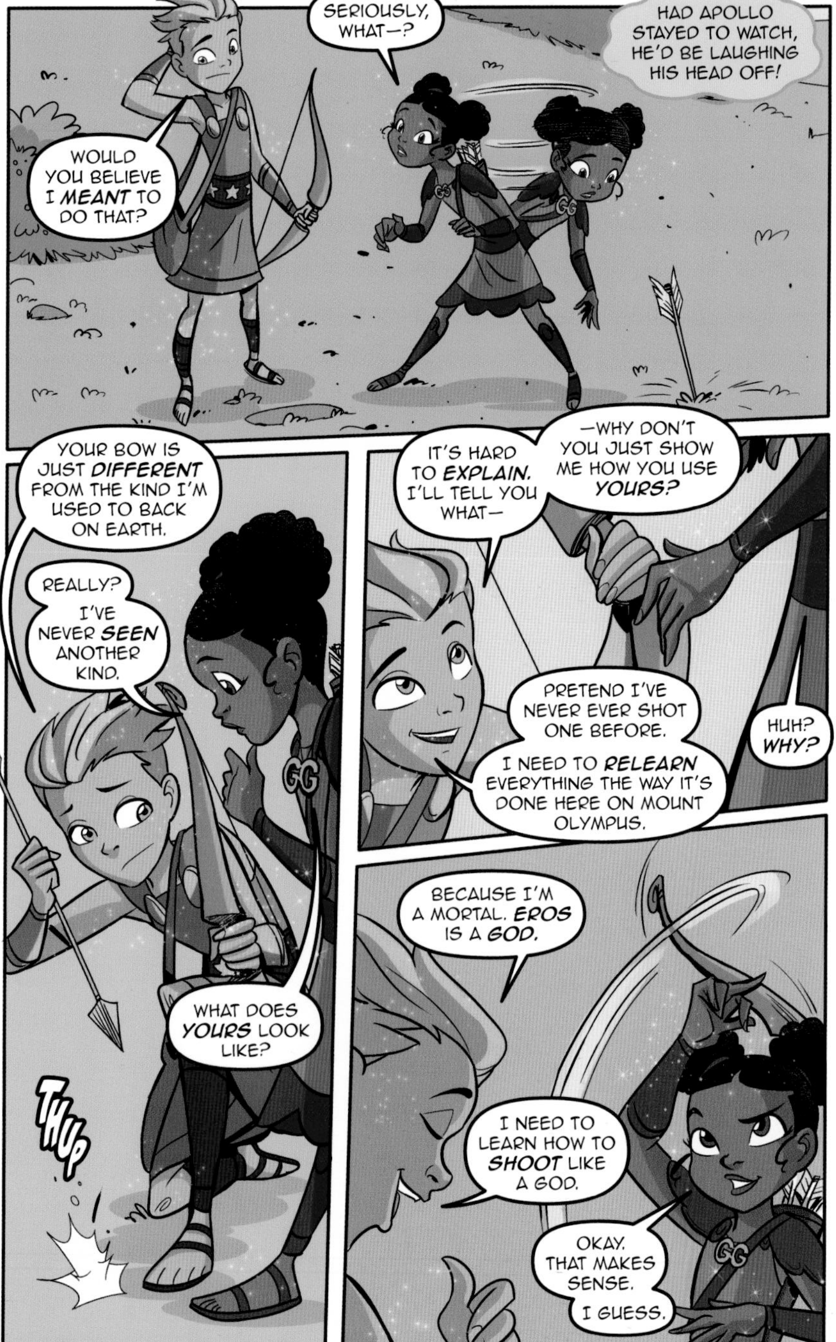
SERIOUSLY, WHAT—?
HAD APOLLO STAYED TO WATCH, HE'D BE LAUGHING HIS HEAD OFF!
WOULD YOU BELIEVE I MEANT TO DO THAT?
YOUR BOW IS JUST DIFFERENT FROM THE KIND I'M USED TO BACK ON EARTH.
REALLY? I'VE NEVER SEEN ANOTHER KIND.
WHAT DOES YOURS LOOK LIKE?
THUP
IT'S HARD TO EXPLAIN. I'LL TELL YOU WHAT—
—WHY DON'T YOU JUST SHOW ME HOW YOU USE YOURS?
PRETEND I'VE NEVER EVER SHOT ONE BEFORE.
I NEED TO RELEARN EVERYTHING THE WAY IT'S DONE HERE ON MOUNT OLYMPUS.
HUH? WHY?
BECAUSE I'M A MORTAL. EROS IS A GOD.
I NEED TO LEARN HOW TO SHOOT LIKE A GOD.
OKAY. THAT MAKES SENSE.
I GUESS.

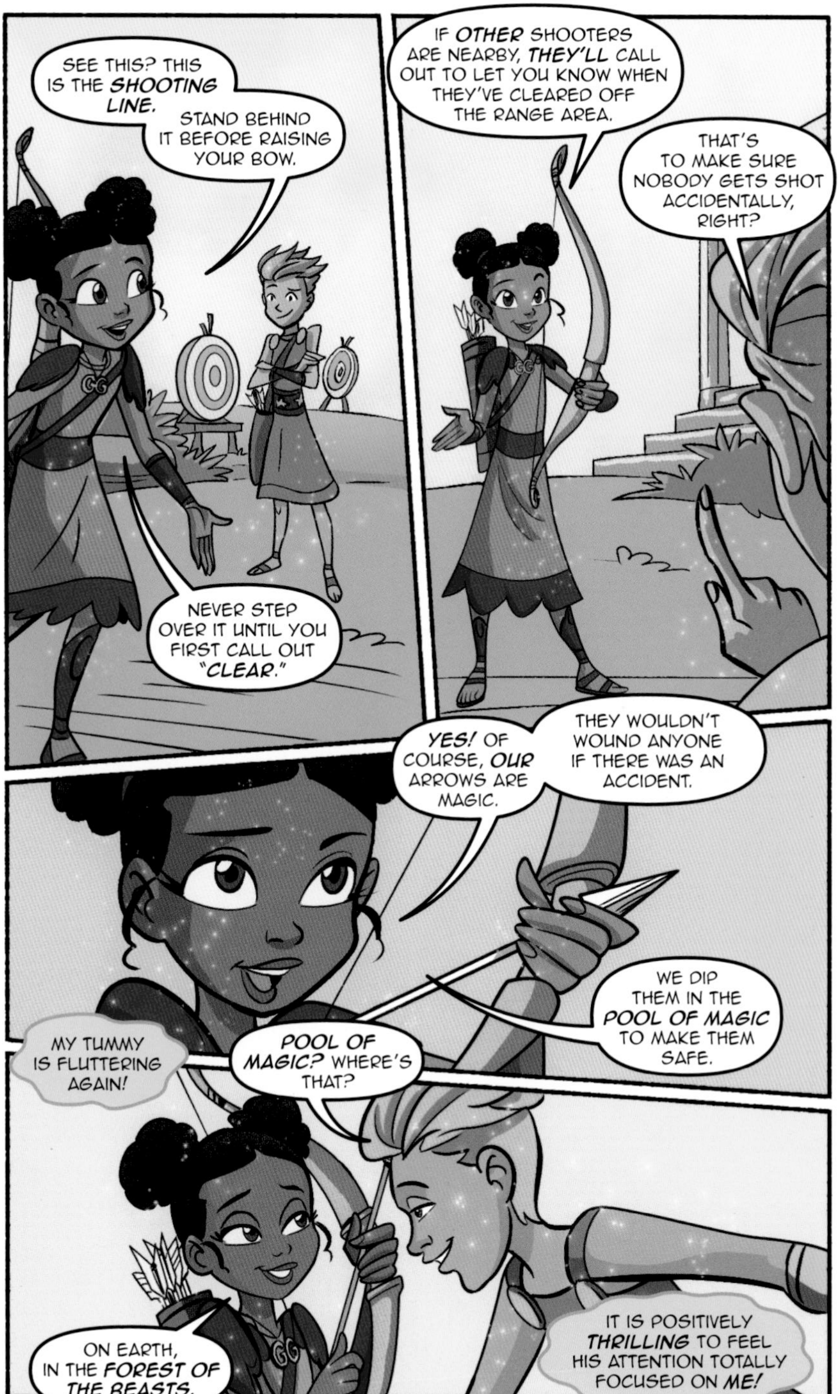
SEE THIS? THIS IS THE SHOOTING LINE.
STAND BEHIND IT BEFORE RAISING YOUR BOW.
NEVER STEP OVER IT UNTIL YOU FIRST CALL OUT "CLEAR."
IF OTHER SHOOTERS ARE NEARBY, THEY'LL CALL OUT TO LET YOU KNOW WHEN THEY'VE CLEARED OFF THE RANGE AREA.
THAT'S TO MAKE SURE NOBODY GETS SHOT ACCIDENTALLY, RIGHT?
YES! OF COURSE, OUR ARROWS ARE MAGIC.
THEY WOULDN'T WOUND ANYONE IF THERE WAS AN ACCIDENT.
WE DIP THEM IN THE POOL OF MAGIC TO MAKE THEM SAFE.
MY TUMMY IS FLUTTERING AGAIN!
POOL OF MAGIC? WHERE'S THAT?
ON EARTH, IN THE FOREST OF THE BEASTS.
IT IS POSITIVELY THRILLING TO FEEL HIS ATTENTION TOTALLY FOCUSED ON ME!

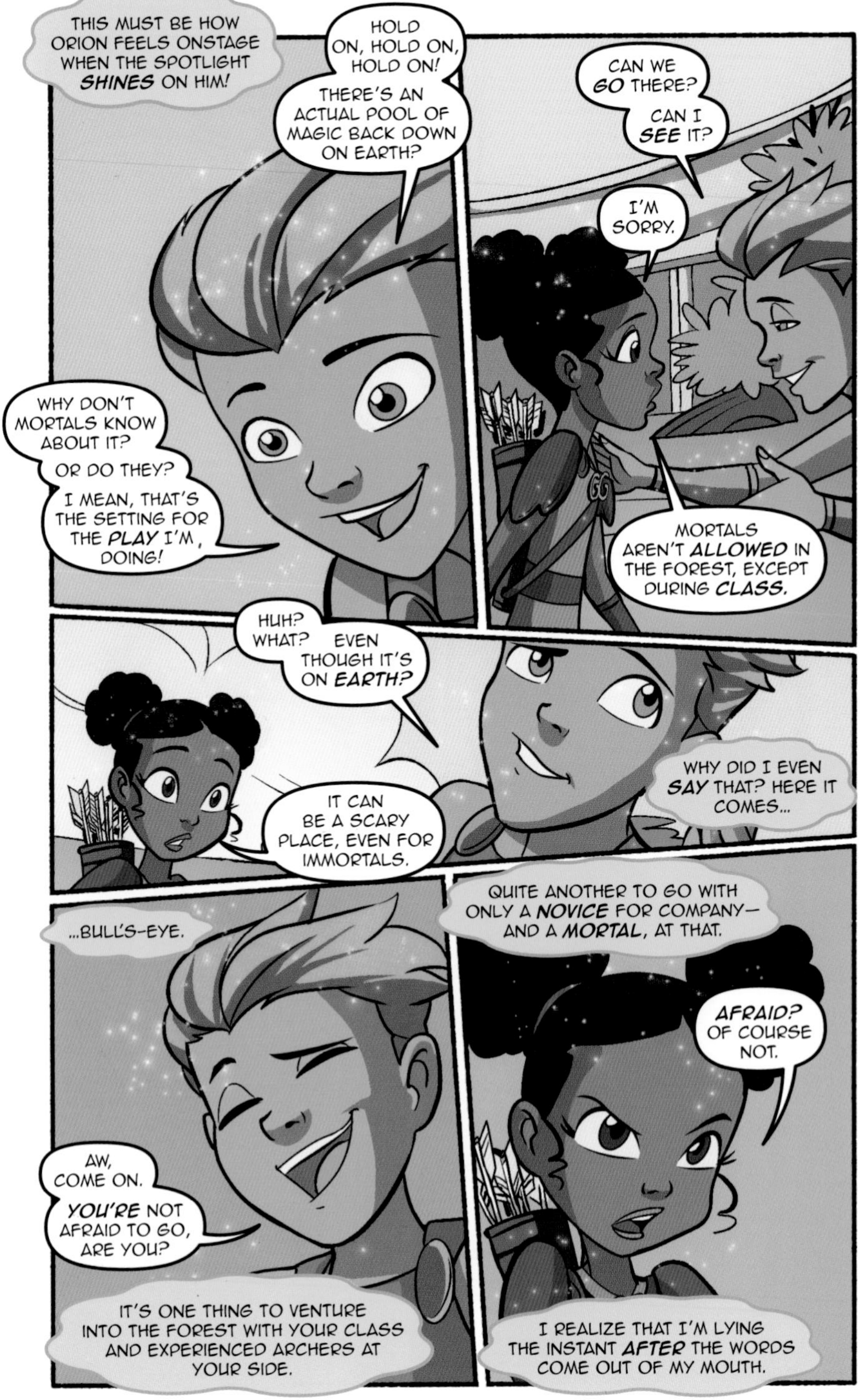

THIS MUST BE HOW ORION FEELS ONSTAGE WHEN THE SPOTLIGHT SHINES ON HIM!
HOLD ON, HOLD ON, HOLD ON!
THERE'S AN ACTUAL POOL OF MAGIC BACK DOWN ON EARTH?
WHY DON'T MORTALS KNOW ABOUT IT?
OR DO THEY?
I MEAN, THAT'S THE SETTING FOR THE PLAY I'M DOING!
CAN WE GO THERE?
CAN I SEE IT?
I'M SORRY.
MORTALS AREN'T ALLOWED IN THE FOREST, EXCEPT DURING CLASS.
HUH? WHAT?
EVEN THOUGH IT'S ON EARTH?
IT CAN BE A SCARY PLACE, EVEN FOR IMMORTALS.
WHY DID I EVEN SAY THAT? HERE IT COMES...
...BULL'S-EYE.
AW, COME ON.
YOU'RE NOT AFRAID TO GO, ARE YOU?
IT'S ONE THING TO VENTURE INTO THE FOREST WITH YOUR CLASS AND EXPERIENCED ARCHERS AT YOUR SIDE.
QUITE ANOTHER TO GO WITH ONLY A NOVICE FOR COMPANY— AND A MORTAL, AT THAT.
AFRAID? OF COURSE NOT.
I REALIZE THAT I'M LYING THE INSTANT AFTER THE WORDS COME OUT OF MY MOUTH.

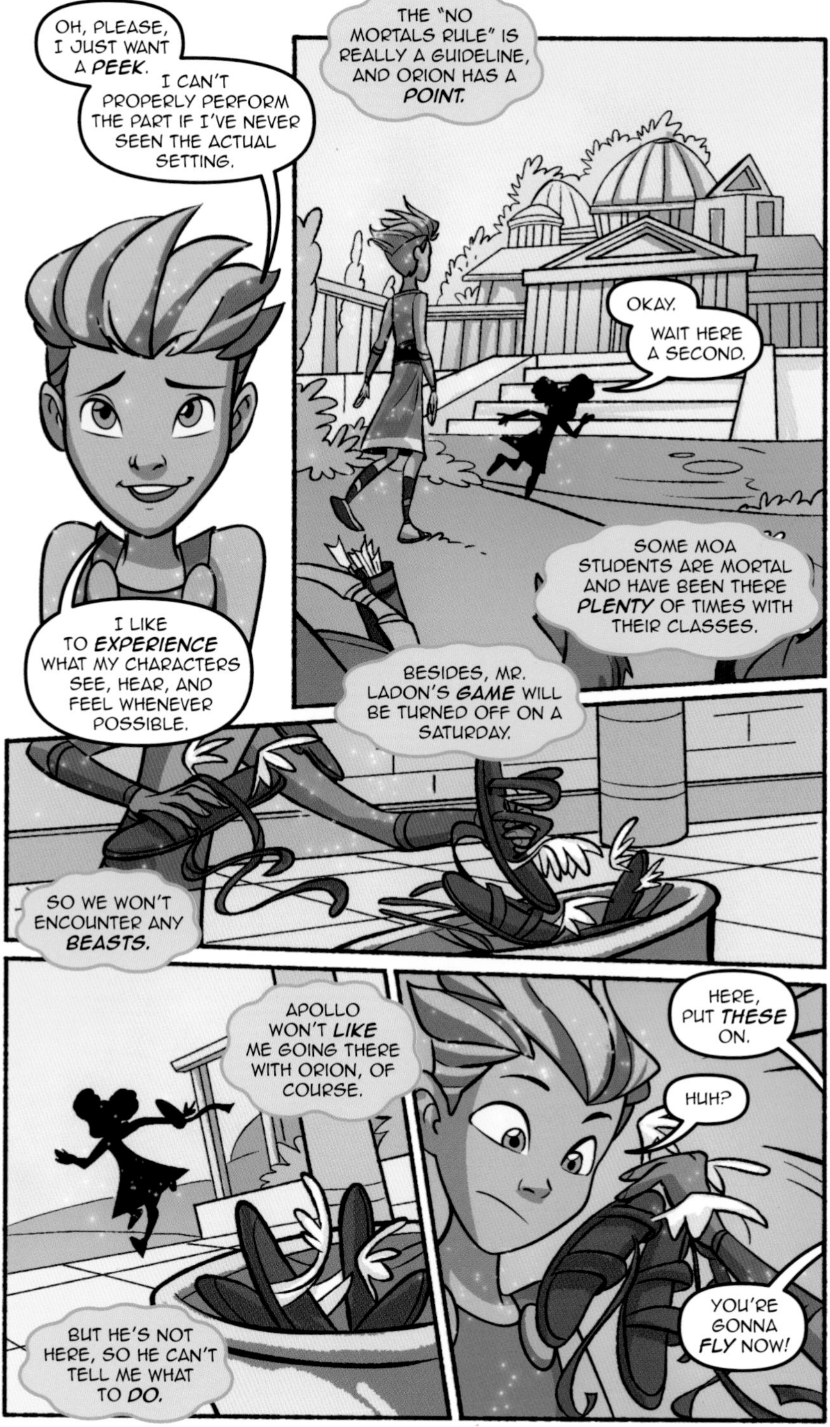
OH, PLEASE, I JUST WANT A PEEK.
I CAN'T PROPERLY PERFORM THE PART IF I'VE NEVER SEEN THE ACTUAL SETTING.
THE "NO MORTALS RULE" IS REALLY A GUIDELINE, AND ORION HAS A POINT.
OKAY.
WAIT HERE A SECOND.
SOME MOA STUDENTS ARE MORTAL AND HAVE BEEN THERE PLENTY OF TIMES WITH THEIR CLASSES.
I LIKE TO EXPERIENCE WHAT MY CHARACTERS SEE, HEAR, AND FEEL WHENEVER POSSIBLE.
BESIDES, MR. LADON'S GAME WILL BE TURNED OFF ON A SATURDAY.
SO WE WON'T ENCOUNTER ANY BEASTS.
APOLLO WON'T LIKE ME GOING THERE WITH ORION, OF COURSE.
BUT HE'S NOT HERE, SO HE CAN'T TELL ME WHAT TO DO.
HERE, PUT THESE ON.
HUH?
YOU'RE GONNA FLY NOW!

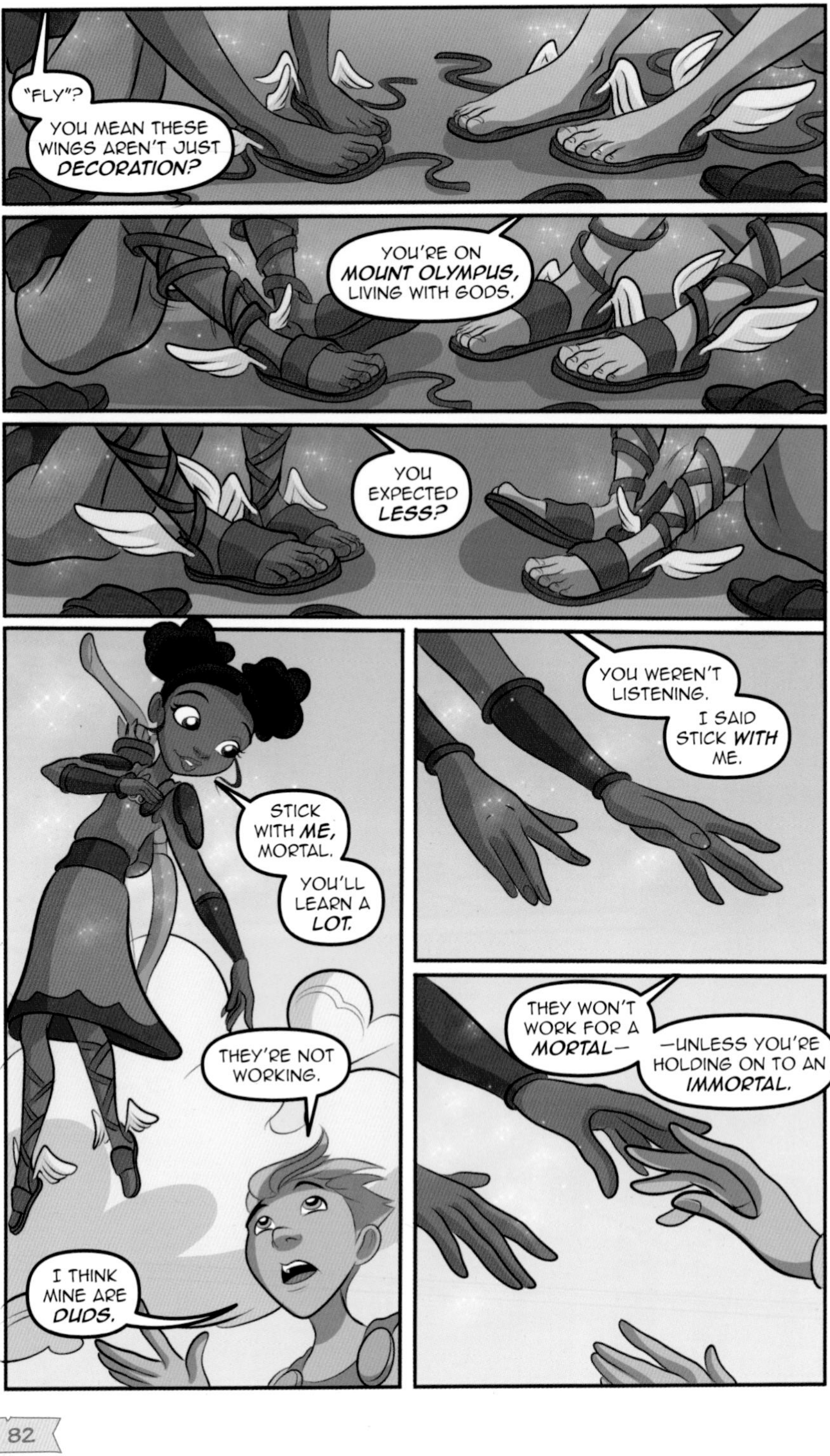
"FLY"?
YOU MEAN THESE WINGS AREN'T JUST DECORATION?
YOU'RE ON MOUNT OLYMPUS, LIVING WITH GODS.
YOU EXPECTED LESS?
STICK WITH ME, MORTAL.
YOU'LL LEARN A LOT.
THEY'RE NOT WORKING.
I THINK MINE ARE DUDS.
YOU WEREN'T LISTENING.
I SAID STICK WITH ME.
THEY WON'T WORK FOR A MORTAL—
—UNLESS YOU'RE HOLDING ON TO AN IMMORTAL.

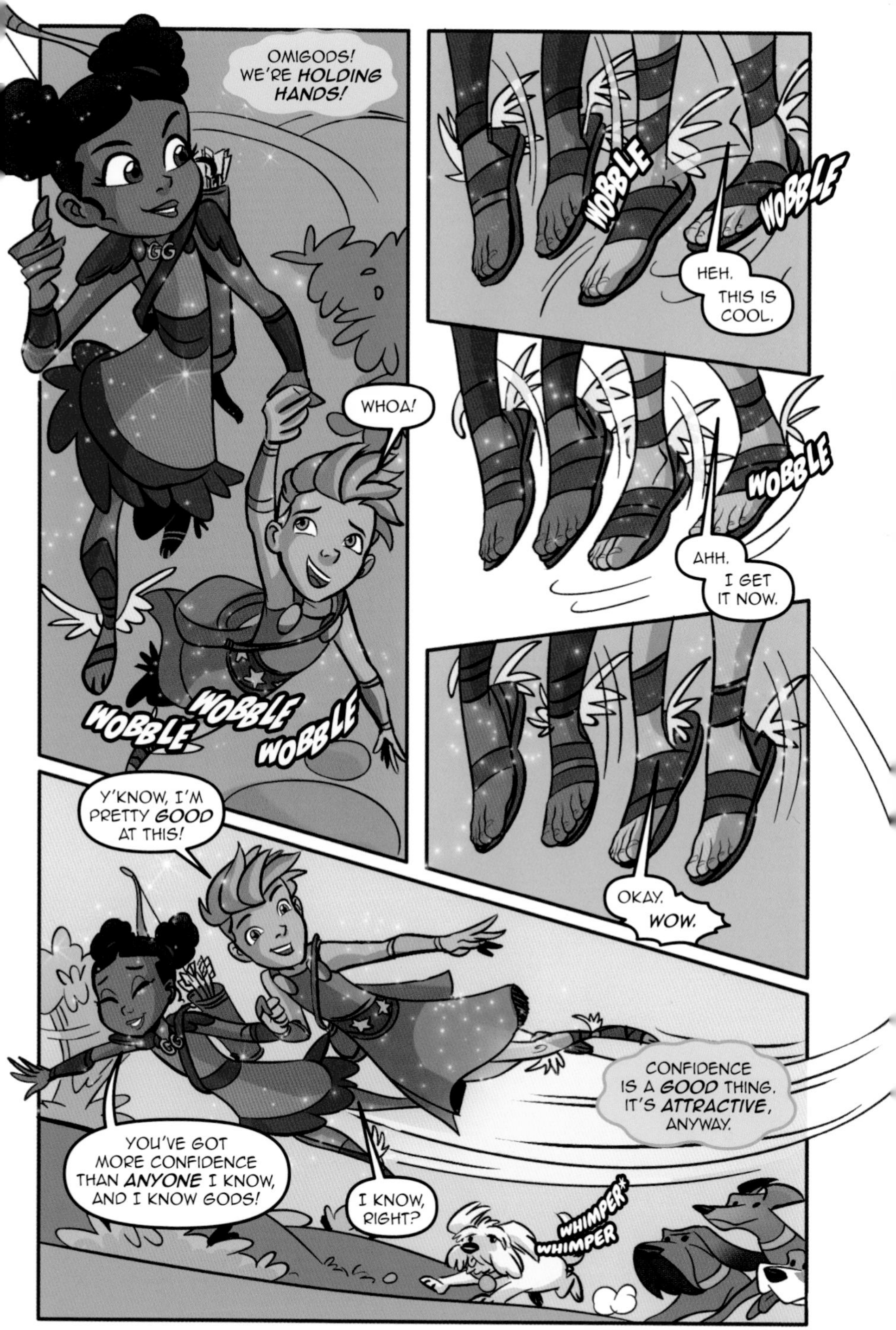
OMIGODS! WE'RE HOLDING HANDS!
WHOA!
WOBBLE
WOBBLE
WOBBLE
WOBBLE
WOBBLE
HEH. THIS IS COOL.
WOBBLE
AHH. I GET IT NOW.
OKAY. WOW.
Y'KNOW, I'M PRETTY GOOD AT THIS!
YOU'VE GOT MORE CONFIDENCE THAN ANYONE I KNOW, AND I KNOW GODS!
I KNOW, RIGHT?
CONFIDENCE IS A GOOD THING. IT'S ATTRACTIVE, ANYWAY.
WHIMPER* WHIMPER

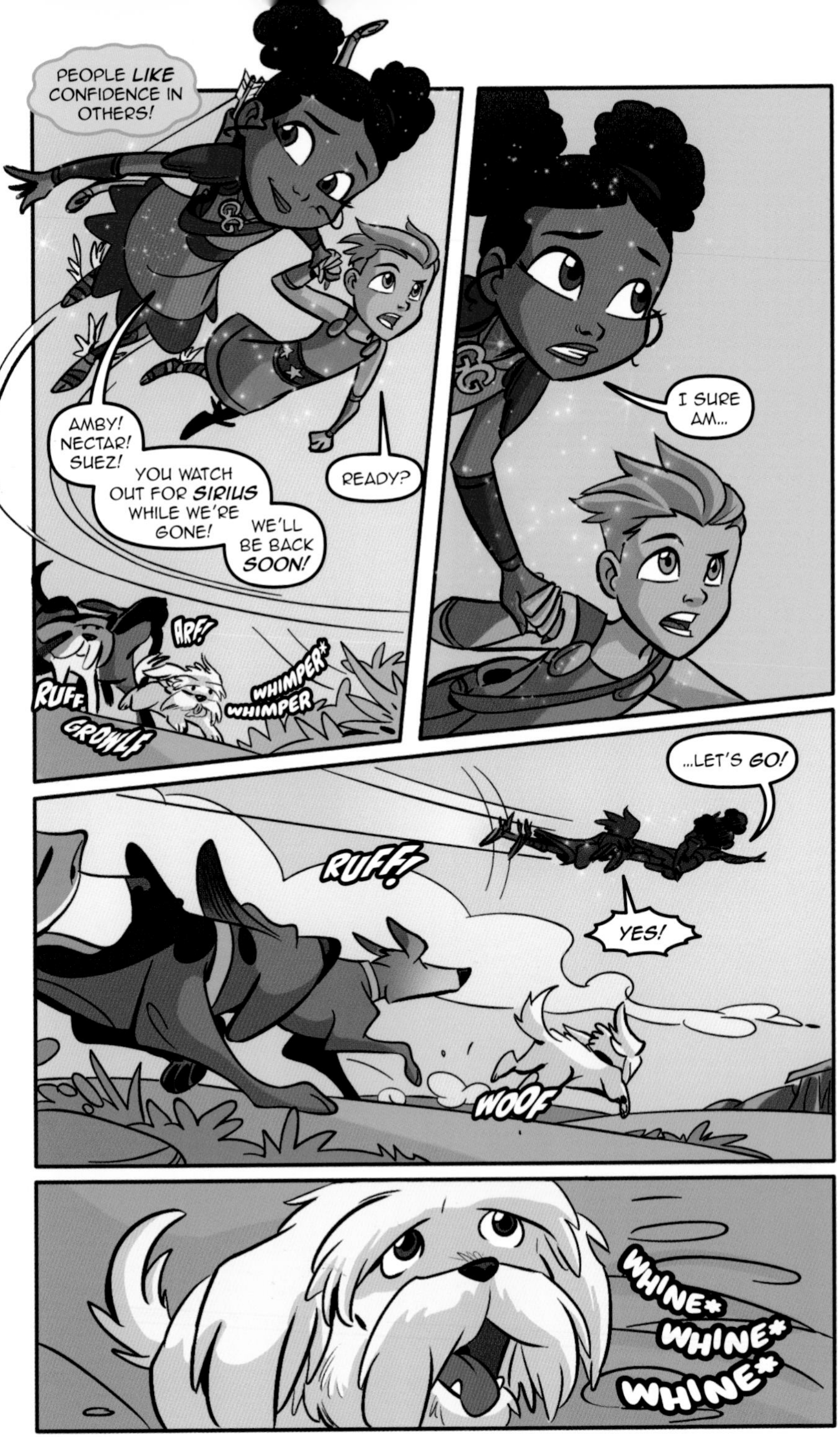
PEOPLE LIKE CONFIDENCE IN OTHERS!
AMBY! NECTAR! SUEZ!
YOU WATCH OUT FOR SIRIUS WHILE WE'RE GONE!
WE'LL BE BACK SOON!
READY?
ARF!
RUFF
GROWL
WHIMPER*
WHIMPER
I SURE AM...
...LET'S GO!
RUFF!
YES!
WOOF
WHINE*
WHINE*
WHINE*

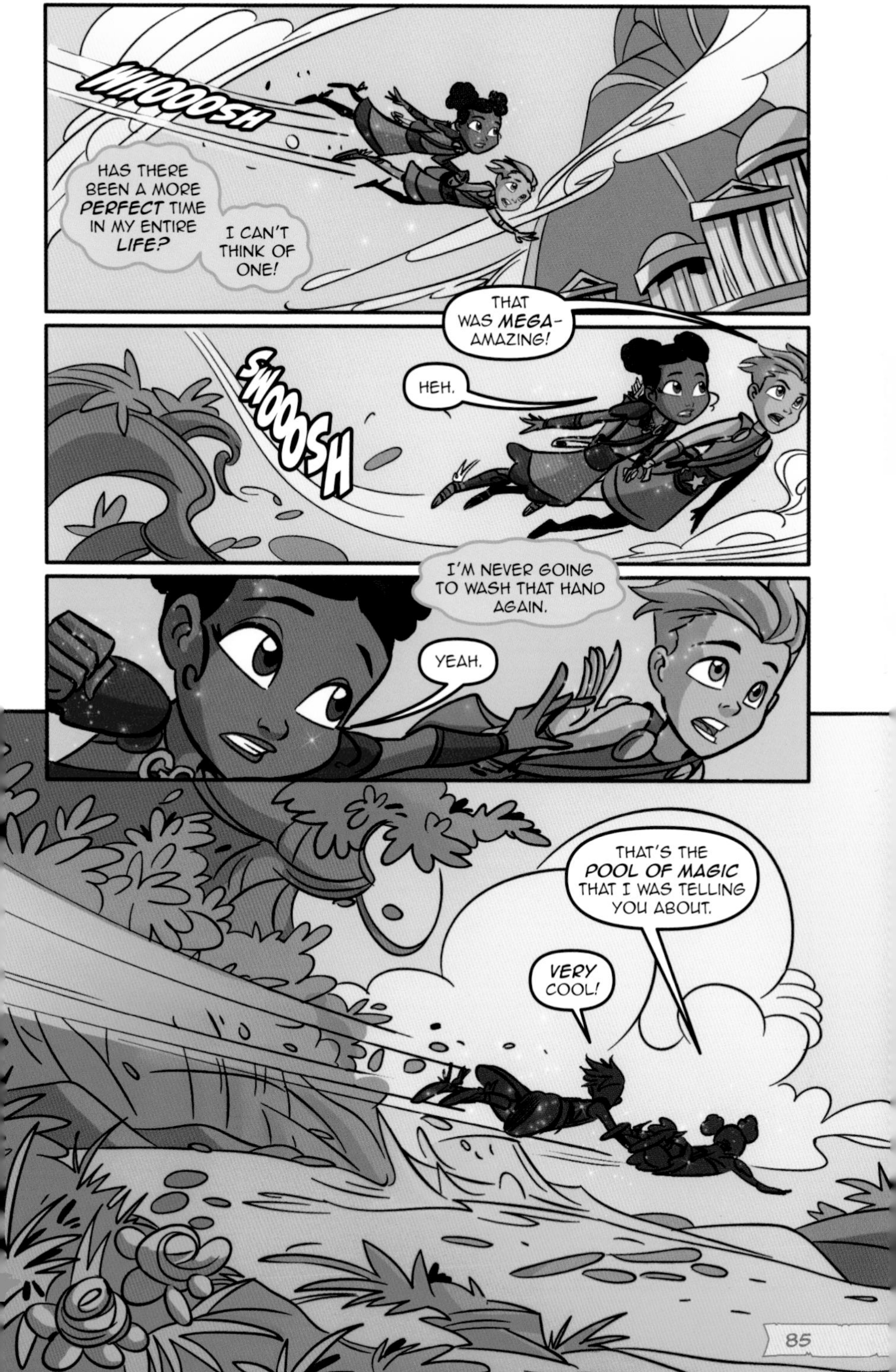
WHOOOSH
HAS THERE BEEN A MORE *PERFECT* TIME IN MY ENTIRE *LIFE?*
I CAN'T THINK OF ONE!
THAT WAS *MEGA*-AMAZING!
HEH.
SWOOOSH
I'M NEVER GOING TO WASH THAT HAND AGAIN.
YEAH.
THAT'S THE *POOL OF MAGIC* THAT I WAS TELLING YOU ABOUT.
VERY COOL!

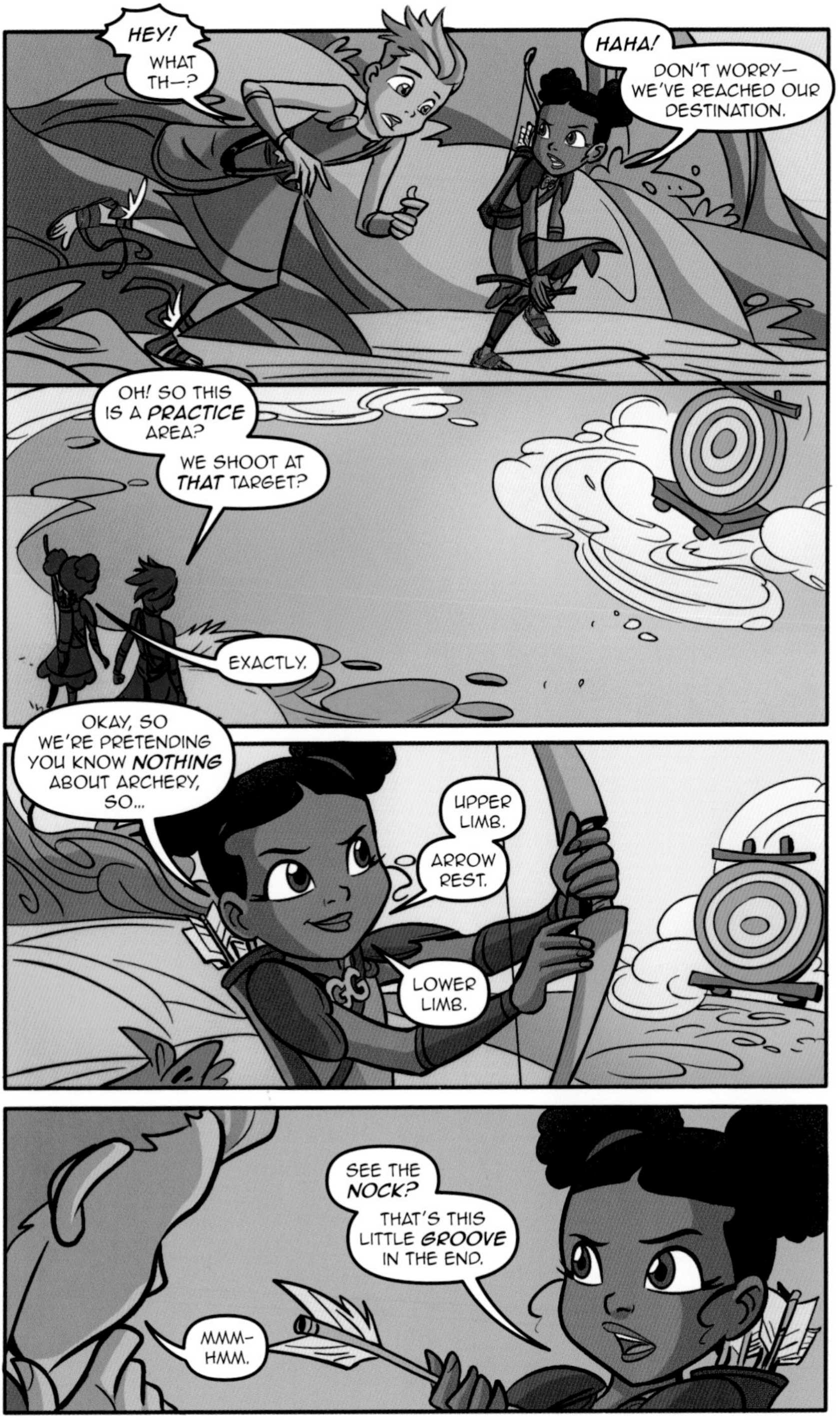
HEY! WHAT TH—?
HAHA! DON'T WORRY—WE'VE REACHED OUR DESTINATION.
OH! SO THIS IS A PRACTICE AREA?
WE SHOOT AT THAT TARGET?
EXACTLY.
OKAY, SO WE'RE PRETENDING YOU KNOW NOTHING ABOUT ARCHERY, SO...
UPPER LIMB.
ARROW REST.
LOWER LIMB.
SEE THE NOCK?
THAT'S THIS LITTLE GROOVE IN THE END.
MMM-HMM.

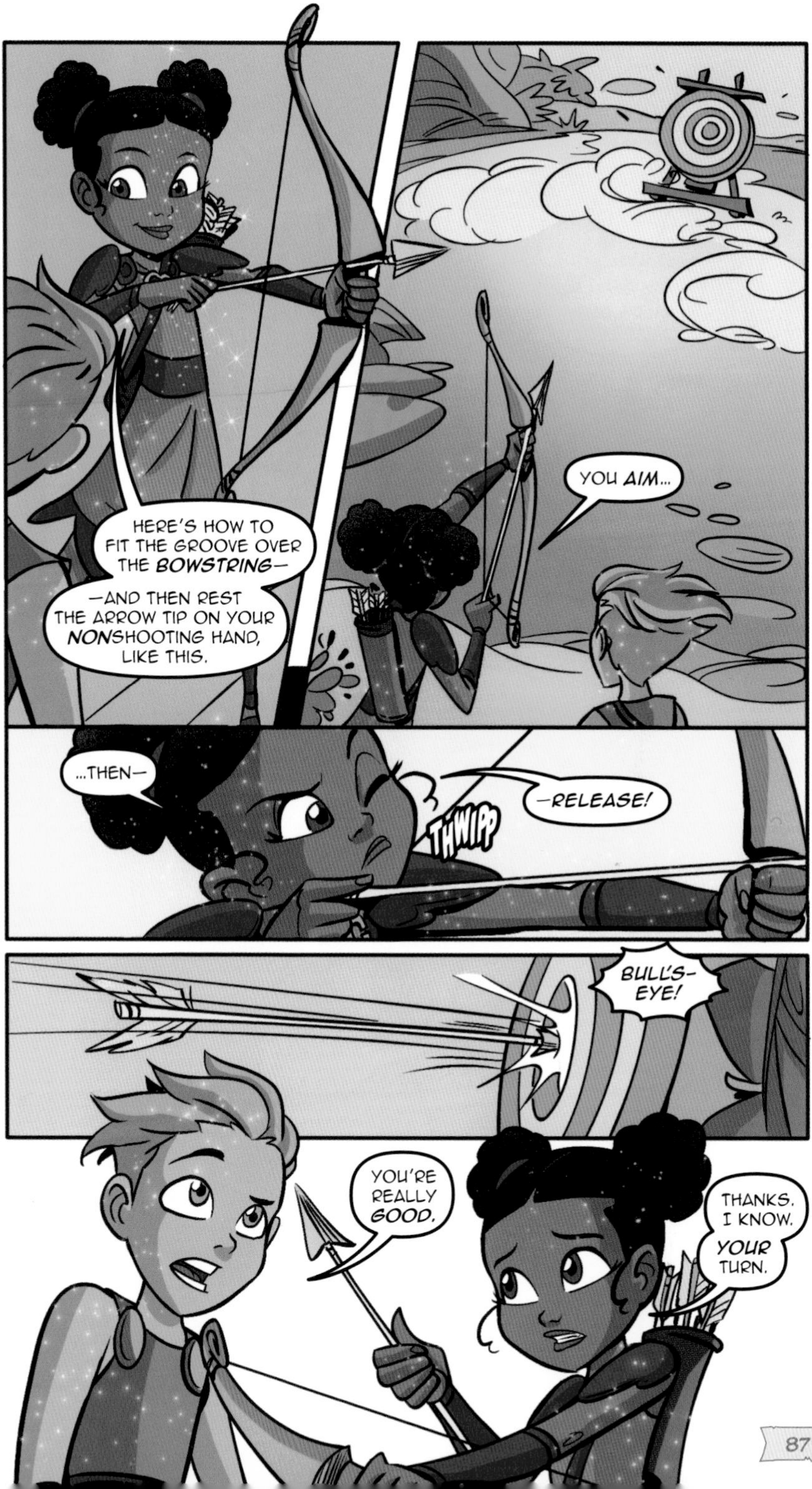
HERE'S HOW TO FIT THE GROOVE OVER THE BOWSTRING—
—AND THEN REST THE ARROW TIP ON YOUR NONSHOOTING HAND, LIKE THIS.
YOU AIM...
...THEN—
THWIPP
—RELEASE!
BULL'S-EYE!
YOU'RE REALLY GOOD.
THANKS. I KNOW. YOUR TURN.

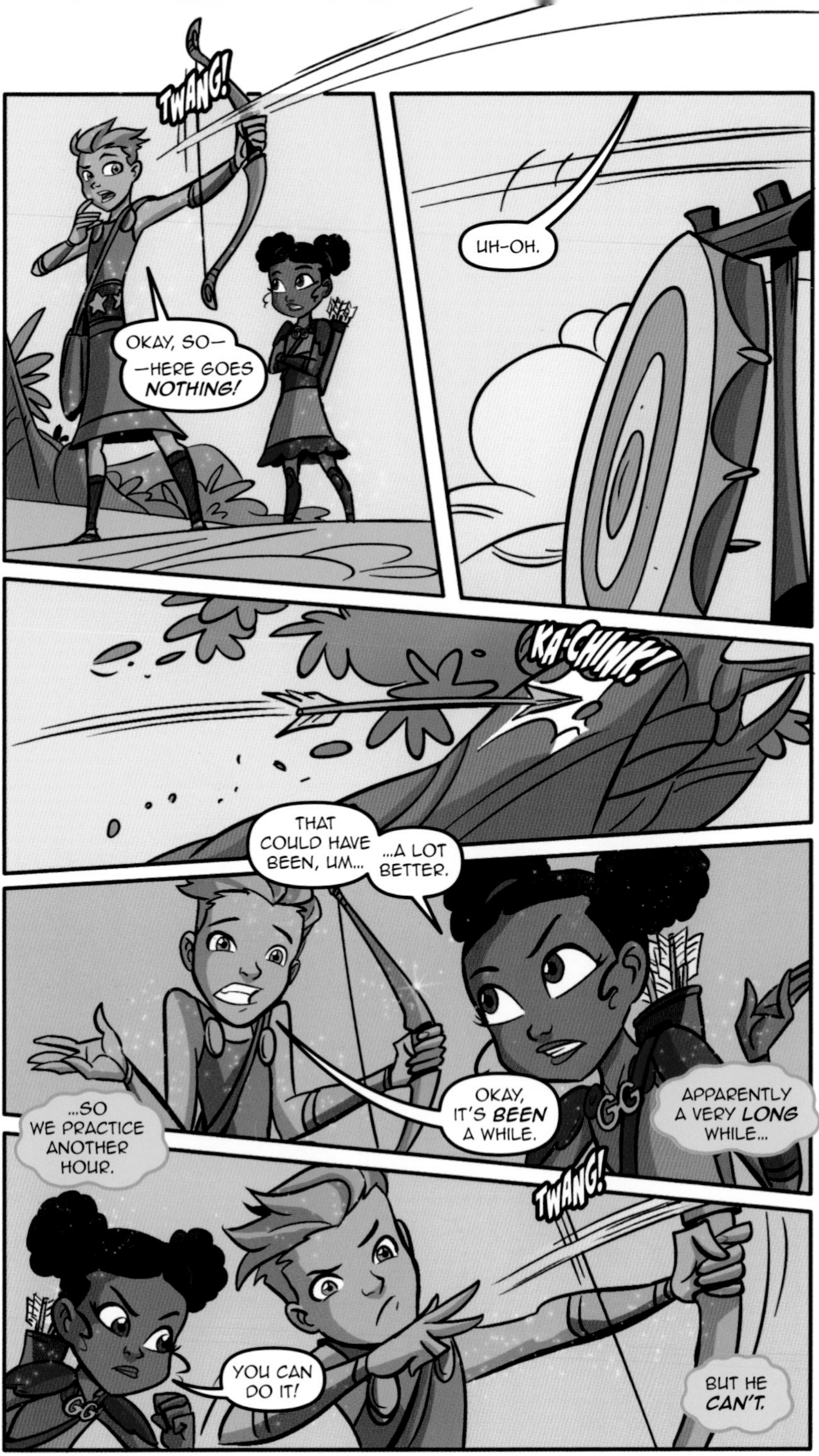
TWANG!
OKAY, SO— —HERE GOES NOTHING!
UH-OH.
KA-CHINK!
THAT COULD HAVE BEEN, UM...
...A LOT BETTER.
OKAY, IT'S BEEN A WHILE.
APPARENTLY A VERY LONG WHILE...
...SO WE PRACTICE ANOTHER HOUR.
TWANG!
YOU CAN DO IT!
BUT HE CAN'T.

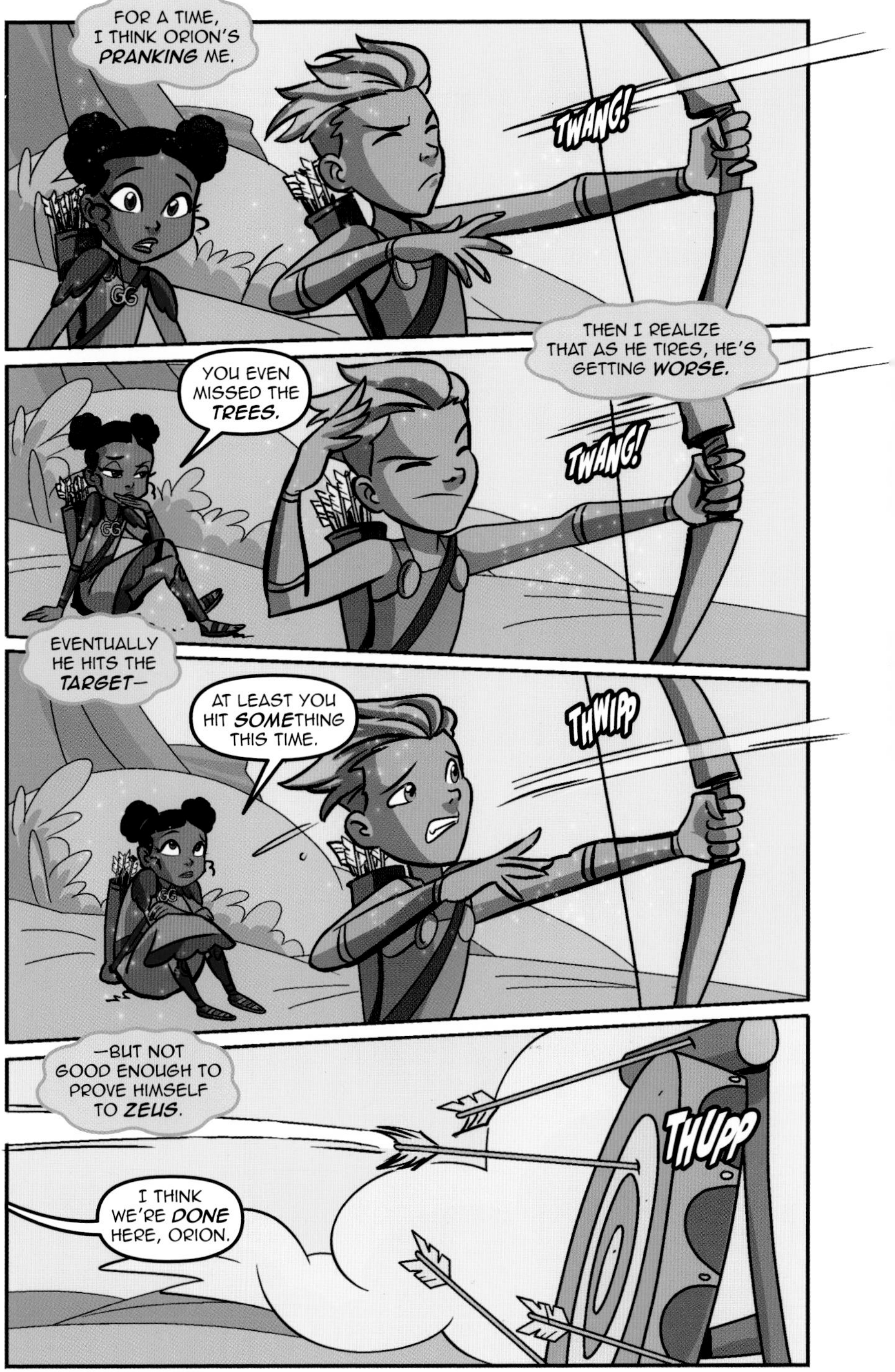
FOR A TIME, I THINK ORION'S PRANKING ME.
TWANG!
THEN I REALIZE THAT AS HE TIRES, HE'S GETTING WORSE.
YOU EVEN MISSED THE TREES.
TWANG!
EVENTUALLY HE HITS THE TARGET—
AT LEAST YOU HIT SOMETHING THIS TIME.
THWIPP
—BUT NOT GOOD ENOUGH TO PROVE HIMSELF TO ZEUS.
THUPP
I THINK WE'RE DONE HERE, ORION.

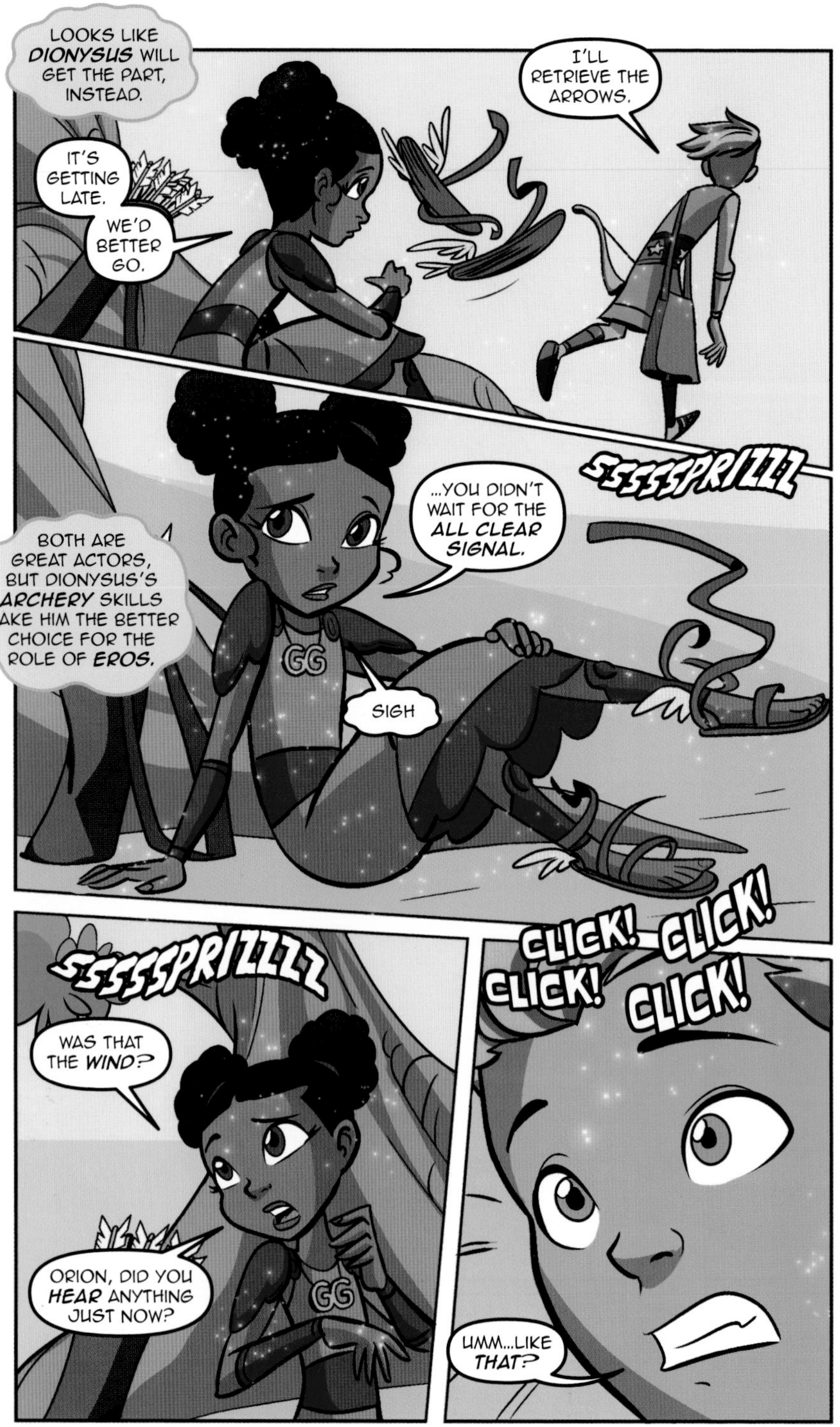
LOOKS LIKE DIONYSUS WILL GET THE PART, INSTEAD.
I'LL RETRIEVE THE ARROWS.
IT'S GETTING LATE.
WE'D BETTER GO.
SSSSSPRIZZZ
...YOU DIDN'T WAIT FOR THE ALL CLEAR SIGNAL.
BOTH ARE GREAT ACTORS, BUT DIONYSUS'S ARCHERY SKILLS MAKE HIM THE BETTER CHOICE FOR THE ROLE OF EROS.
SIGH
SSSSSPRIZZZZZ
WAS THAT THE WIND?
ORION, DID YOU HEAR ANYTHING JUST NOW?
CLICK! CLICK! CLICK! CLICK!
UMM...LIKE THAT?

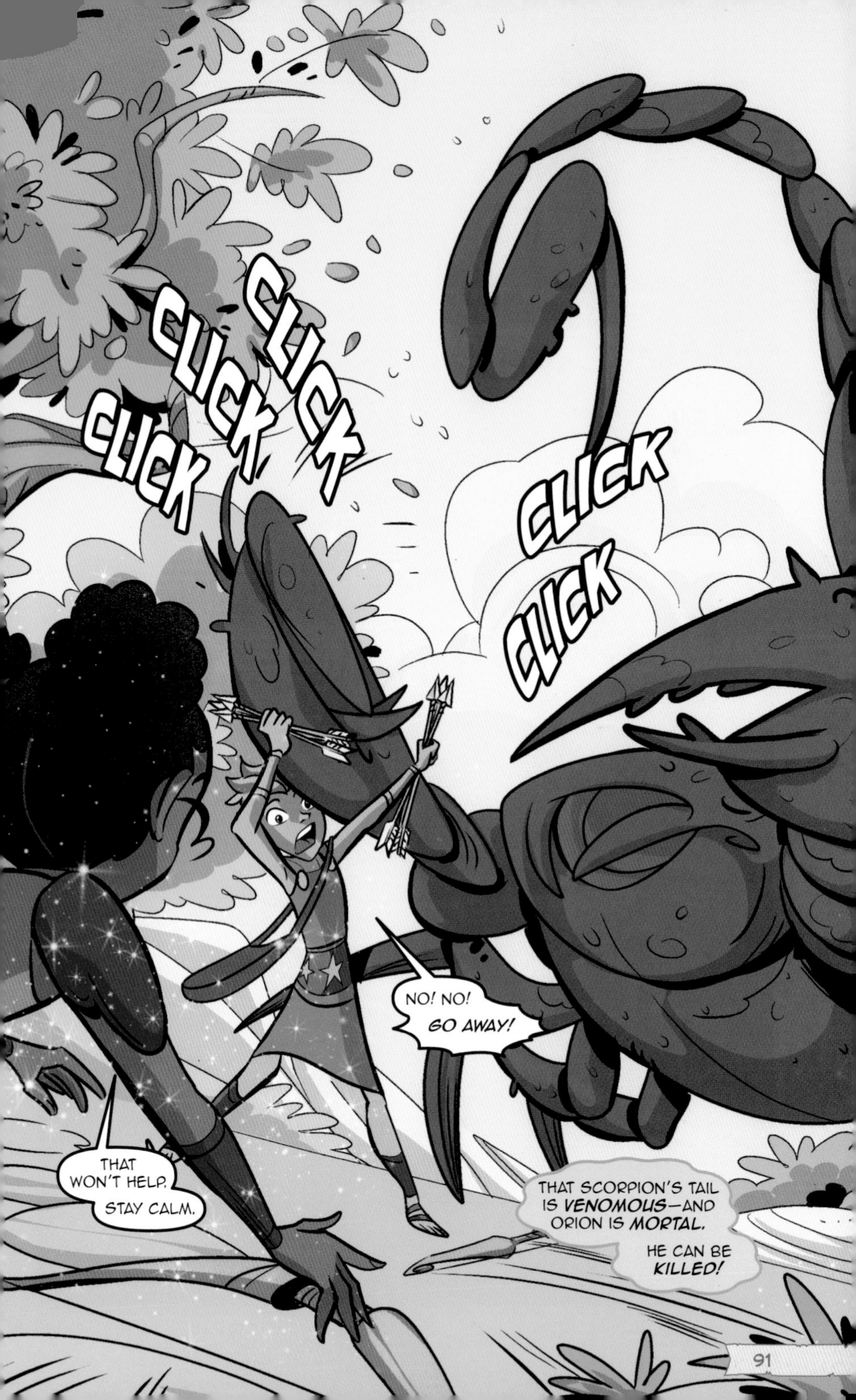
CLICK
CLICK
CLICK
CLICK
CLICK
NO! NO! GO AWAY!
THAT WON'T HELP. STAY CALM.
THAT SCORPION'S TAIL IS VENOMOUS—AND ORION IS MORTAL.
HE CAN BE KILLED!

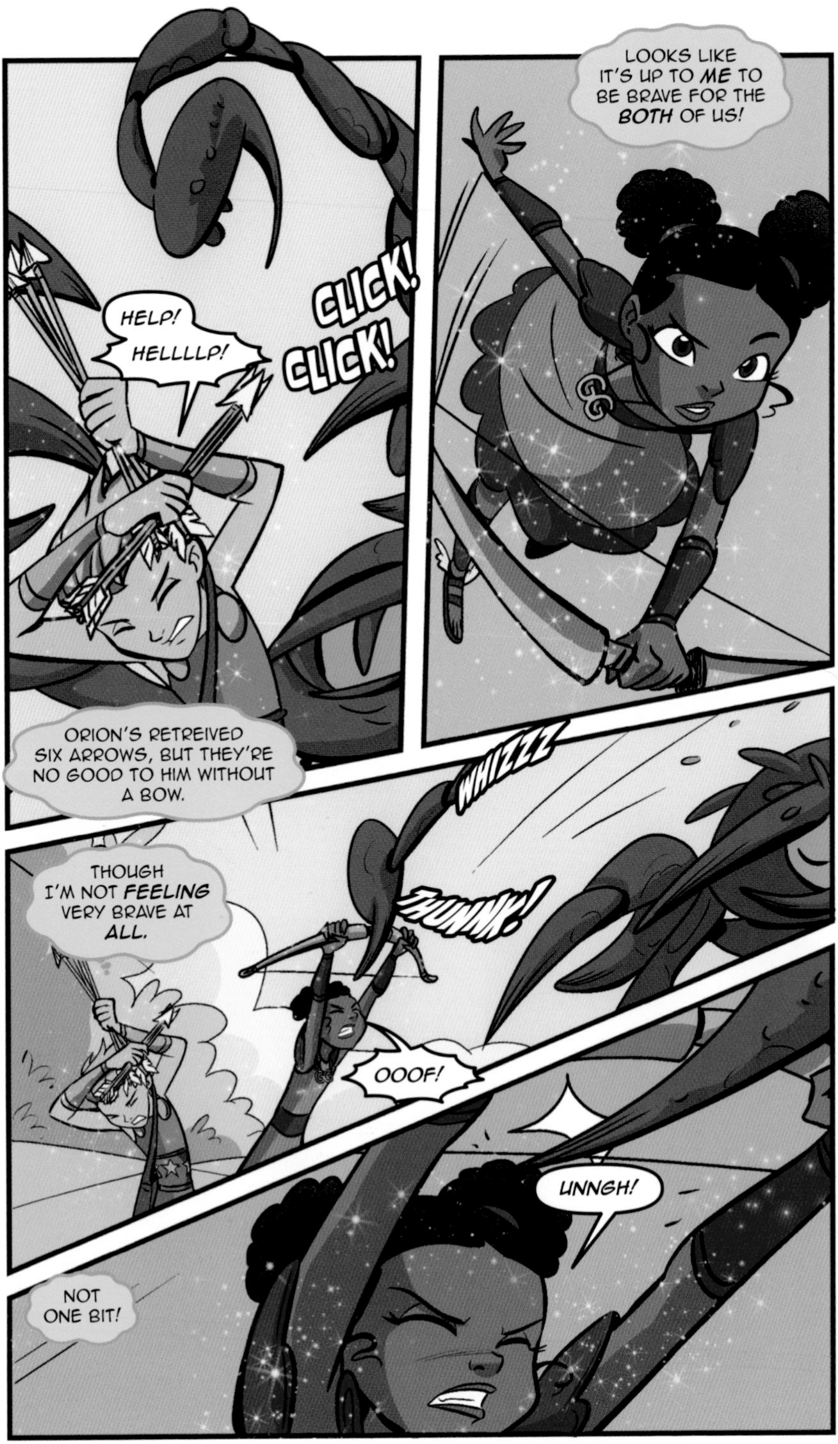
HELP!
HELLLLP!
CLICK!
CLICK!
LOOKS LIKE IT'S UP TO ME TO BE BRAVE FOR THE BOTH OF US!
ORION'S RETREIVED SIX ARROWS, BUT THEY'RE NO GOOD TO HIM WITHOUT A BOW.
WHIZZZ
THUNK!
THOUGH I'M NOT FEELING VERY BRAVE AT ALL.
OOOF!
UNNGH!
NOT ONE BIT!

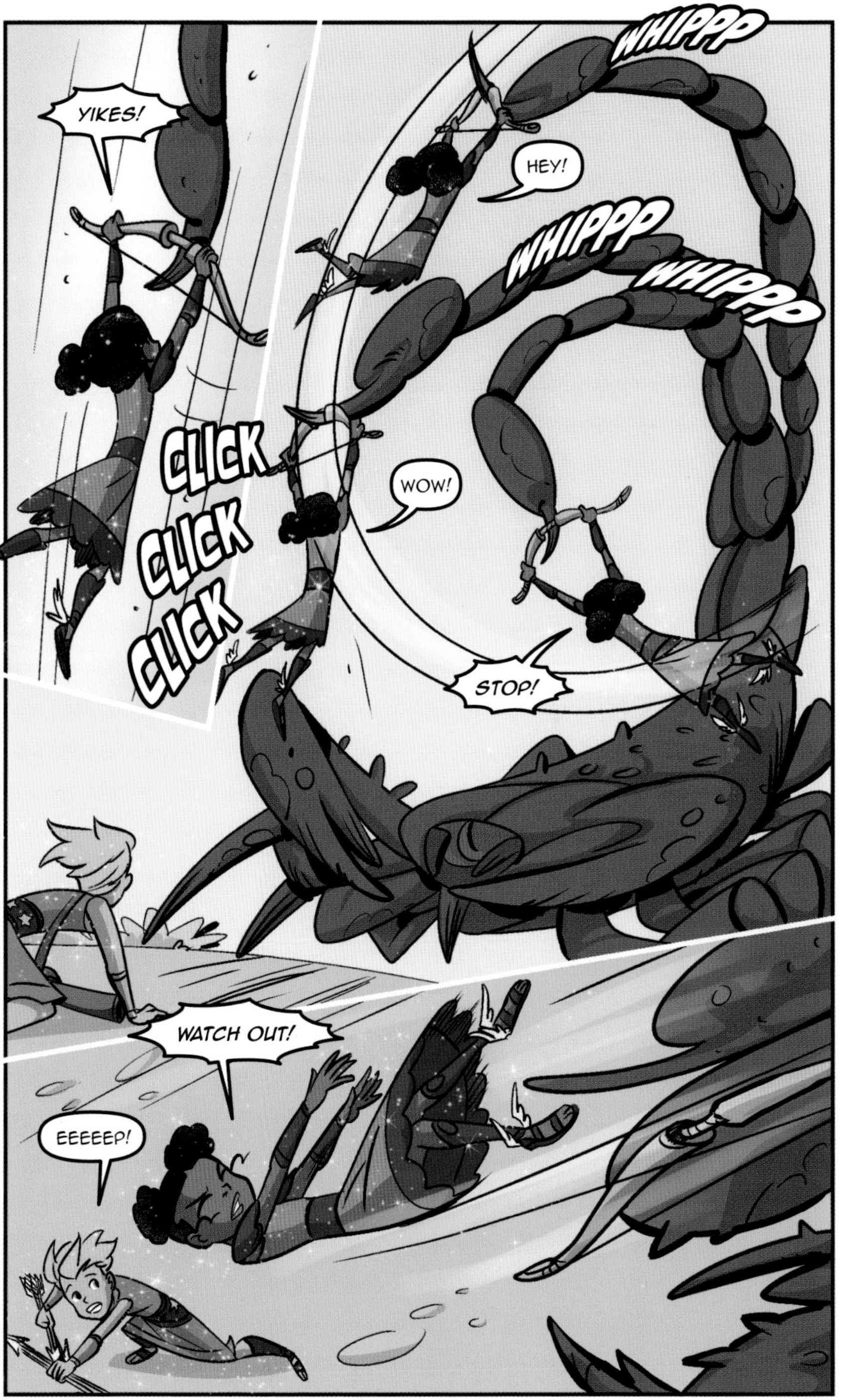
YIKES!
CLICK
CLICK
CLICK
WHIPPP
HEY!
WHIPPP
WHIPPP
WOW!
STOP!
WATCH OUT!
EEEEEP!

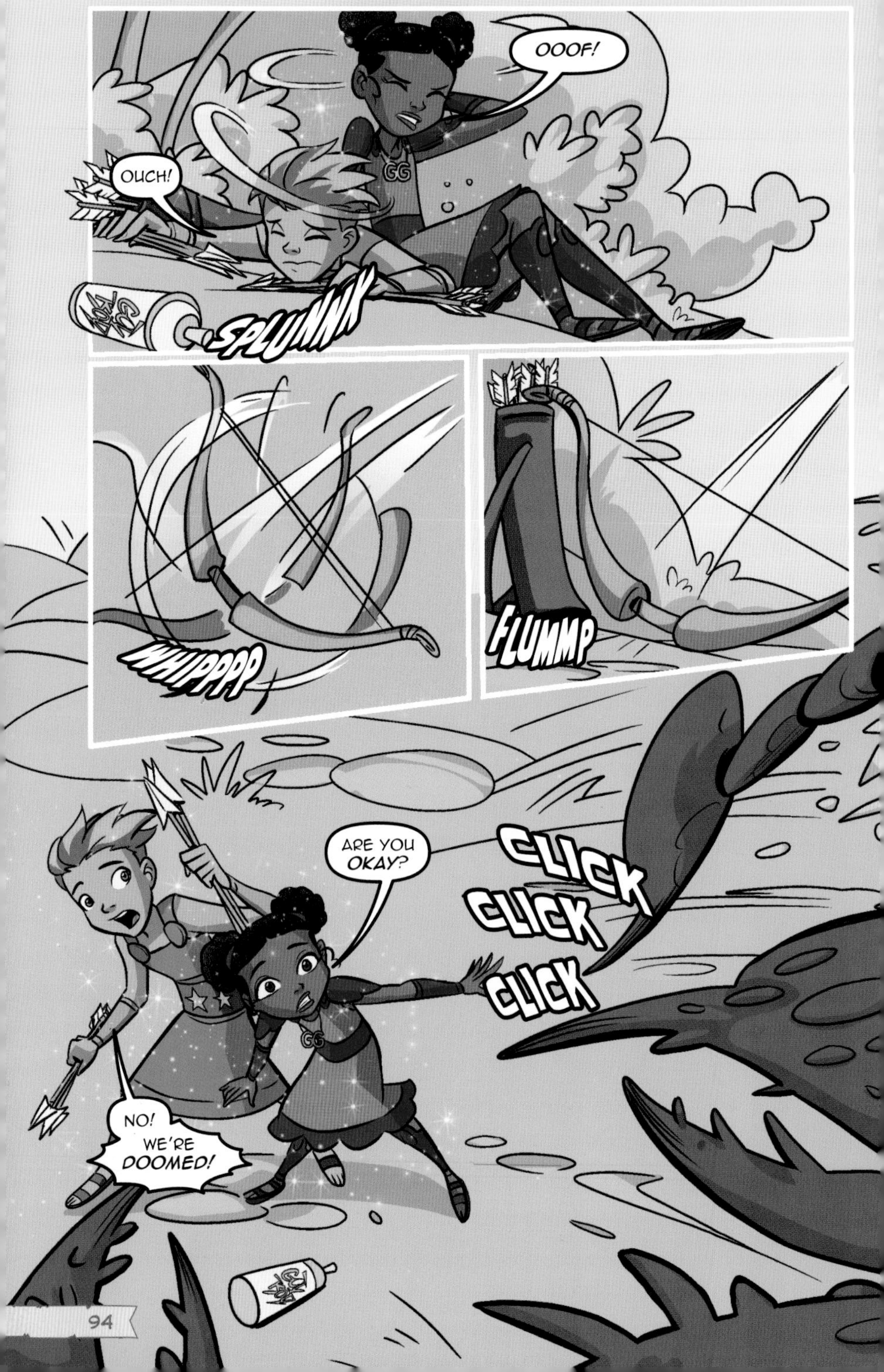
OOOF!
OUCH!
SPLUNNNK
WHIPPPP
FLUMMP
ARE YOU OKAY?
CLICK
CLICK
CLICK
NO! WE'RE DOOMED!

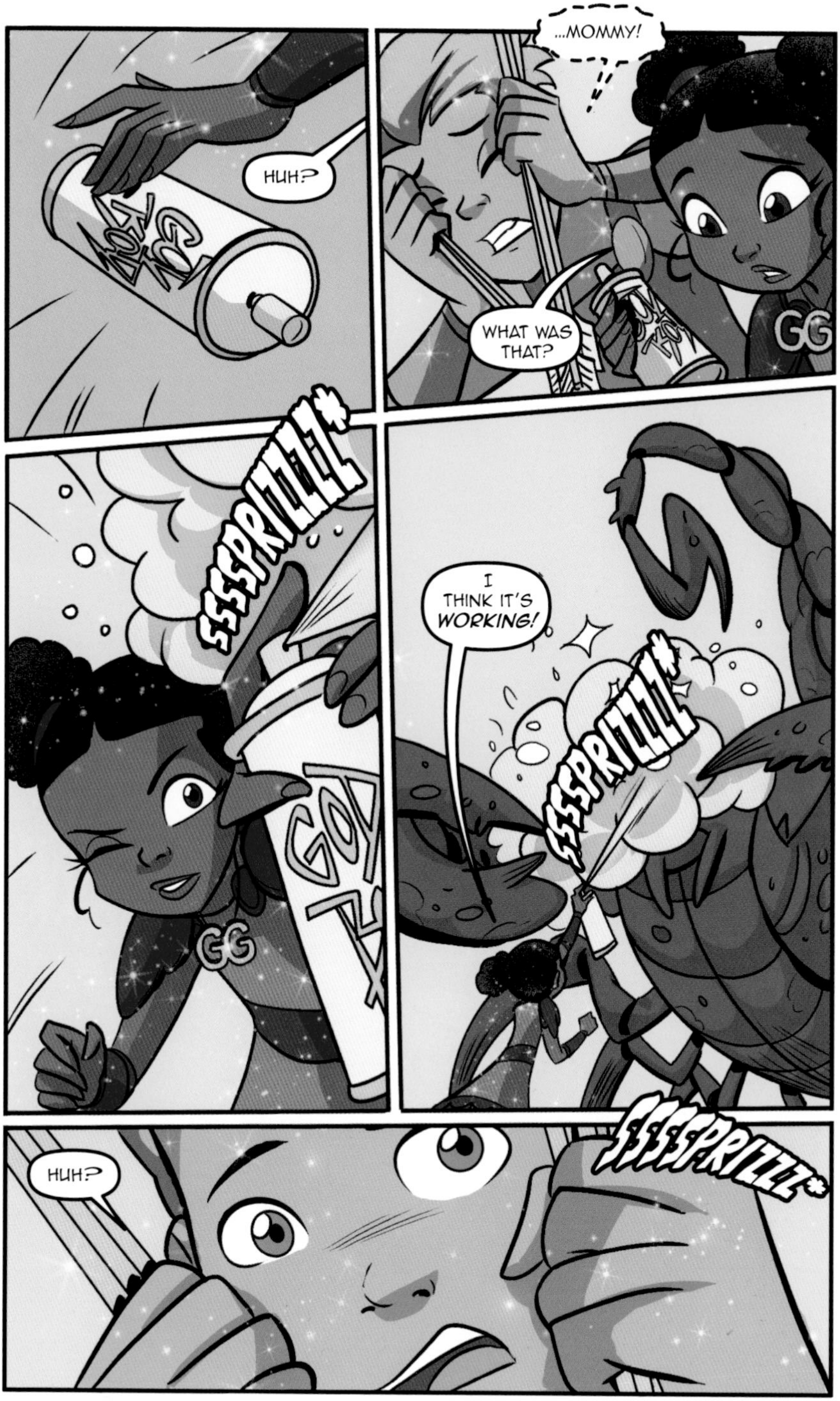
HUH?
...MOMMY!
WHAT WAS THAT?
SSSSPRIZZZ*
I THINK IT'S WORKING!
SSSPRIZZZ*
HUH?
SSSPRIZZZ*

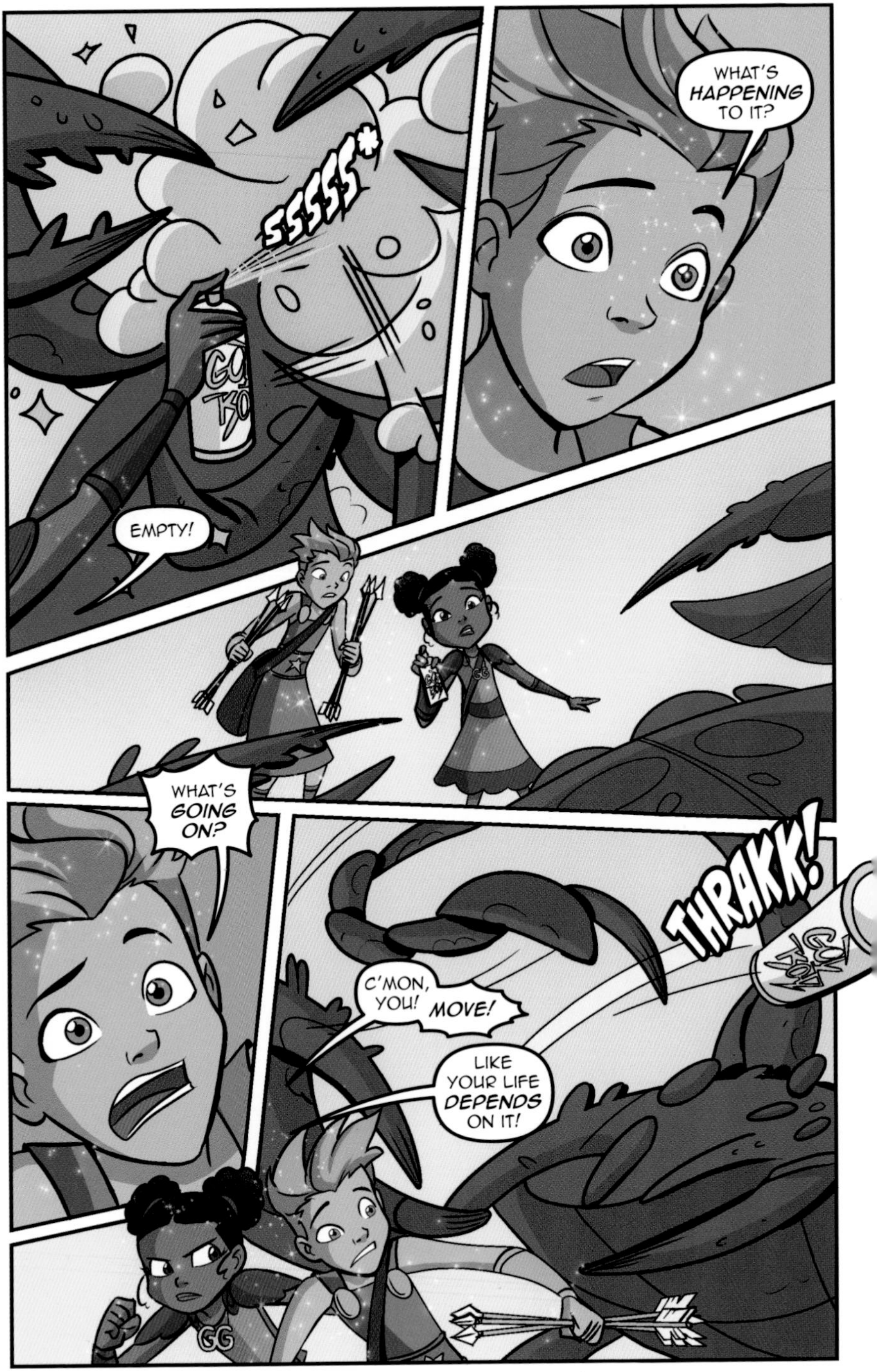
SSSSS*
WHAT'S HAPPENING TO IT?
EMPTY!
WHAT'S GOING ON?
THRAKK!
C'MON, YOU! MOVE!
LIKE YOUR LIFE DEPENDS ON IT!

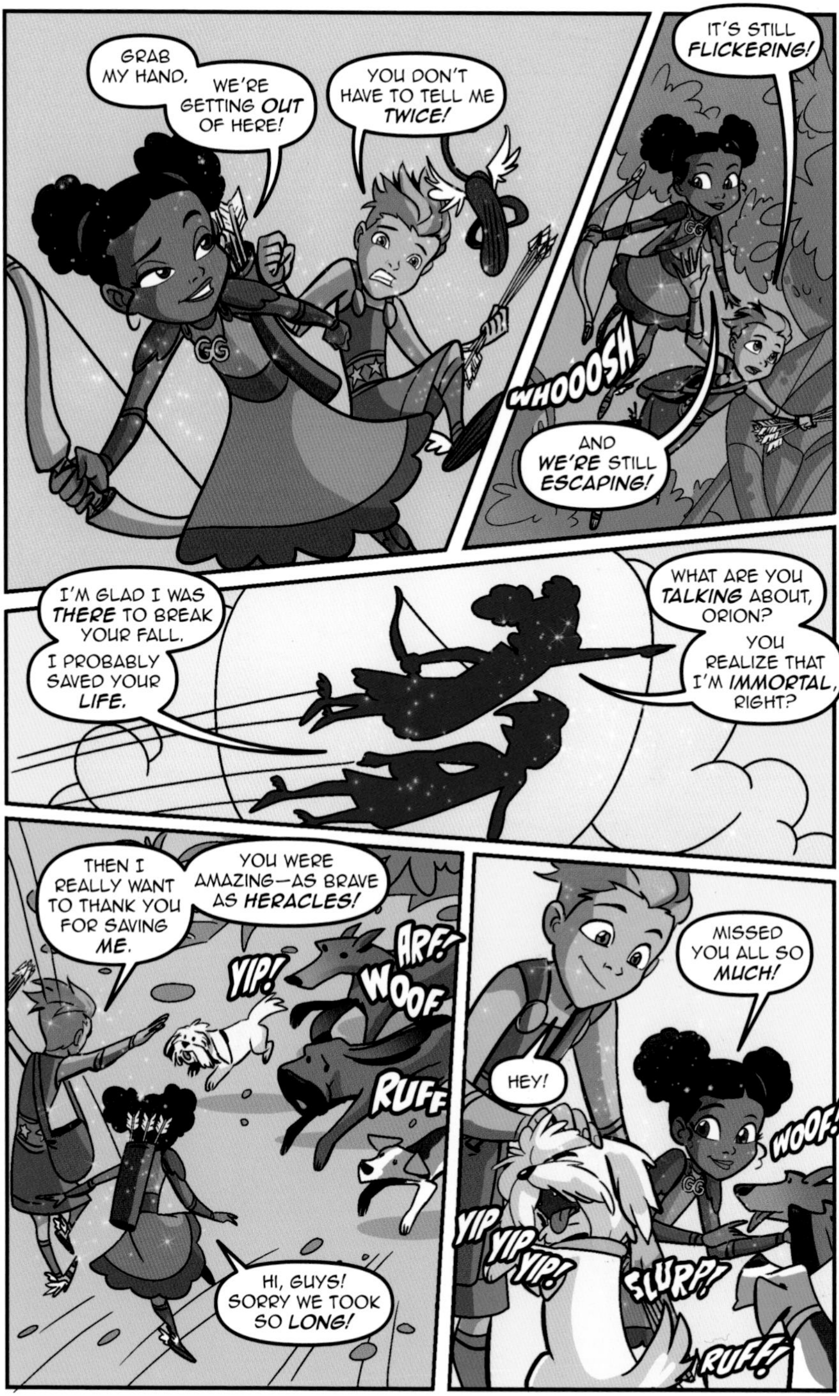
GRAB MY HAND.
WE'RE GETTING OUT OF HERE!
YOU DON'T HAVE TO TELL ME TWICE!
IT'S STILL FLICKERING!
WHOOOSH
AND WE'RE STILL ESCAPING!
I'M GLAD I WAS THERE TO BREAK YOUR FALL.
I PROBABLY SAVED YOUR LIFE.
WHAT ARE YOU TALKING ABOUT, ORION?
YOU REALIZE THAT I'M IMMORTAL, RIGHT?
THEN I REALLY WANT TO THANK YOU FOR SAVING ME.
YOU WERE AMAZING—AS BRAVE AS HERACLES!
YIP!
ARF!
WOOF
RUFF
HI, GUYS! SORRY WE TOOK SO LONG!
MISSED YOU ALL SO MUCH!
HEY!
WOOF!
YIP
YIP
YIP!
SLURP!
RUFF!

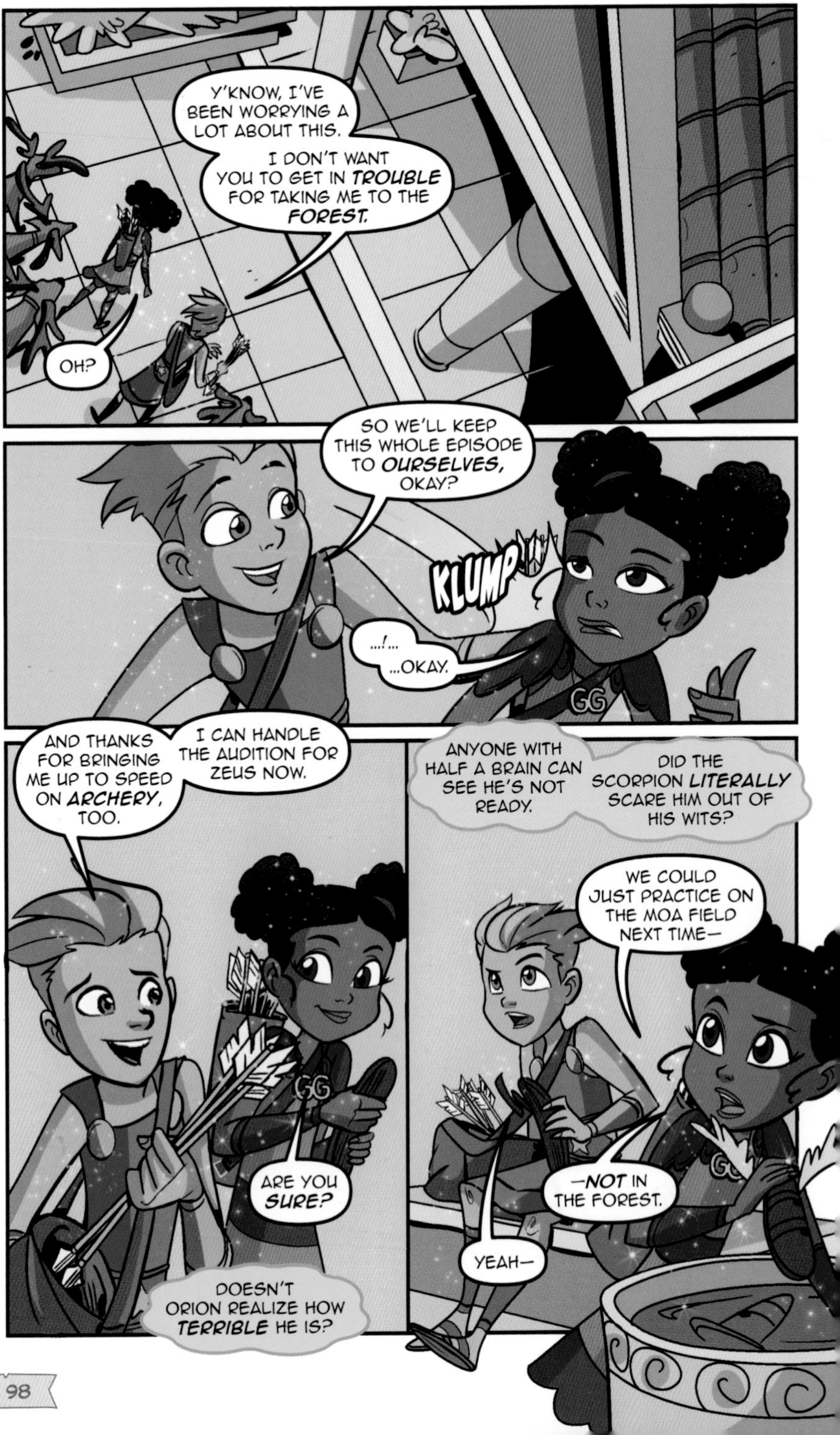

Y'KNOW, I'VE BEEN WORRYING A LOT ABOUT THIS.
I DON'T WANT YOU TO GET IN TROUBLE FOR TAKING ME TO THE FOREST.
OH?
SO WE'LL KEEP THIS WHOLE EPISODE TO OURSELVES, OKAY?
KLUMP
...!...
...OKAY.
AND THANKS FOR BRINGING ME UP TO SPEED ON ARCHERY, TOO.
I CAN HANDLE THE AUDITION FOR ZEUS NOW.
ARE YOU SURE?
DOESN'T ORION REALIZE HOW TERRIBLE HE IS?
ANYONE WITH HALF A BRAIN CAN SEE HE'S NOT READY.
DID THE SCORPION LITERALLY SCARE HIM OUT OF HIS WITS?
WE COULD JUST PRACTICE ON THE MOA FIELD NEXT TIME—
—NOT IN THE FOREST.
YEAH—

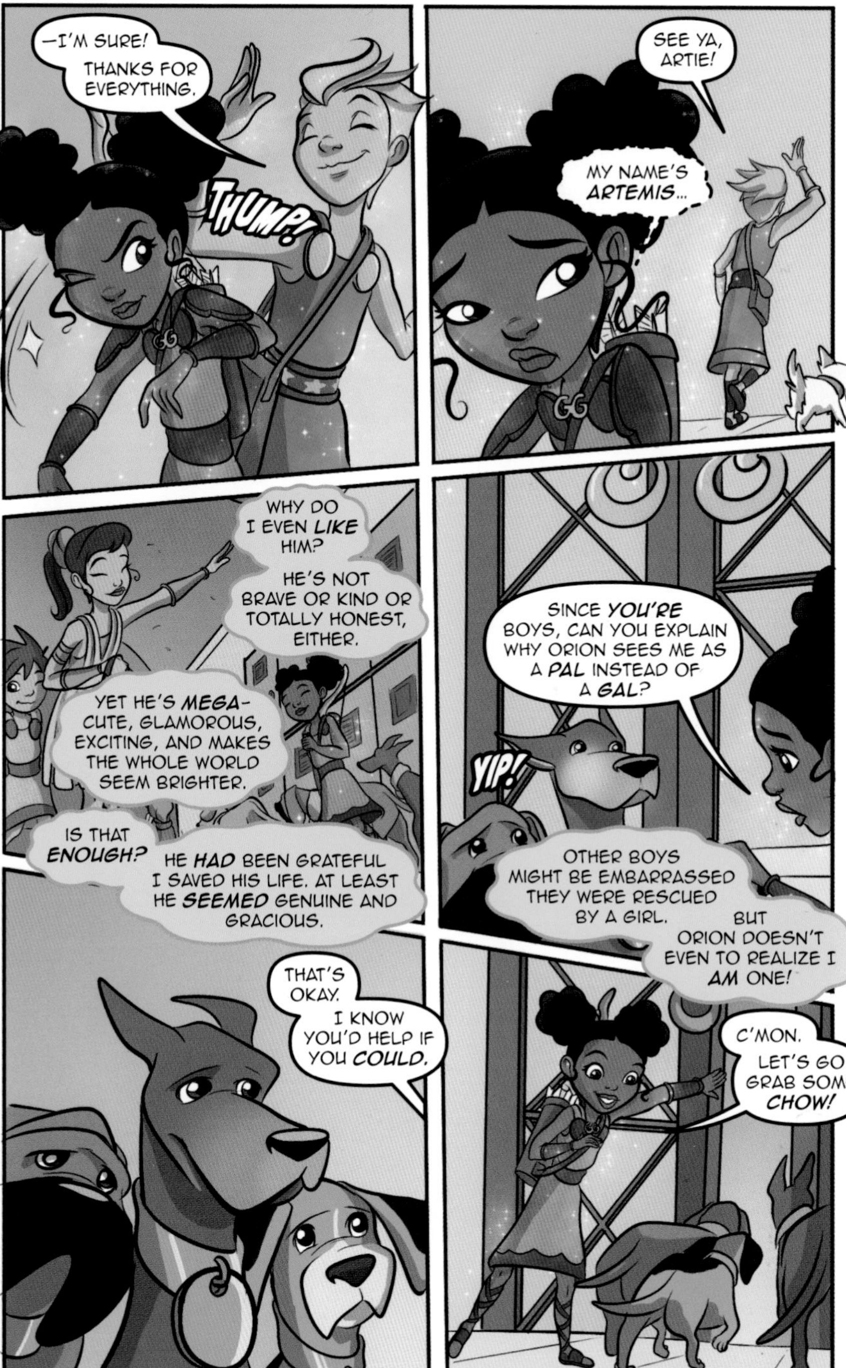
—I'M SURE!
THANKS FOR EVERYTHING.
THUMP!
SEE YA, ARTIE!
MY NAME'S ARTEMIS...
WHY DO I EVEN LIKE HIM?
HE'S NOT BRAVE OR KIND OR TOTALLY HONEST, EITHER.
YET HE'S MEGA-CUTE, GLAMOROUS, EXCITING, AND MAKES THE WHOLE WORLD SEEM BRIGHTER.
IS THAT ENOUGH?
SINCE YOU'RE BOYS, CAN YOU EXPLAIN WHY ORION SEES ME AS A PAL INSTEAD OF A GAL?
YIP!
HE HAD BEEN GRATEFUL I SAVED HIS LIFE. AT LEAST HE SEEMED GENUINE AND GRACIOUS.
OTHER BOYS MIGHT BE EMBARRASSED THEY WERE RESCUED BY A GIRL.
BUT ORION DOESN'T EVEN TO REALIZE I AM ONE!
THAT'S OKAY.
I KNOW YOU'D HELP IF YOU COULD.
C'MON.
LET'S GO GRAB SOME CHOW!

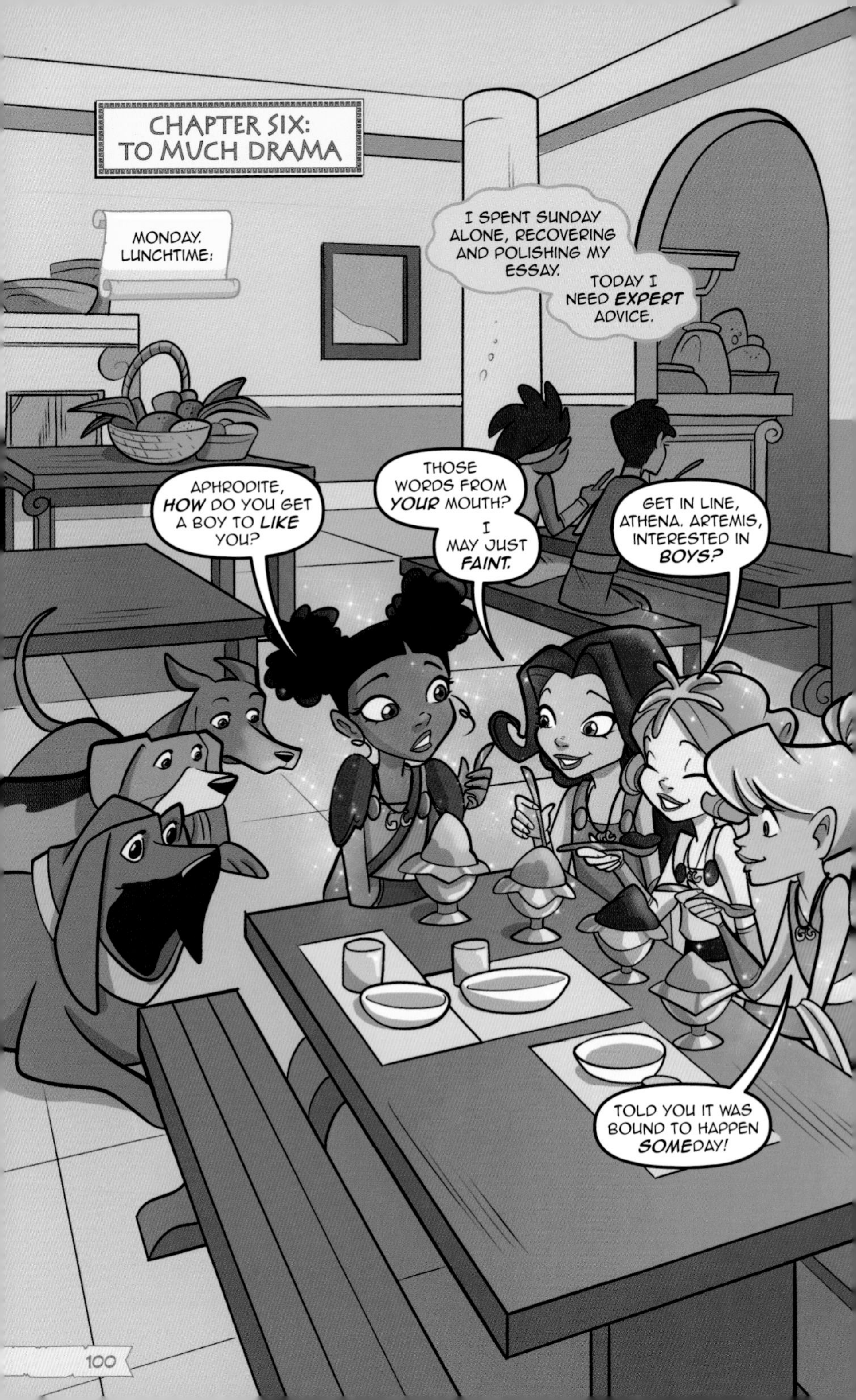
CHAPTER SIX:
TO MUCH DRAMA
MONDAY. LUNCHTIME:
I SPENT SUNDAY ALONE, RECOVERING AND POLISHING MY ESSAY.
TODAY I NEED EXPERT ADVICE.
APHRODITE, HOW DO YOU GET A BOY TO LIKE YOU?
THOSE WORDS FROM YOUR MOUTH?
I MAY JUST FAINT.
GET IN LINE, ATHENA. ARTEMIS, INTERESTED IN BOYS?
TOLD YOU IT WAS BOUND TO HAPPEN SOMEDAY!

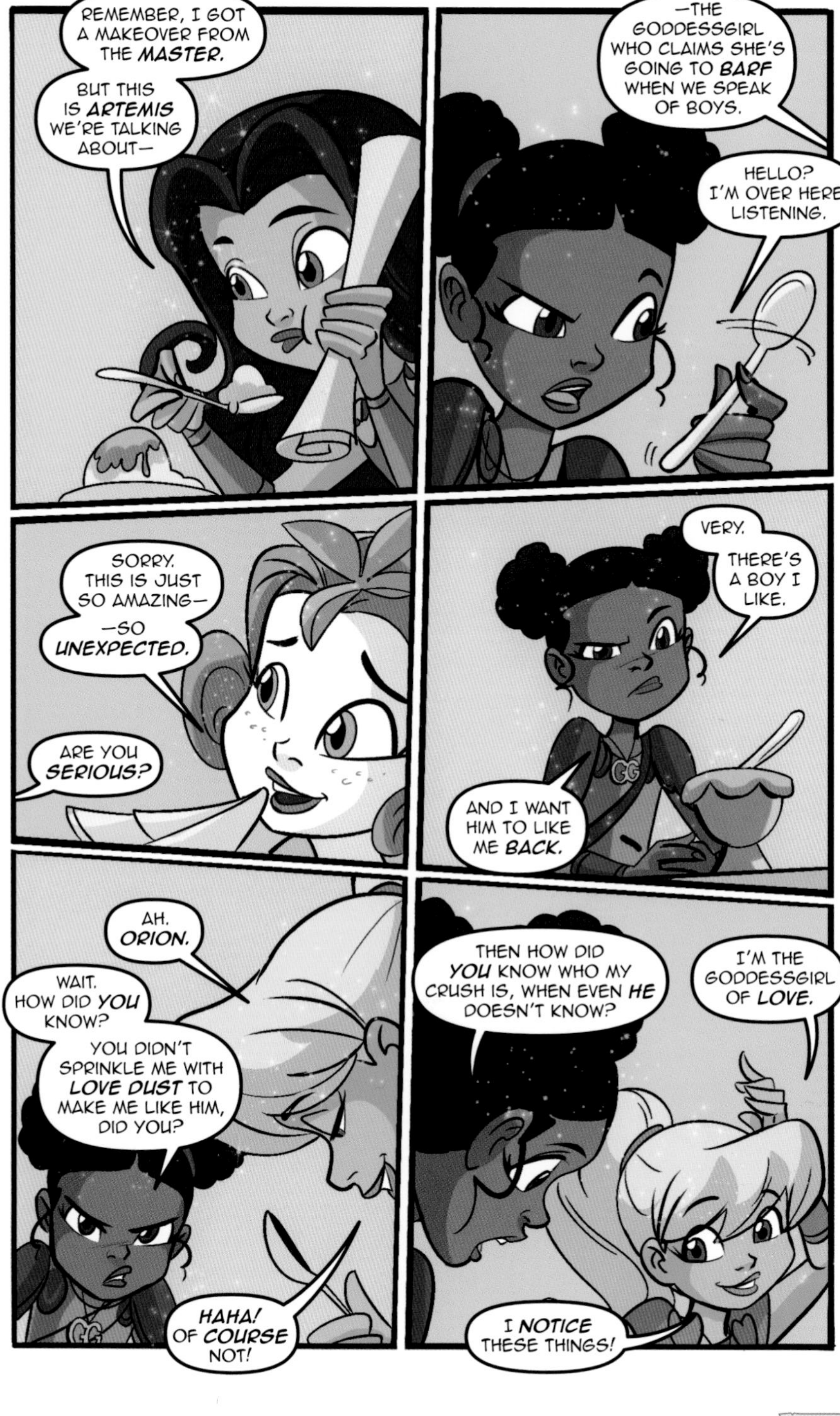
REMEMBER, I GOT A MAKEOVER FROM THE MASTER.
BUT THIS IS ARTEMIS WE'RE TALKING ABOUT—
—THE GODDESSGIRL WHO CLAIMS SHE'S GOING TO BARF WHEN WE SPEAK OF BOYS.
HELLO? I'M OVER HERE. LISTENING.
SORRY. THIS IS JUST SO AMAZING—
—SO UNEXPECTED.
ARE YOU SERIOUS?
VERY.
THERE'S A BOY I LIKE.
AND I WANT HIM TO LIKE ME BACK.
AH. ORION.
WAIT. HOW DID YOU KNOW?
YOU DIDN'T SPRINKLE ME WITH LOVE DUST TO MAKE ME LIKE HIM, DID YOU?
HAHA! OF COURSE NOT!
THEN HOW DID YOU KNOW WHO MY CRUSH IS, WHEN EVEN HE DOESN'T KNOW?
I'M THE GODDESSGIRL OF LOVE.
I NOTICE THESE THINGS!

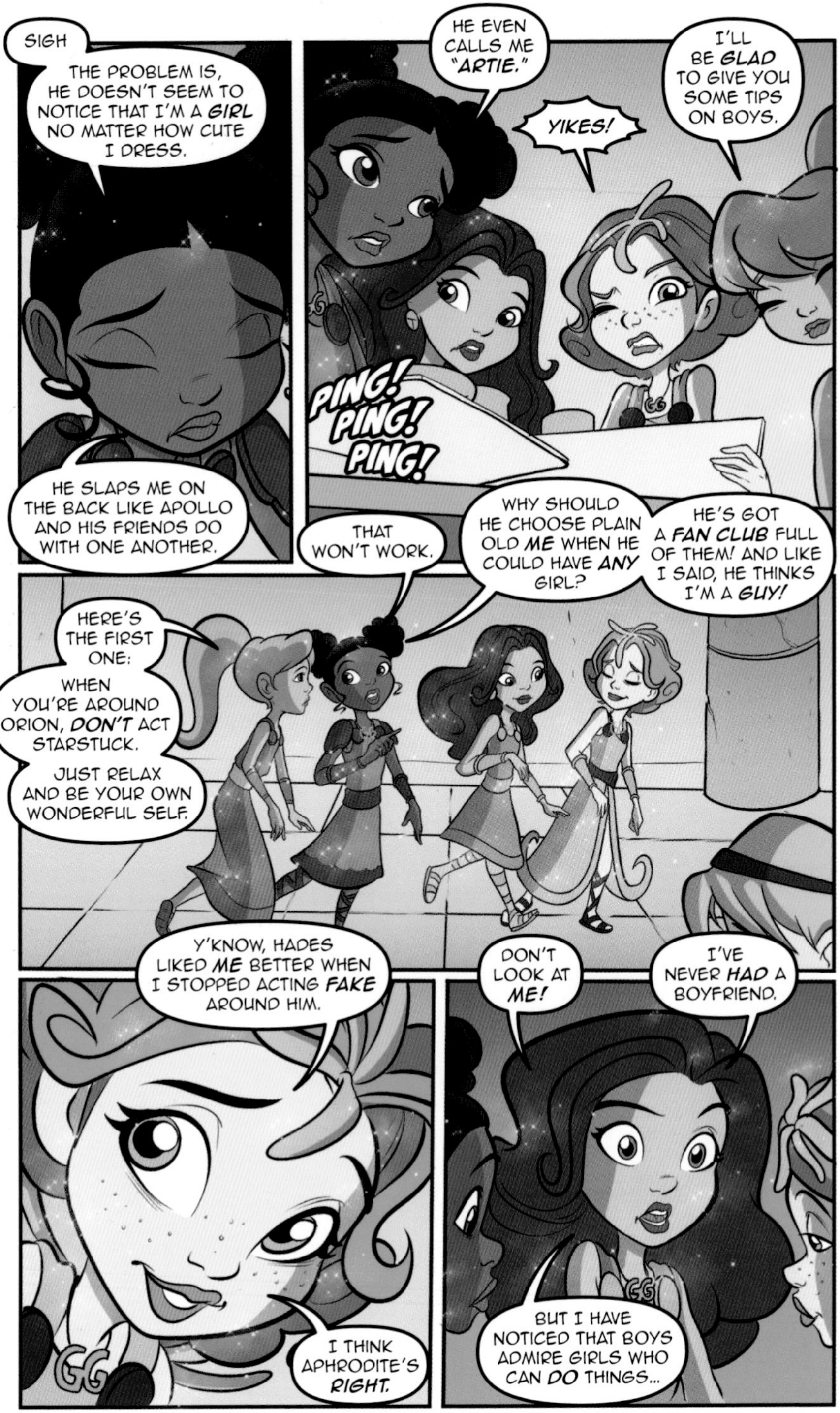
SIGH
THE PROBLEM IS, HE DOESN'T SEEM TO NOTICE THAT I'M A GIRL NO MATTER HOW CUTE I DRESS.
HE SLAPS ME ON THE BACK LIKE APOLLO AND HIS FRIENDS DO WITH ONE ANOTHER.
HE EVEN CALLS ME "ARTIE."
YIKES!
I'LL BE GLAD TO GIVE YOU SOME TIPS ON BOYS.
PING! PING! PING!
THAT WON'T WORK.
WHY SHOULD HE CHOOSE PLAIN OLD ME WHEN HE COULD HAVE ANY GIRL?
HE'S GOT A FAN CLUB FULL OF THEM! AND LIKE I SAID, HE THINKS I'M A GUY!
HERE'S THE FIRST ONE:
WHEN YOU'RE AROUND ORION, DON'T ACT STARSTUCK.
JUST RELAX AND BE YOUR OWN WONDERFUL SELF.
Y'KNOW, HADES LIKED ME BETTER WHEN I STOPPED ACTING FAKE AROUND HIM.
I THINK APHRODITE'S RIGHT.
DON'T LOOK AT ME!
I'VE NEVER HAD A BOYFRIEND.
BUT I HAVE NOTICED THAT BOYS ADMIRE GIRLS WHO CAN DO THINGS...

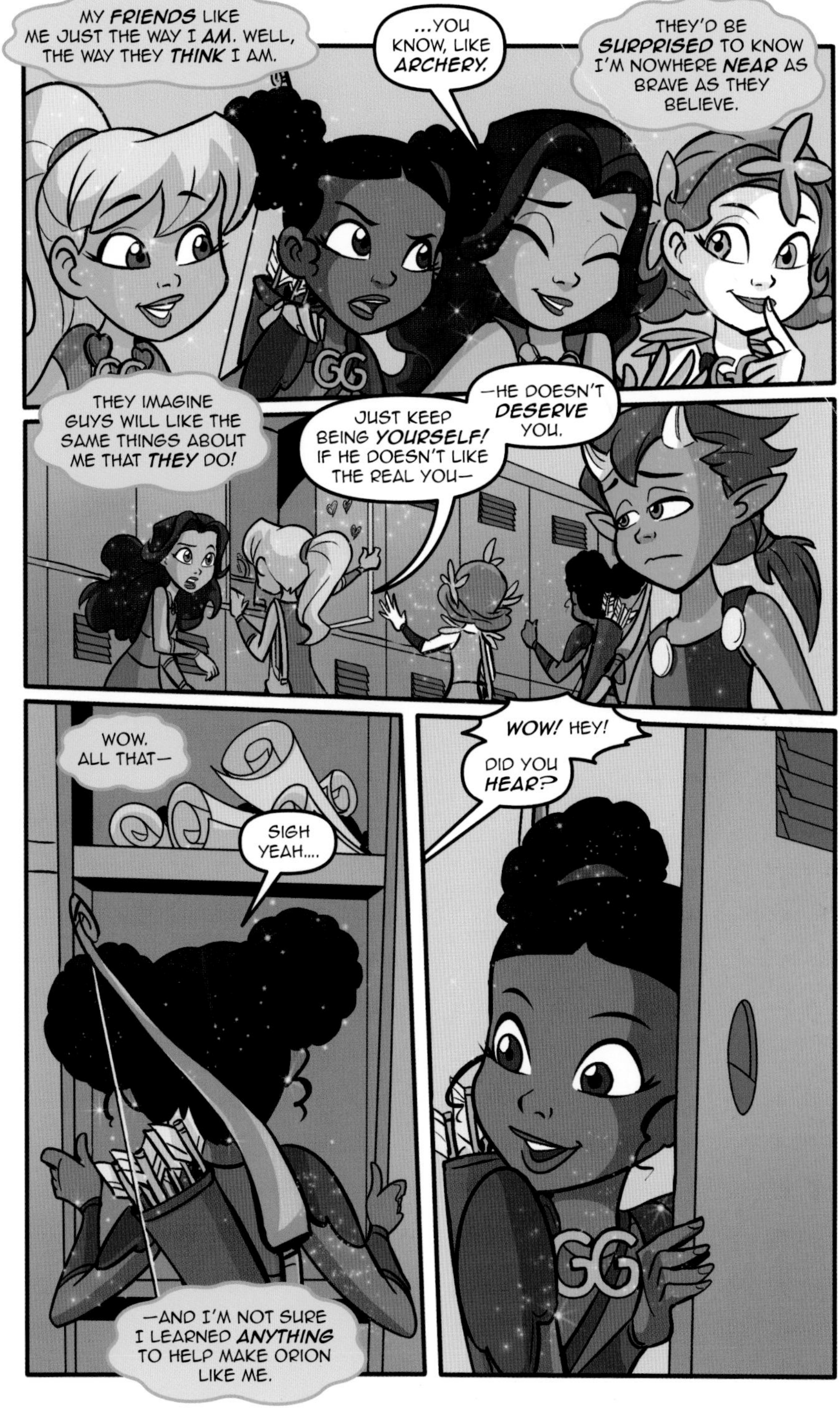
MY FRIENDS LIKE ME JUST THE WAY I AM. WELL, THE WAY THEY THINK I AM.
...YOU KNOW, LIKE ARCHERY.
THEY'D BE SURPRISED TO KNOW I'M NOWHERE NEAR AS BRAVE AS THEY BELIEVE.
THEY IMAGINE GUYS WILL LIKE THE SAME THINGS ABOUT ME THAT THEY DO!
JUST KEEP BEING YOURSELF! IF HE DOESN'T LIKE THE REAL YOU—
—HE DOESN'T DESERVE YOU.
GG
WOW. ALL THAT—
SIGH YEAH....
—AND I'M NOT SURE I LEARNED ANYTHING TO HELP MAKE ORION LIKE ME.
WOW! HEY!
DID YOU HEAR?

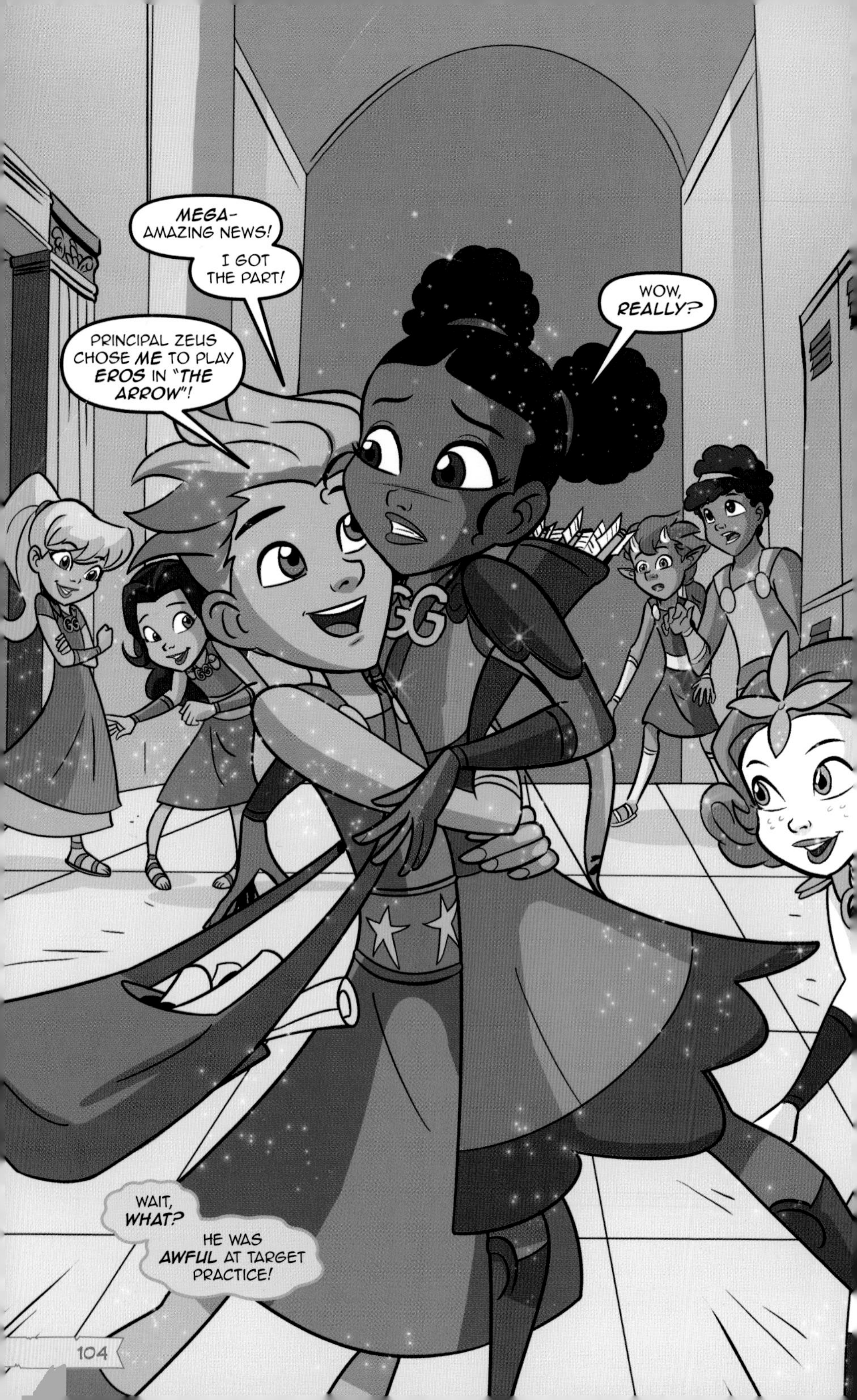
MEGA-AMAZING NEWS!
I GOT THE PART!
PRINCIPAL ZEUS CHOSE ME TO PLAY EROS IN "THE ARROW"!
WOW, REALLY?
WAIT, WHAT?
HE WAS AWFUL AT TARGET PRACTICE!

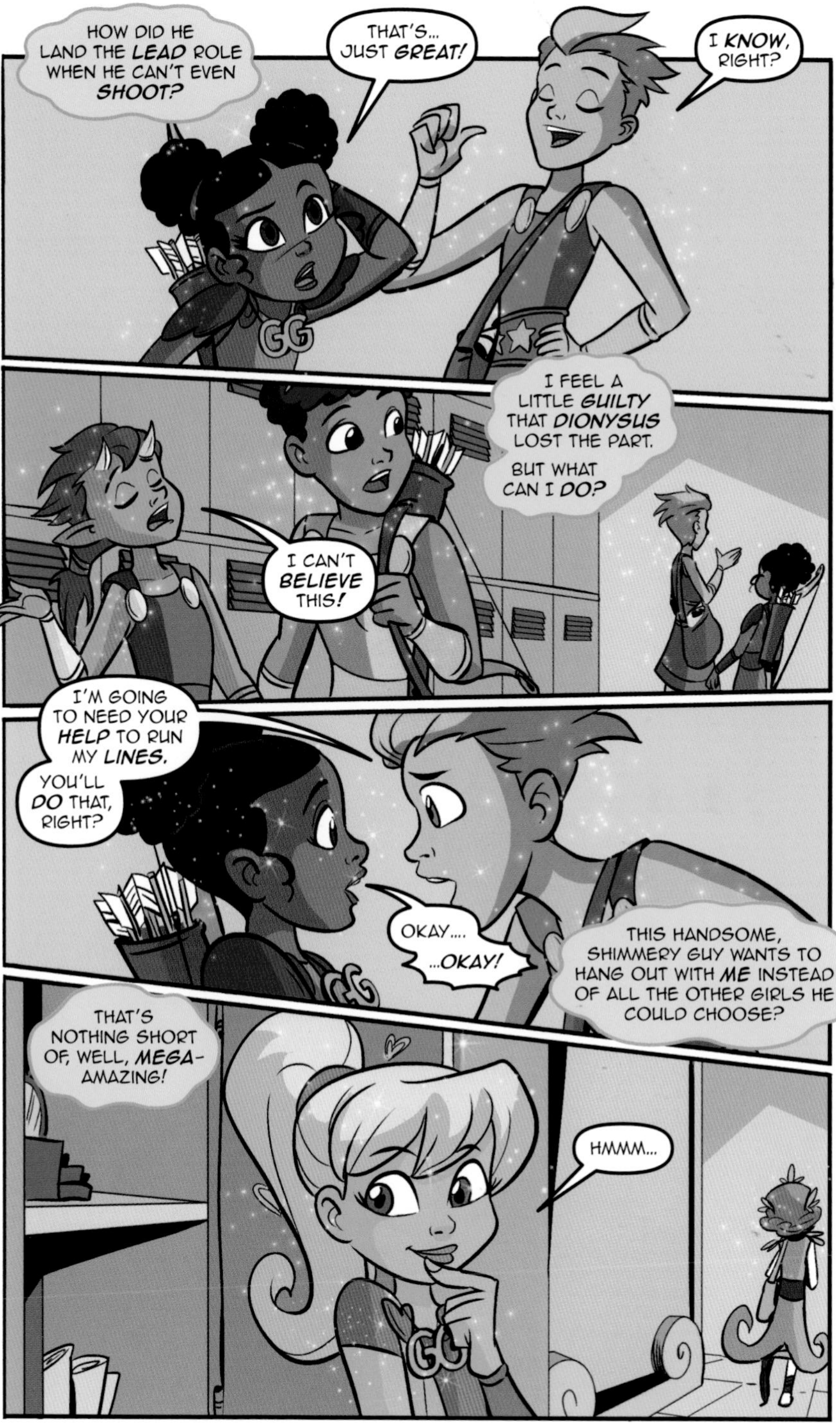
HOW DID HE LAND THE LEAD ROLE WHEN HE CAN'T EVEN SHOOT?
THAT'S... JUST GREAT!
I KNOW, RIGHT?
I FEEL A LITTLE GUILTY THAT DIONYSUS LOST THE PART.
BUT WHAT CAN I DO?
I CAN'T BELIEVE THIS!
I'M GOING TO NEED YOUR HELP TO RUN MY LINES.
YOU'LL DO THAT, RIGHT?
OKAY....
...OKAY!
THIS HANDSOME, SHIMMERY GUY WANTS TO HANG OUT WITH ME INSTEAD OF ALL THE OTHER GIRLS HE COULD CHOOSE?
THAT'S NOTHING SHORT OF, WELL, MEGA-AMAZING!
HMMM...

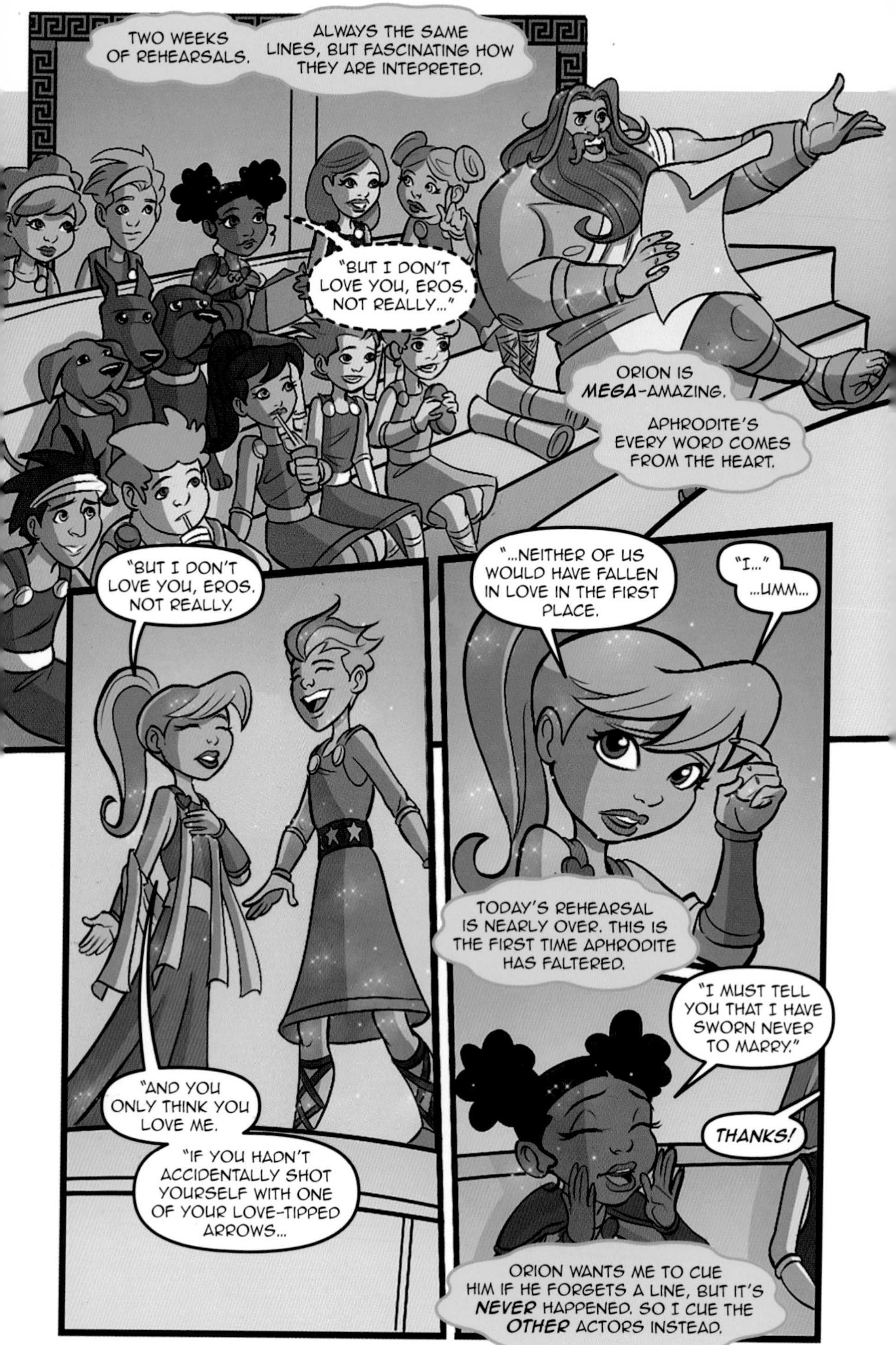
TWO WEEKS OF REHEARSALS.
ALWAYS THE SAME LINES, BUT FASCINATING HOW THEY ARE INTEPRETED.
"BUT I DON'T LOVE YOU, EROS. NOT REALLY..."
ORION IS MEGA-AMAZING.
APHRODITE'S EVERY WORD COMES FROM THE HEART.
"BUT I DON'T LOVE YOU, EROS. NOT REALLY.
"AND YOU ONLY THINK YOU LOVE ME.
"IF YOU HADN'T ACCIDENTALLY SHOT YOURSELF WITH ONE OF YOUR LOVE-TIPPED ARROWS...
"...NEITHER OF US WOULD HAVE FALLEN IN LOVE IN THE FIRST PLACE.
"I..."
...UMM...
TODAY'S REHEARSAL IS NEARLY OVER. THIS IS THE FIRST TIME APHRODITE HAS FALTERED.
"I MUST TELL YOU THAT I HAVE SWORN NEVER TO MARRY."
THANKS!
ORION WANTS ME TO CUE HIM IF HE FORGETS A LINE, BUT IT'S NEVER HAPPENED. SO I CUE THE OTHER ACTORS INSTEAD.

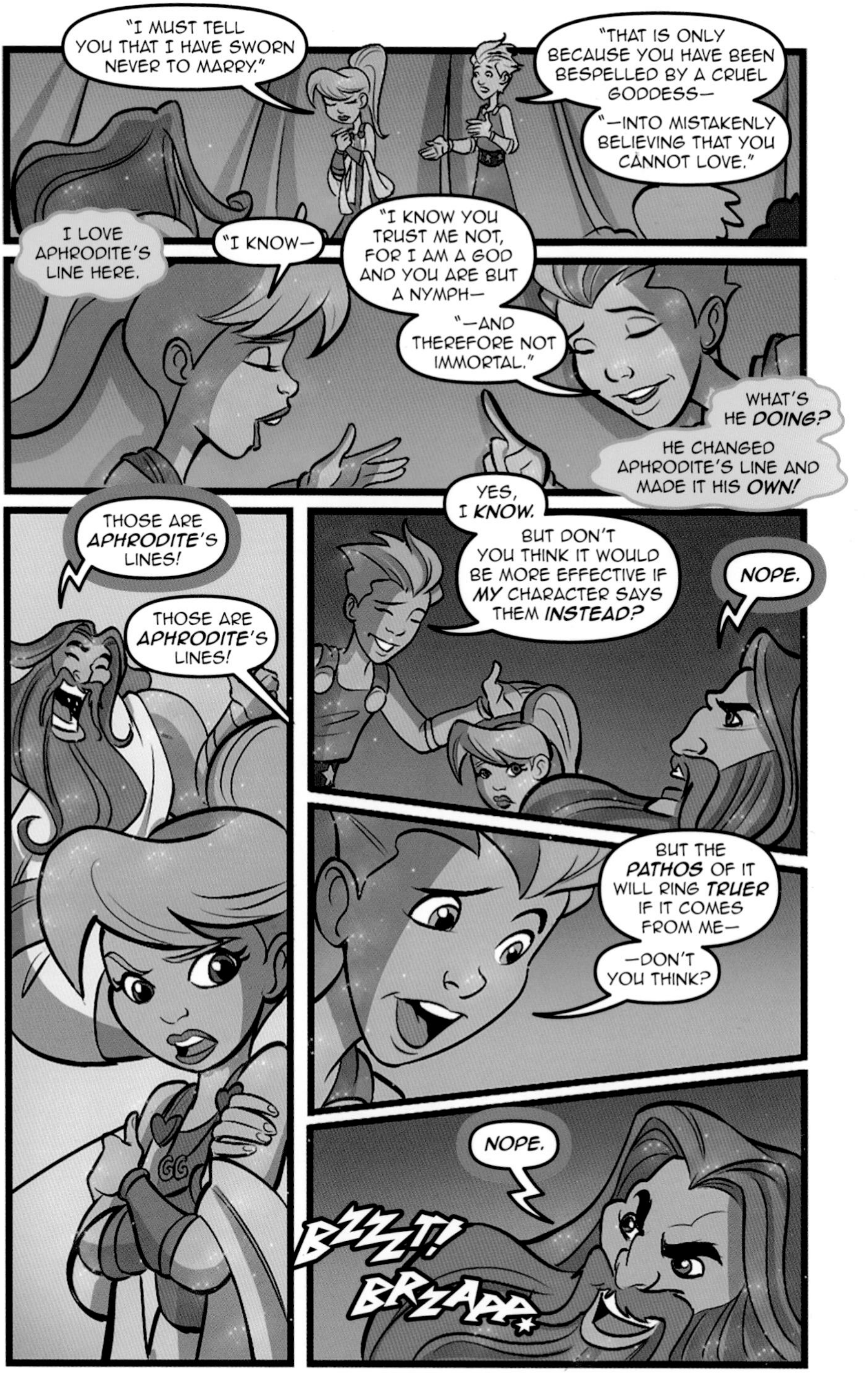
"I MUST TELL YOU THAT I HAVE SWORN NEVER TO MARRY."
"THAT IS ONLY BECAUSE YOU HAVE BEEN BESPELLED BY A CRUEL GODDESS—
"—INTO MISTAKENLY BELIEVING THAT YOU CANNOT LOVE."
I LOVE APHRODITE'S LINE HERE.
"I KNOW—
"I KNOW YOU TRUST ME NOT, FOR I AM A GOD AND YOU ARE BUT A NYMPH—
"—AND THEREFORE NOT IMMORTAL."
WHAT'S HE *DOING?*
HE CHANGED APHRODITE'S LINE AND MADE IT HIS *OWN!*
THOSE ARE *APHRODITE*'S LINES!
THOSE ARE *APHRODITE*'S LINES!
YES, I *KNOW.*
BUT DON'T YOU THINK IT WOULD BE MORE EFFECTIVE IF *MY* CHARACTER SAYS THEM *INSTEAD?*
NOPE.
BUT THE *PATHOS* OF IT WILL RING *TRUER* IF IT COMES FROM ME—
—DON'T YOU THINK?
NOPE.
BZZZT!
BRZAPP

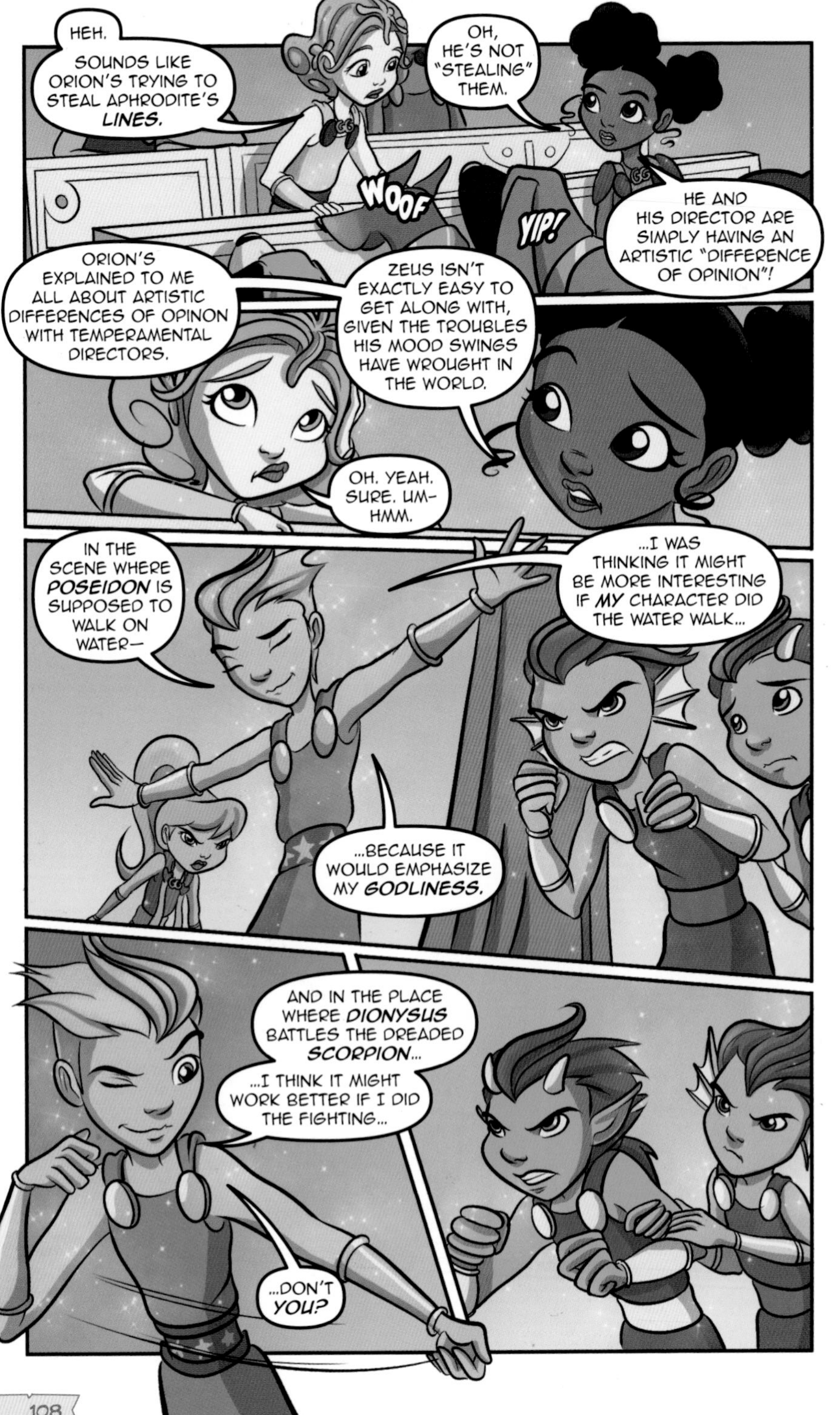
HEH.
SOUNDS LIKE ORION'S TRYING TO STEAL APHRODITE'S LINES.
OH, HE'S NOT "STEALING" THEM.
WOOF
YIP!
HE AND HIS DIRECTOR ARE SIMPLY HAVING AN ARTISTIC "DIFFERENCE OF OPINION"!
ORION'S EXPLAINED TO ME ALL ABOUT ARTISTIC DIFFERENCES OF OPINON WITH TEMPERAMENTAL DIRECTORS.
ZEUS ISN'T EXACTLY EASY TO GET ALONG WITH, GIVEN THE TROUBLES HIS MOOD SWINGS HAVE WROUGHT IN THE WORLD.
OH. YEAH. SURE. UM-HMM.
IN THE SCENE WHERE POSEIDON IS SUPPOSED TO WALK ON WATER—
...I WAS THINKING IT MIGHT BE MORE INTERESTING IF MY CHARACTER DID THE WATER WALK...
...BECAUSE IT WOULD EMPHASIZE MY GODLINESS.
AND IN THE PLACE WHERE DIONYSUS BATTLES THE DREADED SCORPION...
...I THINK IT MIGHT WORK BETTER IF I DID THE FIGHTING...
...DON'T YOU?

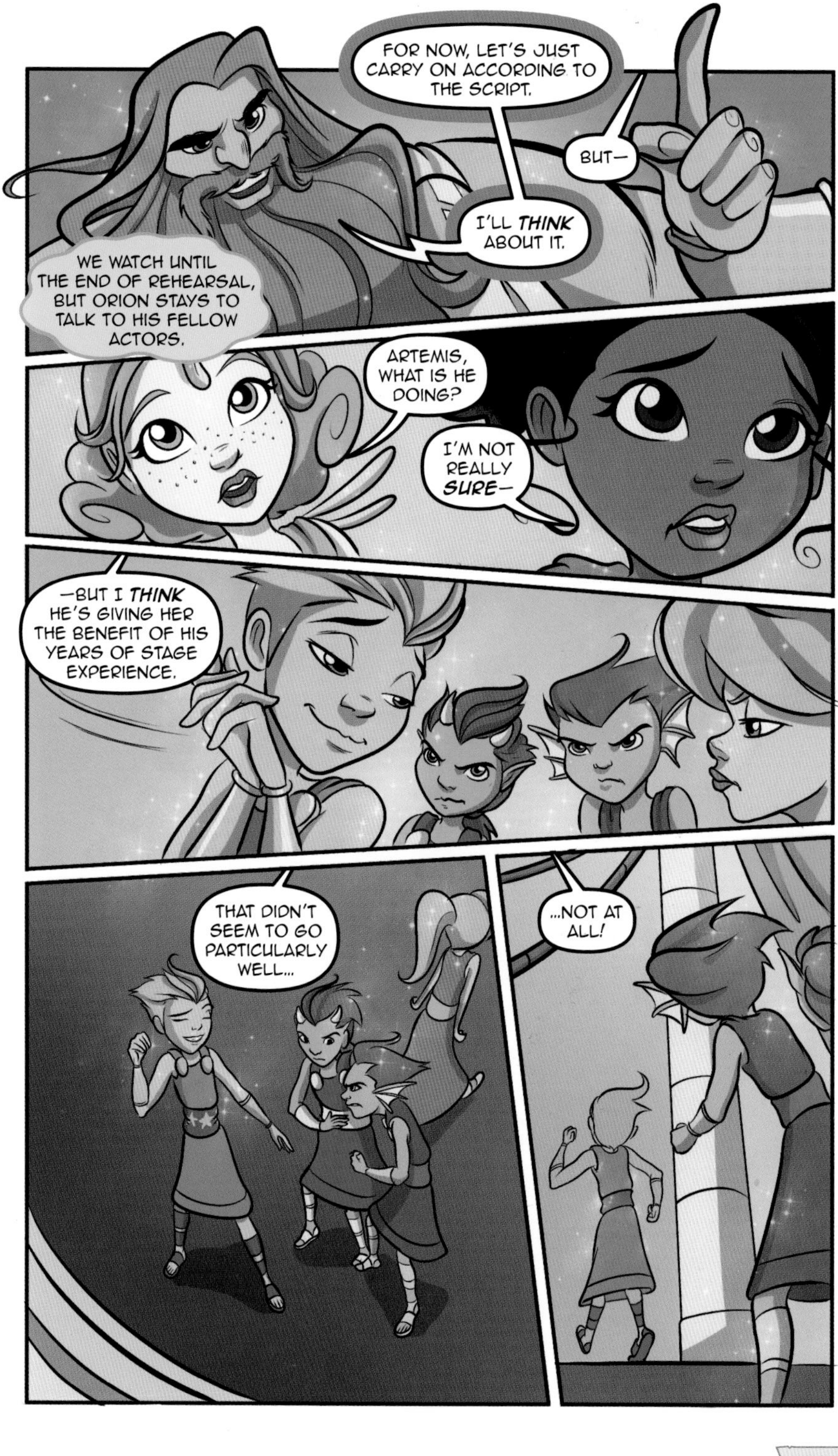
FOR NOW, LET'S JUST CARRY ON ACCORDING TO THE SCRIPT.
BUT—
I'LL *THINK* ABOUT IT.
WE WATCH UNTIL THE END OF REHEARSAL, BUT ORION STAYS TO TALK TO HIS FELLOW ACTORS.
ARTEMIS, WHAT IS HE DOING?
I'M NOT REALLY *SURE*—
—BUT I *THINK* HE'S GIVING HER THE BENEFIT OF HIS YEARS OF STAGE EXPERIENCE.
THAT DIDN'T SEEM TO GO PARTICULARLY WELL...
...NOT AT ALL!

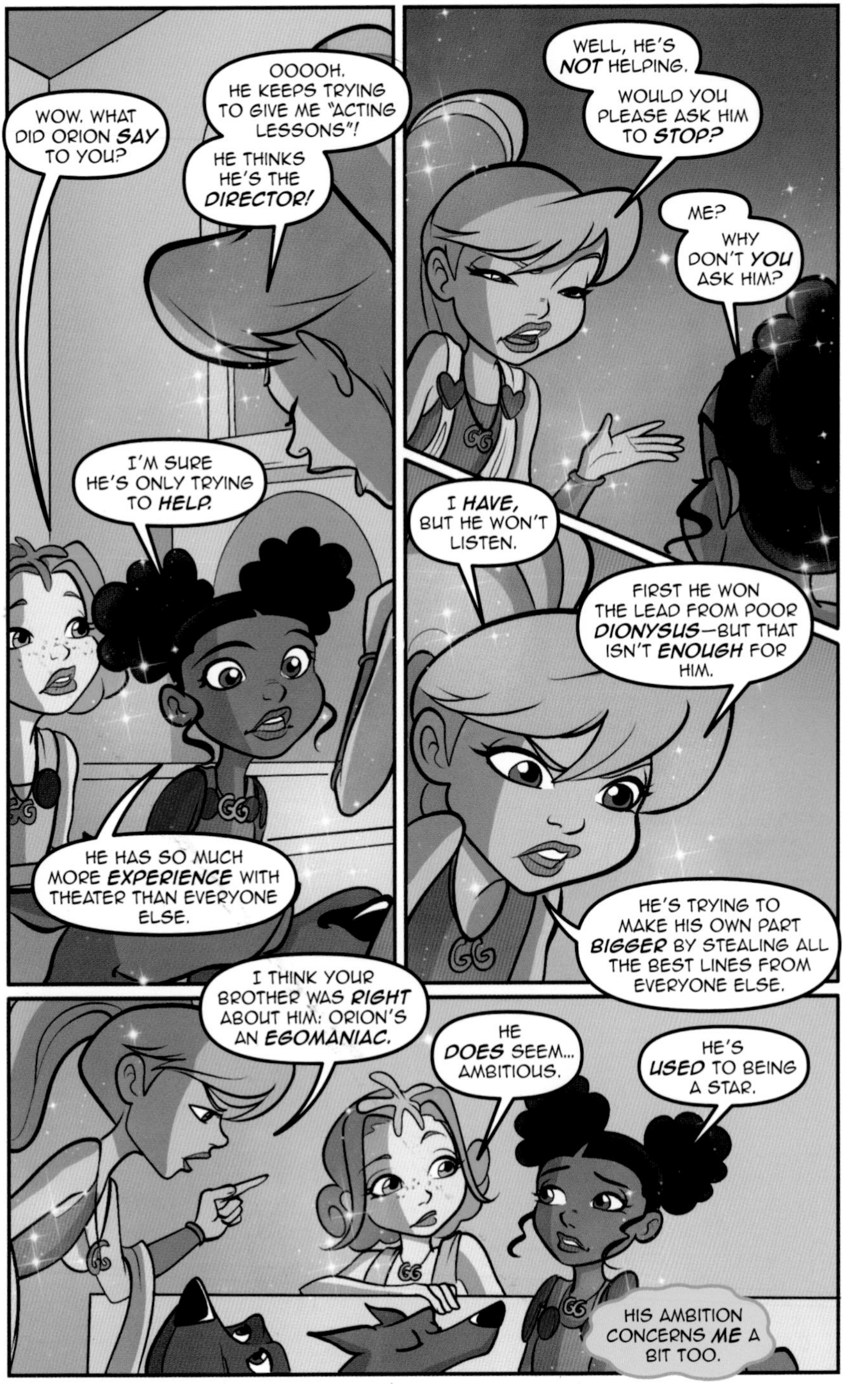
WOW. WHAT DID ORION *SAY* TO YOU?
OOOOH. HE KEEPS TRYING TO GIVE ME "ACTING LESSONS"!
HE THINKS HE'S THE *DIRECTOR!*
I'M SURE HE'S ONLY TRYING TO *HELP.*
HE HAS SO MUCH MORE *EXPERIENCE* WITH THEATER THAN EVERYONE ELSE.
WELL, HE'S *NOT* HELPING.
WOULD YOU PLEASE ASK HIM TO *STOP?*
ME?
WHY DON'T *YOU* ASK HIM?
I *HAVE,* BUT HE WON'T LISTEN.
FIRST HE WON THE LEAD FROM POOR *DIONYSUS*—BUT THAT ISN'T *ENOUGH* FOR HIM.
HE'S TRYING TO MAKE HIS OWN PART *BIGGER* BY STEALING ALL THE BEST LINES FROM EVERYONE ELSE.
I THINK YOUR BROTHER WAS *RIGHT* ABOUT HIM: ORION'S AN *EGOMANIAC.*
HE *DOES* SEEM... AMBITIOUS.
HE'S *USED* TO BEING A STAR.
HIS AMBITION CONCERNS *ME* A BIT TOO.

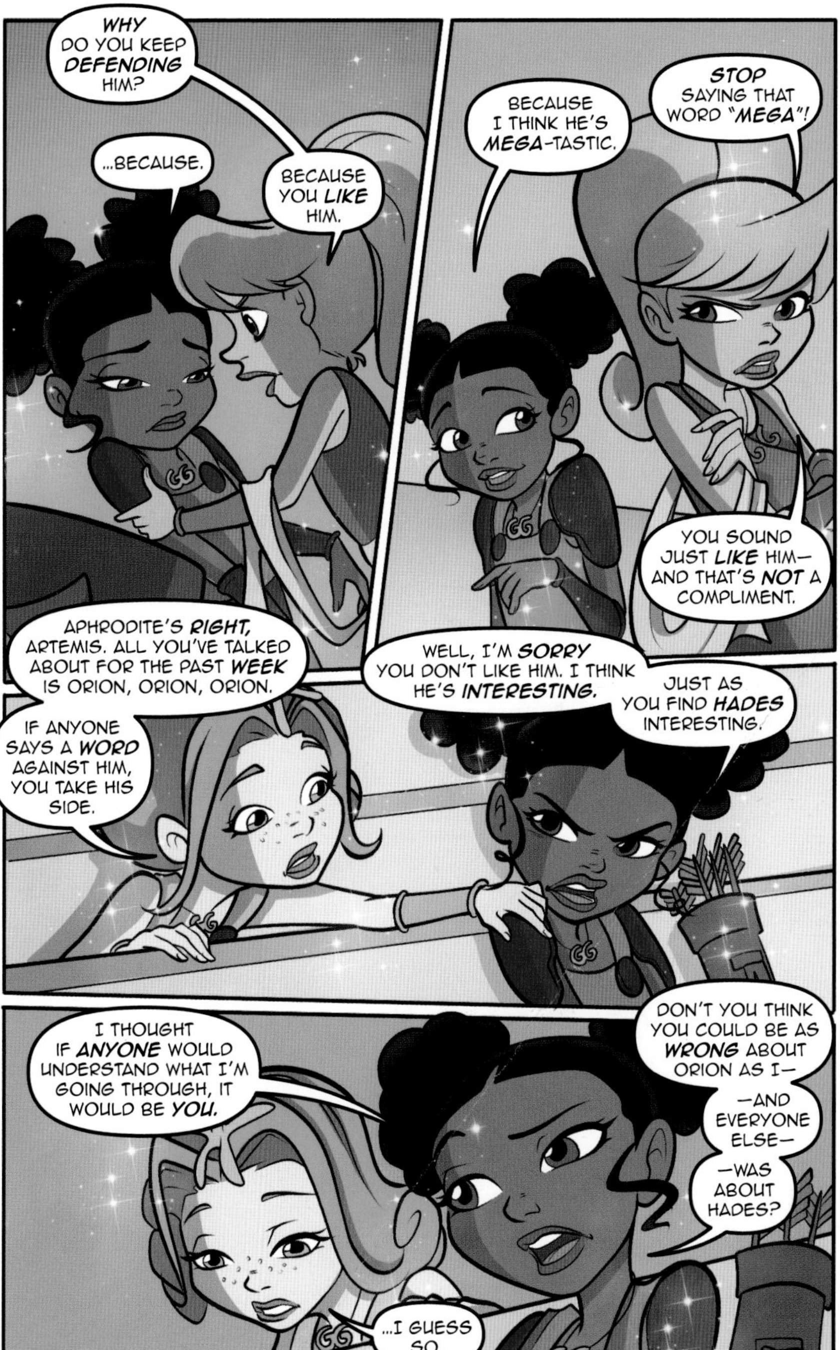
WHY DO YOU KEEP DEFENDING HIM?
...BECAUSE.
BECAUSE YOU LIKE HIM.
BECAUSE I THINK HE'S MEGA-TASTIC.
STOP SAYING THAT WORD "MEGA"!
YOU SOUND JUST LIKE HIM— AND THAT'S NOT A COMPLIMENT.
APHRODITE'S RIGHT, ARTEMIS. ALL YOU'VE TALKED ABOUT FOR THE PAST WEEK IS ORION, ORION, ORION.
IF ANYONE SAYS A WORD AGAINST HIM, YOU TAKE HIS SIDE.
WELL, I'M SORRY YOU DON'T LIKE HIM. I THINK HE'S INTERESTING.
JUST AS YOU FIND HADES INTERESTING.
I THOUGHT IF ANYONE WOULD UNDERSTAND WHAT I'M GOING THROUGH, IT WOULD BE YOU.
DON'T YOU THINK YOU COULD BE AS WRONG ABOUT ORION AS I—
—AND EVERYONE ELSE—
—WAS ABOUT HADES?
...I GUESS SO.

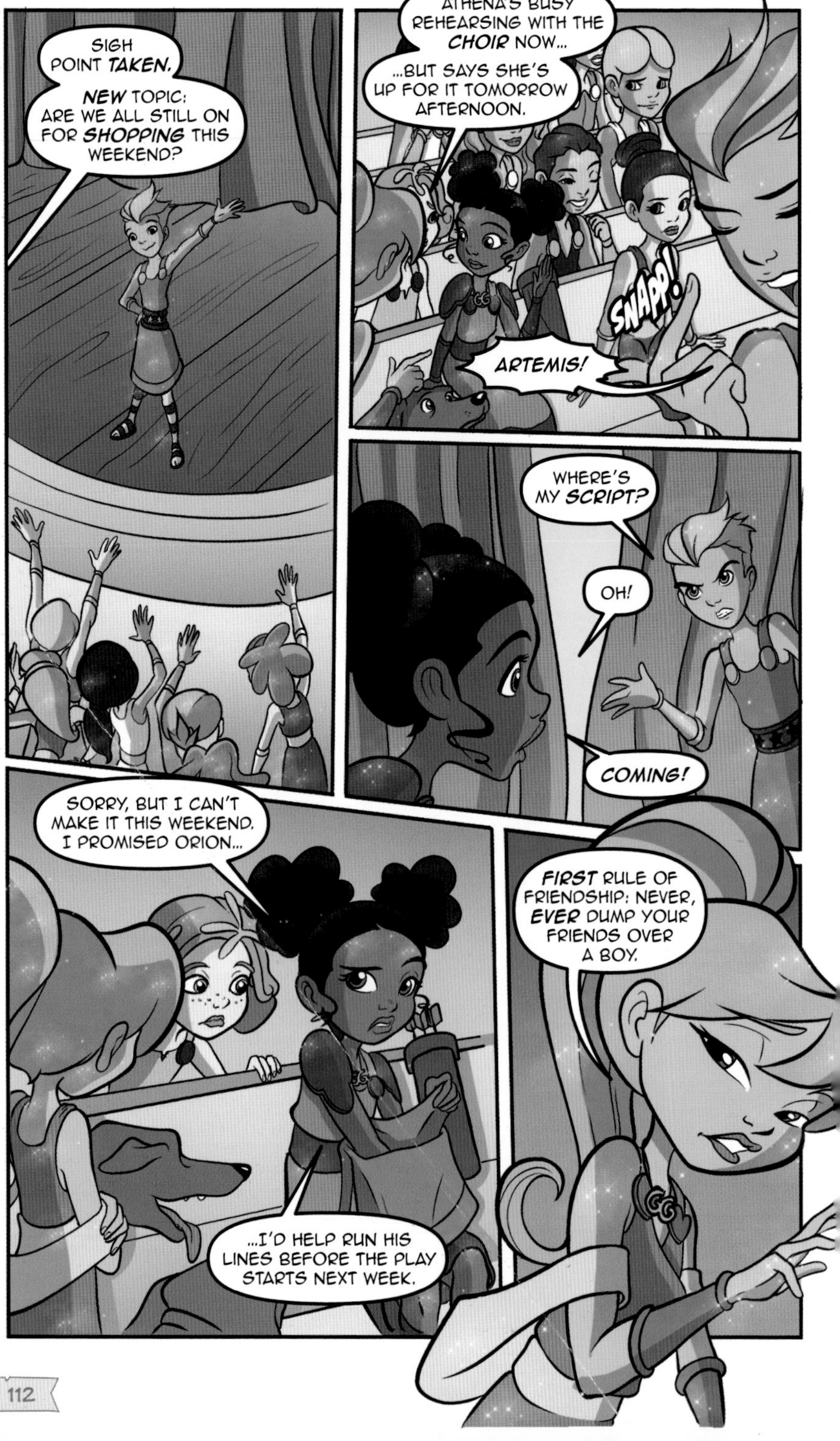
SIGH
POINT TAKEN.
NEW TOPIC: ARE WE ALL STILL ON FOR SHOPPING THIS WEEKEND?
ATHENA'S BUSY REHEARSING WITH THE CHOIR NOW...
...BUT SAYS SHE'S UP FOR IT TOMORROW AFTERNOON.
SNAPP!
ARTEMIS!
WHERE'S MY SCRIPT?
OH!
COMING!
SORRY, BUT I CAN'T MAKE IT THIS WEEKEND. I PROMISED ORION...
...I'D HELP RUN HIS LINES BEFORE THE PLAY STARTS NEXT WEEK.
FIRST RULE OF FRIENDSHIP: NEVER, EVER DUMP YOUR FRIENDS OVER A BOY.

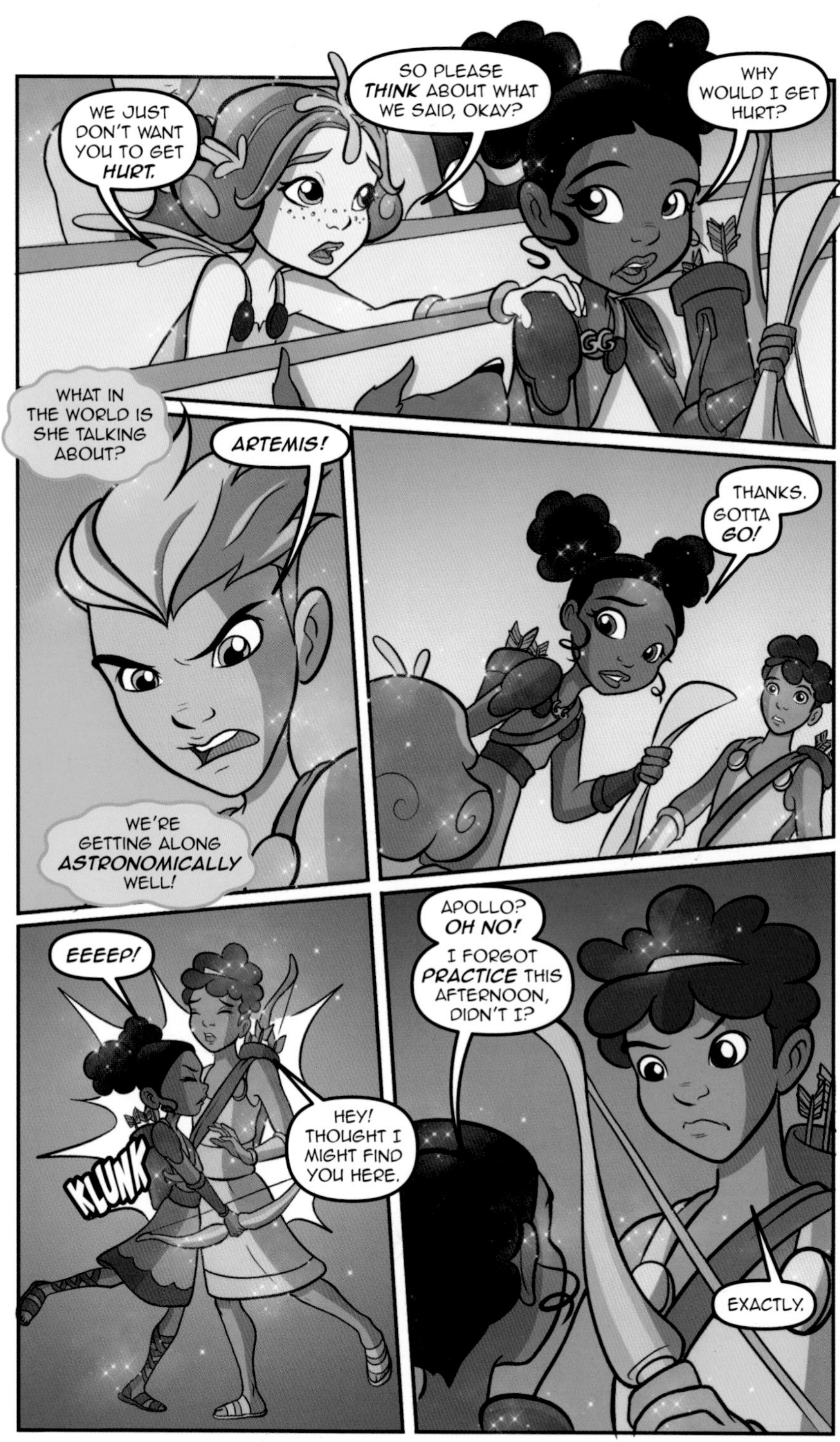
WE JUST DON'T WANT YOU TO GET HURT.
SO PLEASE THINK ABOUT WHAT WE SAID, OKAY?
WHY WOULD I GET HURT?
WHAT IN THE WORLD IS SHE TALKING ABOUT?
ARTEMIS!
WE'RE GETTING ALONG ASTRONOMICALLY WELL!
THANKS. GOTTA GO!
EEEEP!
KLUNK
HEY! THOUGHT I MIGHT FIND YOU HERE.
APOLLO? OH NO!
I FORGOT PRACTICE THIS AFTERNOON, DIDN'T I?
EXACTLY.

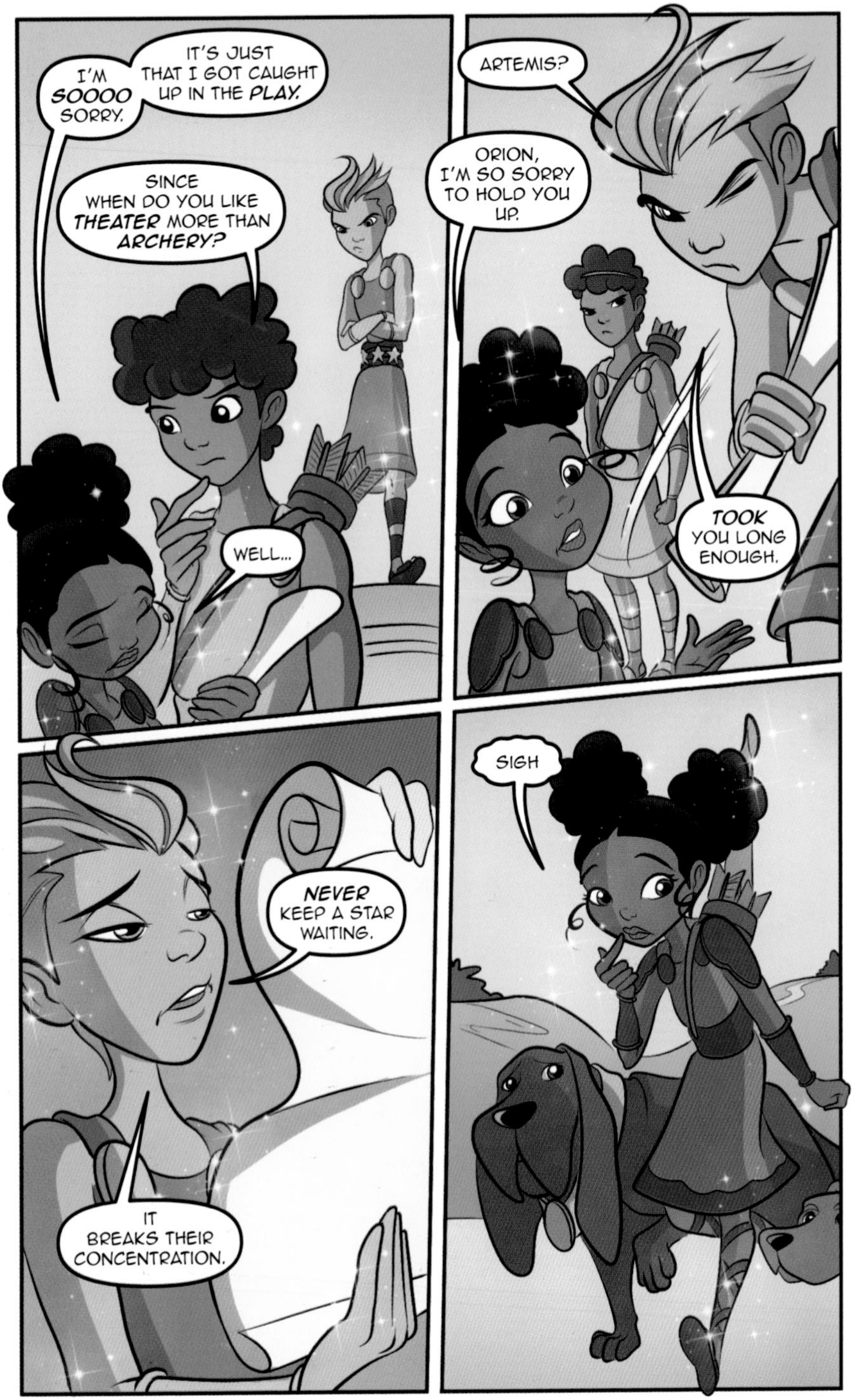
I'M SOOOO SORRY.
IT'S JUST THAT I GOT CAUGHT UP IN THE PLAY.
SINCE WHEN DO YOU LIKE THEATER MORE THAN ARCHERY?
WELL...
ARTEMIS?
ORION, I'M SO SORRY TO HOLD YOU UP.
TOOK YOU LONG ENOUGH.
NEVER KEEP A STAR WAITING.
IT BREAKS THEIR CONCENTRATION.
SIGH

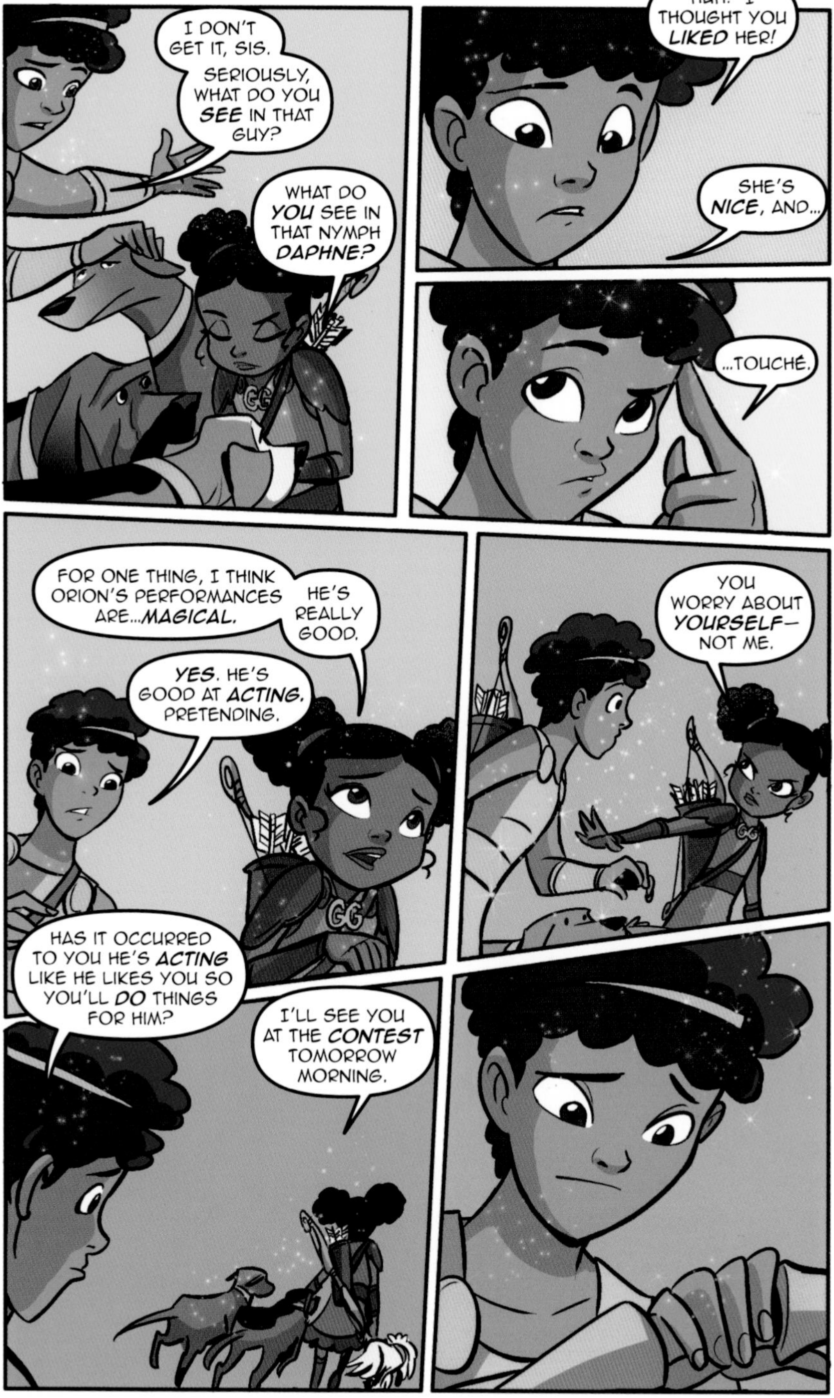
I DON'T GET IT, SIS.
SERIOUSLY, WHAT DO YOU SEE IN THAT GUY?
WHAT DO YOU SEE IN THAT NYMPH DAPHNE?
HUH? I THOUGHT YOU LIKED HER!
SHE'S NICE, AND...
...TOUCHÉ.
FOR ONE THING, I THINK ORION'S PERFORMANCES ARE...MAGICAL.
HE'S REALLY GOOD.
YES. HE'S GOOD AT ACTING. PRETENDING.
YOU WORRY ABOUT YOURSELF— NOT ME.
HAS IT OCCURRED TO YOU HE'S ACTING LIKE HE LIKES YOU SO YOU'LL DO THINGS FOR HIM?
I'LL SEE YOU AT THE CONTEST TOMORROW MORNING.

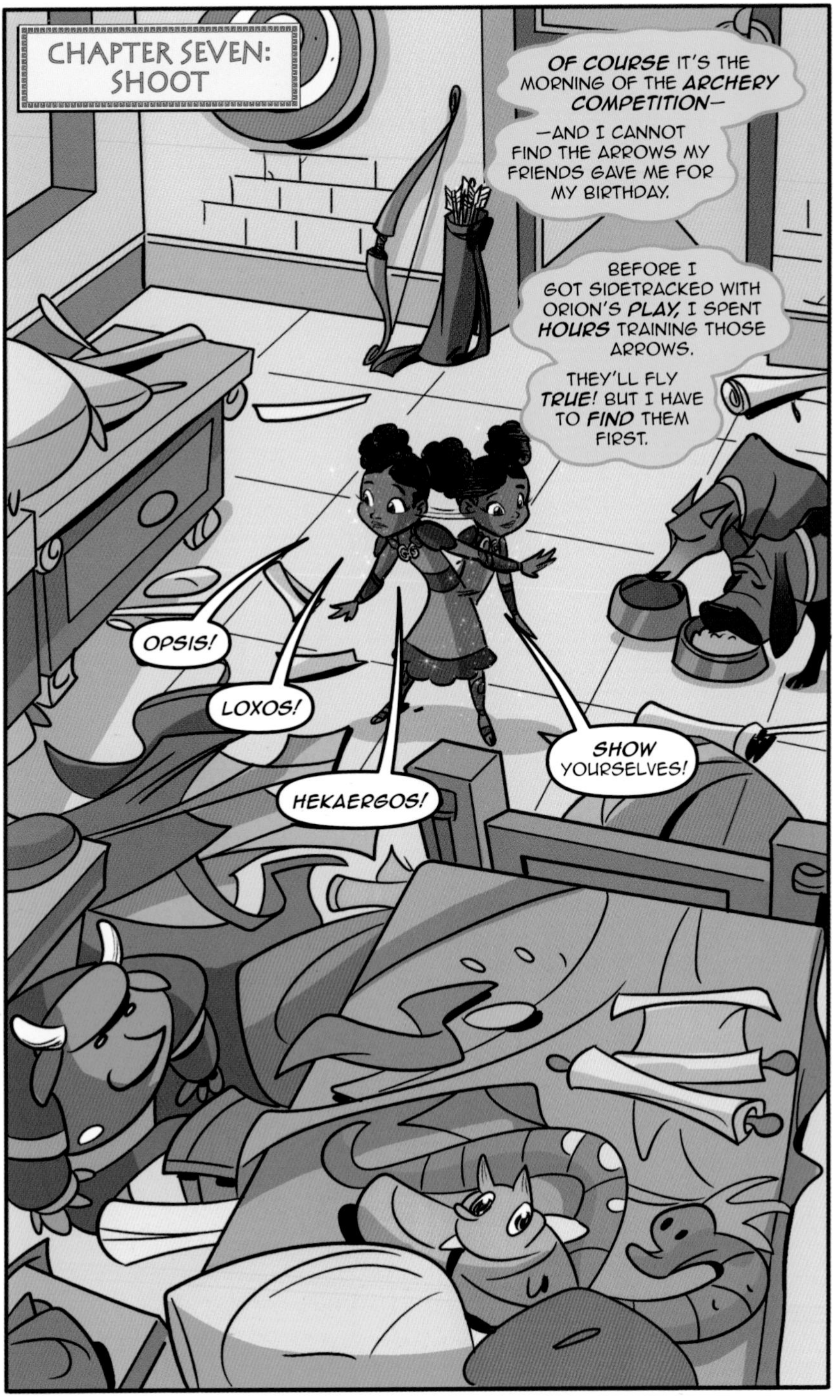
CHAPTER SEVEN: SHOOT
OF COURSE IT'S THE MORNING OF THE ARCHERY COMPETITION—
—AND I CANNOT FIND THE ARROWS MY FRIENDS GAVE ME FOR MY BIRTHDAY.
BEFORE I GOT SIDETRACKED WITH ORION'S PLAY, I SPENT HOURS TRAINING THOSE ARROWS.
THEY'LL FLY TRUE! BUT I HAVE TO FIND THEM FIRST.
OPSIS!
LOXOS!
HEKAERGOS!
SHOW YOURSELVES!

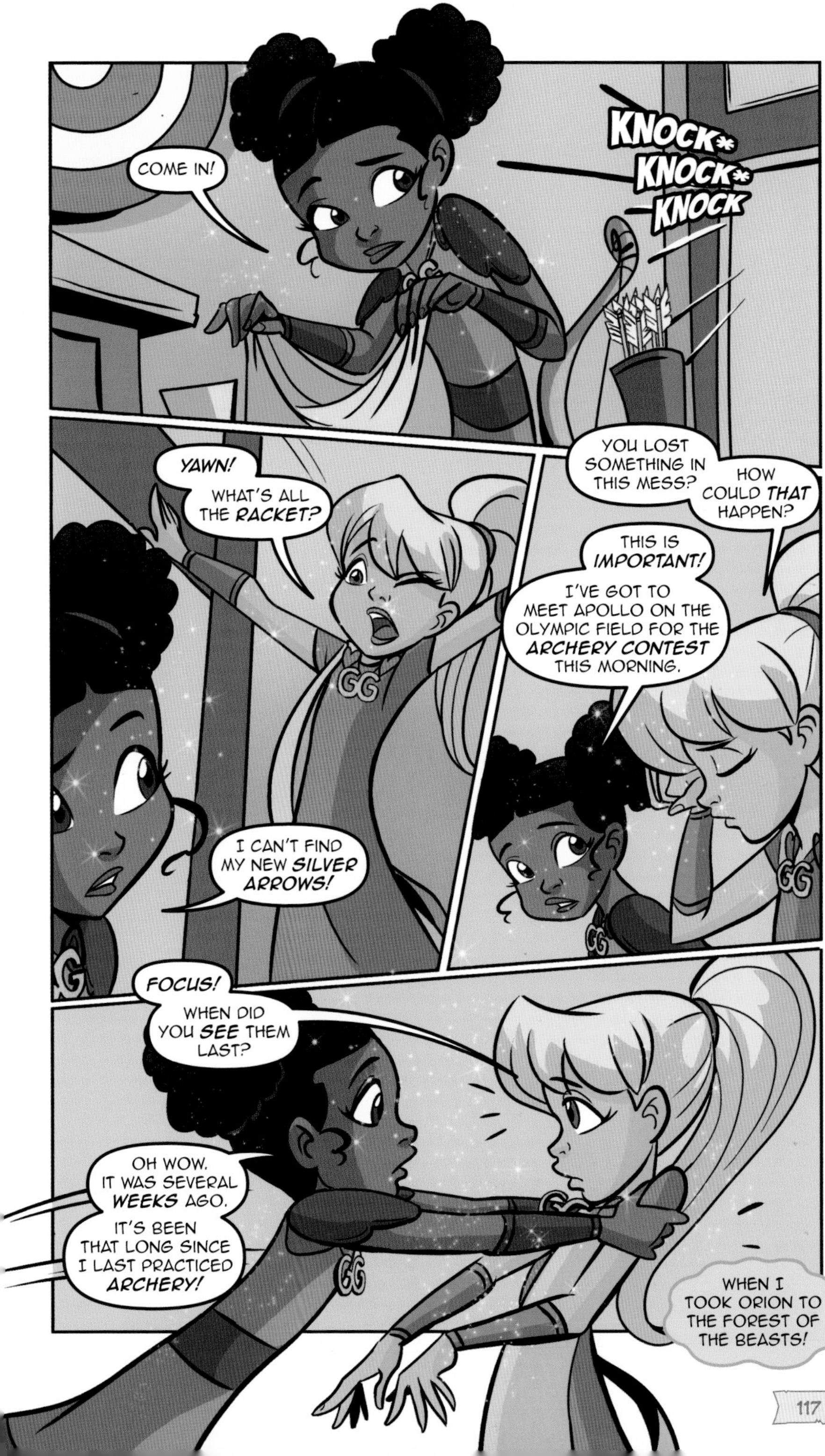
COME IN!
KNOCK KNOCK KNOCK
YAWN!
WHAT'S ALL THE RACKET?
I CAN'T FIND MY NEW SILVER ARROWS!
YOU LOST SOMETHING IN THIS MESS?
HOW COULD THAT HAPPEN?
THIS IS IMPORTANT!
I'VE GOT TO MEET APOLLO ON THE OLYMPIC FIELD FOR THE ARCHERY CONTEST THIS MORNING.
FOCUS!
WHEN DID YOU SEE THEM LAST?
OH WOW. IT WAS SEVERAL WEEKS AGO.
IT'S BEEN THAT LONG SINCE I LAST PRACTICED ARCHERY!
WHEN I TOOK ORION TO THE FOREST OF THE BEASTS!

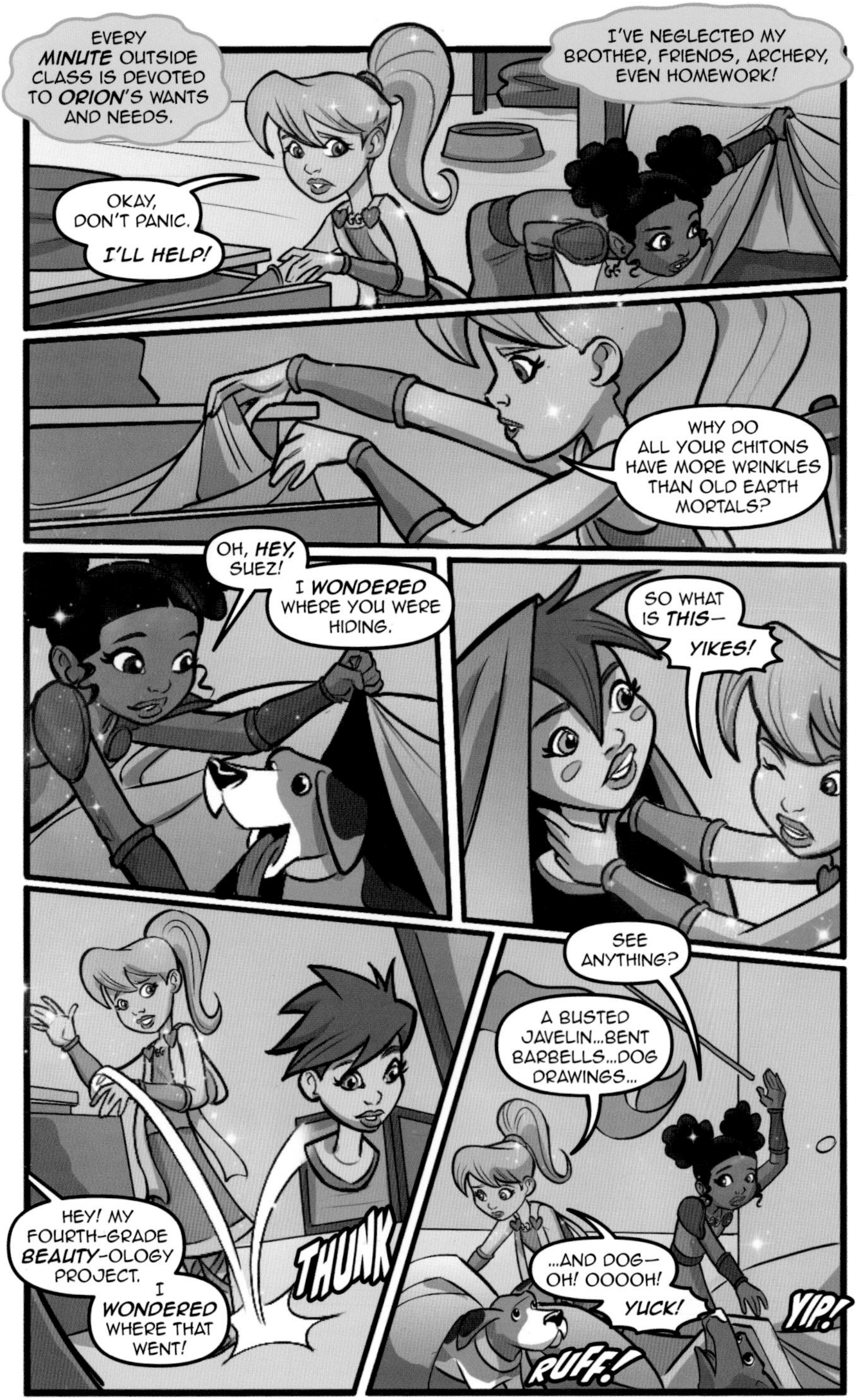

EVERY MINUTE OUTSIDE CLASS IS DEVOTED TO ORION'S WANTS AND NEEDS.
I'VE NEGLECTED MY BROTHER, FRIENDS, ARCHERY, EVEN HOMEWORK!
OKAY, DON'T PANIC.
I'LL HELP!
WHY DO ALL YOUR CHITONS HAVE MORE WRINKLES THAN OLD EARTH MORTALS?
OH, HEY, SUEZ!
I WONDERED WHERE YOU WERE HIDING.
SO WHAT IS THIS—
YIKES!
HEY! MY FOURTH-GRADE BEAUTY-OLOGY PROJECT.
I WONDERED WHERE THAT WENT!
THUNK
SEE ANYTHING?
A BUSTED JAVELIN...BENT BARBELLS...DOG DRAWINGS...
...AND DOG—OH! OOOOH!
YUCK!
YIP!
RUFF!

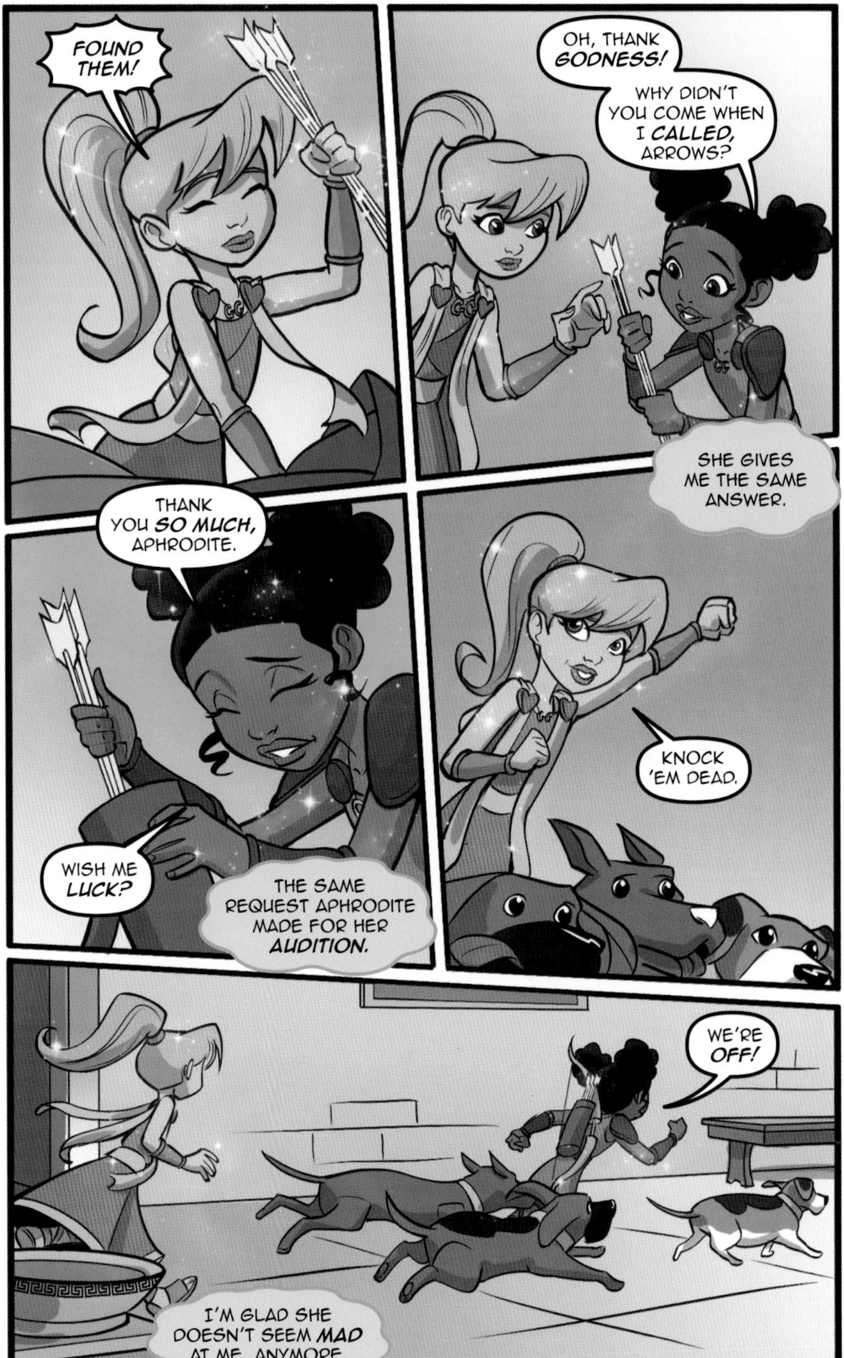
FOUND THEM!
OH, THANK GODNESS!
WHY DIDN'T YOU COME WHEN I CALLED, ARROWS?
SHE GIVES ME THE SAME ANSWER.
THANK YOU SO MUCH, APHRODITE.
WISH ME LUCK?
THE SAME REQUEST APHRODITE MADE FOR HER AUDITION.
KNOCK 'EM DEAD.
WE'RE OFF!
I'M GLAD SHE DOESN'T SEEM MAD AT ME, ANYMORE.

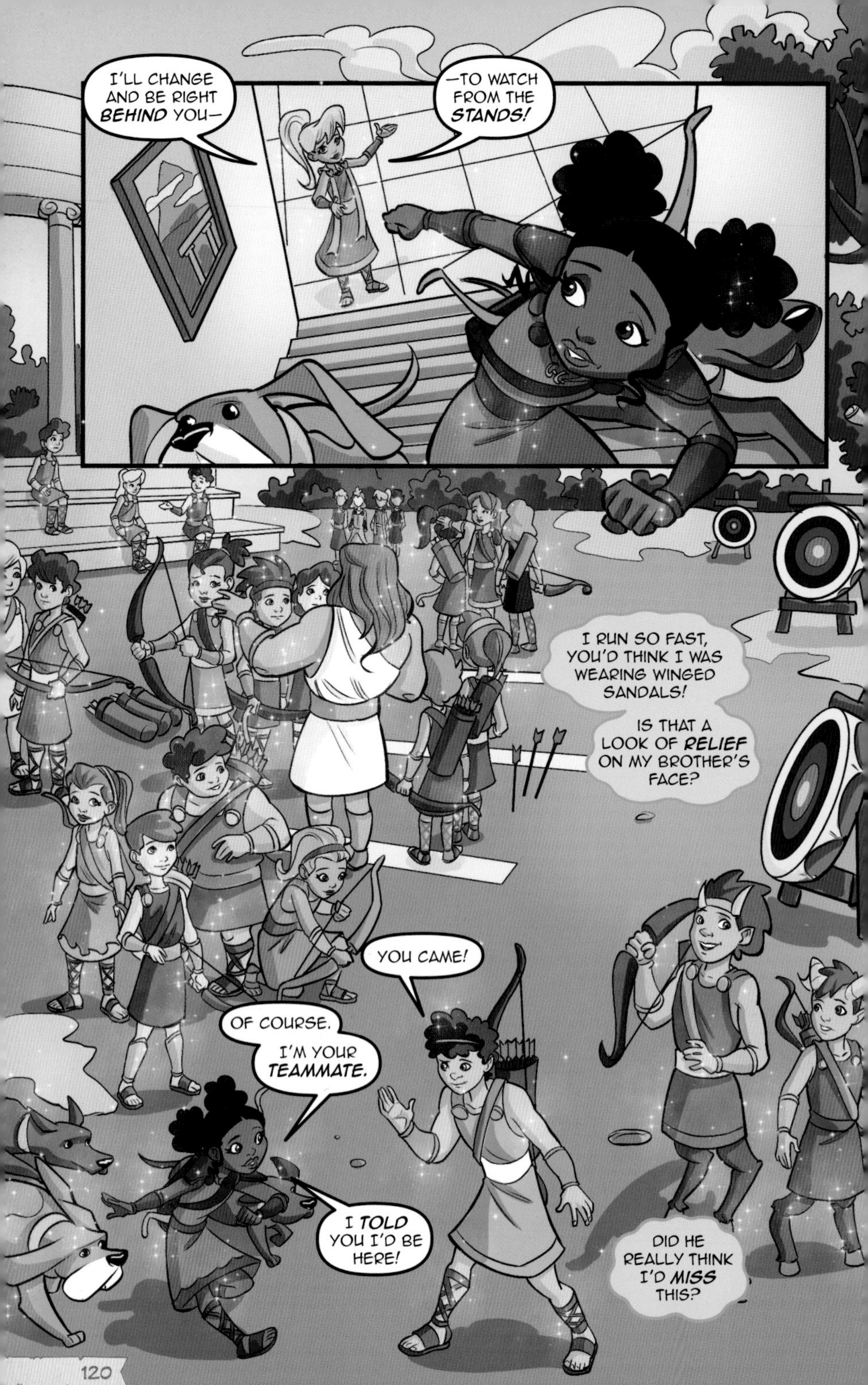

I'LL CHANGE AND BE RIGHT BEHIND YOU—
—TO WATCH FROM THE STANDS!
I RUN SO FAST, YOU'D THINK I WAS WEARING WINGED SANDALS!
IS THAT A LOOK OF RELIEF ON MY BROTHER'S FACE?
YOU CAME!
OF COURSE.
I'M YOUR TEAMMATE.
I TOLD YOU I'D BE HERE!
DID HE REALLY THINK I'D MISS THIS?

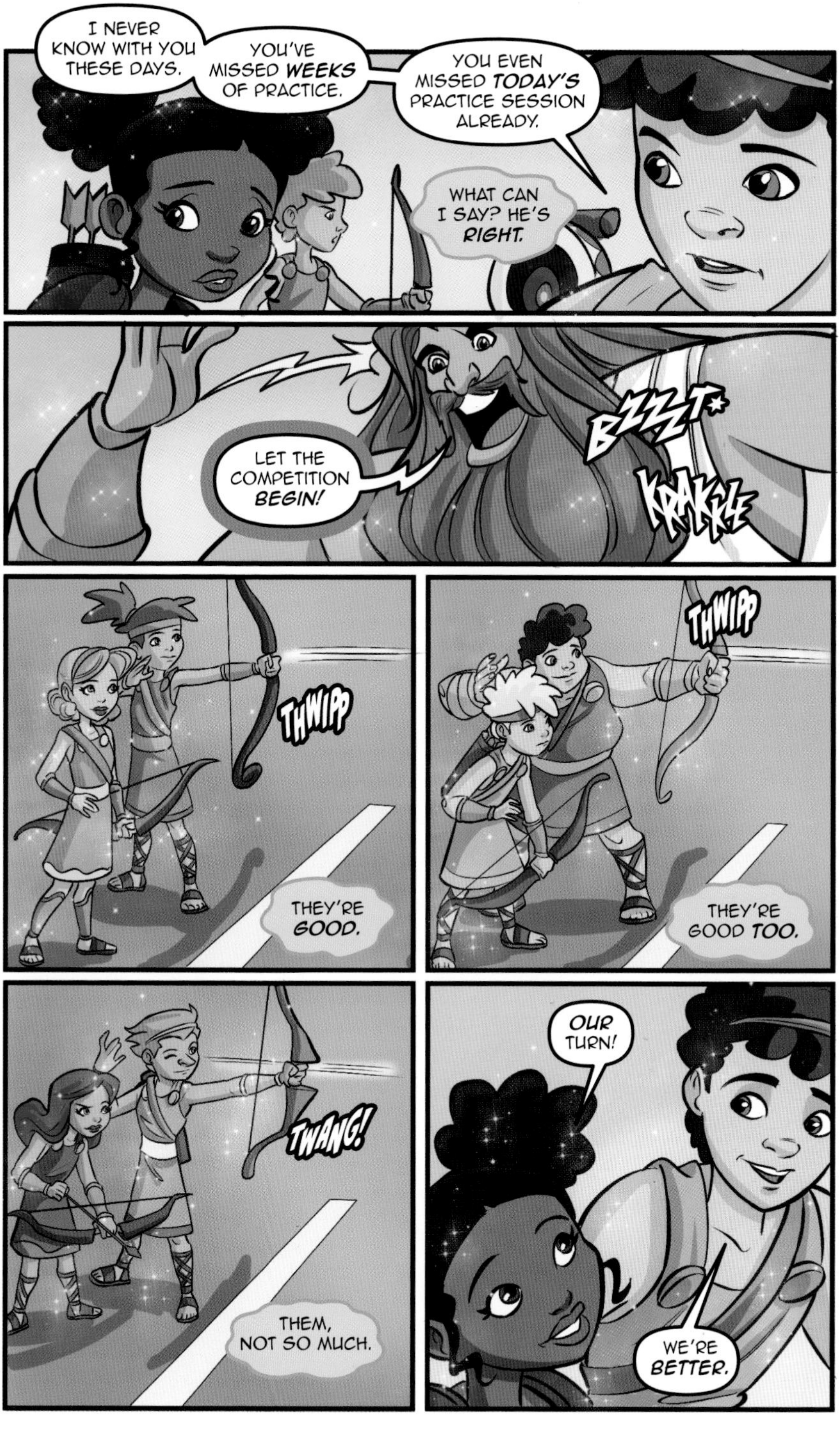
I NEVER KNOW WITH YOU THESE DAYS.
YOU'VE MISSED **WEEKS** OF PRACTICE.
YOU EVEN MISSED **TODAY'S** PRACTICE SESSION ALREADY.
WHAT CAN I SAY? HE'S **RIGHT.**
LET THE COMPETITION **BEGIN!**
BZZZT*
KRAKKLE
THWIPP
THEY'RE **GOOD.**
THWIPP
THEY'RE GOOD **TOO.**
TWANG!
THEM, NOT SO MUCH.
OUR TURN!
WE'RE **BETTER.**

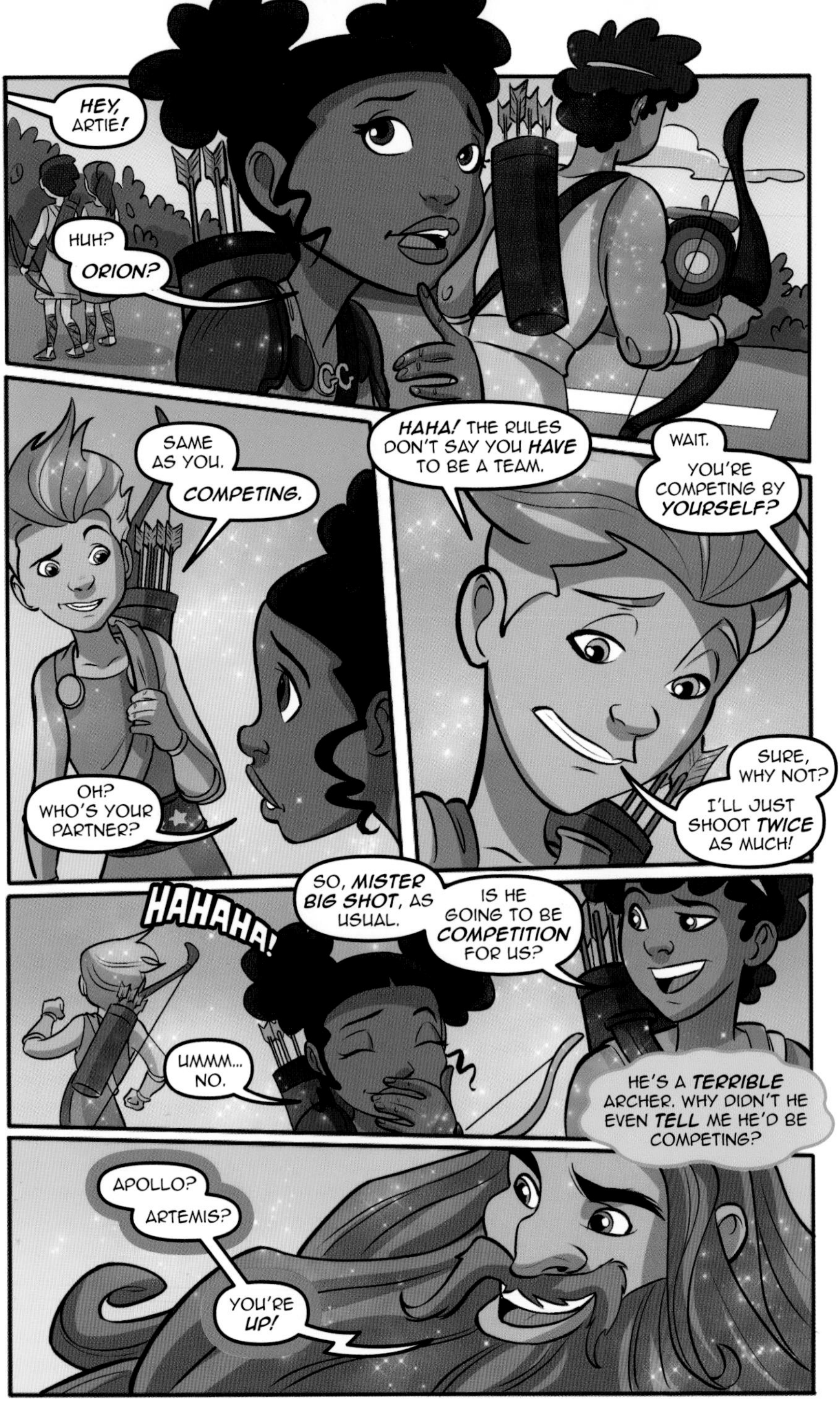
HEY, ARTIE!
HUH? ORION?
SAME AS YOU. COMPETING.
OH? WHO'S YOUR PARTNER?
HAHA! THE RULES DON'T SAY YOU HAVE TO BE A TEAM.
WAIT. YOU'RE COMPETING BY YOURSELF?
SURE, WHY NOT? I'LL JUST SHOOT TWICE AS MUCH!
HAHAHA!
SO, MISTER BIG SHOT, AS USUAL.
IS HE GOING TO BE COMPETITION FOR US?
UMMM... NO.
HE'S A TERRIBLE ARCHER. WHY DIDN'T HE EVEN TELL ME HE'D BE COMPETING?
APOLLO? ARTEMIS?
YOU'RE UP!

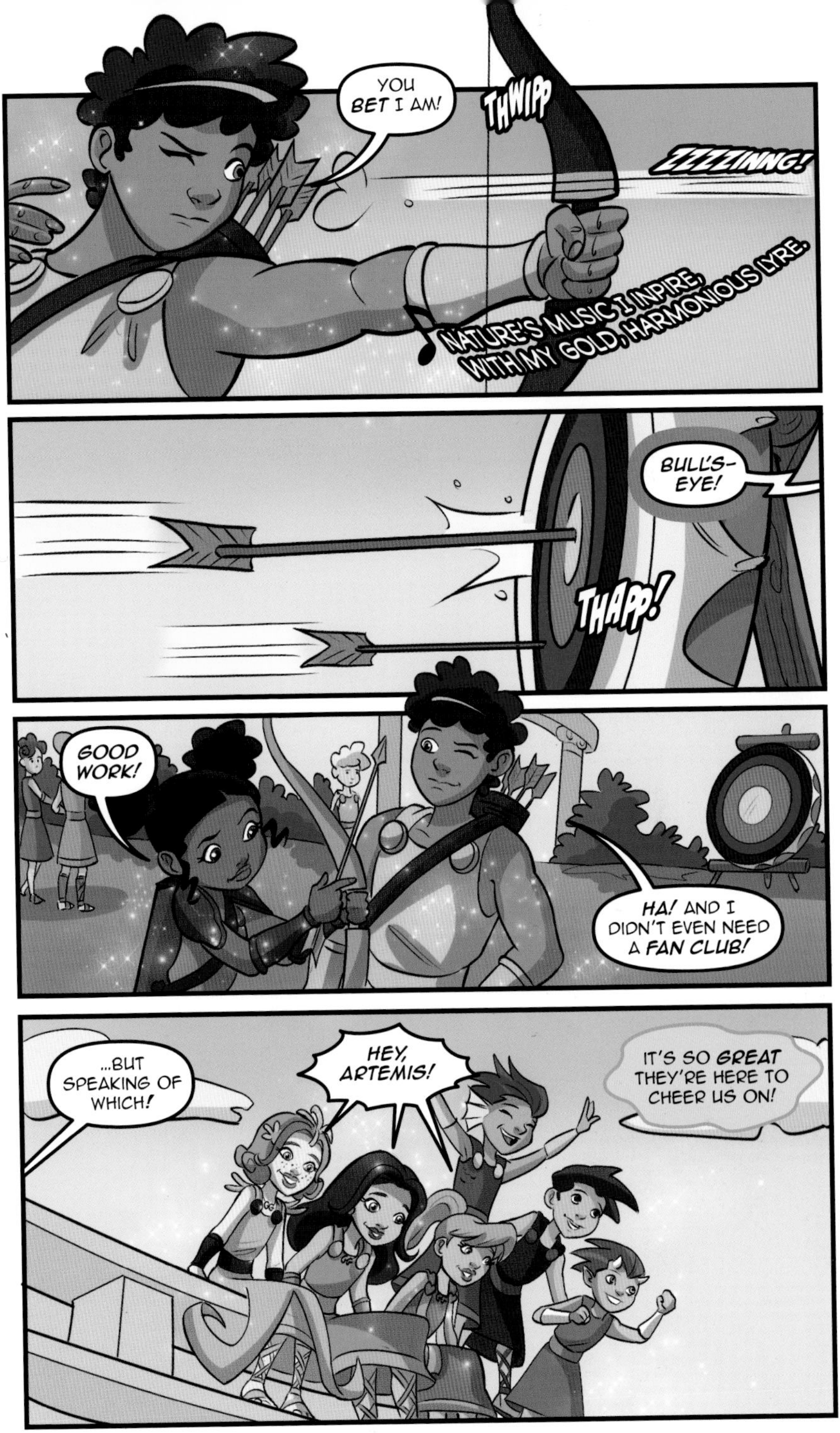

YOU BET I AM!
THWIPP
ZZZZINNG!
NATURE'S MUSIC I INPIRE, WITH MY GOLD, HARMONIOUS LYRE.
BULL'S-EYE!
THAPP!
GOOD WORK!
HA! AND I DIDN'T EVEN NEED A FAN CLUB!
...BUT SPEAKING OF WHICH!
HEY, ARTEMIS!
IT'S SO GREAT THEY'RE HERE TO CHEER US ON!

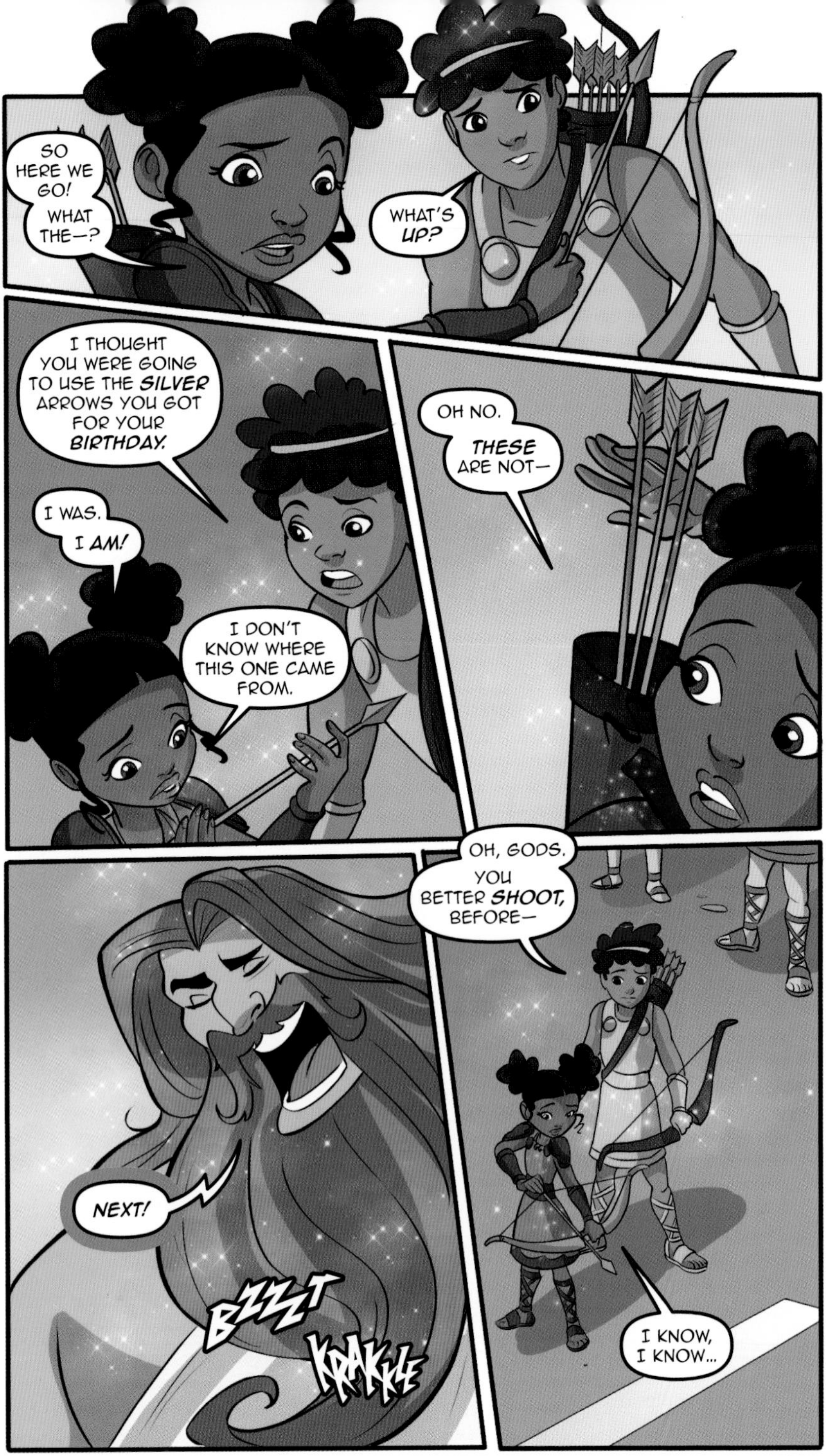
SO HERE WE GO!
WHAT THE—?
WHAT'S UP?
I THOUGHT YOU WERE GOING TO USE THE SILVER ARROWS YOU GOT FOR YOUR BIRTHDAY.
I WAS.
I AM!
I DON'T KNOW WHERE THIS ONE CAME FROM.
OH NO.
THESE ARE NOT—
NEXT!
BZZZT
KRAKKLE
OH, GODS.
YOU BETTER SHOOT, BEFORE—
I KNOW, I KNOW...

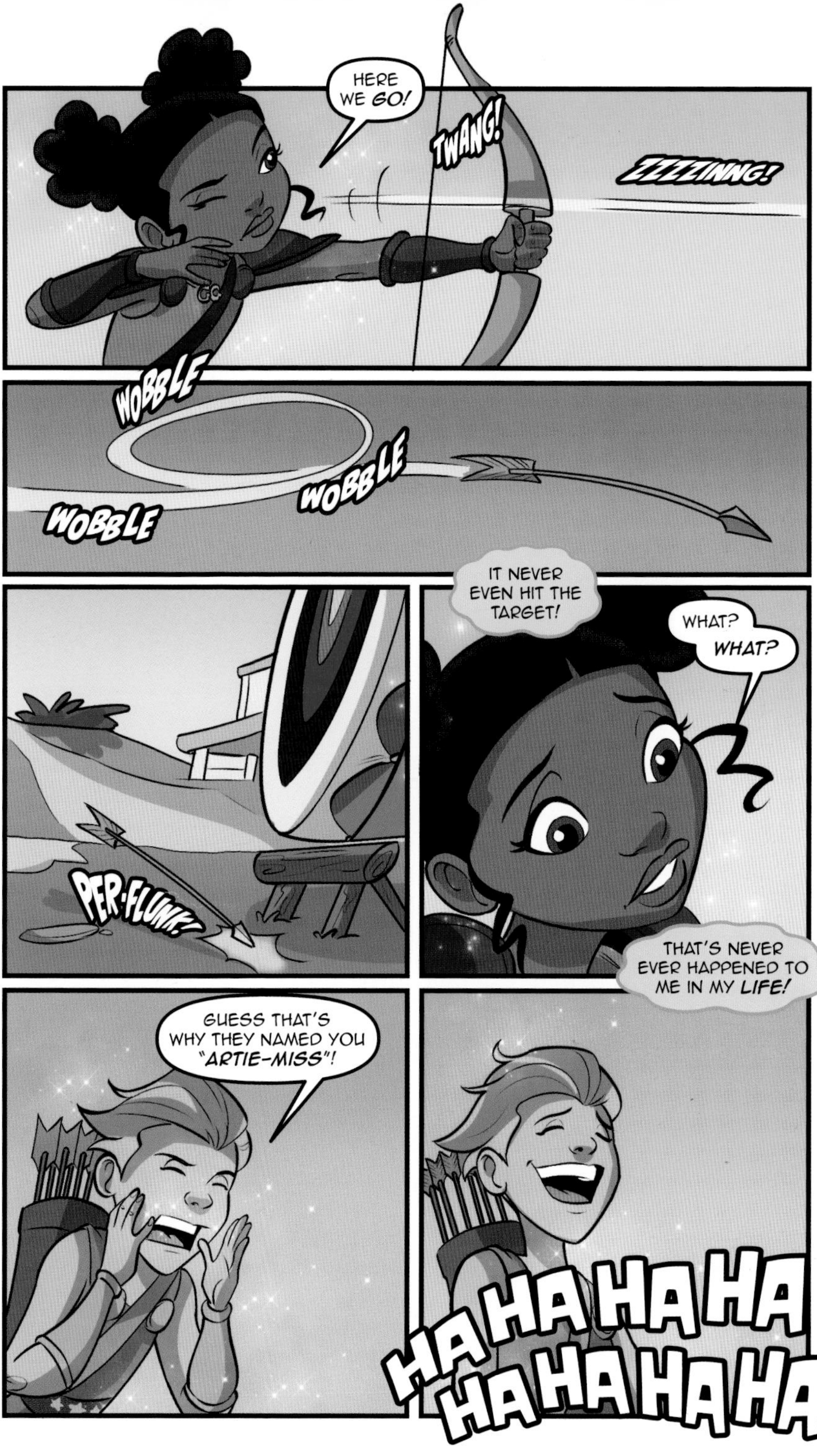
HERE WE GO!
TWANG!
ZZZZINNG!
WOBBLE
WOBBLE
WOBBLE
PER-FLUNK!
IT NEVER EVEN HIT THE TARGET!
WHAT? WHAT?
THAT'S NEVER EVER HAPPENED TO ME IN MY LIFE!
GUESS THAT'S WHY THEY NAMED YOU "ARTIE-MISS"!
HA HA HA HA HA
HA HA HA HA HA

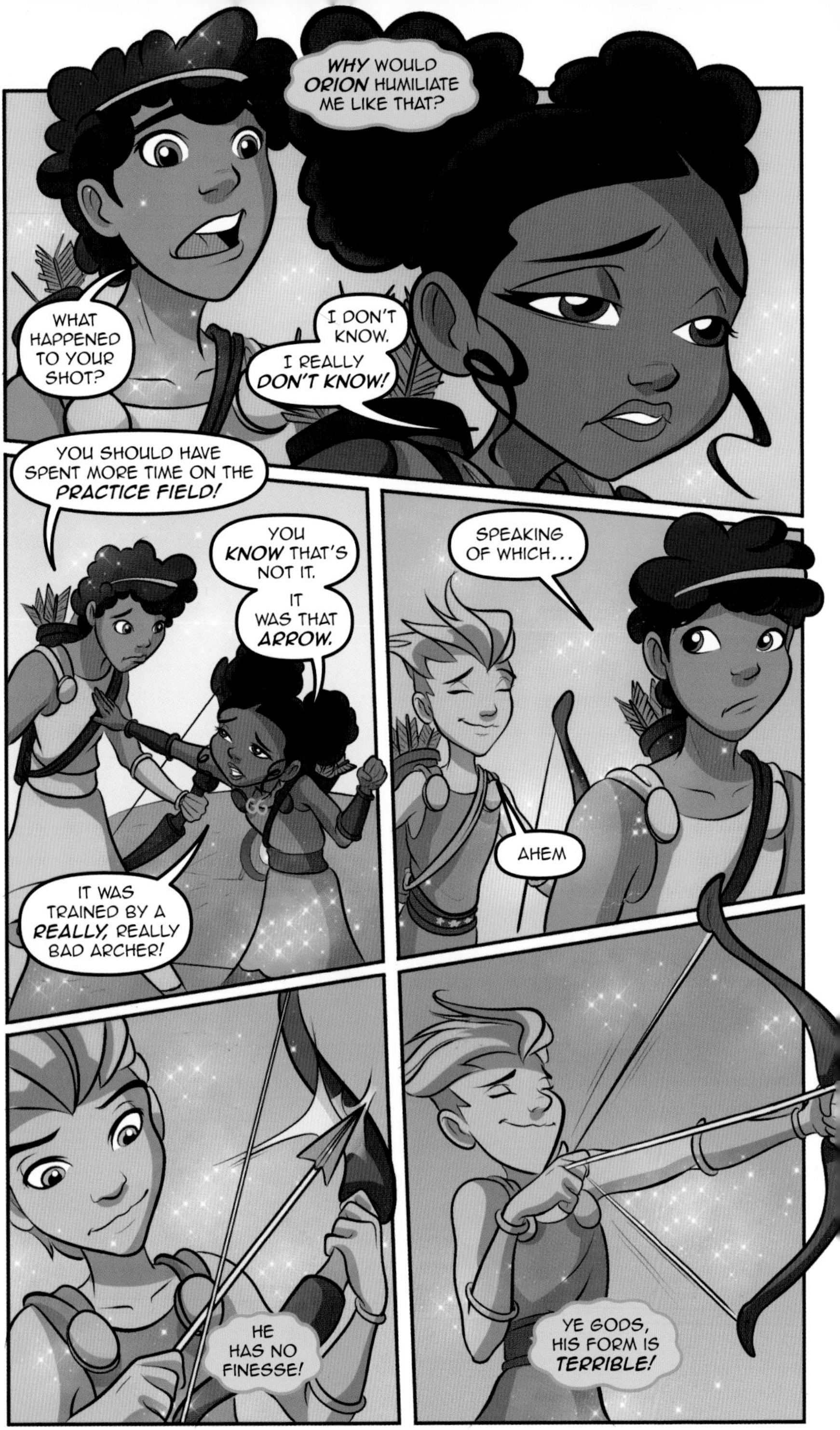

WHY WOULD ORION HUMILIATE ME LIKE THAT?
WHAT HAPPENED TO YOUR SHOT?
I DON'T KNOW.
I REALLY DON'T KNOW!
YOU SHOULD HAVE SPENT MORE TIME ON THE PRACTICE FIELD!
YOU KNOW THAT'S NOT IT.
IT WAS THAT ARROW.
IT WAS TRAINED BY A REALLY, REALLY BAD ARCHER!
SPEAKING OF WHICH...
AHEM
HE HAS NO FINESSE!
YE GODS, HIS FORM IS TERRIBLE!

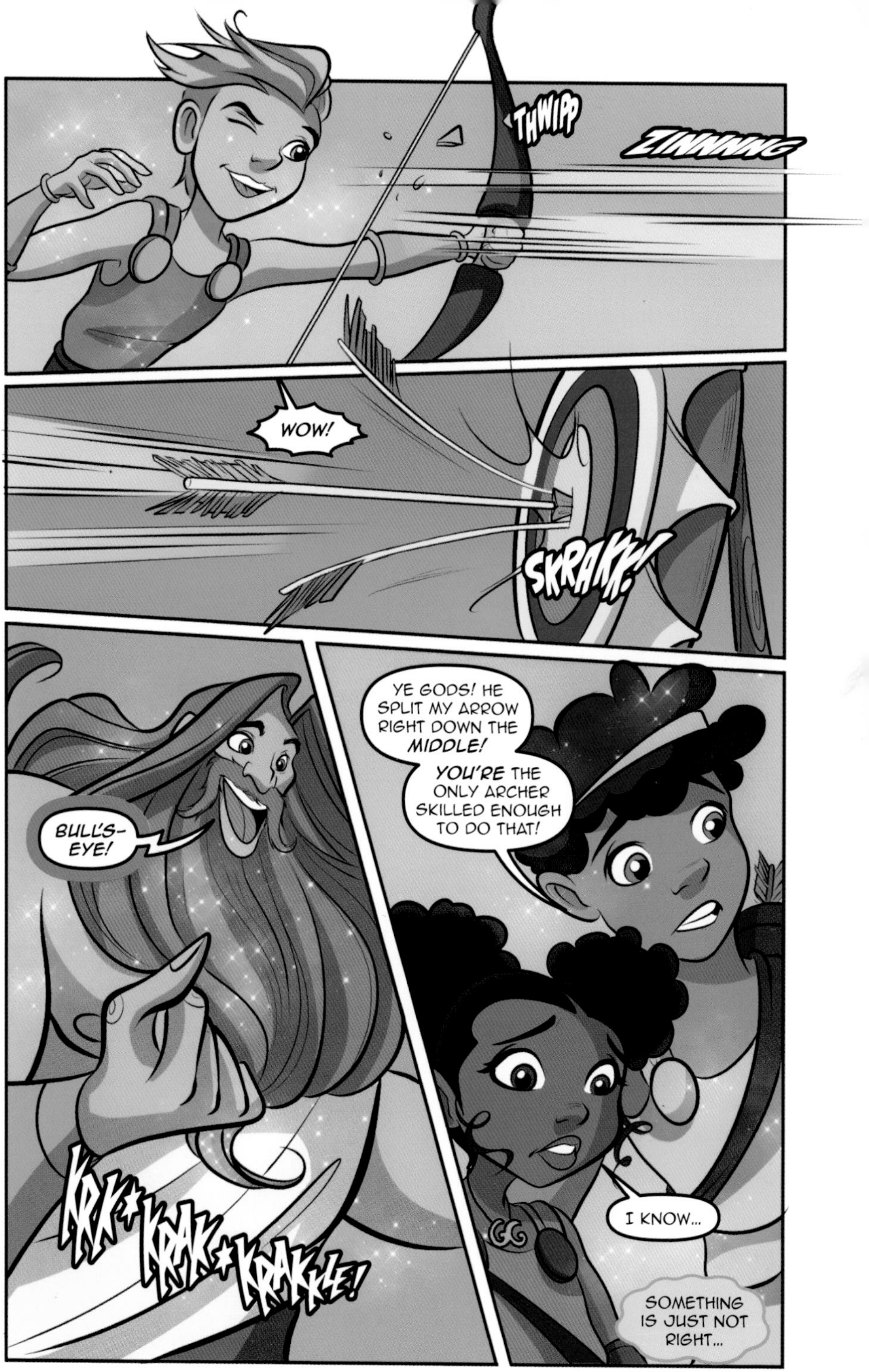
THWIPP
ZINNNNG
WOW!
SKRAKK!
BULL'S-EYE!
YE GODS! HE SPLIT MY ARROW RIGHT DOWN THE MIDDLE!
YOU'RE THE ONLY ARCHER SKILLED ENOUGH TO DO THAT!
KRK*KRAK*KRAKKLE!
I KNOW...
SOMETHING IS JUST NOT RIGHT...

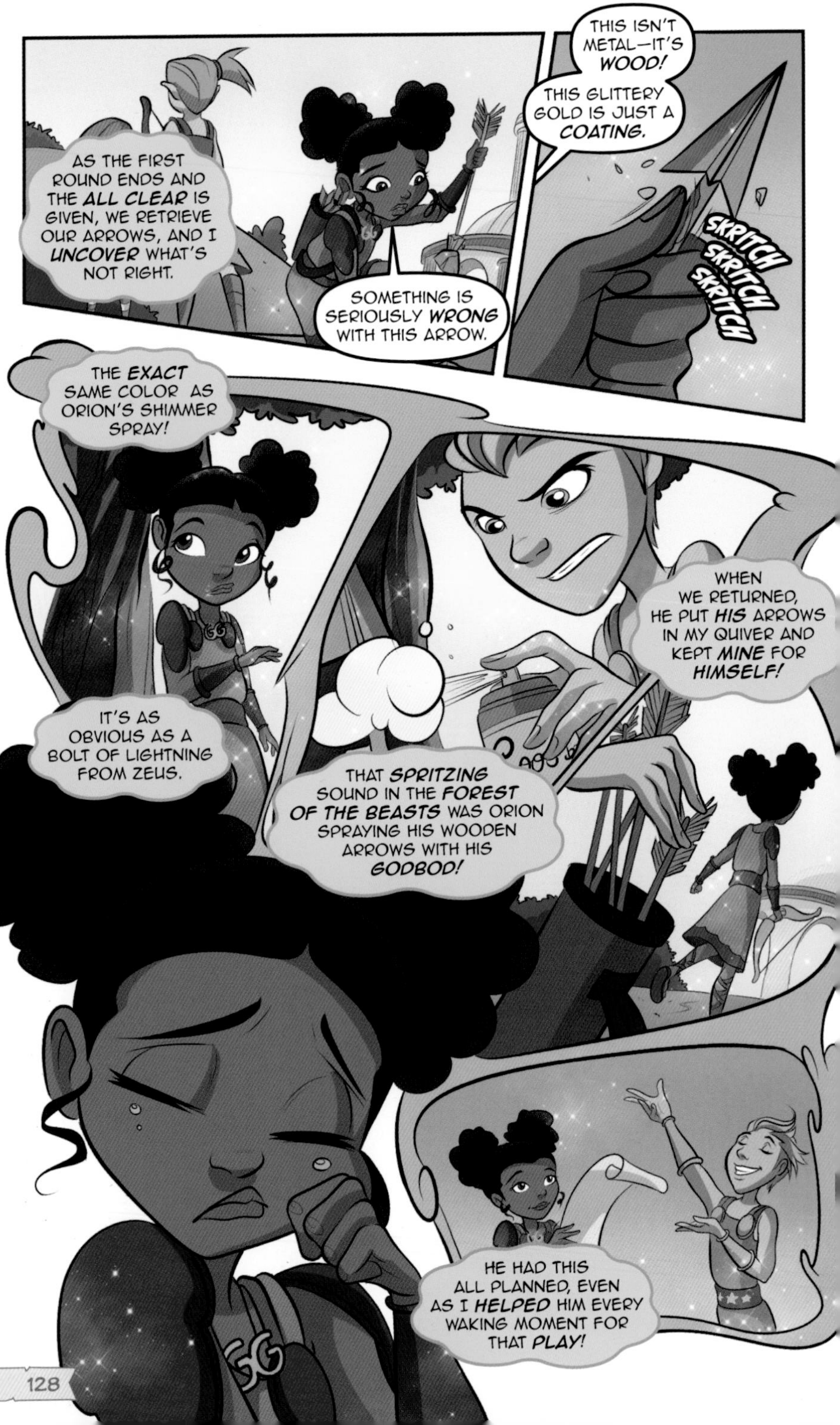

AS THE FIRST ROUND ENDS AND THE ALL CLEAR IS GIVEN, WE RETRIEVE OUR ARROWS, AND I UNCOVER WHAT'S NOT RIGHT.
SOMETHING IS SERIOUSLY WRONG WITH THIS ARROW.
THIS ISN'T METAL—IT'S WOOD!
THIS GLITTERY GOLD IS JUST A COATING.
SKRITCH SKRITCH SKRITCH
THE EXACT SAME COLOR AS ORION'S SHIMMER SPRAY!
IT'S AS OBVIOUS AS A BOLT OF LIGHTNING FROM ZEUS.
THAT SPRITZING SOUND IN THE FOREST OF THE BEASTS WAS ORION SPRAYING HIS WOODEN ARROWS WITH HIS GODBOD!
WHEN WE RETURNED, HE PUT HIS ARROWS IN MY QUIVER AND KEPT MINE FOR HIMSELF!
HE HAD THIS ALL PLANNED, EVEN AS I HELPED HIM EVERY WAKING MOMENT FOR THAT PLAY!

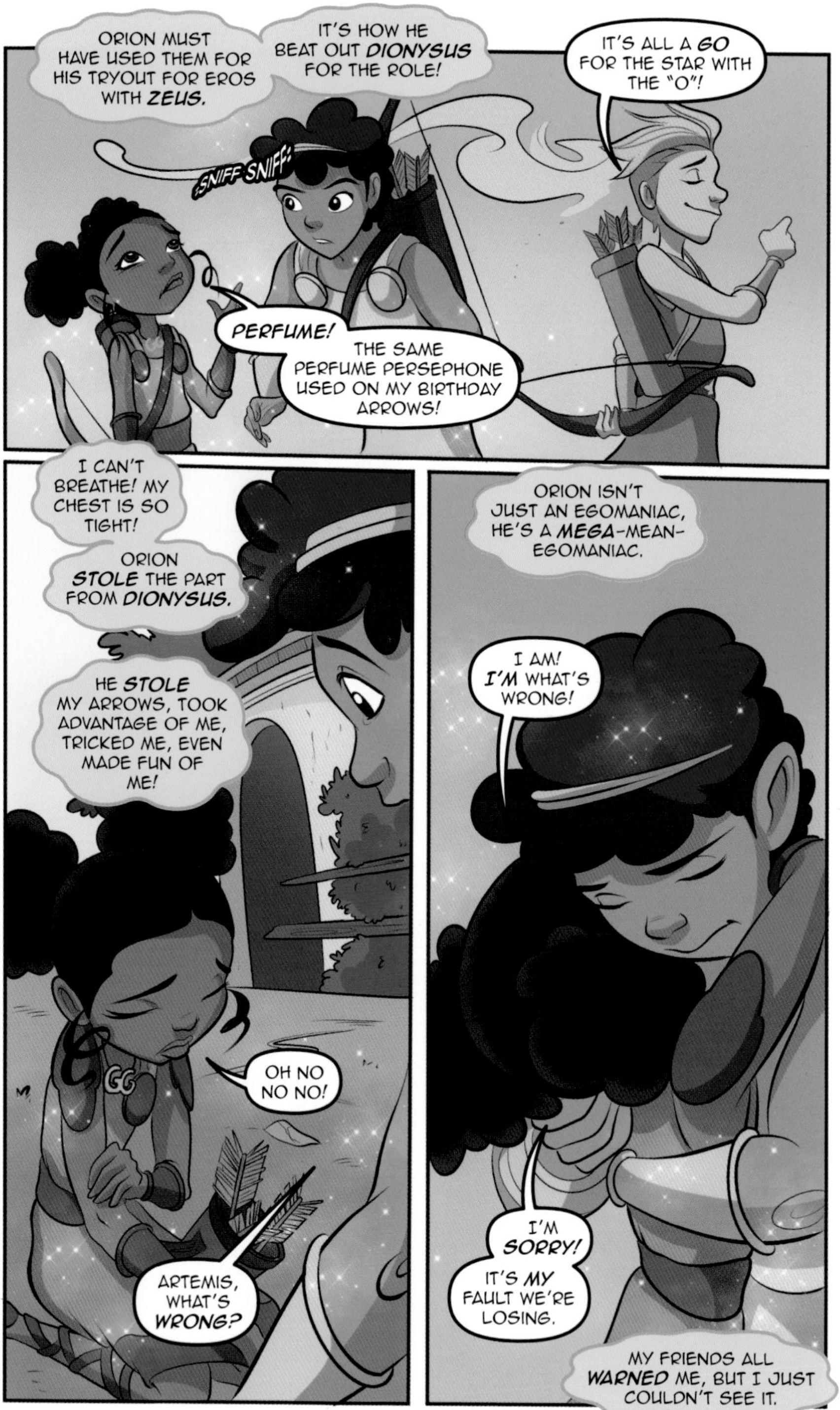

ORION MUST HAVE USED THEM FOR HIS TRYOUT FOR EROS WITH ZEUS.
IT'S HOW HE BEAT OUT DIONYSUS FOR THE ROLE!
IT'S ALL A GO FOR THE STAR WITH THE "O"!
SNIFF SNIFF
PERFUME!
THE SAME PERFUME PERSEPHONE USED ON MY BIRTHDAY ARROWS!
I CAN'T BREATHE! MY CHEST IS SO TIGHT!
ORION STOLE THE PART FROM DIONYSUS.
HE STOLE MY ARROWS, TOOK ADVANTAGE OF ME, TRICKED ME, EVEN MADE FUN OF ME!
OH NO NO NO!
ARTEMIS, WHAT'S WRONG?
ORION ISN'T JUST AN EGOMANIAC, HE'S A MEGA-MEAN-EGOMANIAC.
I AM! I'M WHAT'S WRONG!
I'M SORRY!
IT'S MY FAULT WE'RE LOSING.
MY FRIENDS ALL WARNED ME, BUT I JUST COULDN'T SEE IT.

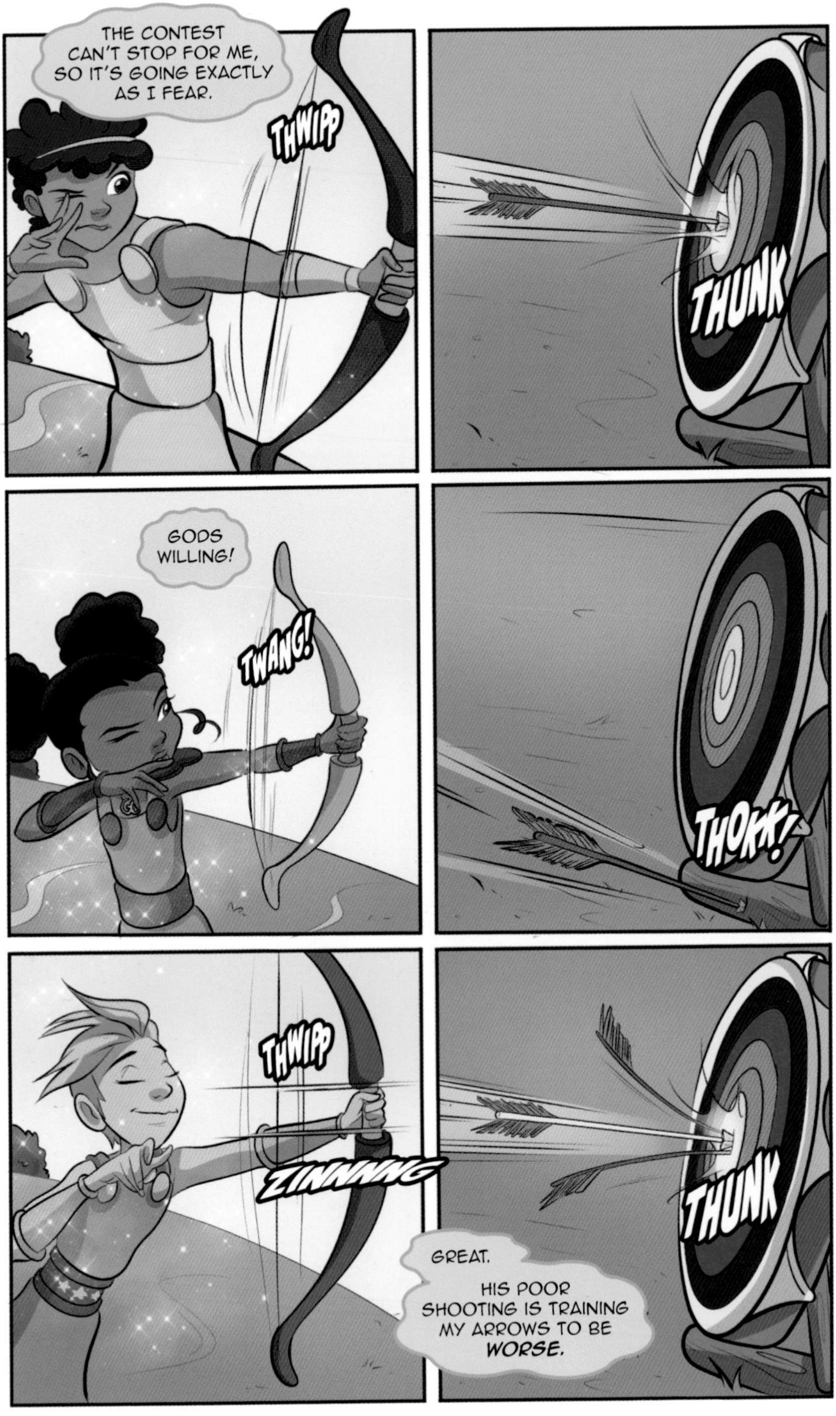
THE CONTEST CAN'T STOP FOR ME, SO IT'S GOING EXACTLY AS I FEAR.
THWIPP
THUNK
GODS WILLING!
TWANG!
THOKK!
THWIPP
ZINNNNG
THUNK
GREAT.
HIS POOR SHOOTING IS TRAINING MY ARROWS TO BE *WORSE.*

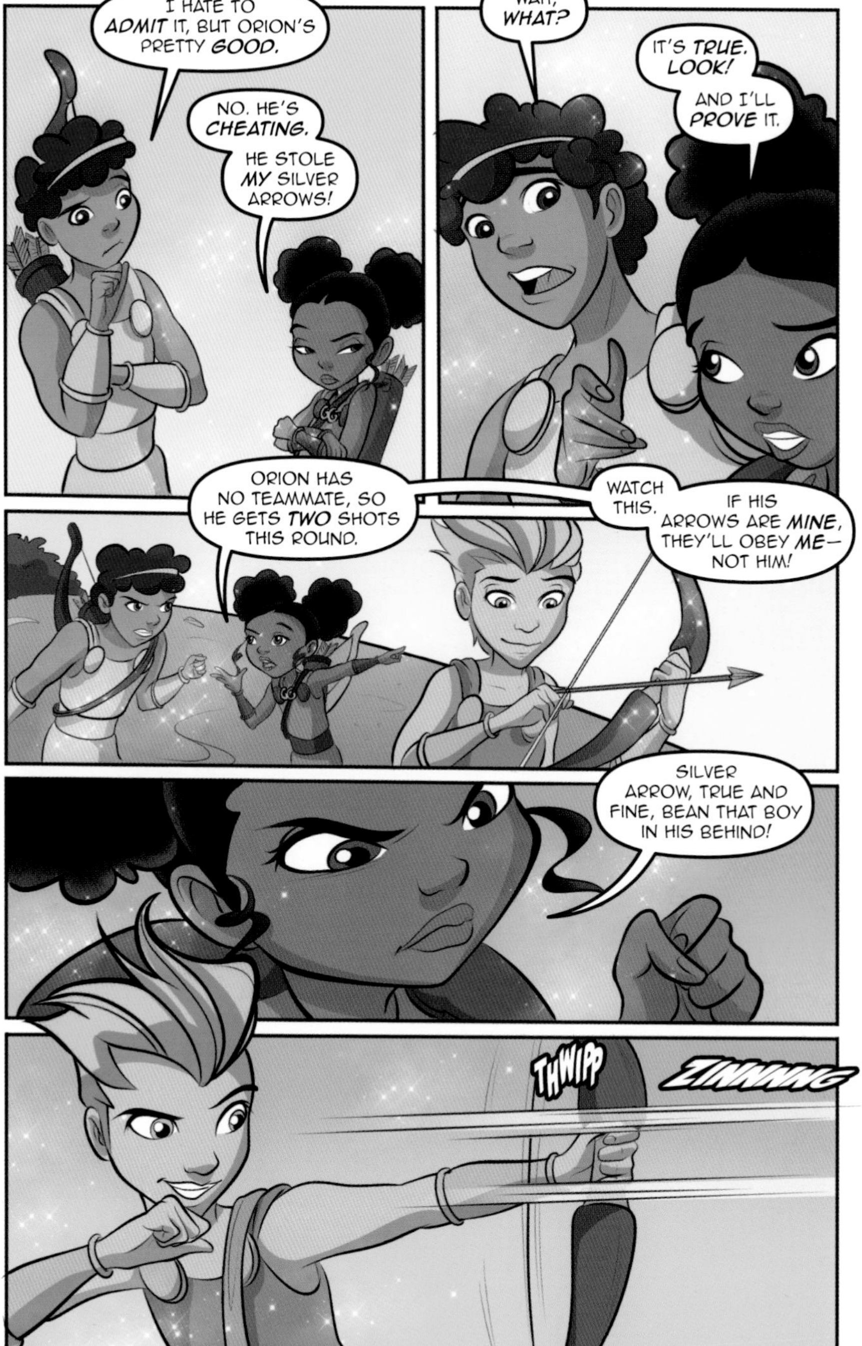
I HATE TO ADMIT IT, BUT ORION'S PRETTY GOOD.
NO. HE'S CHEATING.
HE STOLE MY SILVER ARROWS!
WAIT, WHAT?
IT'S TRUE. LOOK!
AND I'LL PROVE IT.
ORION HAS NO TEAMMATE, SO HE GETS TWO SHOTS THIS ROUND.
WATCH THIS.
IF HIS ARROWS ARE MINE, THEY'LL OBEY ME— NOT HIM!
SILVER ARROW, TRUE AND FINE, BEAN THAT BOY IN HIS BEHIND!
THWIPP
ZINNNNG

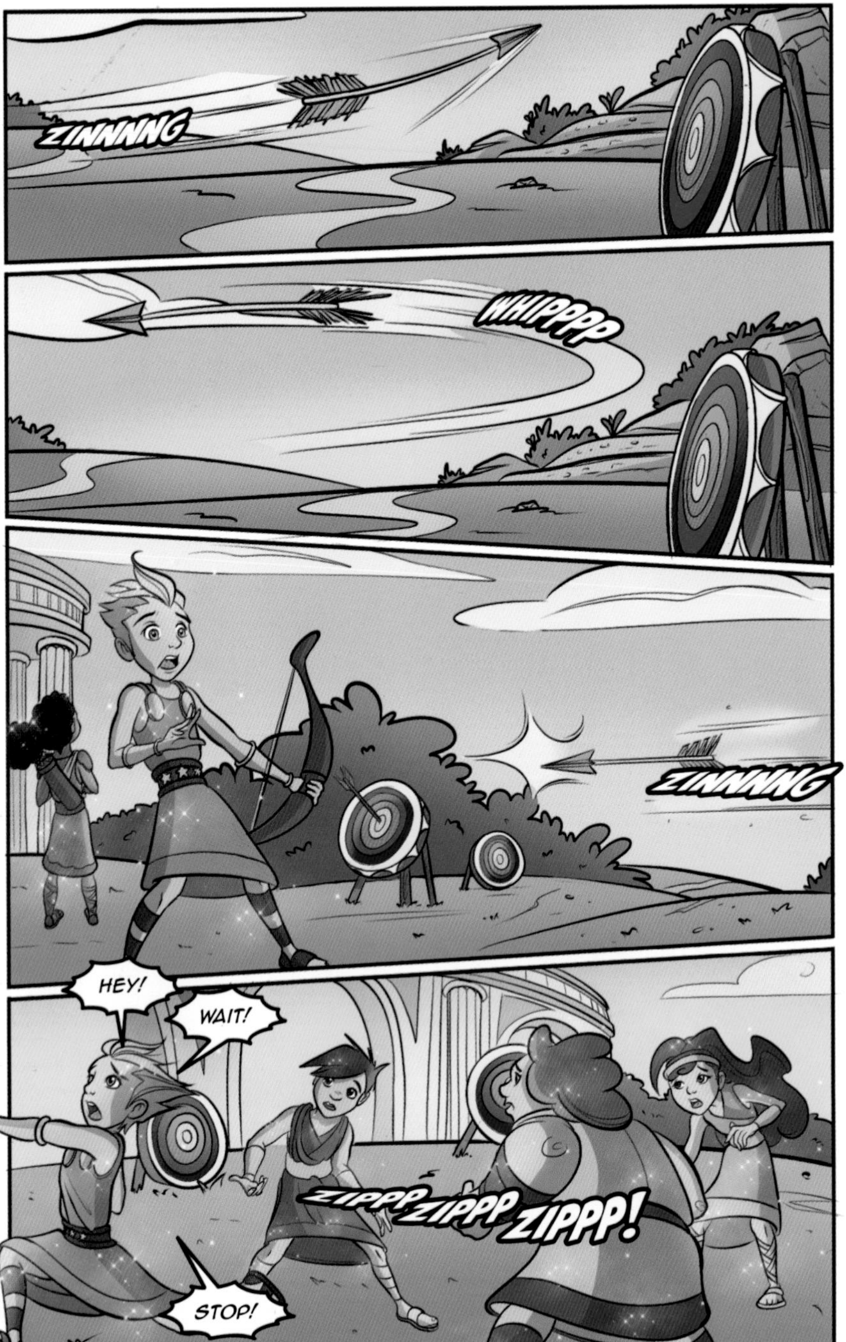
ZINNNNG
WHIPPPP
ZINNNNG
HEY!
WAIT!
ZIPPP ZIPPP ZIPPP!
STOP!

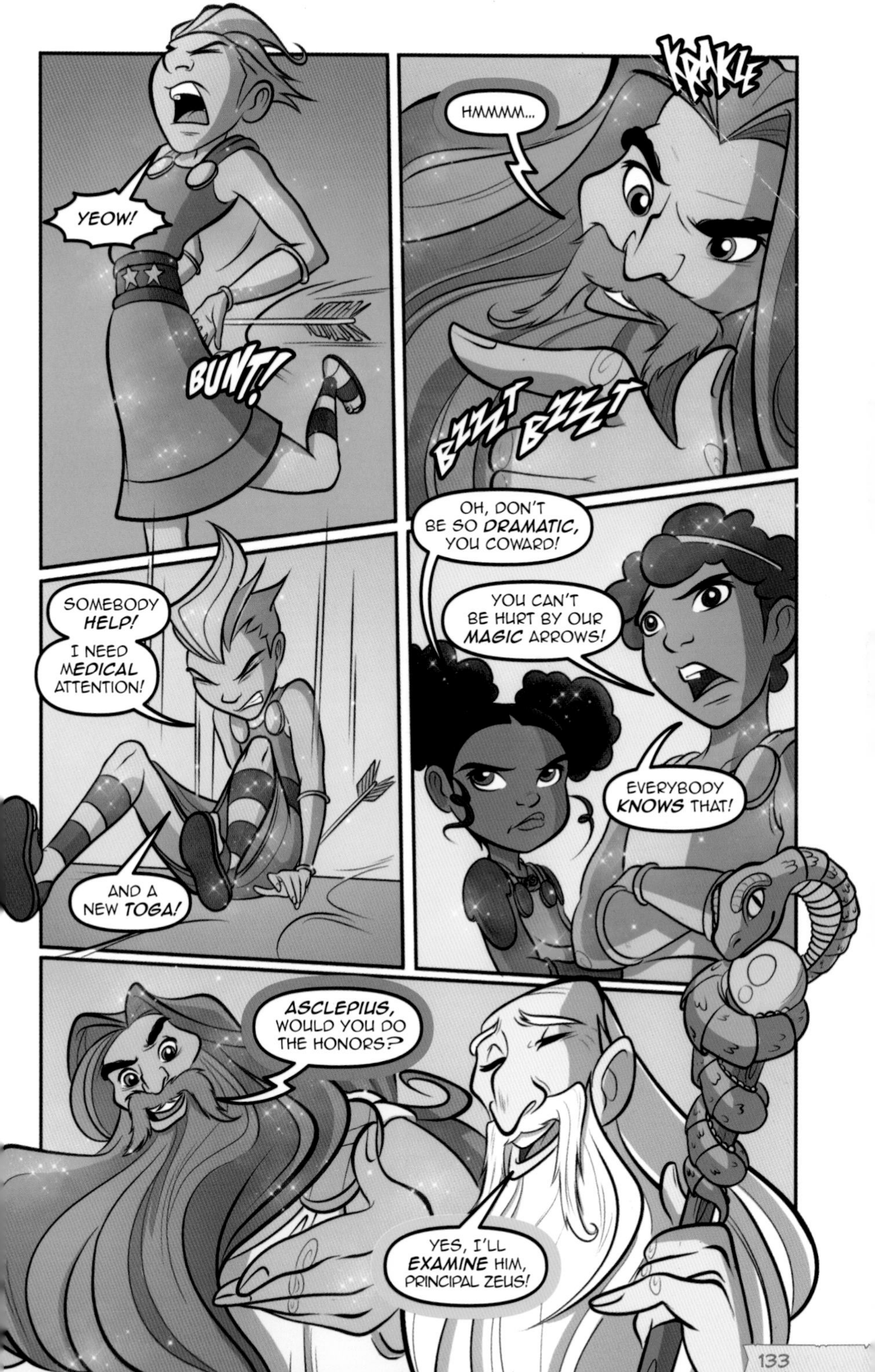
YEOW!
BUNT!
HMMMM...
KRAKLE
BZZZT BZZZT
SOMEBODY HELP!
I NEED MEDICAL ATTENTION!
AND A NEW TOGA!
OH, DON'T BE SO DRAMATIC, YOU COWARD!
YOU CAN'T BE HURT BY OUR MAGIC ARROWS!
EVERYBODY KNOWS THAT!
ASCLEPIUS, WOULD YOU DO THE HONORS?
YES, I'LL EXAMINE HIM, PRINCIPAL ZEUS!

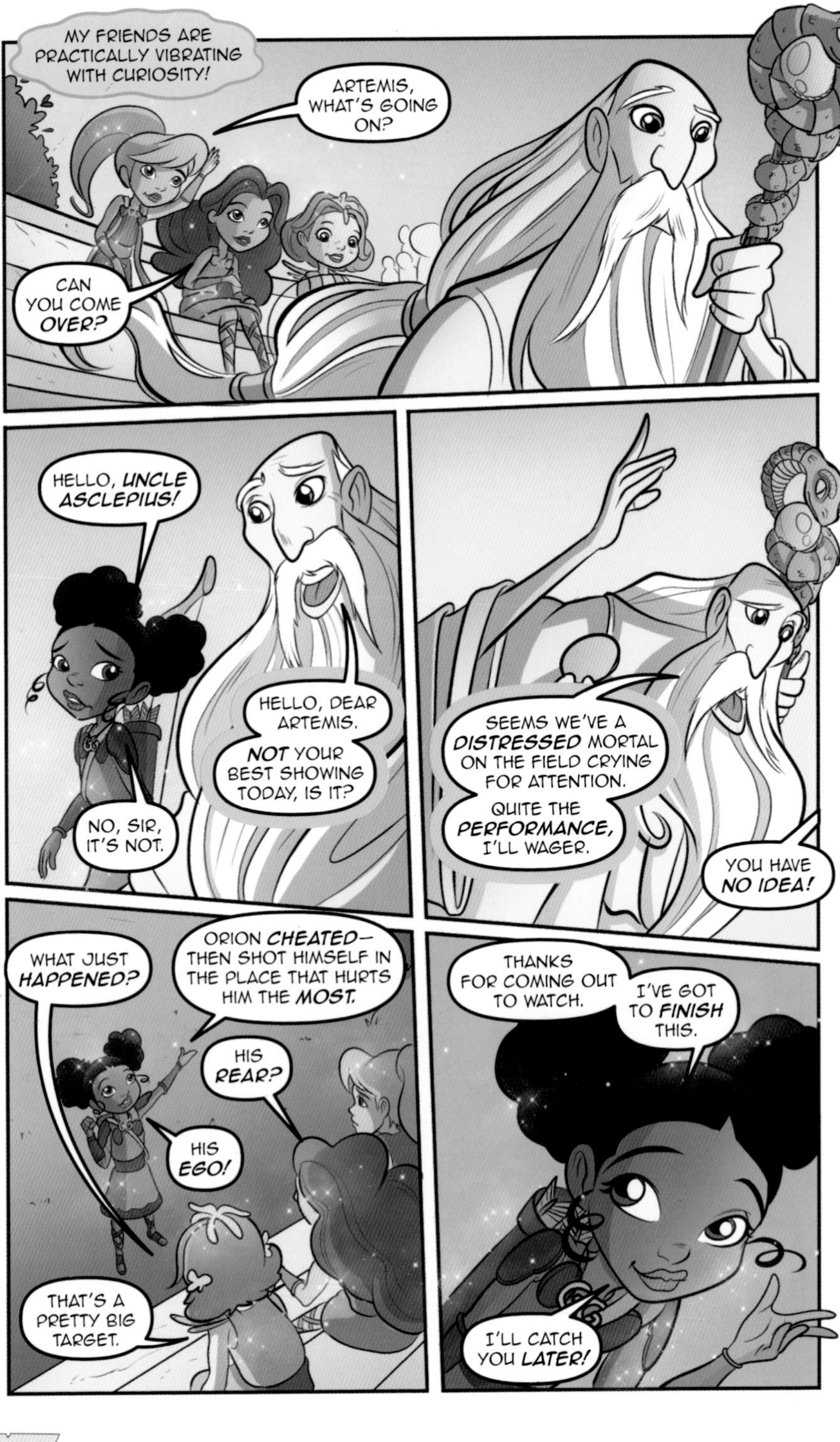
MY FRIENDS ARE PRACTICALLY VIBRATING WITH CURIOSITY!
ARTEMIS, WHAT'S GOING ON?
CAN YOU COME OVER?
HELLO, UNCLE ASCLEPIUS!
HELLO, DEAR ARTEMIS.
NOT YOUR BEST SHOWING TODAY, IS IT?
NO, SIR, IT'S NOT.
SEEMS WE'VE A DISTRESSED MORTAL ON THE FIELD CRYING FOR ATTENTION.
QUITE THE PERFORMANCE, I'LL WAGER.
YOU HAVE NO IDEA!
WHAT JUST HAPPENED?
ORION CHEATED—THEN SHOT HIMSELF IN THE PLACE THAT HURTS HIM THE MOST.
HIS REAR?
HIS EGO!
THAT'S A PRETTY BIG TARGET.
THANKS FOR COMING OUT TO WATCH.
I'VE GOT TO FINISH THIS.
I'LL CATCH YOU LATER!

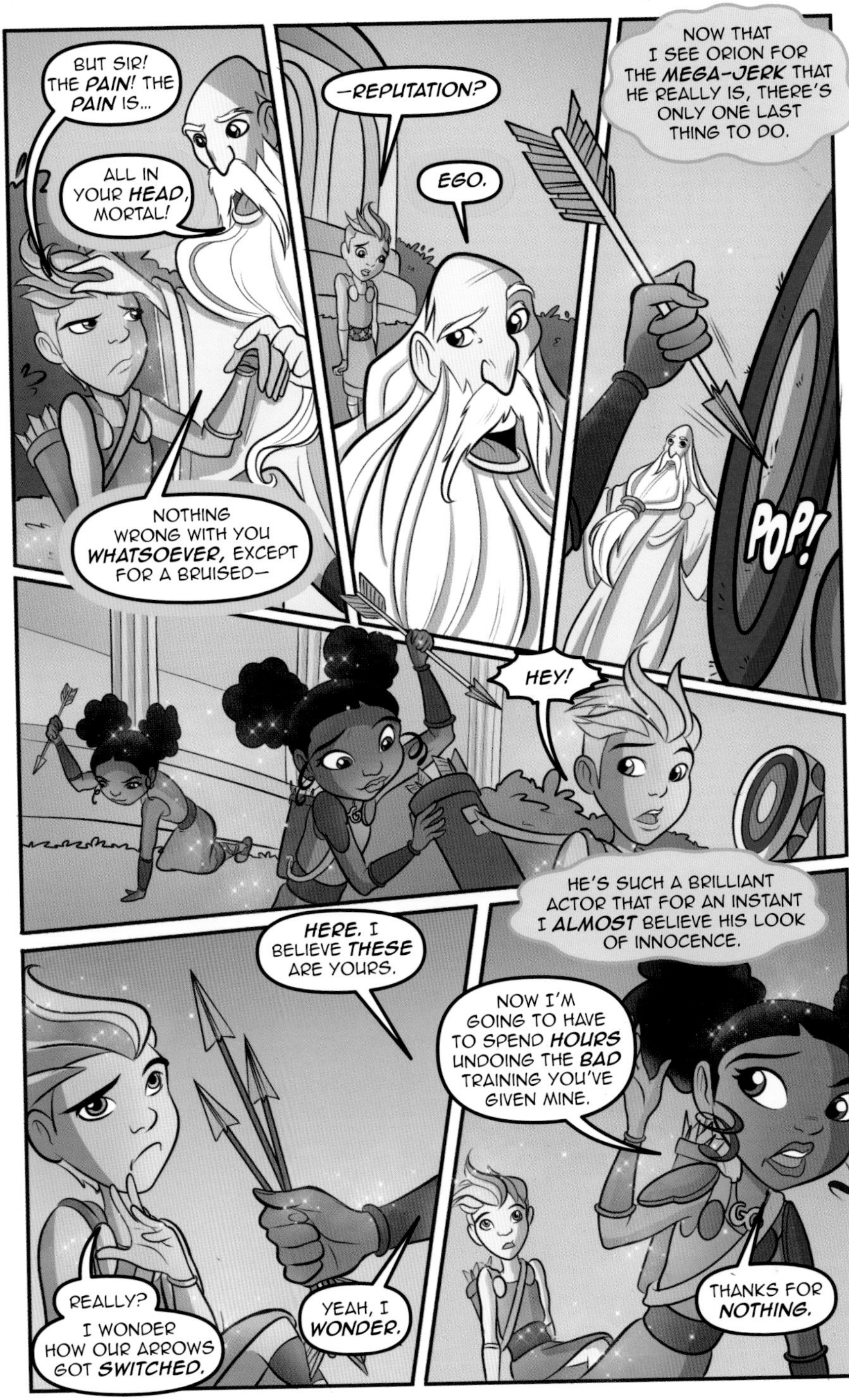
BUT SIR! THE PAIN! THE PAIN IS...
ALL IN YOUR HEAD, MORTAL!
NOTHING WRONG WITH YOU WHATSOEVER, EXCEPT FOR A BRUISED—
—REPUTATION?
EGO.
NOW THAT I SEE ORION FOR THE MEGA-JERK THAT HE REALLY IS, THERE'S ONLY ONE LAST THING TO DO.
POP!
HEY!
HE'S SUCH A BRILLIANT ACTOR THAT FOR AN INSTANT I ALMOST BELIEVE HIS LOOK OF INNOCENCE.
HERE. I BELIEVE THESE ARE YOURS.
REALLY? I WONDER HOW OUR ARROWS GOT SWITCHED.
YEAH, I WONDER.
NOW I'M GOING TO HAVE TO SPEND HOURS UNDOING THE BAD TRAINING YOU'VE GIVEN MINE.
THANKS FOR NOTHING.

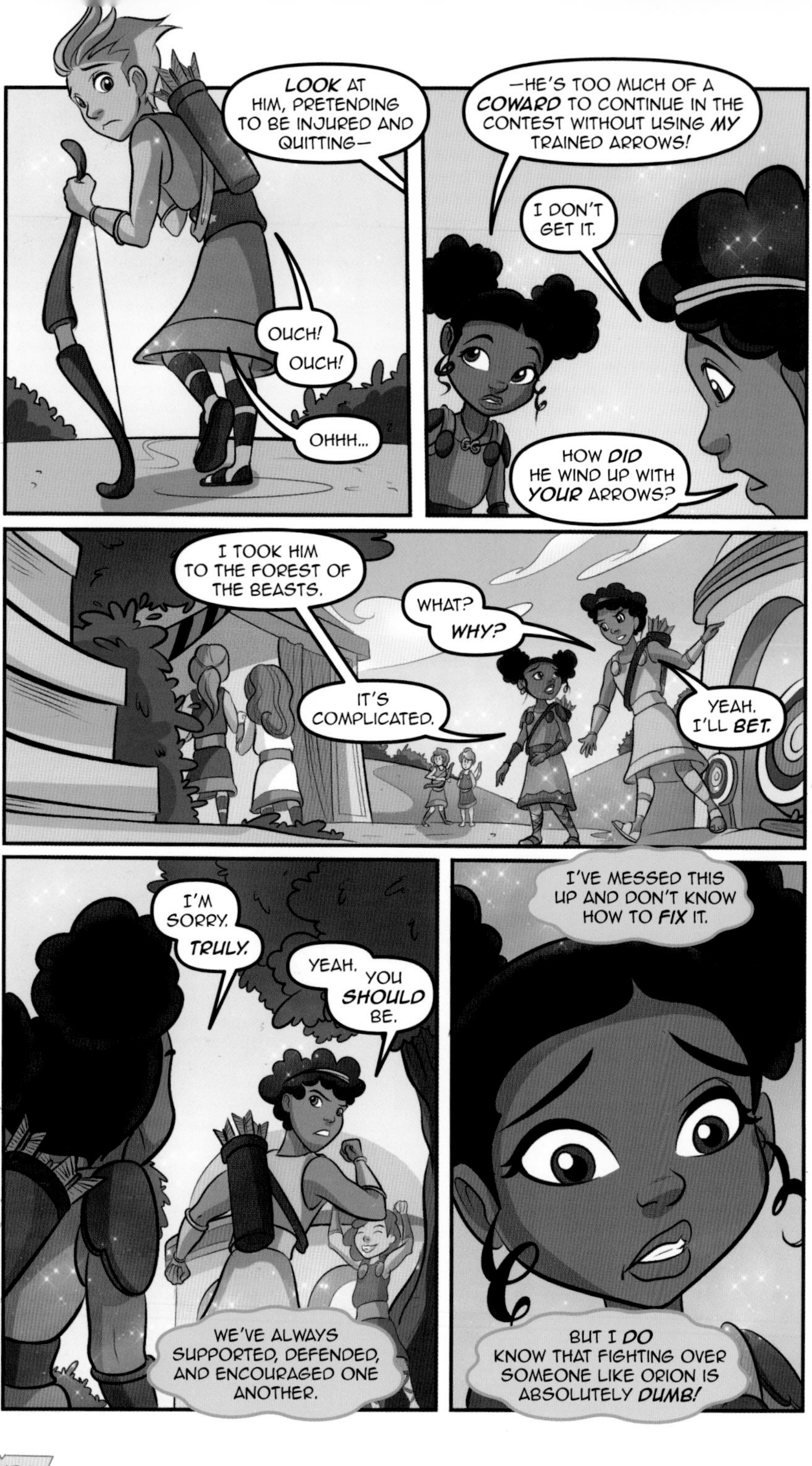
LOOK AT HIM, PRETENDING TO BE INJURED AND QUITTING—
—HE'S TOO MUCH OF A COWARD TO CONTINUE IN THE CONTEST WITHOUT USING MY TRAINED ARROWS!
OUCH!
OUCH!
OHHH...
I DON'T GET IT.
HOW DID HE WIND UP WITH YOUR ARROWS?
I TOOK HIM TO THE FOREST OF THE BEASTS.
WHAT? WHY?
IT'S COMPLICATED.
YEAH. I'LL BET.
I'M SORRY. TRULY.
YEAH. YOU SHOULD BE.
WE'VE ALWAYS SUPPORTED, DEFENDED, AND ENCOURAGED ONE ANOTHER.
I'VE MESSED THIS UP AND DON'T KNOW HOW TO FIX IT.
BUT I DO KNOW THAT FIGHTING OVER SOMEONE LIKE ORION IS ABSOLUTELY DUMB!

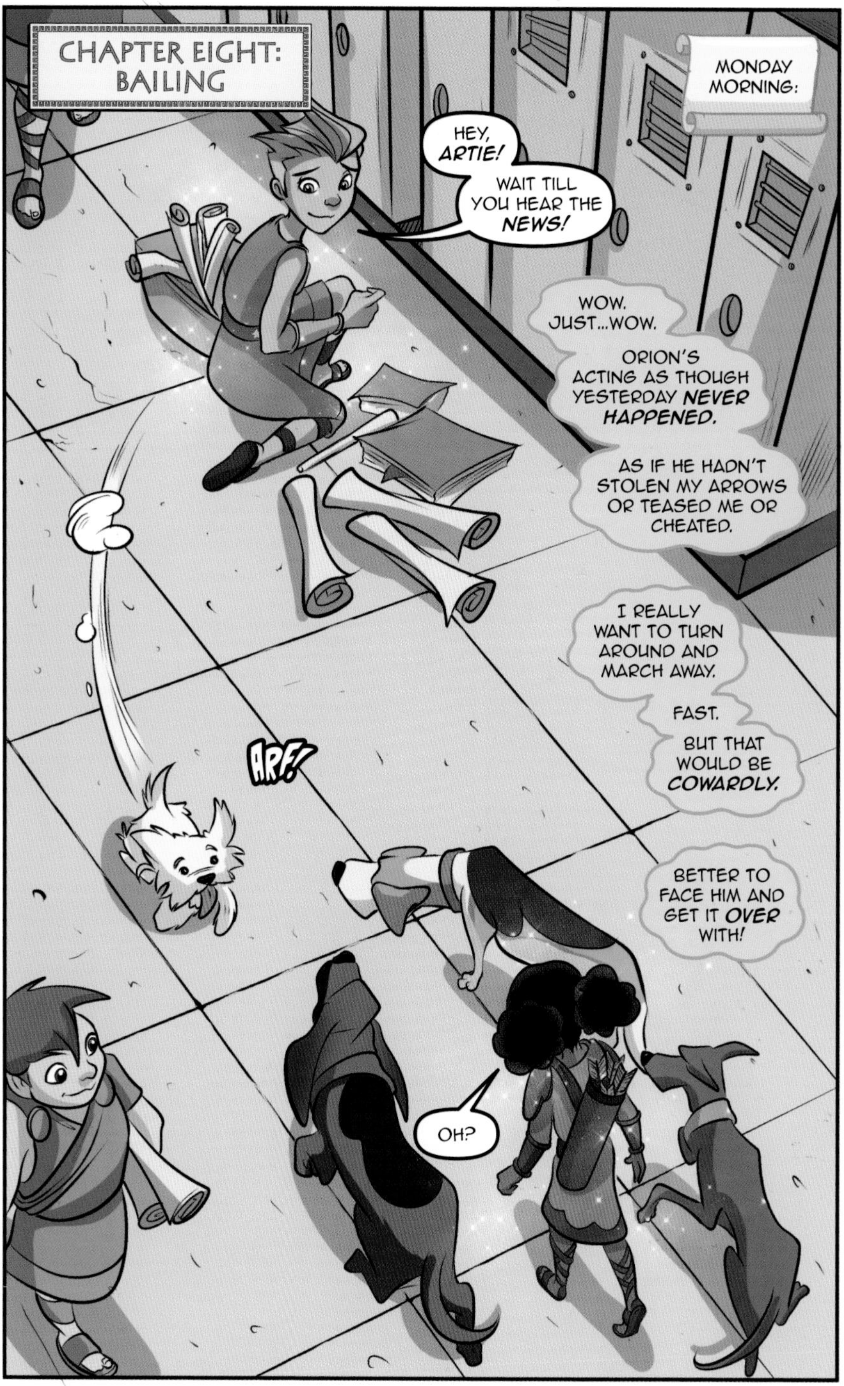
CHAPTER EIGHT: BAILING
MONDAY MORNING:
HEY, ARTIE!
WAIT TILL YOU HEAR THE NEWS!
WOW. JUST...WOW.
ORION'S ACTING AS THOUGH YESTERDAY NEVER HAPPENED.
AS IF HE HADN'T STOLEN MY ARROWS OR TEASED ME OR CHEATED.
I REALLY WANT TO TURN AROUND AND MARCH AWAY.
FAST.
BUT THAT WOULD BE COWARDLY.
ARF!
BETTER TO FACE HIM AND GET IT OVER WITH!
OH?

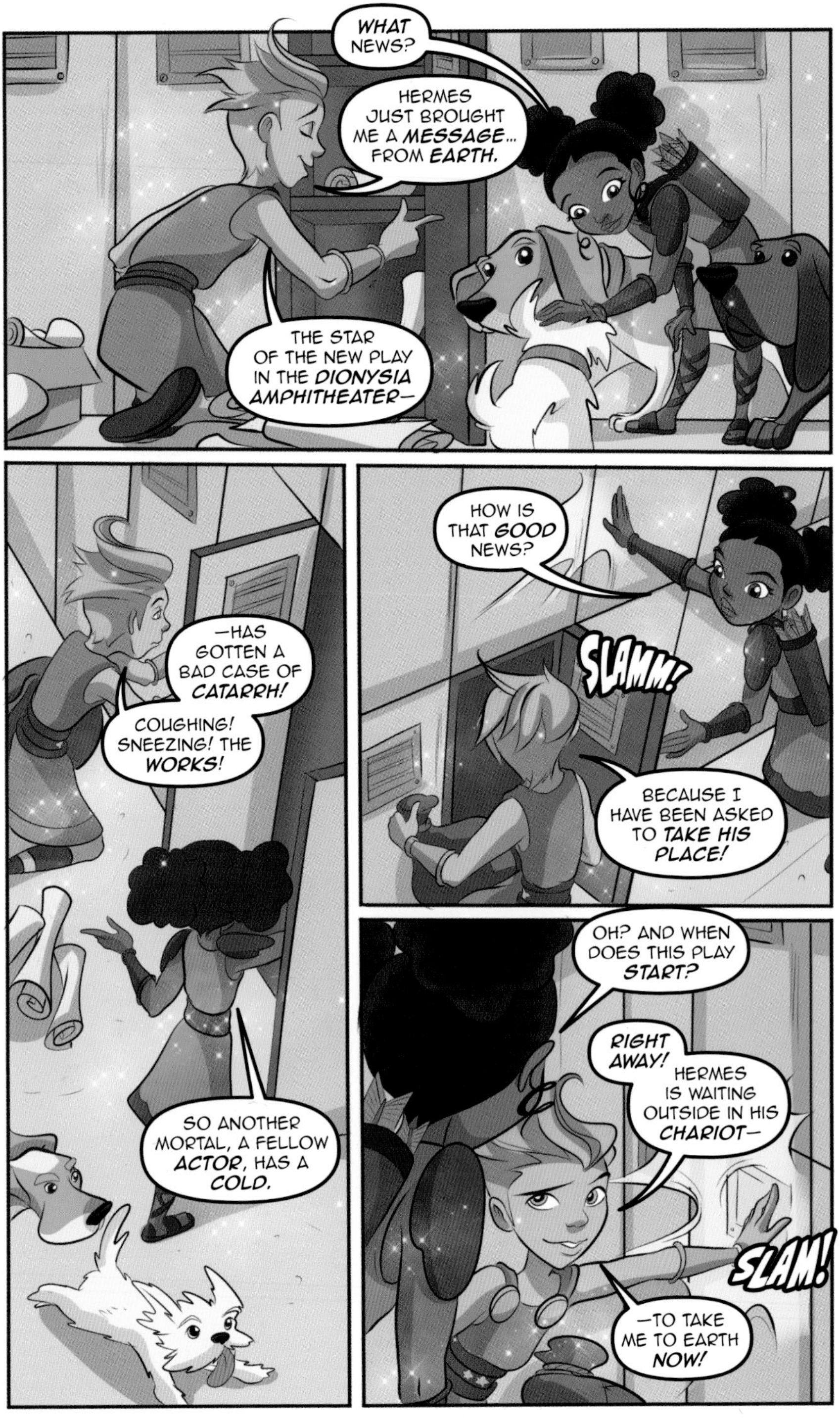
WHAT NEWS?
HERMES JUST BROUGHT ME A MESSAGE... FROM EARTH.
THE STAR OF THE NEW PLAY IN THE DIONYSIA AMPHITHEATER—
—HAS GOTTEN A BAD CASE OF CATARRH!
COUGHING! SNEEZING! THE WORKS!
SO ANOTHER MORTAL, A FELLOW ACTOR, HAS A COLD.
HOW IS THAT GOOD NEWS?
SLAMM!
BECAUSE I HAVE BEEN ASKED TO TAKE HIS PLACE!
OH? AND WHEN DOES THIS PLAY START?
RIGHT AWAY!
HERMES IS WAITING OUTSIDE IN HIS CHARIOT—
SLAM!
—TO TAKE ME TO EARTH NOW!

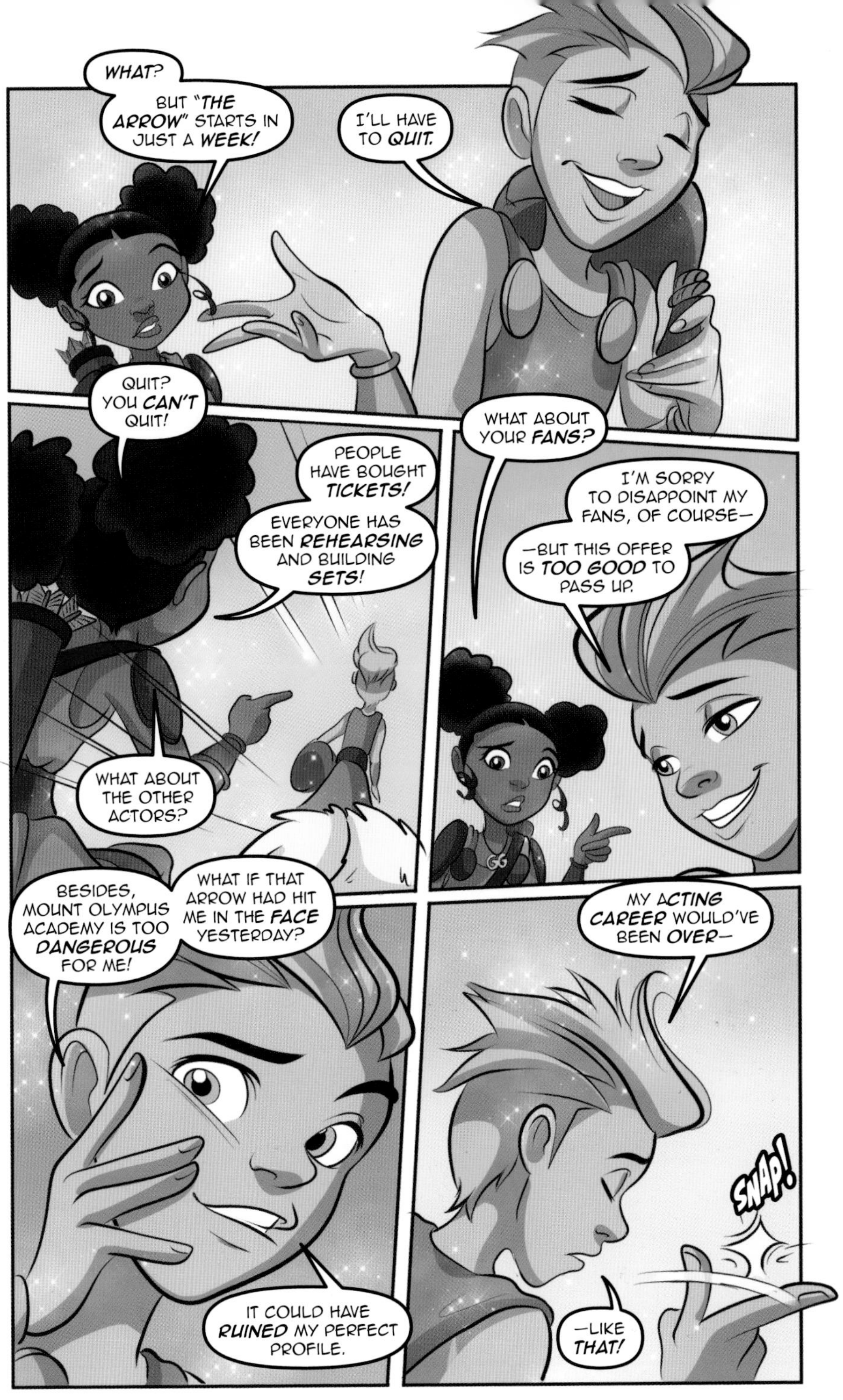
WHAT?
BUT "THE ARROW" STARTS IN JUST A WEEK!
I'LL HAVE TO QUIT.
QUIT? YOU CAN'T QUIT!
PEOPLE HAVE BOUGHT TICKETS!
EVERYONE HAS BEEN REHEARSING AND BUILDING SETS!
WHAT ABOUT THE OTHER ACTORS?
WHAT ABOUT YOUR FANS?
I'M SORRY TO DISAPPOINT MY FANS, OF COURSE—
—BUT THIS OFFER IS TOO GOOD TO PASS UP.
GG
BESIDES, MOUNT OLYMPUS ACADEMY IS TOO DANGEROUS FOR ME!
WHAT IF THAT ARROW HAD HIT ME IN THE FACE YESTERDAY?
IT COULD HAVE RUINED MY PERFECT PROFILE.
MY ACTING CAREER WOULD'VE BEEN OVER—
SNAP!
—LIKE THAT!

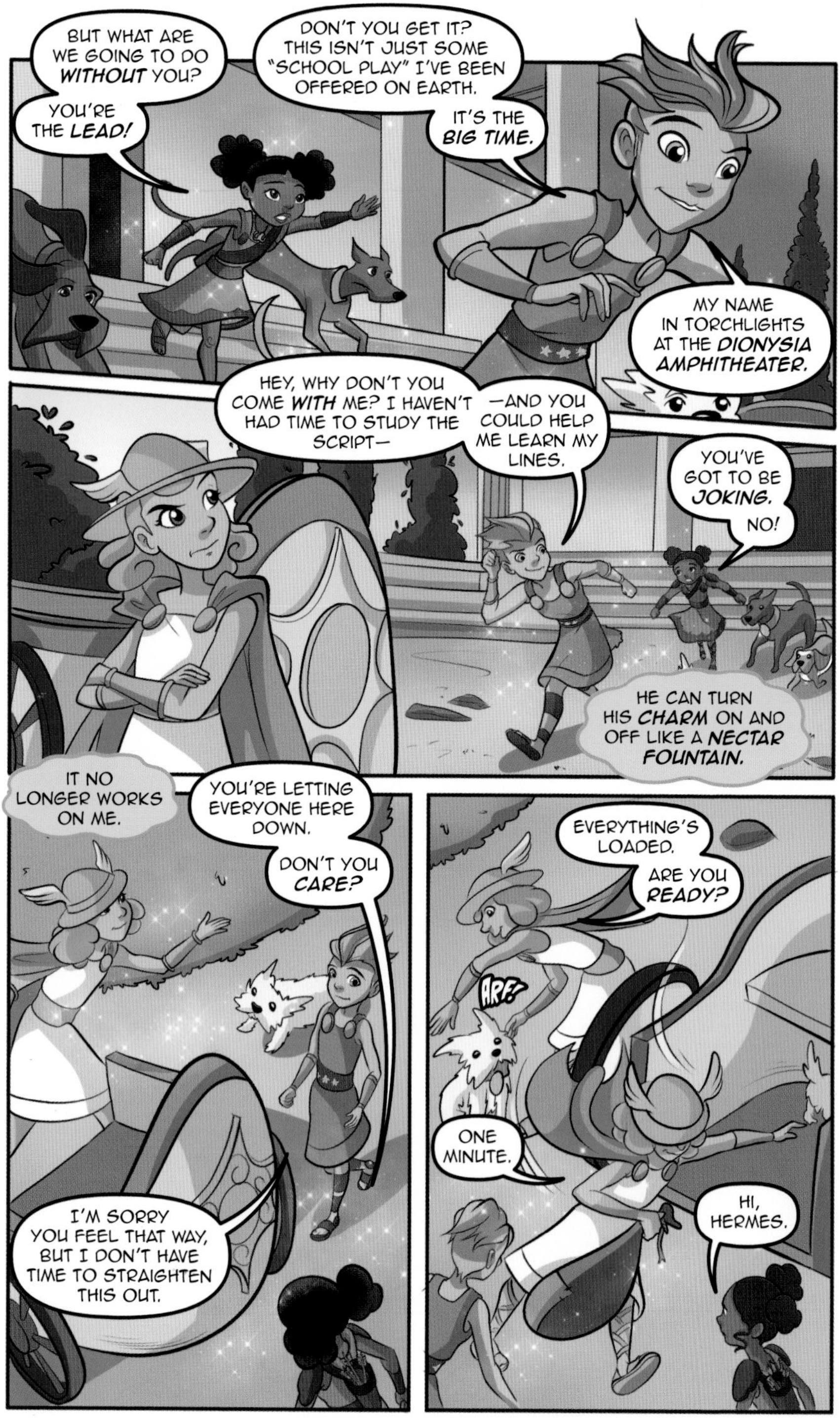

BUT WHAT ARE WE GOING TO DO *WITHOUT* YOU?
YOU'RE THE *LEAD!*
DON'T YOU GET IT? THIS ISN'T JUST SOME "SCHOOL PLAY" I'VE BEEN OFFERED ON EARTH.
IT'S THE *BIG TIME.*
MY NAME IN TORCHLIGHTS AT THE *DIONYSIA AMPHITHEATER.*
HEY, WHY DON'T YOU COME *WITH* ME? I HAVEN'T HAD TIME TO STUDY THE SCRIPT—
—AND YOU COULD HELP ME LEARN MY LINES.
YOU'VE GOT TO BE *JOKING.*
NO!
HE CAN TURN HIS *CHARM* ON AND OFF LIKE A *NECTAR FOUNTAIN.*
IT NO LONGER WORKS ON ME.
YOU'RE LETTING EVERYONE HERE DOWN.
DON'T YOU *CARE?*
I'M SORRY YOU FEEL THAT WAY, BUT I DON'T HAVE TIME TO STRAIGHTEN THIS OUT.
EVERYTHING'S LOADED.
ARE YOU *READY?*
ARF!
ONE MINUTE.
HI, HERMES.

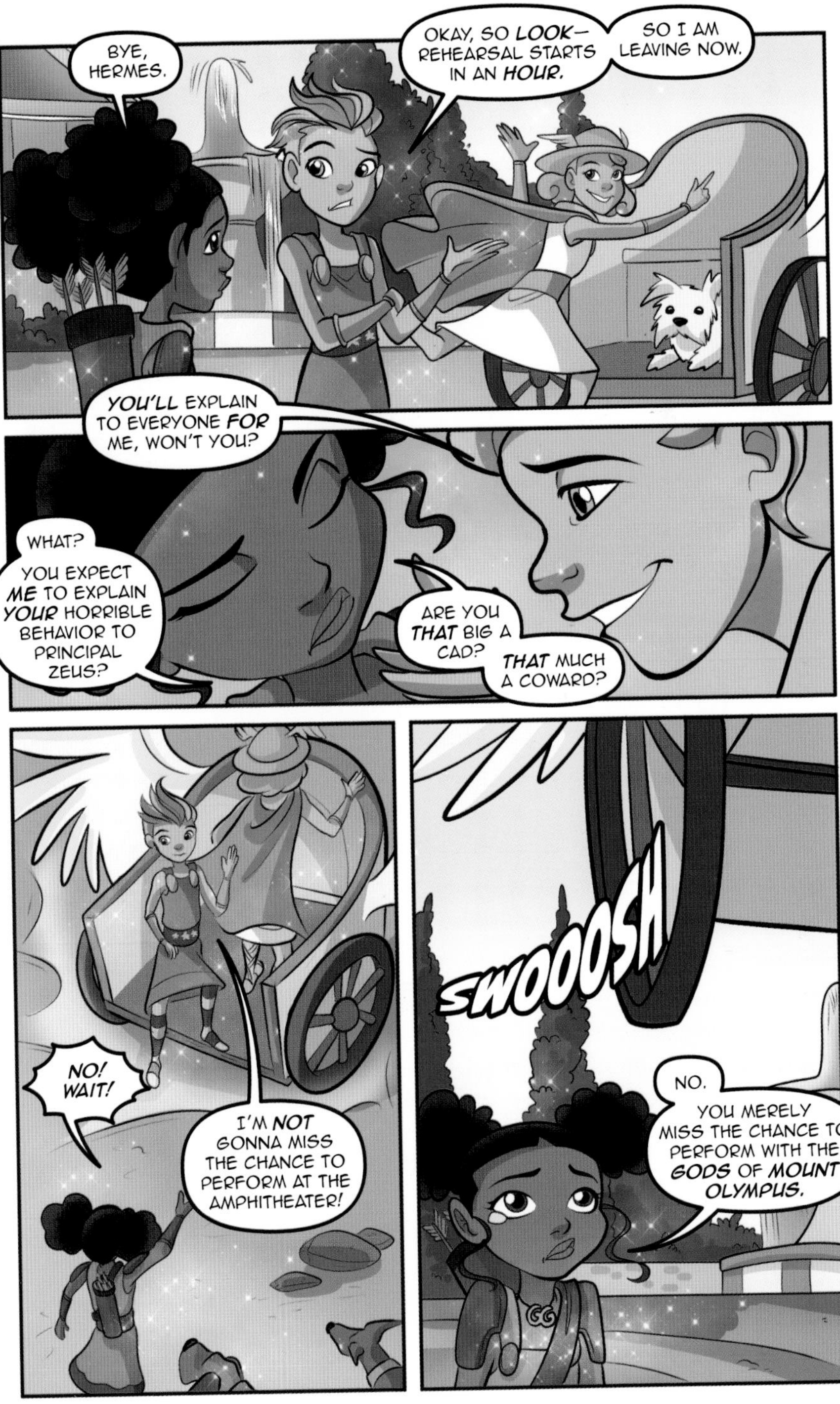

BYE, HERMES.
OKAY, SO LOOK—REHEARSAL STARTS IN AN HOUR.
SO I AM LEAVING NOW.
YOU'LL EXPLAIN TO EVERYONE FOR ME, WON'T YOU?
WHAT?
YOU EXPECT ME TO EXPLAIN YOUR HORRIBLE BEHAVIOR TO PRINCIPAL ZEUS?
ARE YOU THAT BIG A CAD?
THAT MUCH A COWARD?
NO! WAIT!
I'M NOT GONNA MISS THE CHANCE TO PERFORM AT THE AMPHITHEATER!
SWOOOSH
NO.
YOU MERELY MISS THE CHANCE TO PERFORM WITH THE GODS OF MOUNT OLYMPUS.

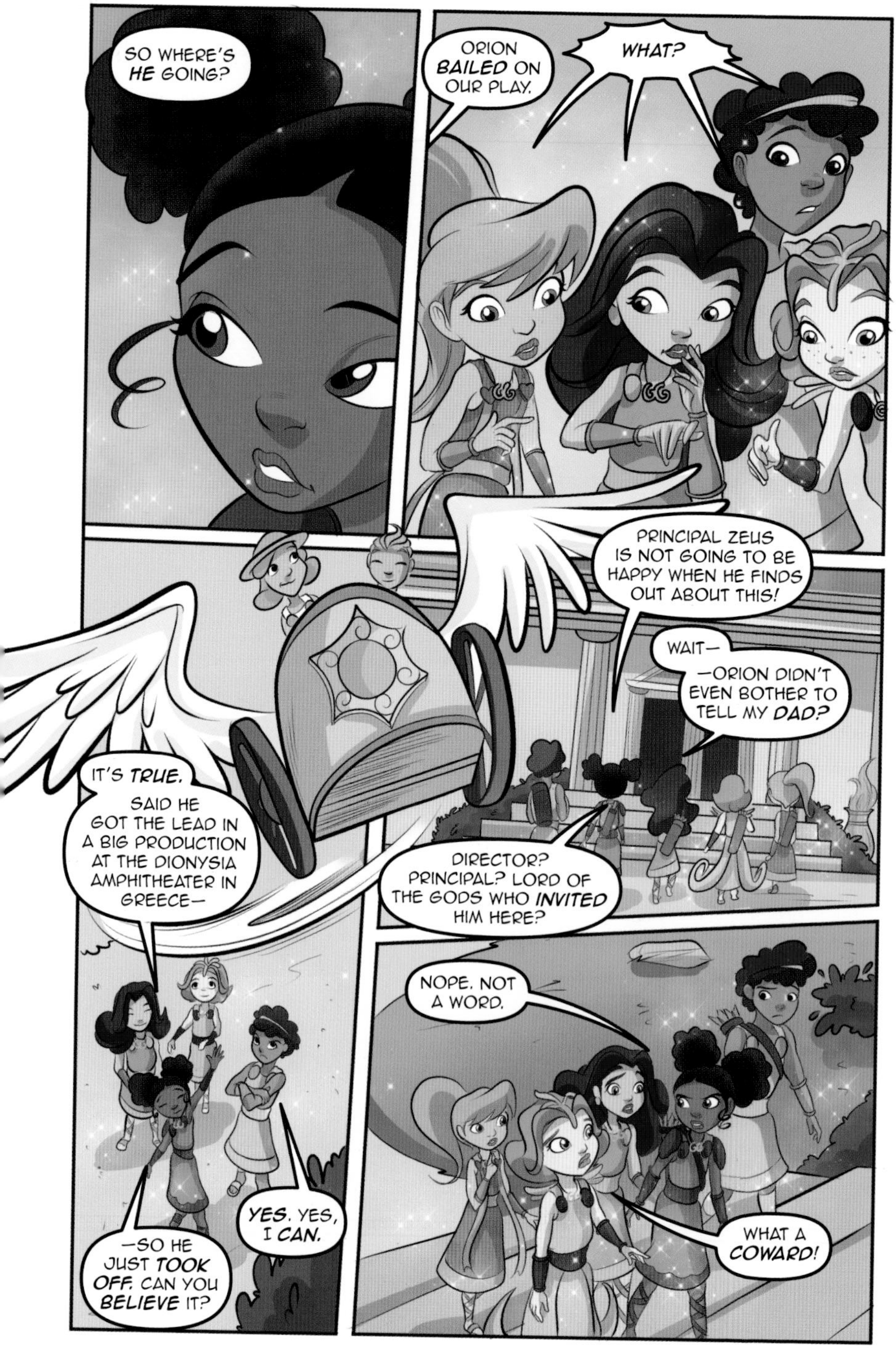
SO WHERE'S HE GOING?
ORION BAILED ON OUR PLAY.
WHAT?
PRINCIPAL ZEUS IS NOT GOING TO BE HAPPY WHEN HE FINDS OUT ABOUT THIS!
WAIT—
—ORION DIDN'T EVEN BOTHER TO TELL MY DAD?
DIRECTOR? PRINCIPAL? LORD OF THE GODS WHO INVITED HIM HERE?
IT'S TRUE.
SAID HE GOT THE LEAD IN A BIG PRODUCTION AT THE DIONYSIA AMPHITHEATER IN GREECE—
—SO HE JUST TOOK OFF. CAN YOU BELIEVE IT?
YES. YES, I CAN.
NOPE. NOT A WORD.
WHAT A COWARD!

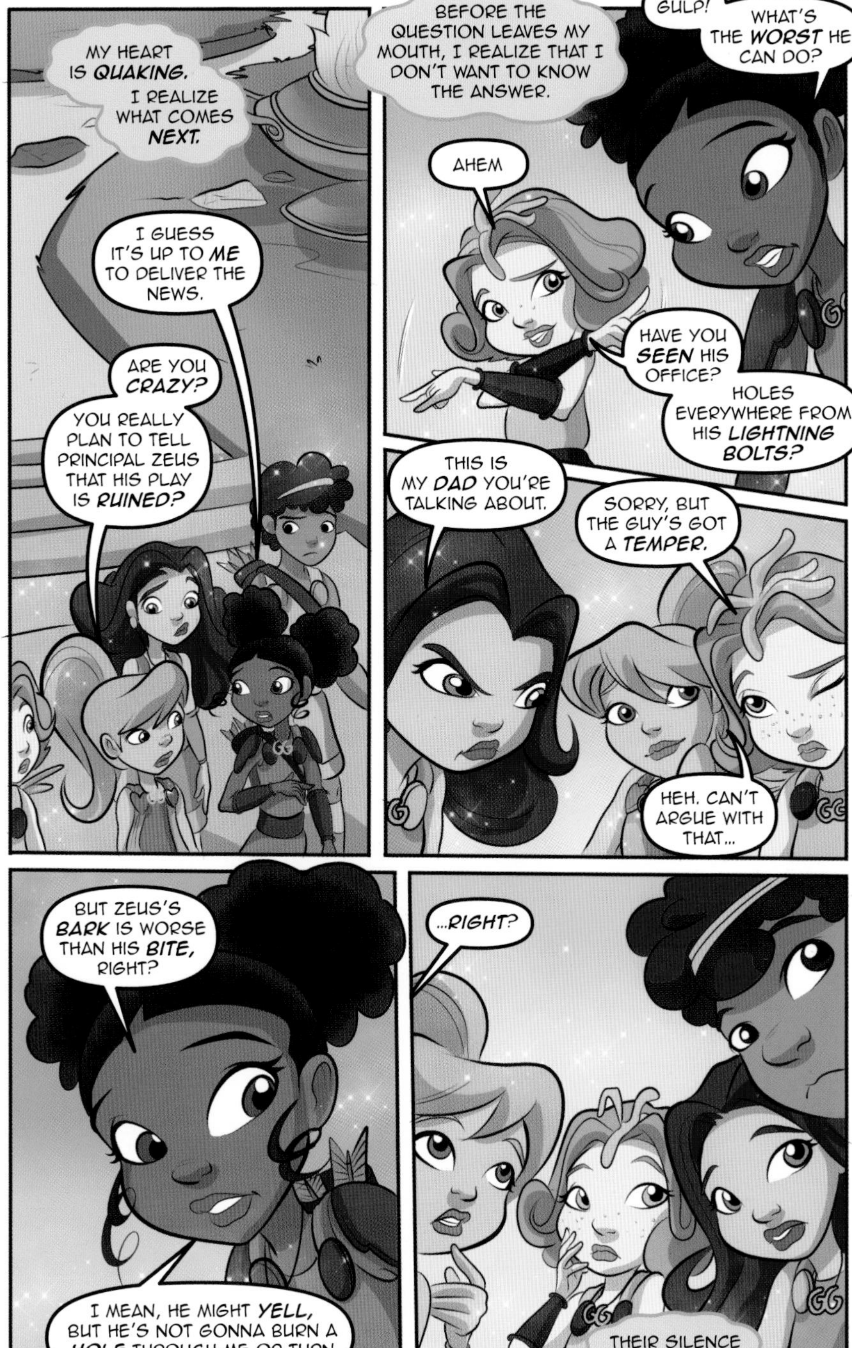
MY HEART IS QUAKING.
I REALIZE WHAT COMES NEXT.
I GUESS IT'S UP TO ME TO DELIVER THE NEWS.
ARE YOU CRAZY?
YOU REALLY PLAN TO TELL PRINCIPAL ZEUS THAT HIS PLAY IS RUINED?
BEFORE THE QUESTION LEAVES MY MOUTH, I REALIZE THAT I DON'T WANT TO KNOW THE ANSWER.
GULP!
WHAT'S THE WORST HE CAN DO?
AHEM
HAVE YOU SEEN HIS OFFICE?
HOLES EVERYWHERE FROM HIS LIGHTNING BOLTS?
THIS IS MY DAD YOU'RE TALKING ABOUT.
SORRY, BUT THE GUY'S GOT A TEMPER.
HEH. CAN'T ARGUE WITH THAT...
BUT ZEUS'S BARK IS WORSE THAN HIS BITE, RIGHT?
I MEAN, HE MIGHT YELL, BUT HE'S NOT GONNA BURN A HOLE THROUGH ME OR TURN ME INTO A TOAD...
...RIGHT?
THEIR SILENCE IS DEAFENING.

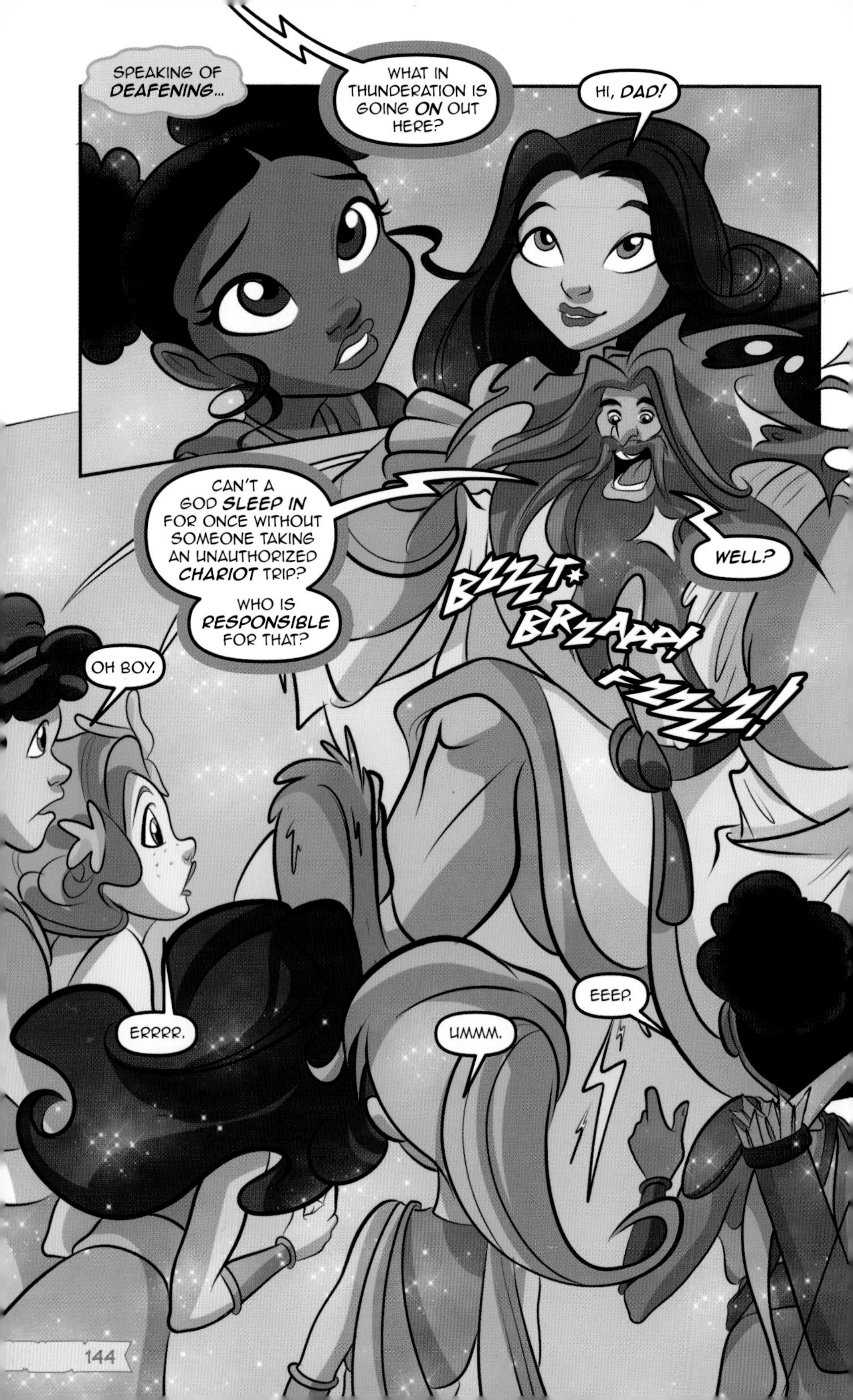
SPEAKING OF DEAFENING...
WHAT IN THUNDERATION IS GOING ON OUT HERE?
HI, DAD!
CAN'T A GOD SLEEP IN FOR ONCE WITHOUT SOMEONE TAKING AN UNAUTHORIZED CHARIOT TRIP?
WHO IS RESPONSIBLE FOR THAT?
WELL?
BZZZT* BRZAPP! FZZZZ!
OH BOY.
EEEP.
ERRRR.
UMMM.

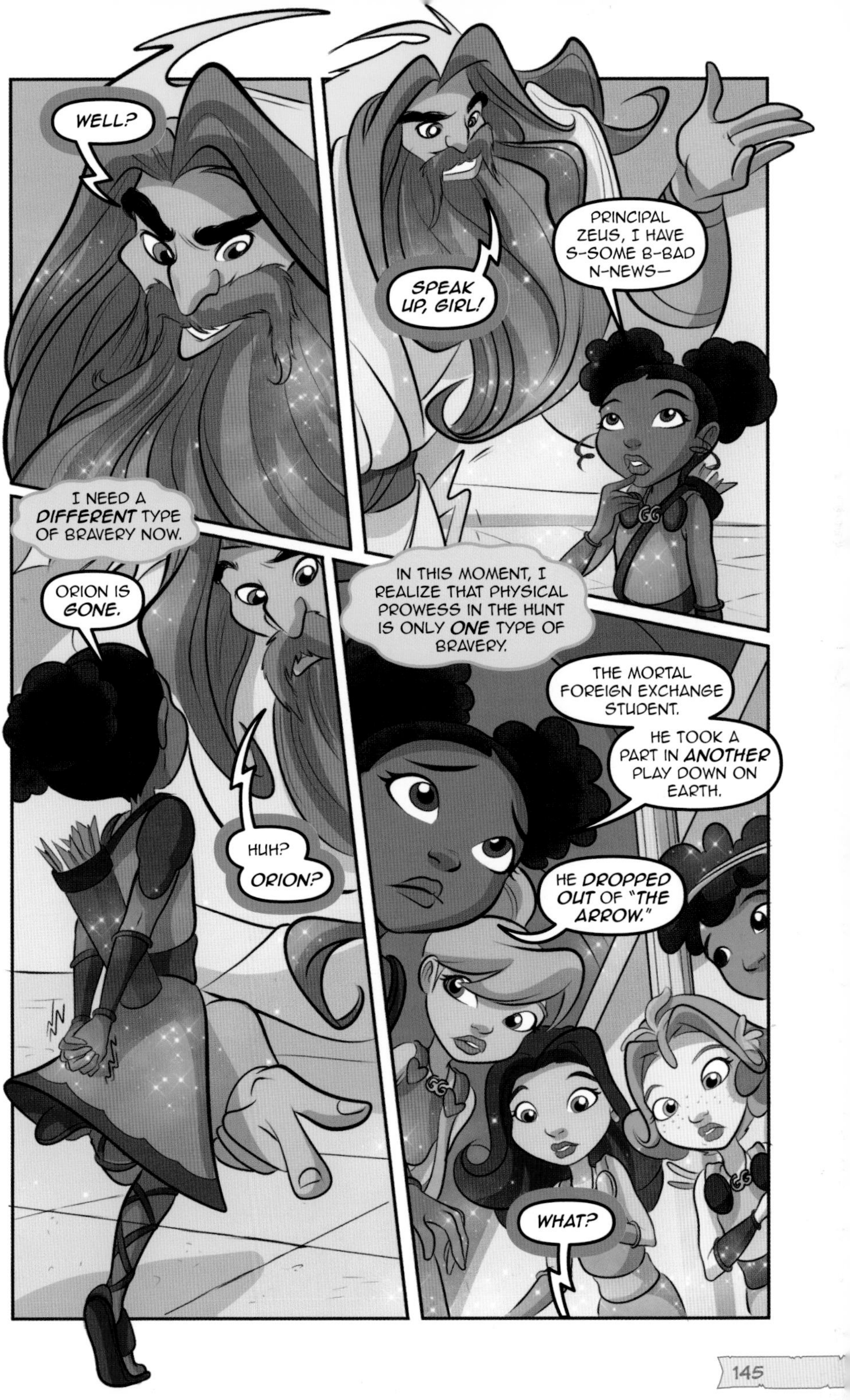
WELL?
SPEAK UP, GIRL!
PRINCIPAL ZEUS, I HAVE S-SOME B-BAD N-NEWS—
I NEED A DIFFERENT TYPE OF BRAVERY NOW.
ORION IS GONE.
HUH? ORION?
IN THIS MOMENT, I REALIZE THAT PHYSICAL PROWESS IN THE HUNT IS ONLY ONE TYPE OF BRAVERY.
THE MORTAL FOREIGN EXCHANGE STUDENT.
HE TOOK A PART IN ANOTHER PLAY DOWN ON EARTH.
HE DROPPED OUT OF "THE ARROW."
WHAT?

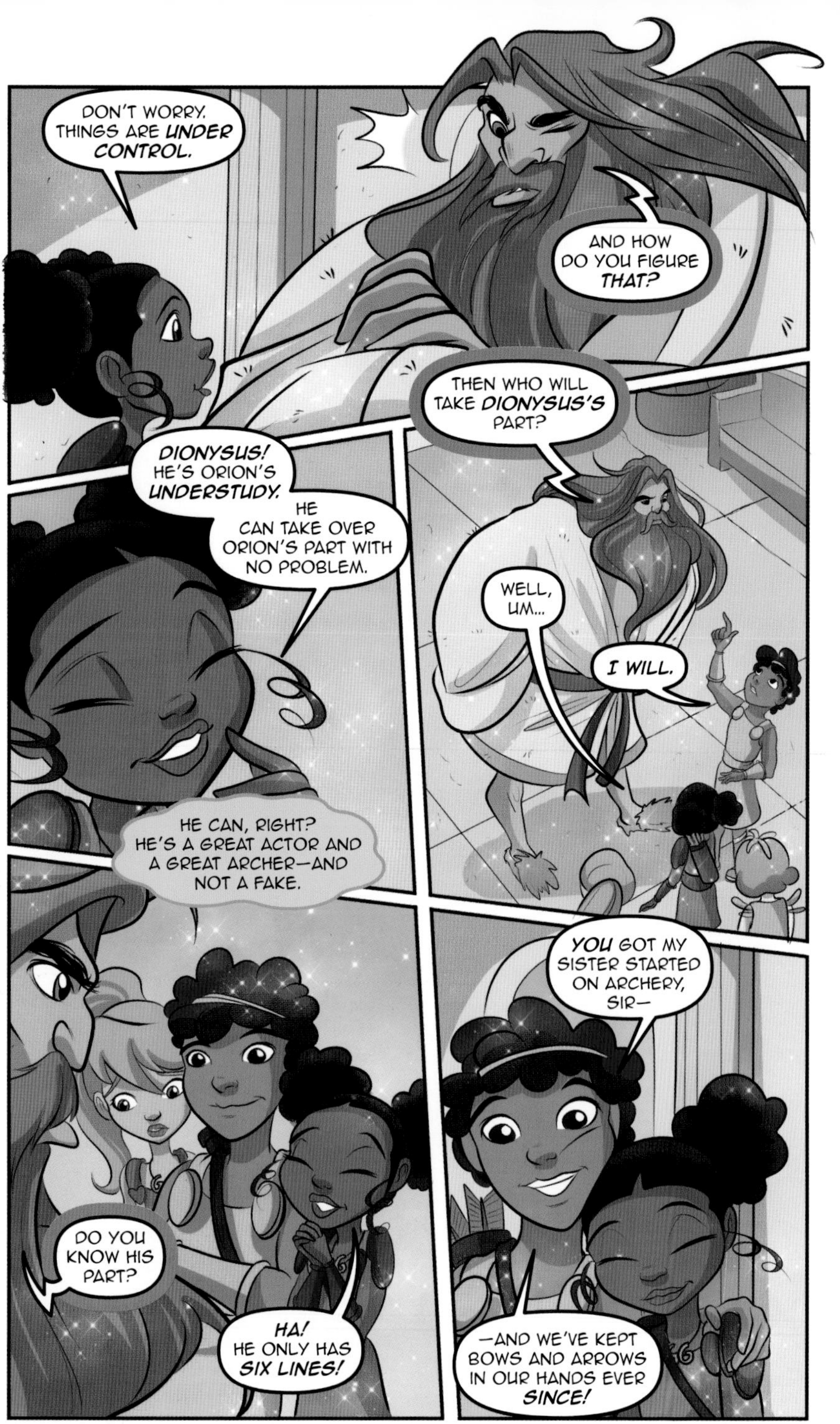
DON'T WORRY. THINGS ARE UNDER CONTROL.
AND HOW DO YOU FIGURE THAT?
THEN WHO WILL TAKE DIONYSUS'S PART?
DIONYSUS! HE'S ORION'S UNDERSTUDY.
HE CAN TAKE OVER ORION'S PART WITH NO PROBLEM.
WELL, UM...
I WILL.
HE CAN, RIGHT? HE'S A GREAT ACTOR AND A GREAT ARCHER—AND NOT A FAKE.
DO YOU KNOW HIS PART?
HA! HE ONLY HAS SIX LINES!
YOU GOT MY SISTER STARTED ON ARCHERY, SIR—
—AND WE'VE KEPT BOWS AND ARROWS IN OUR HANDS EVER SINCE!

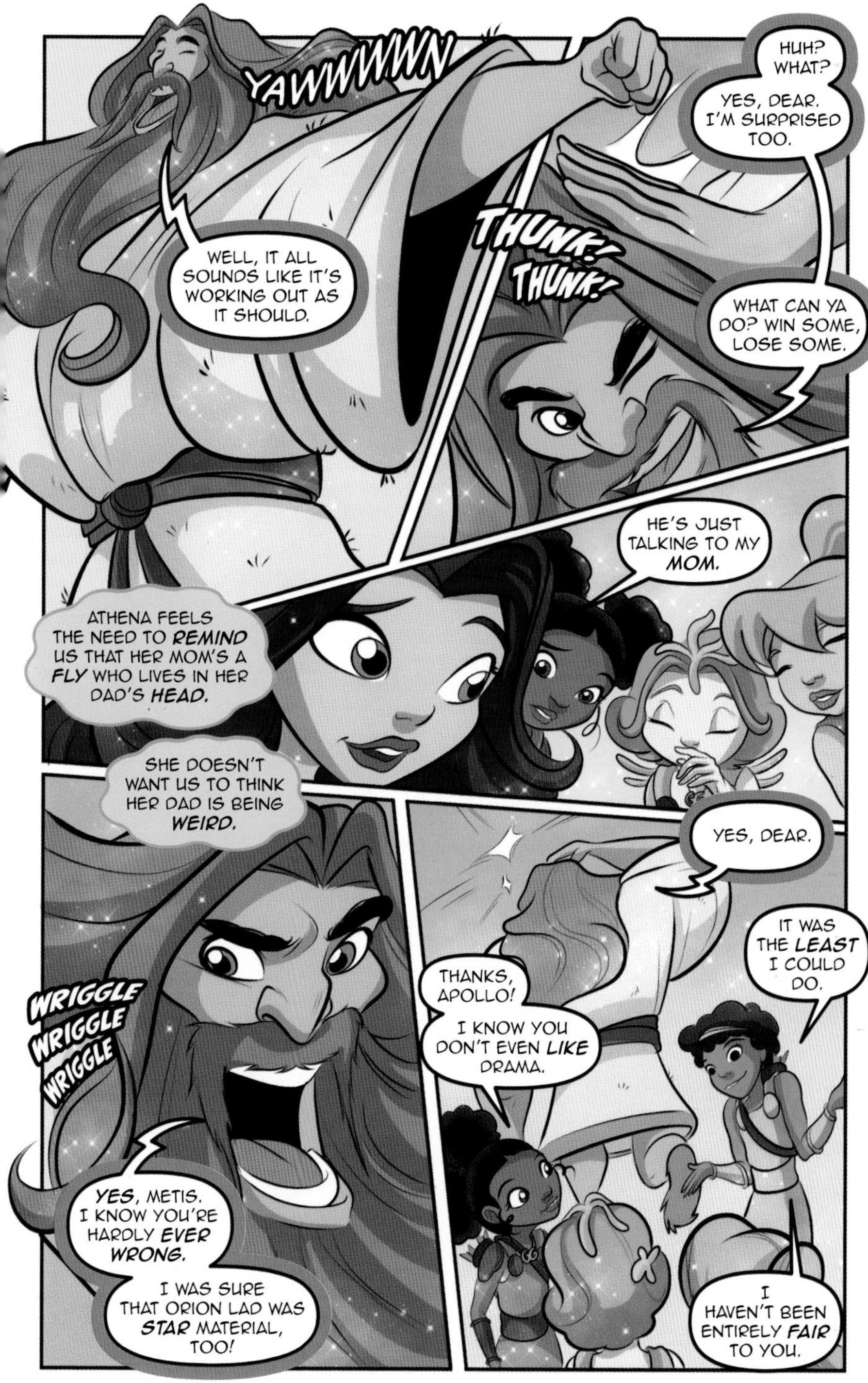
YAWWWWN
WELL, IT ALL SOUNDS LIKE IT'S WORKING OUT AS IT SHOULD.
HUH? WHAT?
YES, DEAR. I'M SURPRISED TOO.
THUNK! THUNK!
WHAT CAN YA DO? WIN SOME, LOSE SOME.
HE'S JUST TALKING TO MY MOM.
ATHENA FEELS THE NEED TO REMIND US THAT HER MOM'S A FLY WHO LIVES IN HER DAD'S HEAD.
SHE DOESN'T WANT US TO THINK HER DAD IS BEING WEIRD.
WRIGGLE WRIGGLE WRIGGLE
YES, METIS. I KNOW YOU'RE HARDLY EVER WRONG.
I WAS SURE THAT ORION LAD WAS STAR MATERIAL, TOO!
YES, DEAR.
THANKS, APOLLO!
I KNOW YOU DON'T EVEN LIKE DRAMA.
IT WAS THE LEAST I COULD DO.
I HAVEN'T BEEN ENTIRELY FAIR TO YOU.

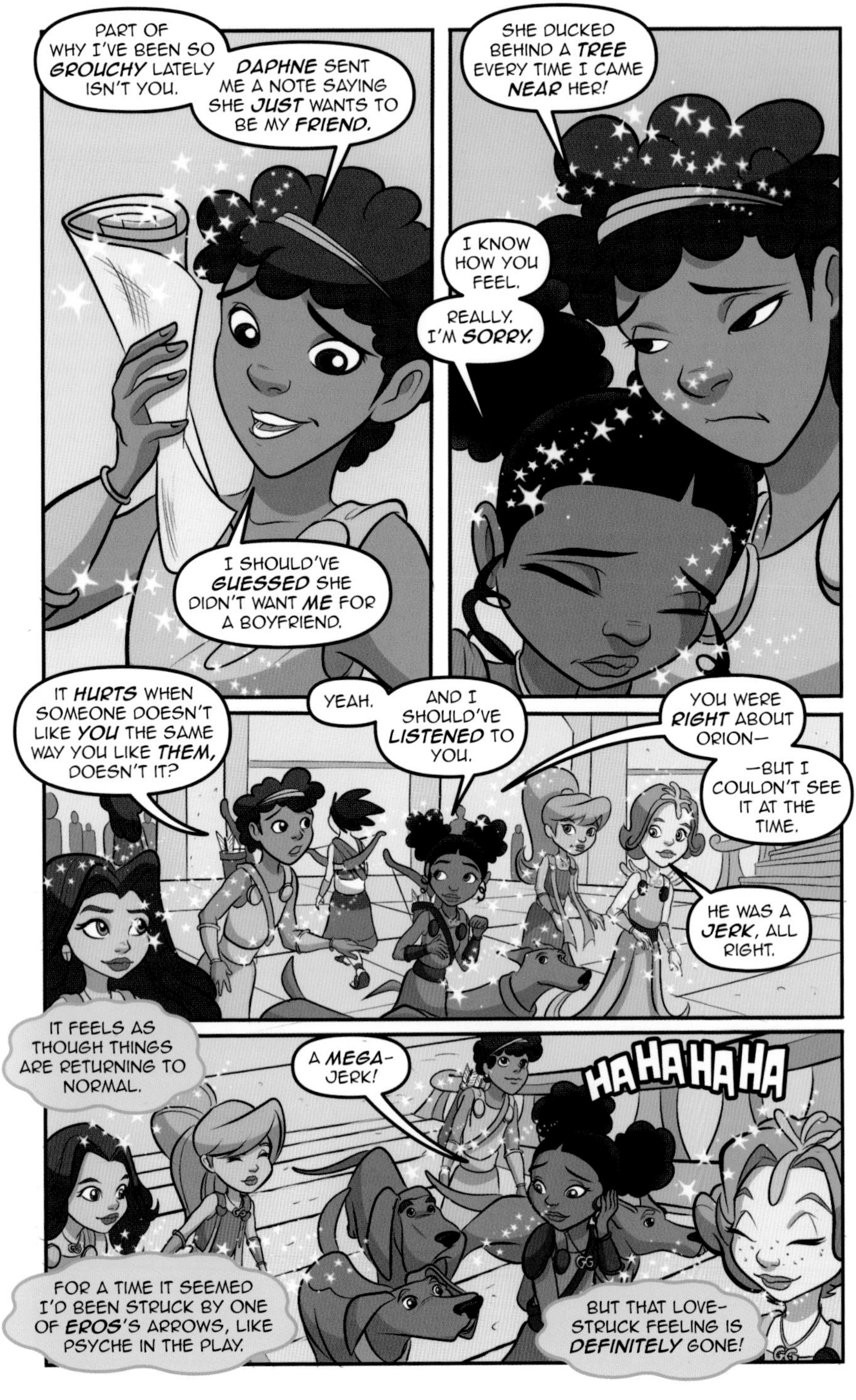
PART OF WHY I'VE BEEN SO GROUCHY LATELY ISN'T YOU.
DAPHNE SENT ME A NOTE SAYING SHE JUST WANTS TO BE MY FRIEND.
I SHOULD'VE GUESSED SHE DIDN'T WANT ME FOR A BOYFRIEND.
SHE DUCKED BEHIND A TREE EVERY TIME I CAME NEAR HER!
I KNOW HOW YOU FEEL.
REALLY. I'M SORRY.
IT HURTS WHEN SOMEONE DOESN'T LIKE YOU THE SAME WAY YOU LIKE THEM, DOESN'T IT?
YEAH.
AND I SHOULD'VE LISTENED TO YOU.
YOU WERE RIGHT ABOUT ORION—
—BUT I COULDN'T SEE IT AT THE TIME.
HE WAS A JERK, ALL RIGHT.
IT FEELS AS THOUGH THINGS ARE RETURNING TO NORMAL.
A MEGA-JERK!
HA HA HA HA
FOR A TIME IT SEEMED I'D BEEN STRUCK BY ONE OF EROS'S ARROWS, LIKE PSYCHE IN THE PLAY.
BUT THAT LOVE-STRUCK FEELING IS DEFINITELY GONE!

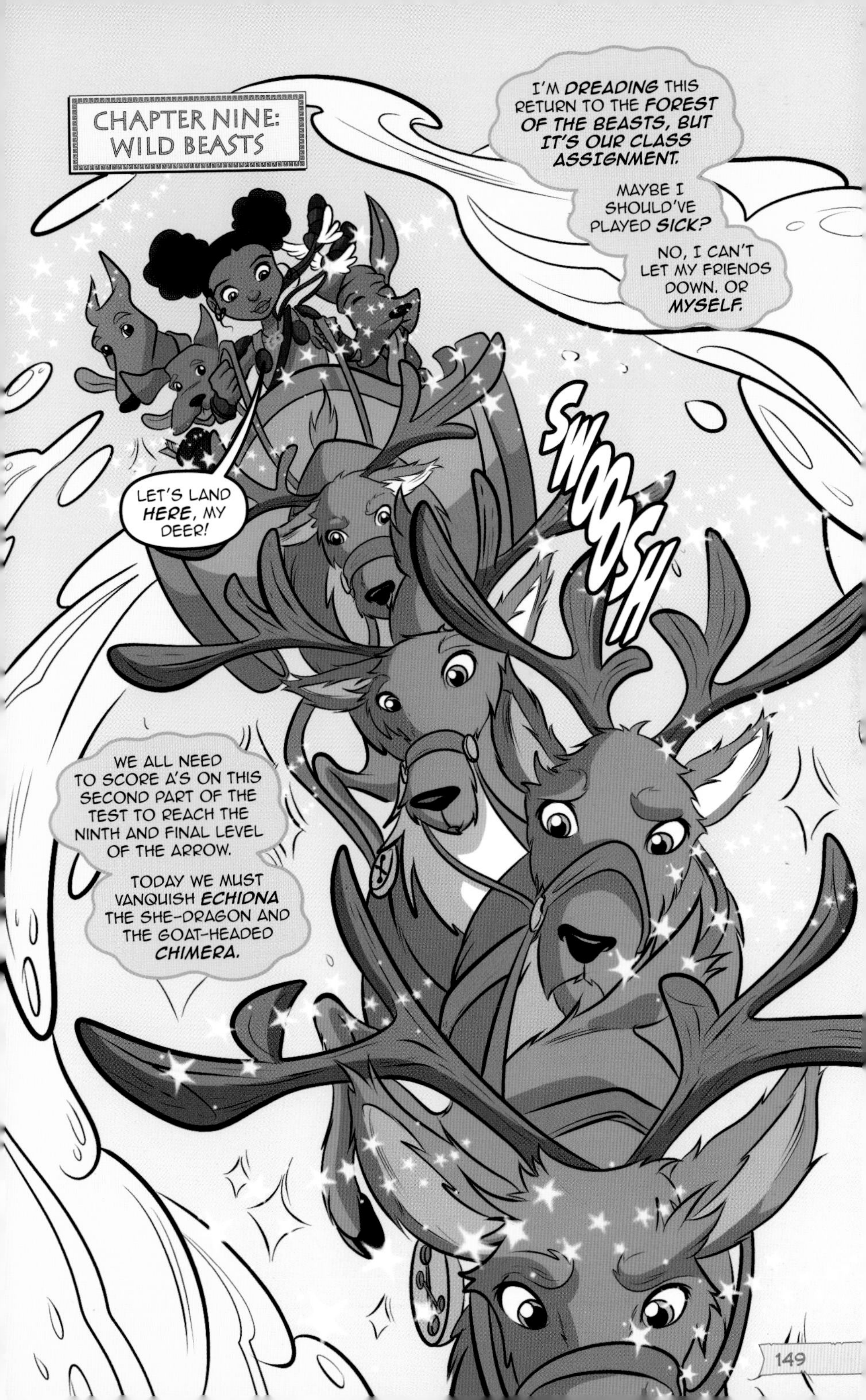
CHAPTER NINE: WILD BEASTS
I'M DREADING THIS RETURN TO THE FOREST OF THE BEASTS, BUT IT'S OUR CLASS ASSIGNMENT.
MAYBE I SHOULD'VE PLAYED SICK?
NO, I CAN'T LET MY FRIENDS DOWN. OR MYSELF.
LET'S LAND HERE, MY DEER!
SWOOOSH
WE ALL NEED TO SCORE A'S ON THIS SECOND PART OF THE TEST TO REACH THE NINTH AND FINAL LEVEL OF THE ARROW.
TODAY WE MUST VANQUISH ECHIDNA THE SHE-DRAGON AND THE GOAT-HEADED CHIMERA.

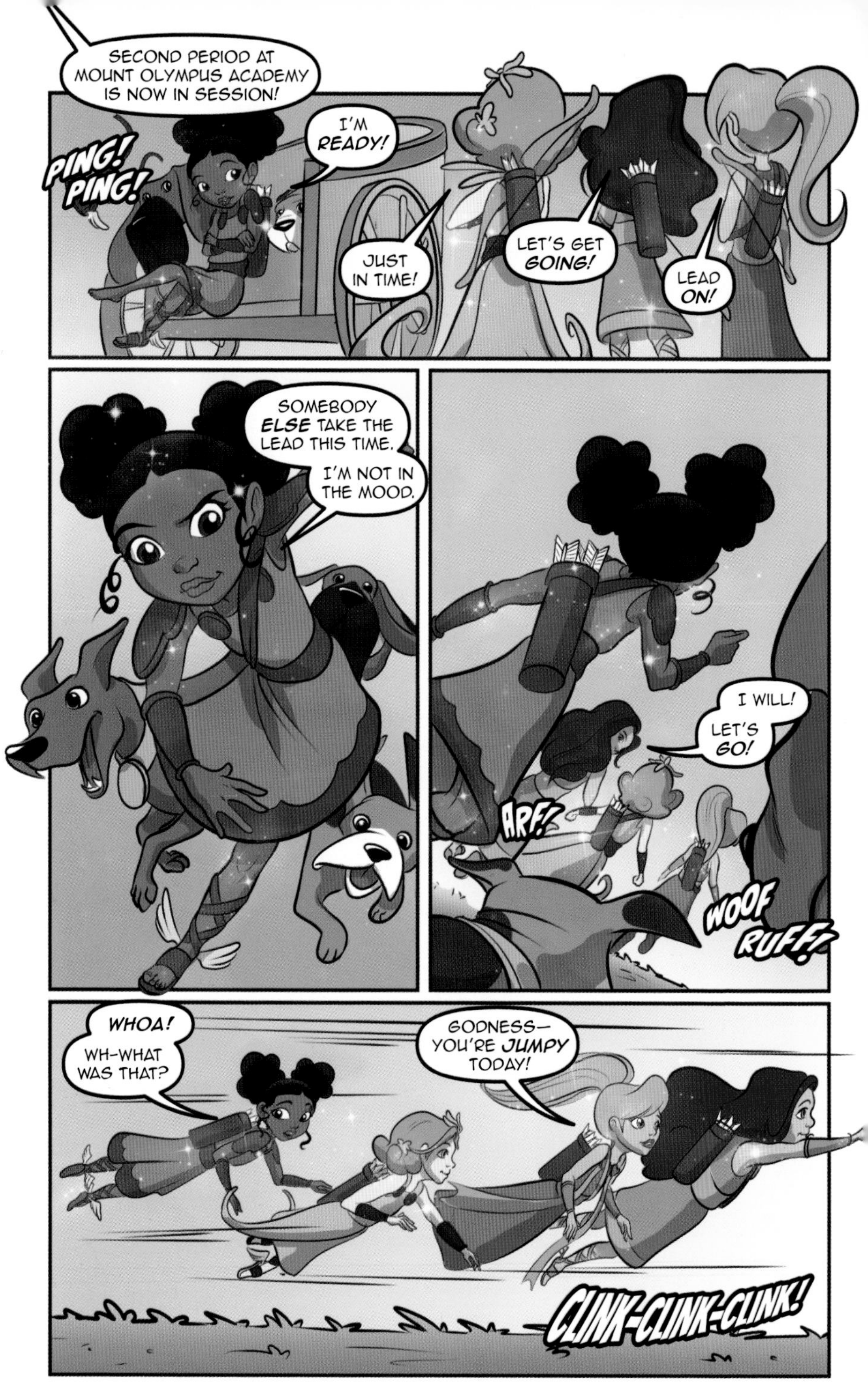
SECOND PERIOD AT MOUNT OLYMPUS ACADEMY IS NOW IN SESSION!
PING! PING!
I'M READY!
JUST IN TIME!
LET'S GET GOING!
LEAD ON!
SOMEBODY ELSE TAKE THE LEAD THIS TIME.
I'M NOT IN THE MOOD.
I WILL!
LET'S GO!
ARF!
WOOF
RUFF!
WHOA!
WH-WHAT WAS THAT?
GODNESS— YOU'RE JUMPY TODAY!
CLINK-CLINK-CLINK!

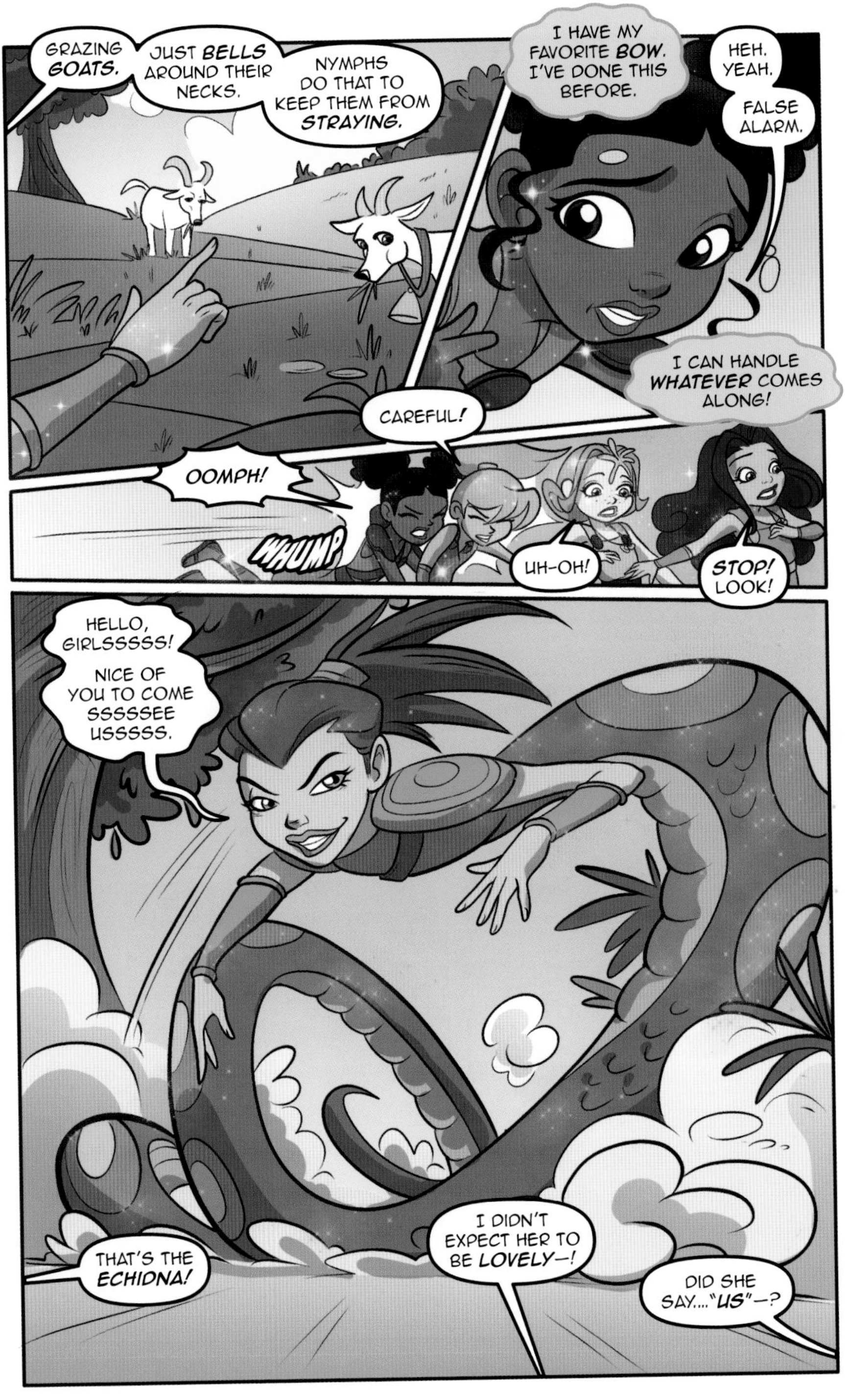
GRAZING GOATS.
JUST BELLS AROUND THEIR NECKS.
NYMPHS DO THAT TO KEEP THEM FROM STRAYING.
I HAVE MY FAVORITE BOW. I'VE DONE THIS BEFORE.
HEH. YEAH.
FALSE ALARM.
I CAN HANDLE WHATEVER COMES ALONG!
CAREFUL!
OOMPH!
WHUMP
UH-OH!
STOP! LOOK!
HELLO, GIRLSSSSS!
NICE OF YOU TO COME SSSSSEE USSSSS.
THAT'S THE ECHIDNA!
I DIDN'T EXPECT HER TO BE LOVELY—!
DID SHE SAY...."US"—?

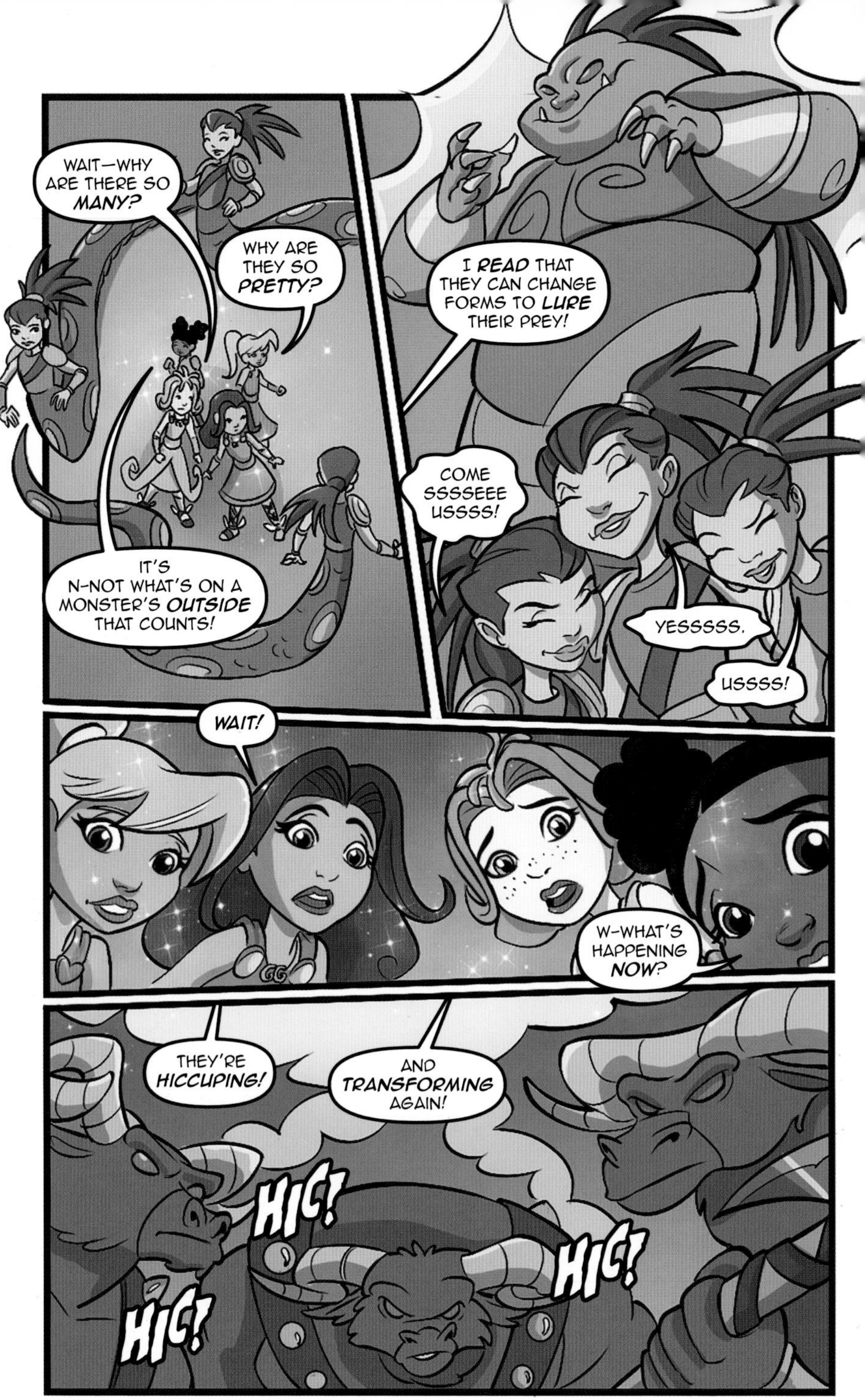
WAIT—WHY ARE THERE SO *MANY?*
WHY ARE THEY SO *PRETTY?*
IT'S N-NOT WHAT'S ON A MONSTER'S *OUTSIDE* THAT COUNTS!
I *READ* THAT THEY CAN CHANGE FORMS TO *LURE* THEIR PREY!
COME SSSSEEE USSSS!
YESSSSS.
USSSS!
WAIT!
W-WHAT'S HAPPENING *NOW?*
THEY'RE *HICCUPING!*
AND *TRANSFORMING* AGAIN!
HIC!
HIC!
HIC!

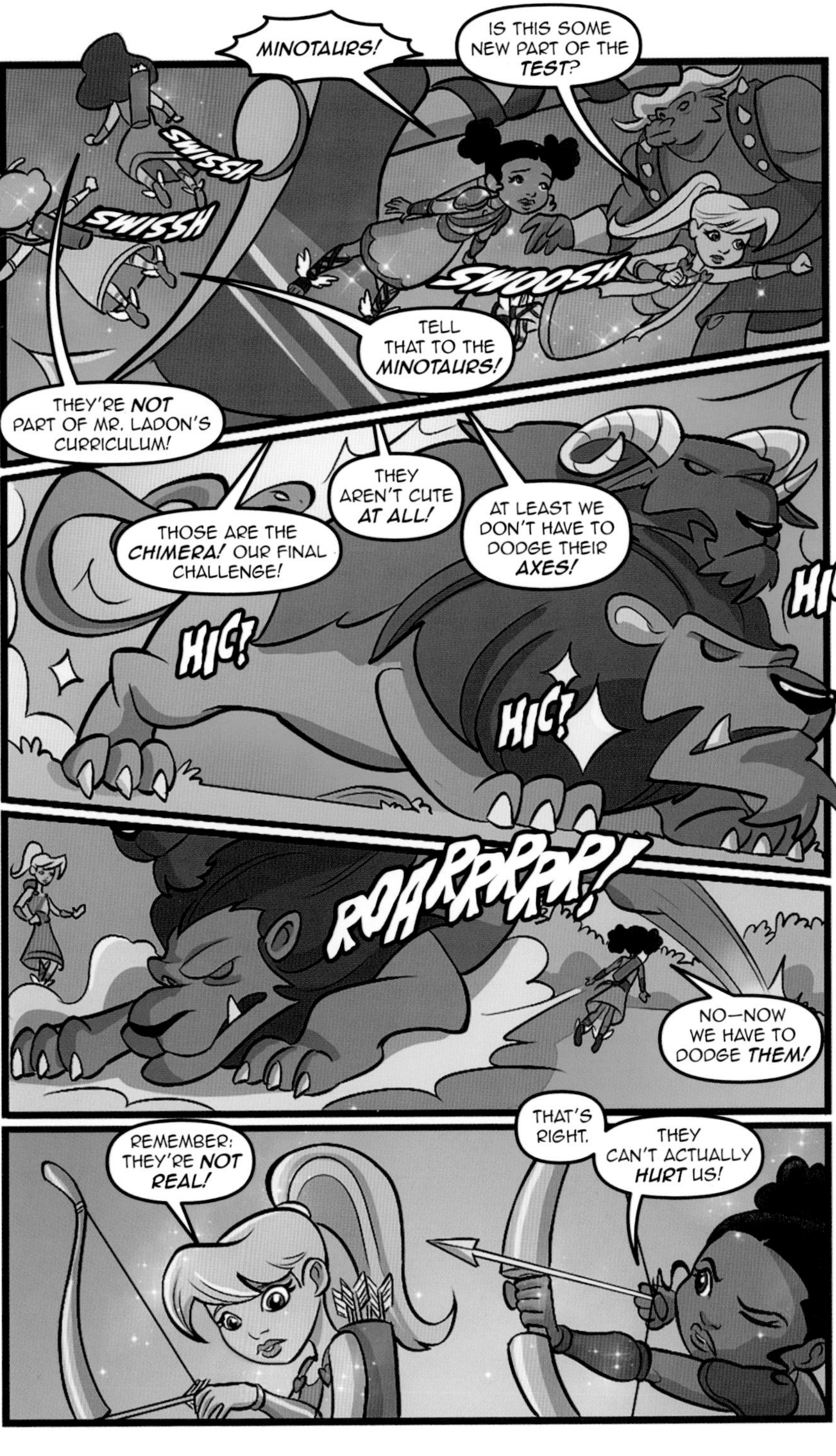
MINOTAURS!
IS THIS SOME NEW PART OF THE TEST?
SWISSH
SWISSH
SWOOSH
TELL THAT TO THE MINOTAURS!
THEY'RE NOT PART OF MR. LADON'S CURRICULUM!
THOSE ARE THE CHIMERA! OUR FINAL CHALLENGE!
THEY AREN'T CUTE AT ALL!
AT LEAST WE DON'T HAVE TO DODGE THEIR AXES!
HIC!
HIC!
HIC!
ROARRRRRR!
NO—NOW WE HAVE TO DODGE THEM!
REMEMBER: THEY'RE NOT REAL!
THAT'S RIGHT.
THEY CAN'T ACTUALLY HURT US!

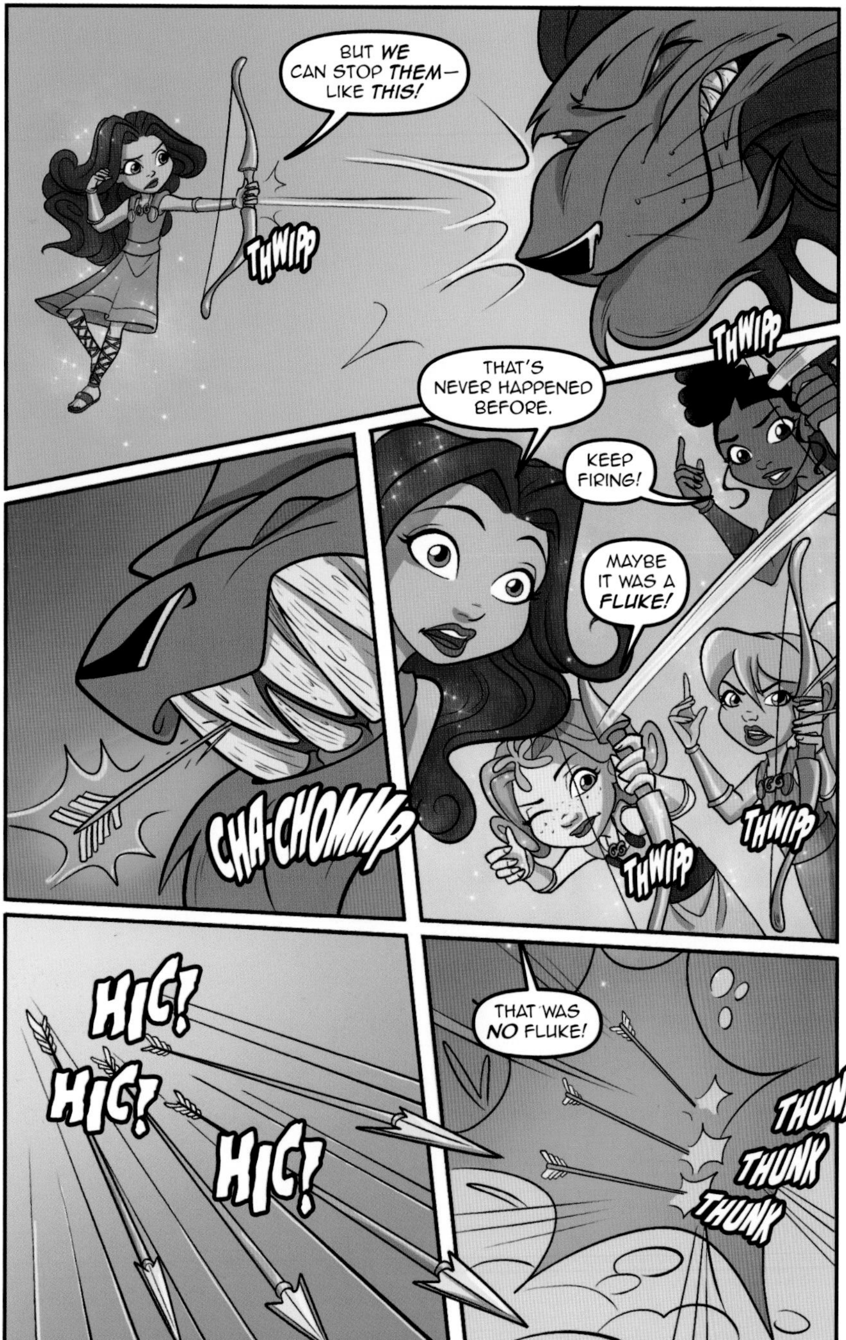
BUT WE CAN STOP THEM— LIKE THIS!
THWIPP
THWIPP
THAT'S NEVER HAPPENED BEFORE.
KEEP FIRING!
MAYBE IT WAS A FLUKE!
CHA-CHOMMP
THWIPP
THWIPP
HIC!
HIC!
HIC!
THAT WAS NO FLUKE!
THUNK
THUNK
THUNK

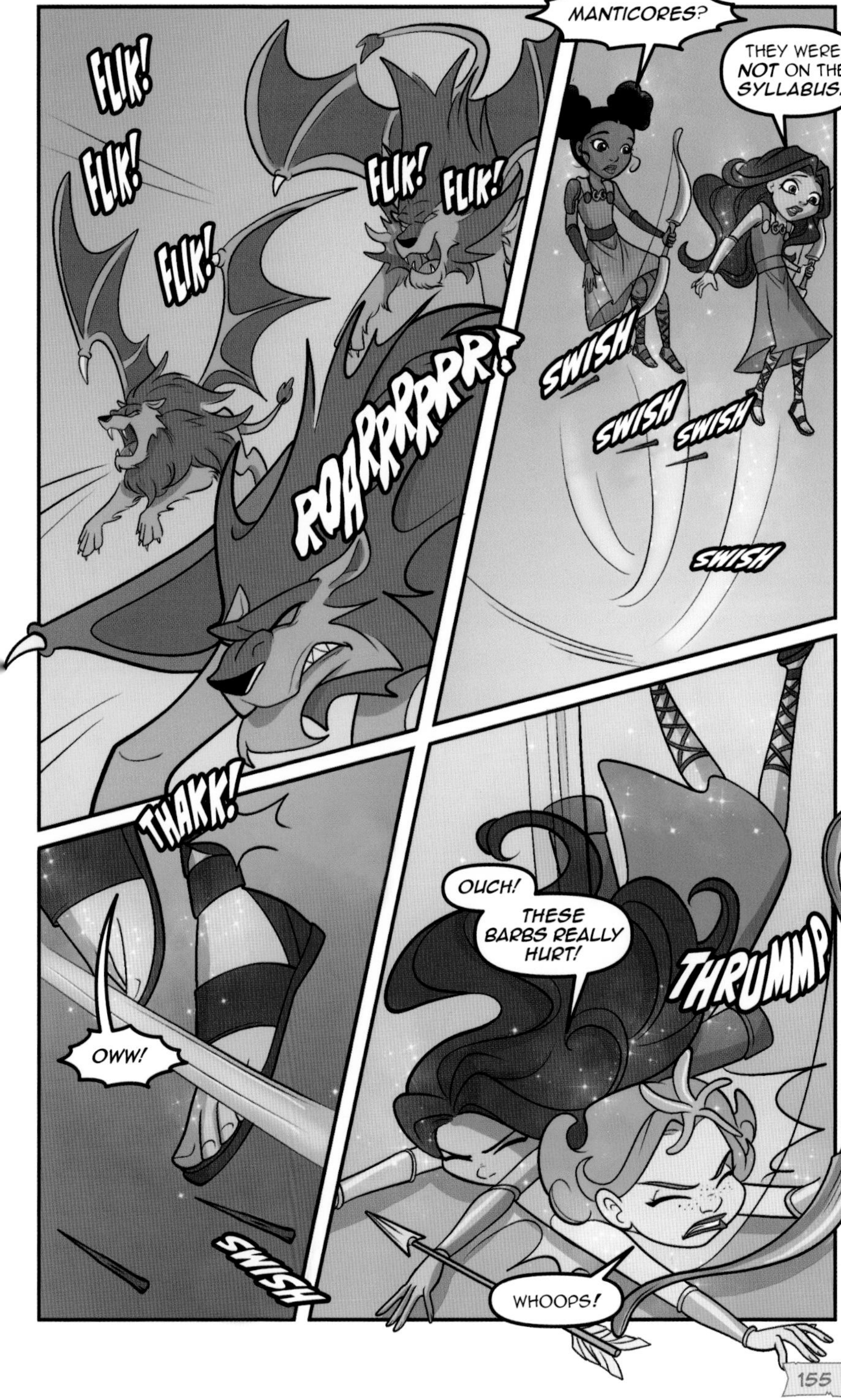
FLIK!
FLIK!
FLIK!
FLIK!
FLIK!
ROARRRRRR!
MANTICORES?
THEY WERE NOT ON THE SYLLABUS!
SWISH
SWISH
SWISH
SWISH
THAKK!
OWW!
SWISH
OUCH!
THESE BARBS REALLY HURT!
THRUMMP
WHOOPS!

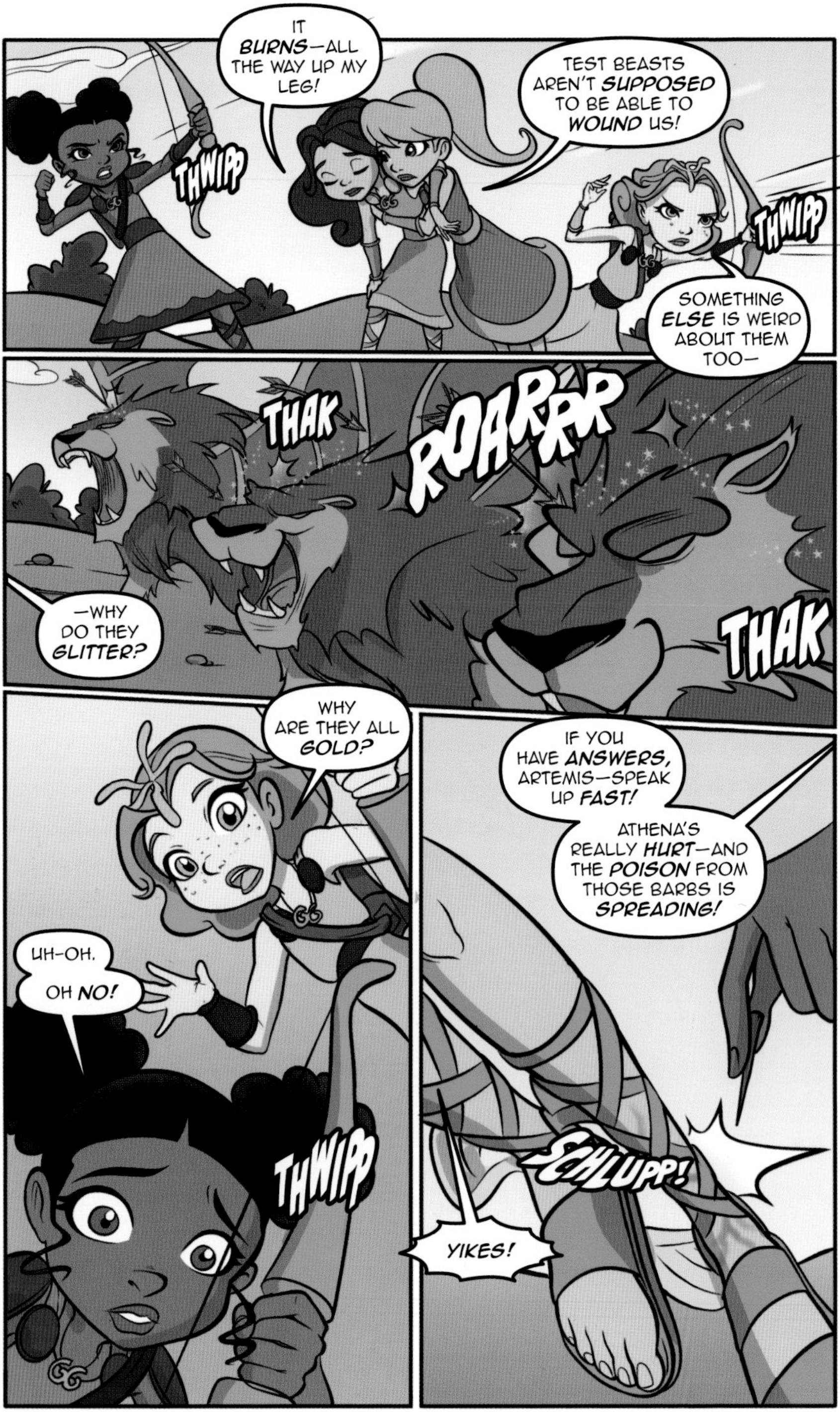

IT BURNS—ALL THE WAY UP MY LEG!
TEST BEASTS AREN'T SUPPOSED TO BE ABLE TO WOUND US!
THWIPP
THWIPP
SOMETHING ELSE IS WEIRD ABOUT THEM TOO—
THAK
ROARRRR
—WHY DO THEY GLITTER?
THAK
WHY ARE THEY ALL GOLD?
IF YOU HAVE ANSWERS, ARTEMIS—SPEAK UP FAST!
ATHENA'S REALLY HURT—AND THE POISON FROM THOSE BARBS IS SPREADING!
UH-OH.
OH NO!
THWIPP
SCHLUPP!
YIKES!

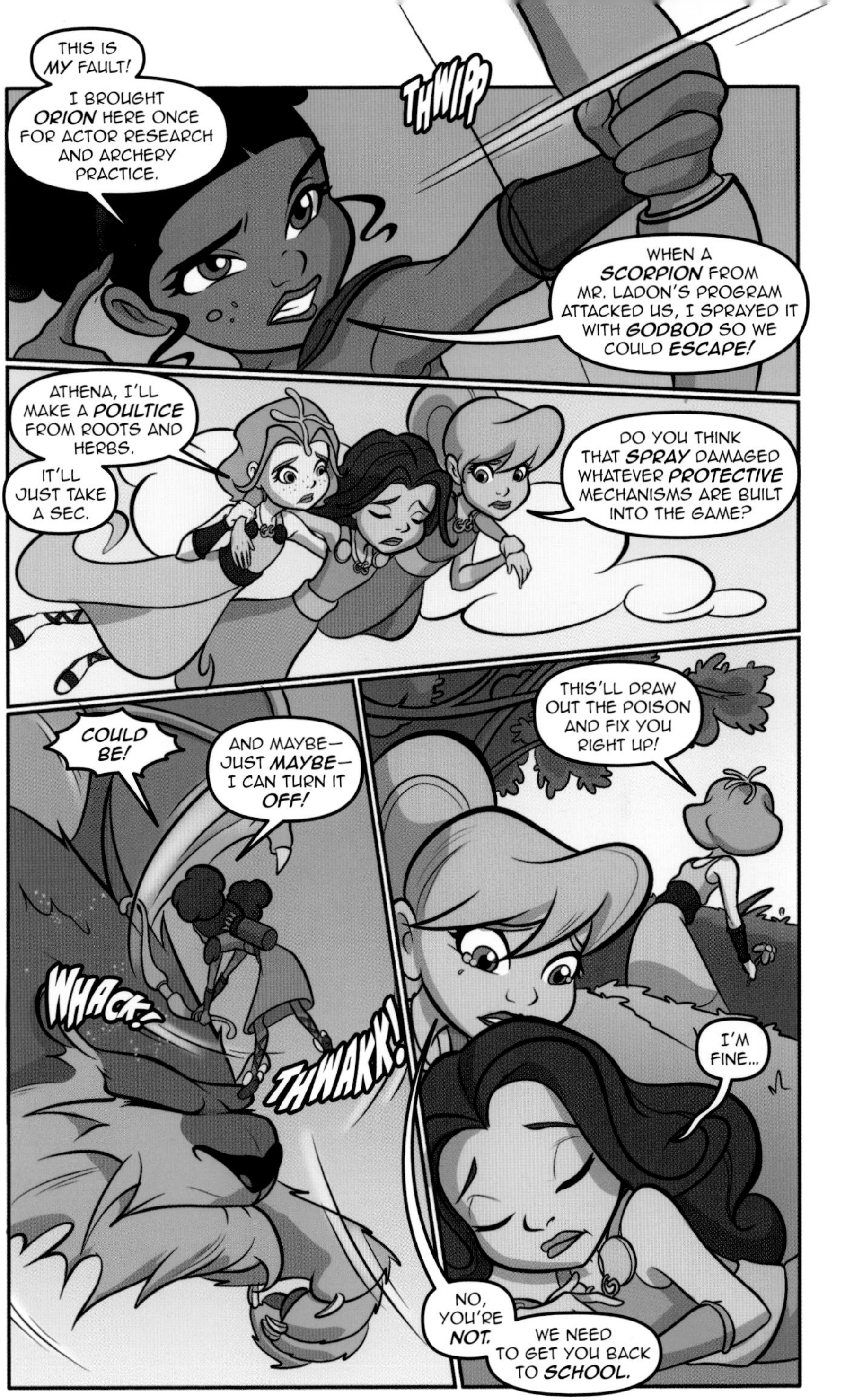
THIS IS MY FAULT!
I BROUGHT ORION HERE ONCE FOR ACTOR RESEARCH AND ARCHERY PRACTICE.
THWIPP
WHEN A SCORPION FROM MR. LADON'S PROGRAM ATTACKED US, I SPRAYED IT WITH GODBOD SO WE COULD ESCAPE!
ATHENA, I'LL MAKE A POULTICE FROM ROOTS AND HERBS.
IT'LL JUST TAKE A SEC.
DO YOU THINK THAT SPRAY DAMAGED WHATEVER PROTECTIVE MECHANISMS ARE BUILT INTO THE GAME?
COULD BE!
AND MAYBE— JUST MAYBE— I CAN TURN IT OFF!
WHACK!
THWAKK!
THIS'LL DRAW OUT THE POISON AND FIX YOU RIGHT UP!
I'M FINE...
NO, YOU'RE NOT.
WE NEED TO GET YOU BACK TO SCHOOL.

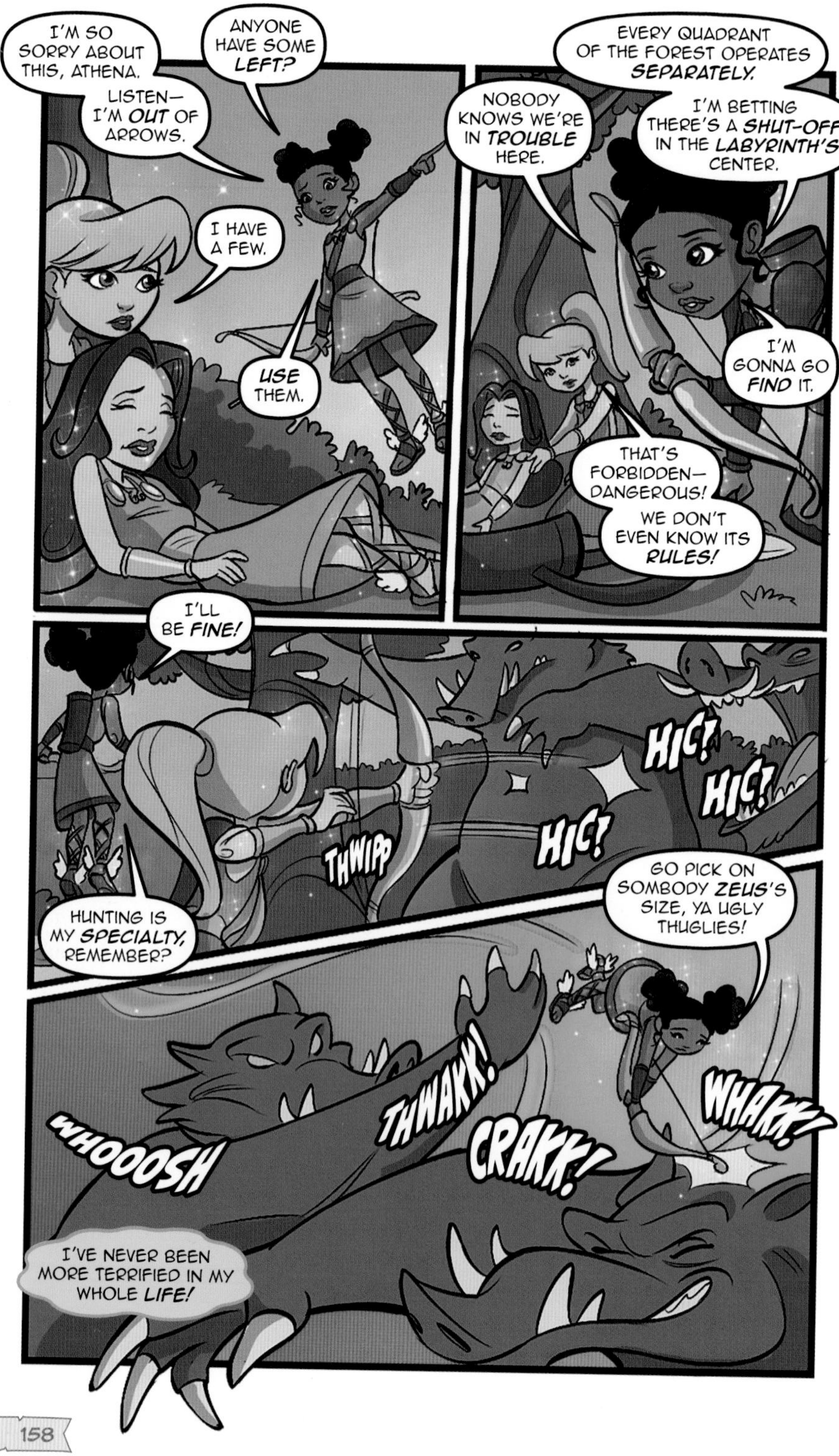
I'M SO SORRY ABOUT THIS, ATHENA.
ANYONE HAVE SOME LEFT?
LISTEN— I'M OUT OF ARROWS.
I HAVE A FEW.
USE THEM.
EVERY QUADRANT OF THE FOREST OPERATES SEPARATELY.
NOBODY KNOWS WE'RE IN TROUBLE HERE.
I'M BETTING THERE'S A SHUT-OFF IN THE LABYRINTH'S CENTER.
I'M GONNA GO FIND IT.
THAT'S FORBIDDEN— DANGEROUS!
WE DON'T EVEN KNOW ITS RULES!
I'LL BE FINE!
HIC!
HIC!
HIC!
THWIPP
HUNTING IS MY SPECIALTY, REMEMBER?
GO PICK ON SOMBODY ZEUS'S SIZE, YA UGLY THUGLIES!
WHOOOSH
THWAKK!
CRAKK!
WHAKK!
I'VE NEVER BEEN MORE TERRIFIED IN MY WHOLE LIFE!

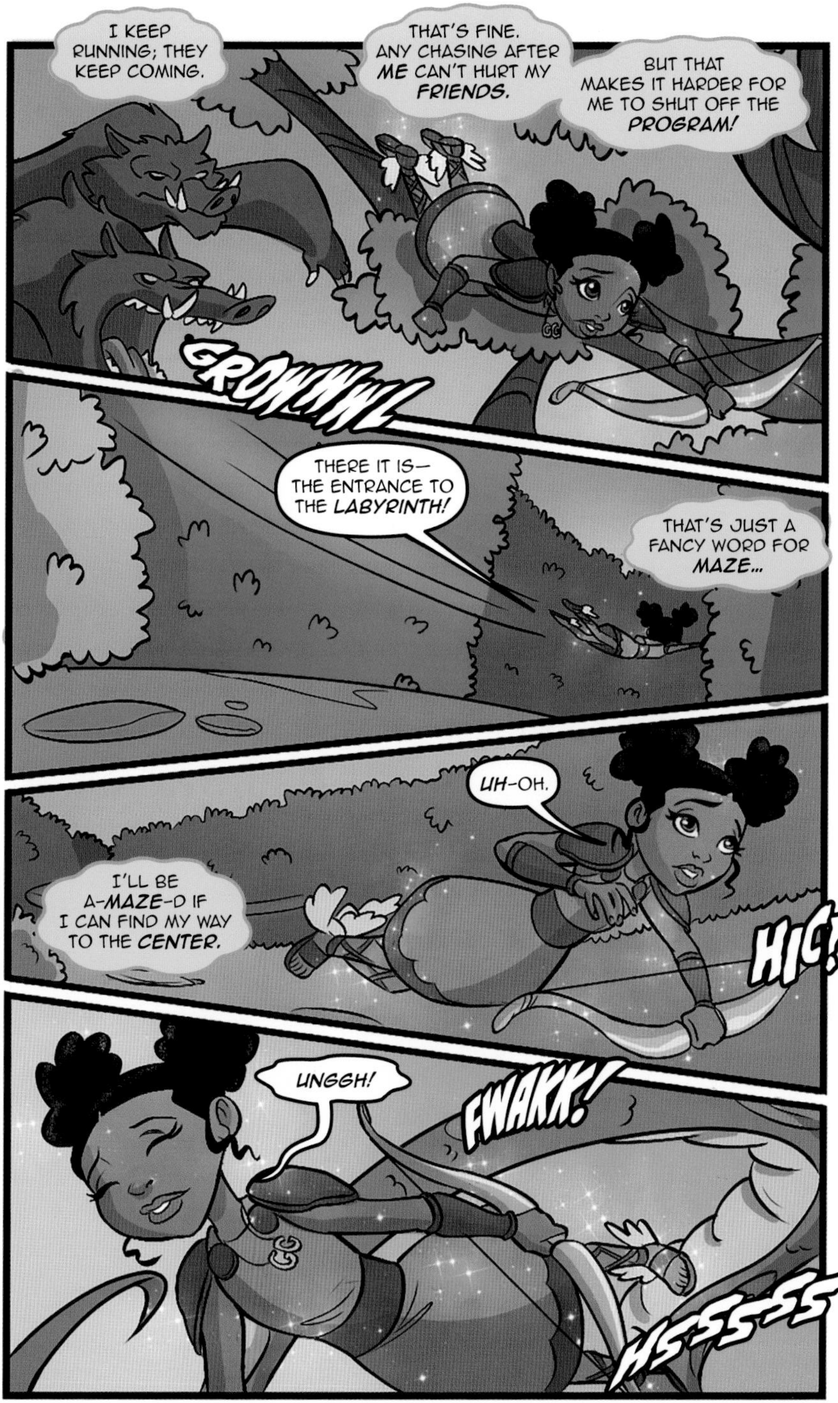
I KEEP RUNNING; THEY KEEP COMING.
THAT'S FINE. ANY CHASING AFTER ME CAN'T HURT MY FRIENDS.
BUT THAT MAKES IT HARDER FOR ME TO SHUT OFF THE PROGRAM!
GROWWWL
THERE IT IS— THE ENTRANCE TO THE LABYRINTH!
THAT'S JUST A FANCY WORD FOR MAZE...
UH-OH.
I'LL BE A-MAZE-D IF I CAN FIND MY WAY TO THE CENTER.
HIC!
UNGGH!
FWAKK!
HSSSSS

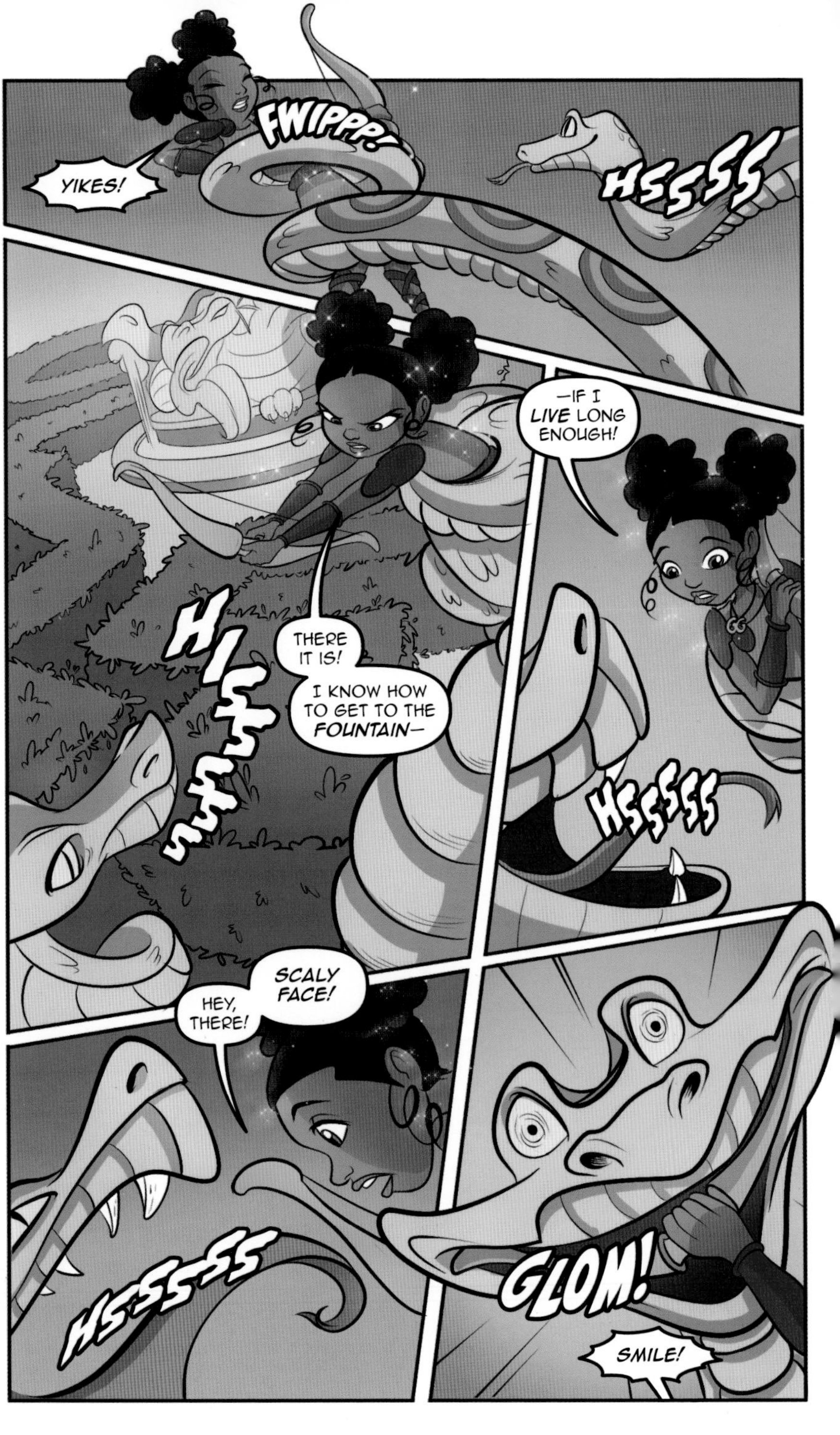
FWIPPP!
YIKES!
HSSSSS
THERE IT IS!
I KNOW HOW TO GET TO THE *FOUNTAIN*—
HISSSSS
—IF I *LIVE* LONG ENOUGH!
HSSSSS
HEY, THERE!
SCALY FACE!
HSSSSSS
GLOM!
SMILE!

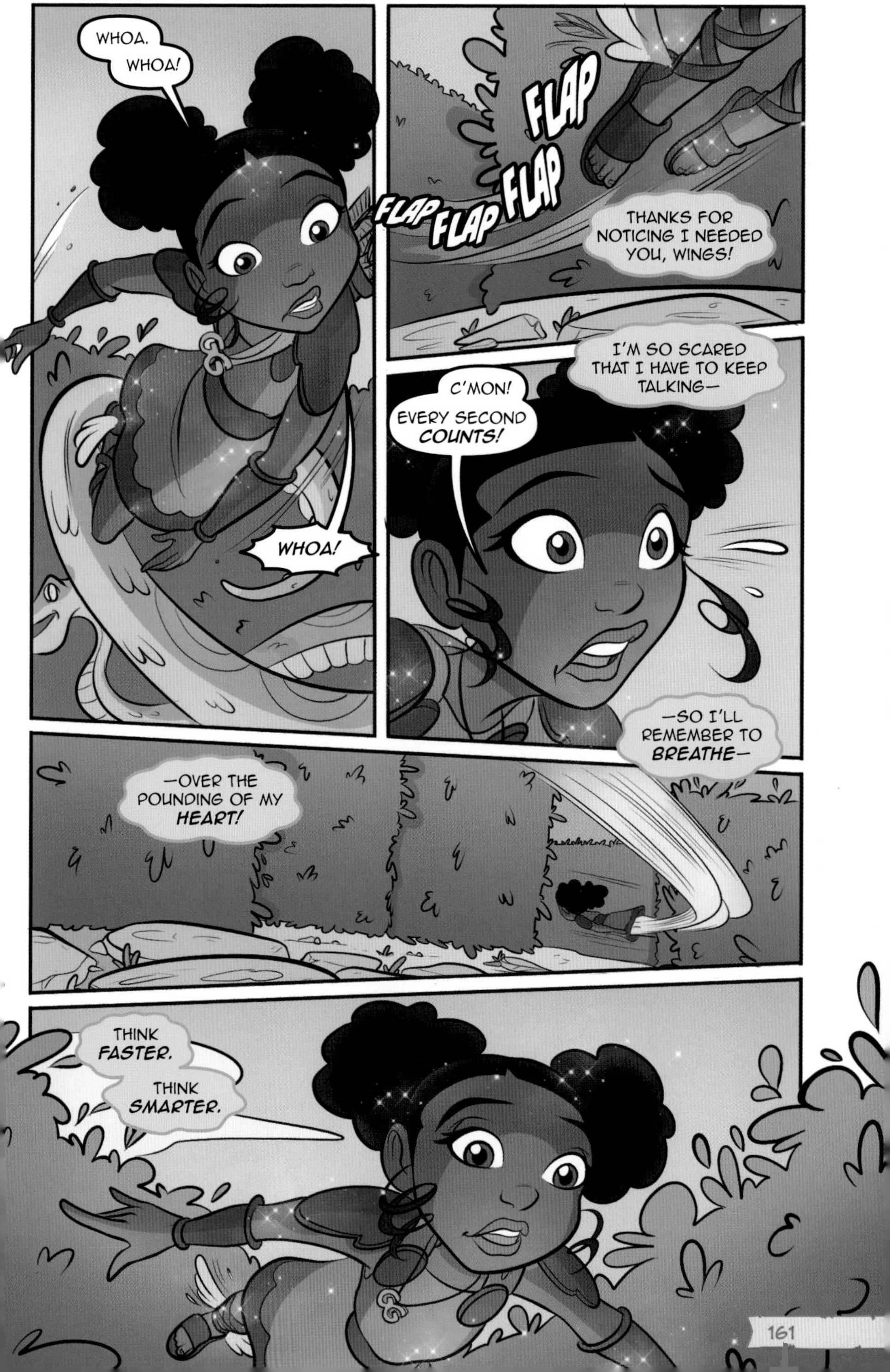
WHOA.
WHOA!
FLAP FLAP FLAP FLAP FLAP
THANKS FOR NOTICING I NEEDED YOU, WINGS!
WHOA!
I'M SO SCARED THAT I HAVE TO KEEP TALKING—
C'MON! EVERY SECOND COUNTS!
—SO I'LL REMEMBER TO BREATHE—
—OVER THE POUNDING OF MY HEART!
THINK FASTER.
THINK SMARTER.

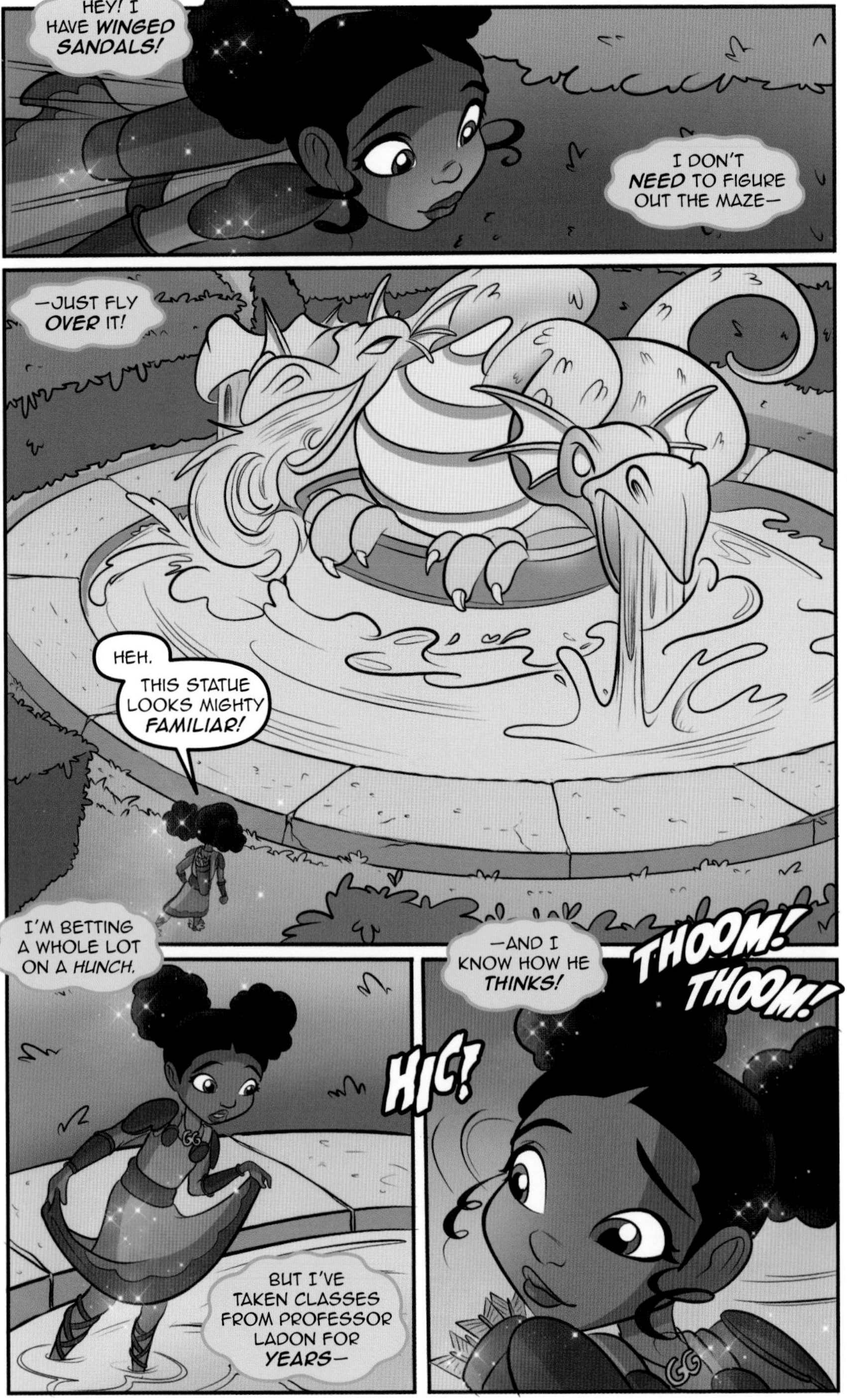
HEY! I HAVE WINGED SANDALS!
I DON'T NEED TO FIGURE OUT THE MAZE—
—JUST FLY OVER IT!
HEH. THIS STATUE LOOKS MIGHTY FAMILIAR!
I'M BETTING A WHOLE LOT ON A HUNCH.
BUT I'VE TAKEN CLASSES FROM PROFESSOR LADON FOR YEARS—
—AND I KNOW HOW HE THINKS!
THOOM! THOOM!
HIC!

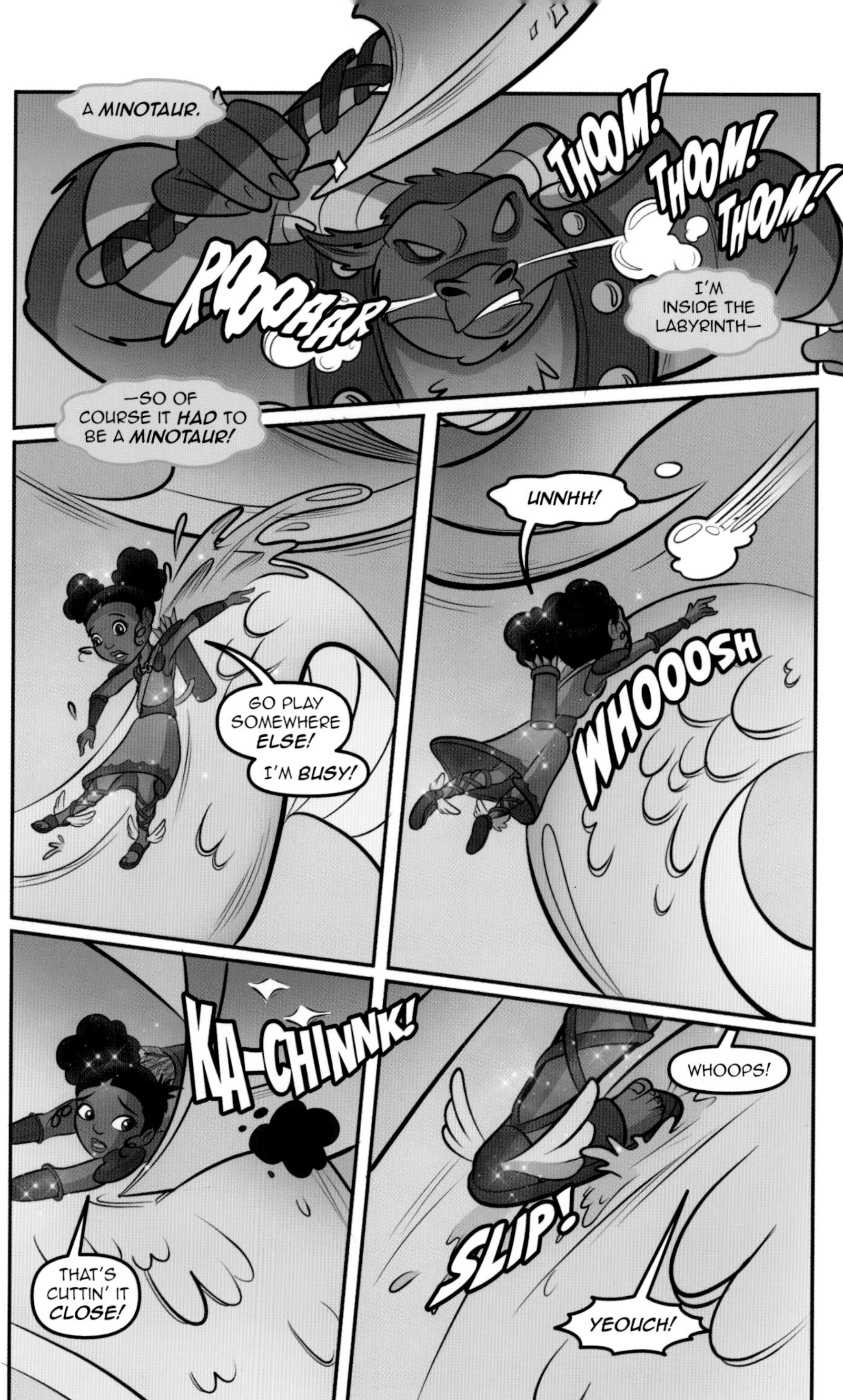
A MINOTAUR.
THOOM! THOOM! THOOM!
ROOOAAAR
I'M INSIDE THE LABYRINTH—
—SO OF COURSE IT HAD TO BE A MINOTAUR!
GO PLAY SOMEWHERE ELSE!
I'M BUSY!
UNNHH!
WHOOOOSH
KA-CHINNK!
THAT'S CUTTIN' IT CLOSE!
WHOOPS!
SLIP!
YEOUCH!

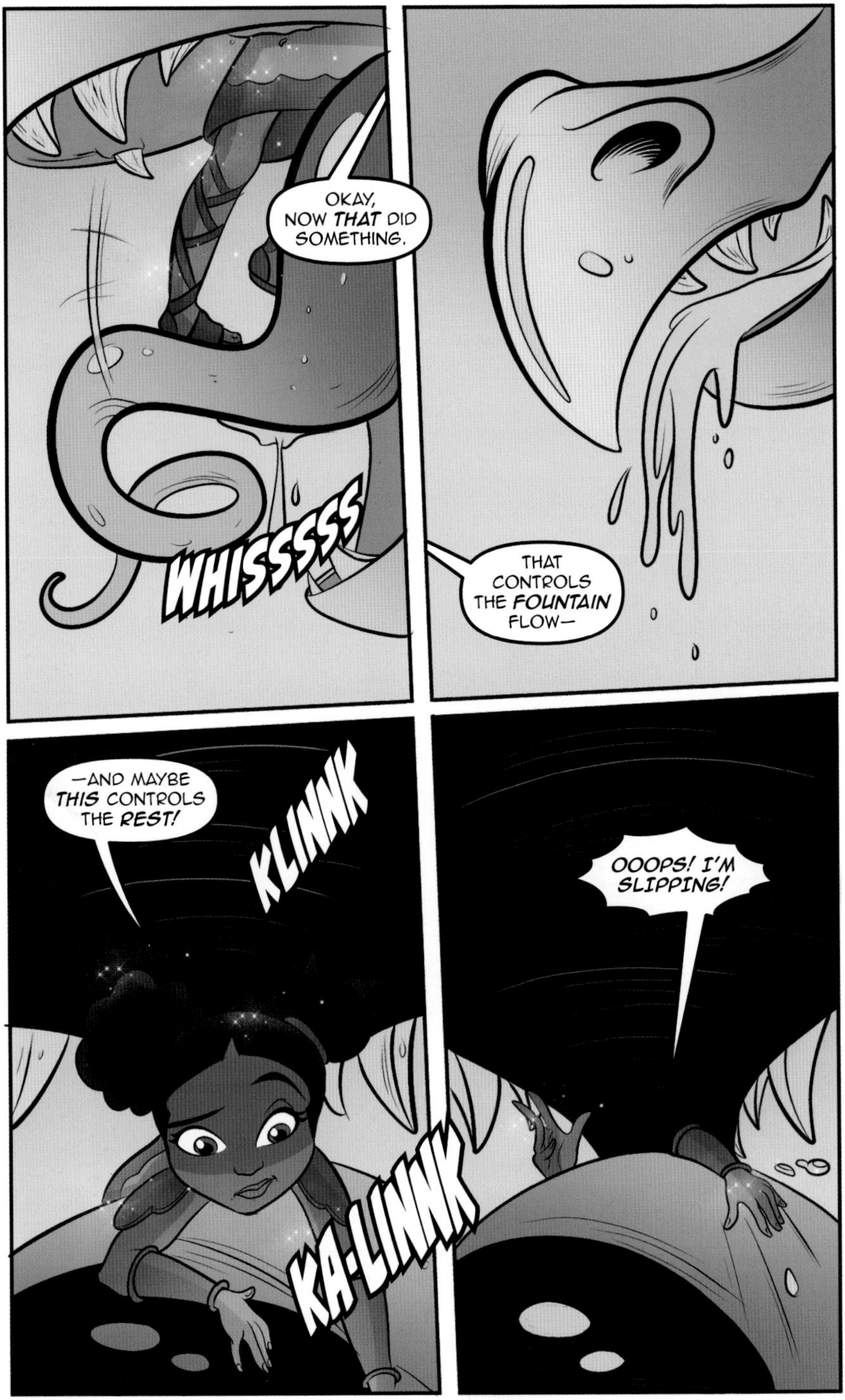
OKAY, NOW THAT DID SOMETHING.
WHISSSSS
THAT CONTROLS THE FOUNTAIN FLOW—
—AND MAYBE THIS CONTROLS THE REST!
KLINNK
KA-LINNK
OOOPS! I'M SLIPPING!

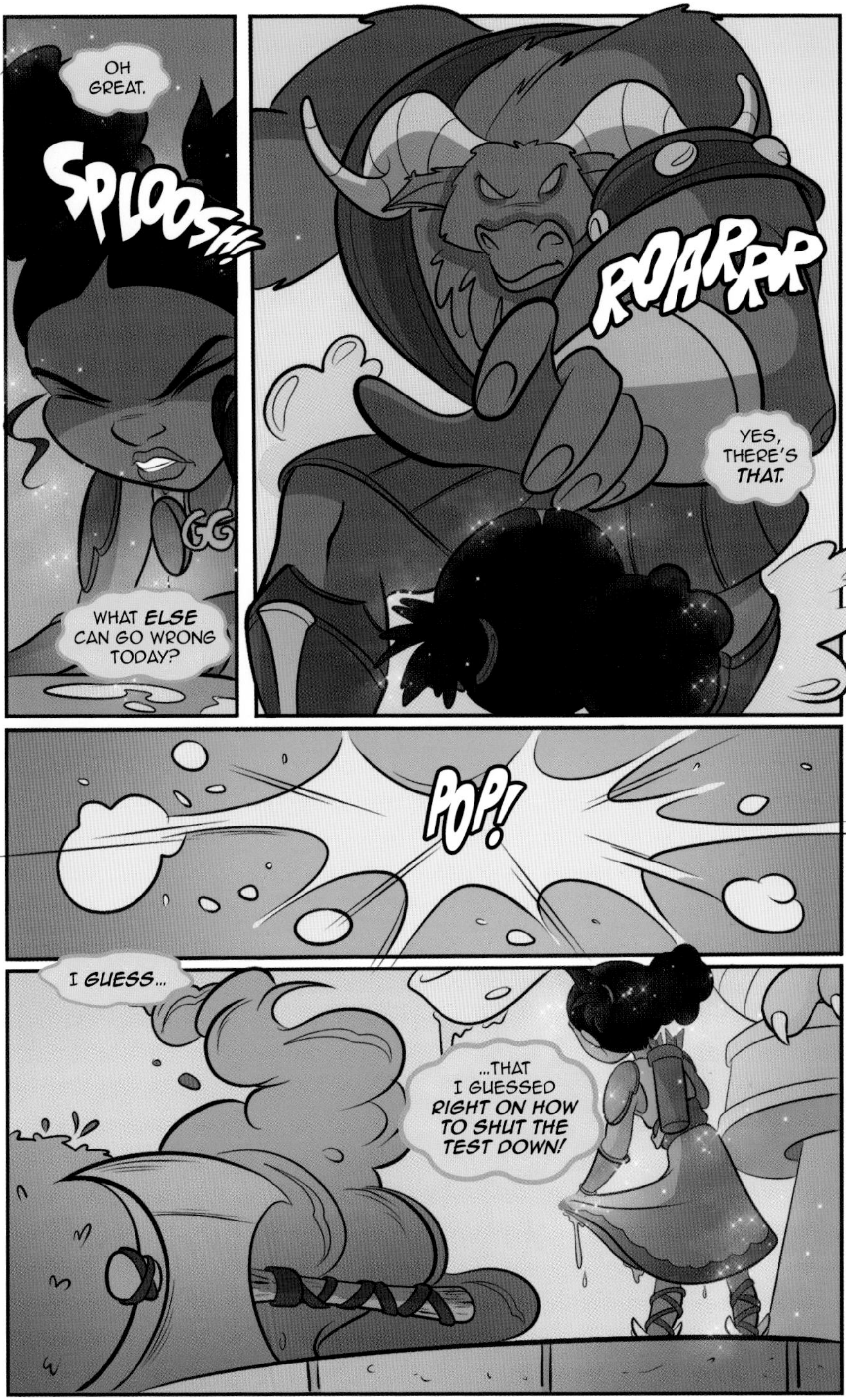
OH GREAT.
SPLOOSH!
WHAT ELSE CAN GO WRONG TODAY?
ROARRRR
YES, THERE'S THAT.
POP!
I GUESS...
...THAT I GUESSED RIGHT ON HOW TO SHUT THE TEST DOWN!

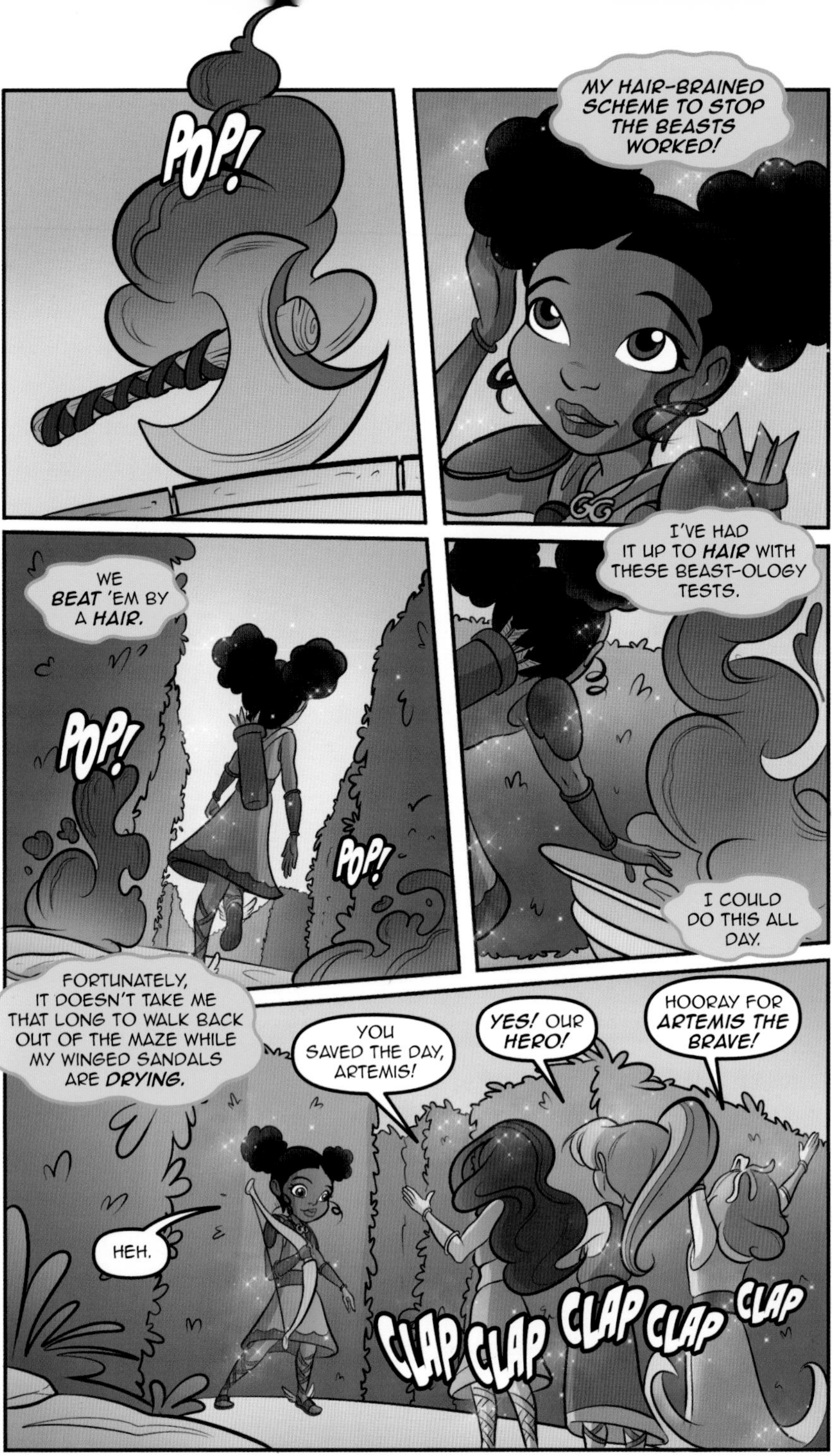
POP!
MY HAIR-BRAINED SCHEME TO STOP THE BEASTS WORKED!
WE BEAT 'EM BY A HAIR.
POP!
POP!
I'VE HAD IT UP TO HAIR WITH THESE BEAST-OLOGY TESTS.
I COULD DO THIS ALL DAY.
FORTUNATELY, IT DOESN'T TAKE ME THAT LONG TO WALK BACK OUT OF THE MAZE WHILE MY WINGED SANDALS ARE DRYING.
YOU SAVED THE DAY, ARTEMIS!
YES! OUR HERO!
HOORAY FOR ARTEMIS THE BRAVE!
HEH.
CLAP CLAP CLAP CLAP CLAP

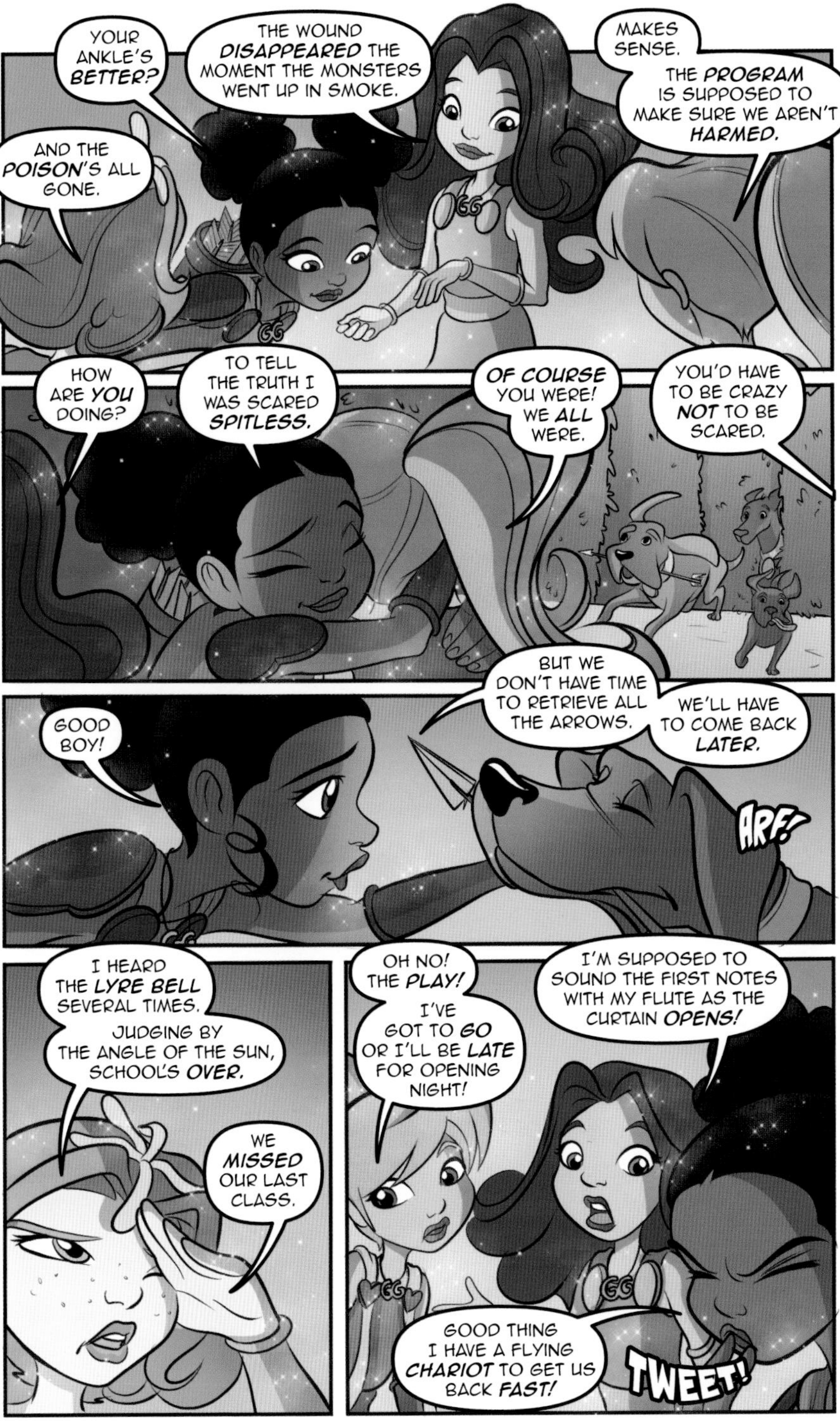
YOUR ANKLE'S BETTER?
THE WOUND DISAPPEARED THE MOMENT THE MONSTERS WENT UP IN SMOKE.
AND THE POISON'S ALL GONE.
MAKES SENSE.
THE PROGRAM IS SUPPOSED TO MAKE SURE WE AREN'T HARMED.
HOW ARE YOU DOING?
TO TELL THE TRUTH I WAS SCARED SPITLESS.
OF COURSE YOU WERE! WE ALL WERE.
YOU'D HAVE TO BE CRAZY NOT TO BE SCARED.
GOOD BOY!
BUT WE DON'T HAVE TIME TO RETRIEVE ALL THE ARROWS.
WE'LL HAVE TO COME BACK LATER.
ARF!
I HEARD THE LYRE BELL SEVERAL TIMES.
JUDGING BY THE ANGLE OF THE SUN, SCHOOL'S OVER.
WE MISSED OUR LAST CLASS.
OH NO! THE PLAY!
I'VE GOT TO GO OR I'LL BE LATE FOR OPENING NIGHT!
I'M SUPPOSED TO SOUND THE FIRST NOTES WITH MY FLUTE AS THE CURTAIN OPENS!
GOOD THING I HAVE A FLYING CHARIOT TO GET US BACK FAST!
TWEET!

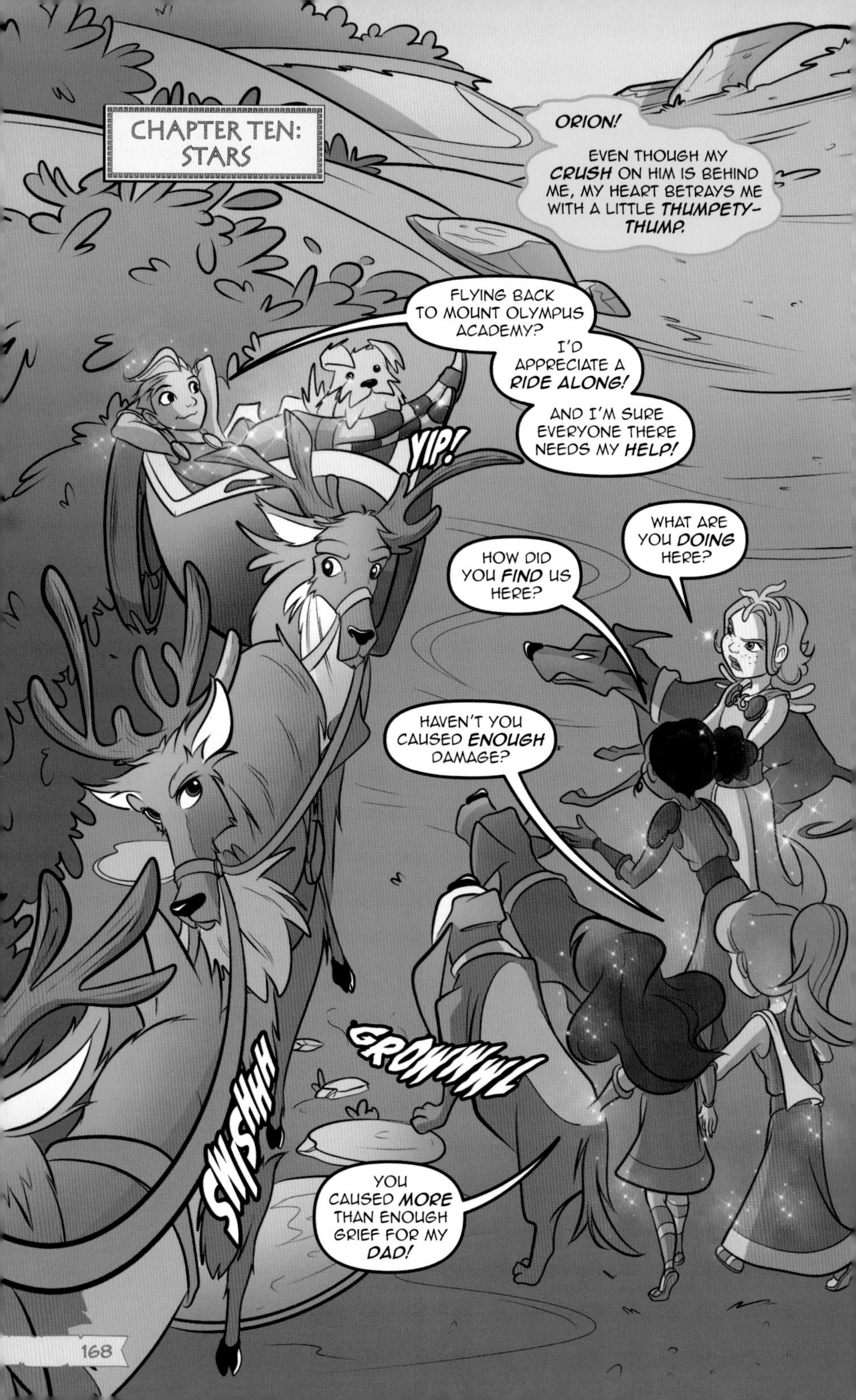
CHAPTER TEN: STARS
ORION!
EVEN THOUGH MY CRUSH ON HIM IS BEHIND ME, MY HEART BETRAYS ME WITH A LITTLE THUMPETY-THUMP.
FLYING BACK TO MOUNT OLYMPUS ACADEMY?
I'D APPRECIATE A RIDE ALONG!
AND I'M SURE EVERYONE THERE NEEDS MY HELP!
YIP!
WHAT ARE YOU DOING HERE?
HOW DID YOU FIND US HERE?
HAVEN'T YOU CAUSED ENOUGH DAMAGE?
GROWWWL
SWISHHH
YOU CAUSED MORE THAN ENOUGH GRIEF FOR MY DAD!

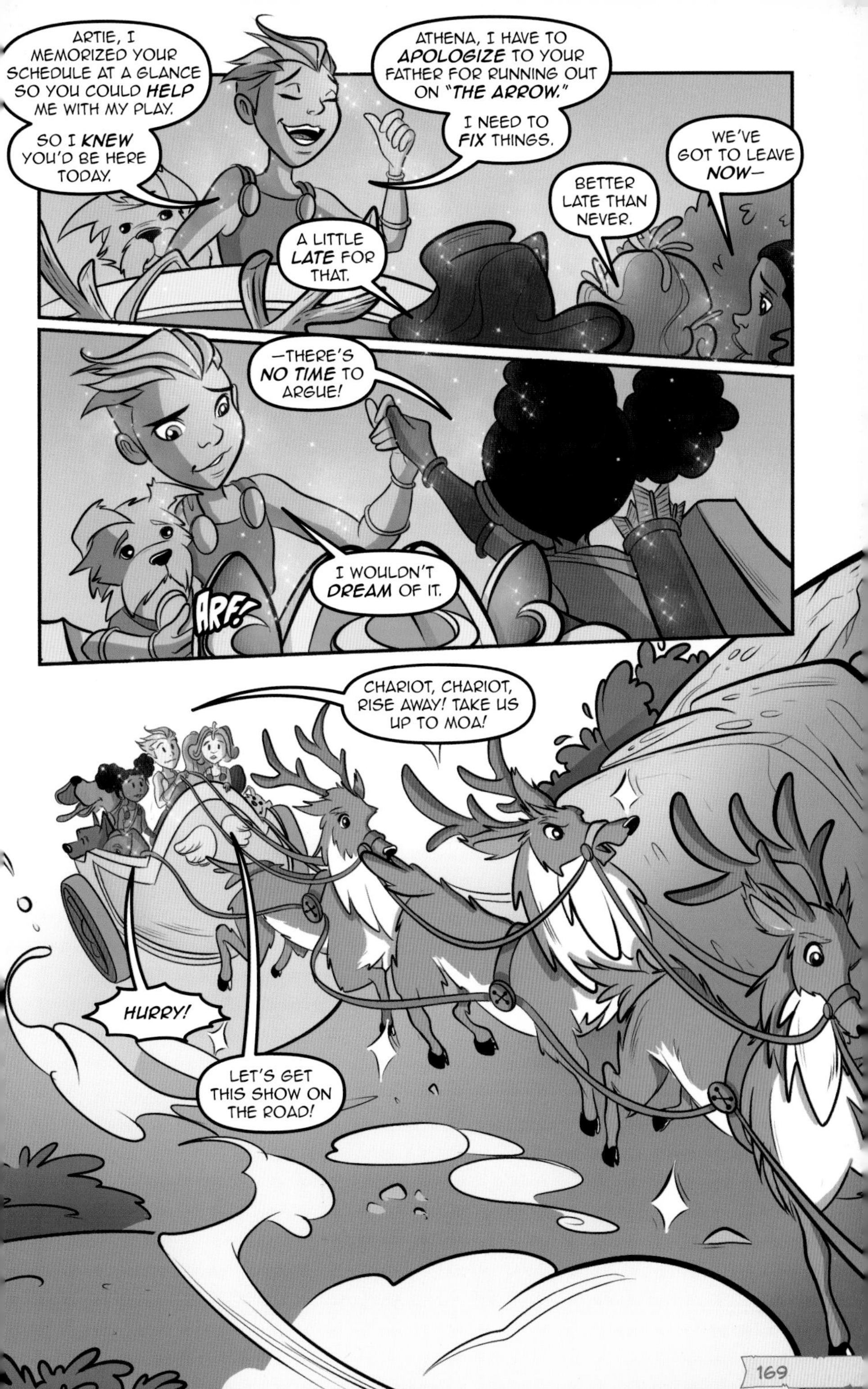
ARTIE, I MEMORIZED YOUR SCHEDULE AT A GLANCE SO YOU COULD **HELP** ME WITH MY PLAY.
SO I **KNEW** YOU'D BE HERE TODAY.
ATHENA, I HAVE TO **APOLOGIZE** TO YOUR FATHER FOR RUNNING OUT ON "**THE ARROW.**"
I NEED TO **FIX** THINGS.
A LITTLE **LATE** FOR THAT.
BETTER LATE THAN NEVER.
WE'VE GOT TO LEAVE **NOW**—
—THERE'S **NO TIME** TO ARGUE!
I WOULDN'T **DREAM** OF IT.
ARF!
CHARIOT, CHARIOT, RISE AWAY! TAKE US UP TO MOA!
HURRY!
LET'S GET THIS SHOW ON THE ROAD!

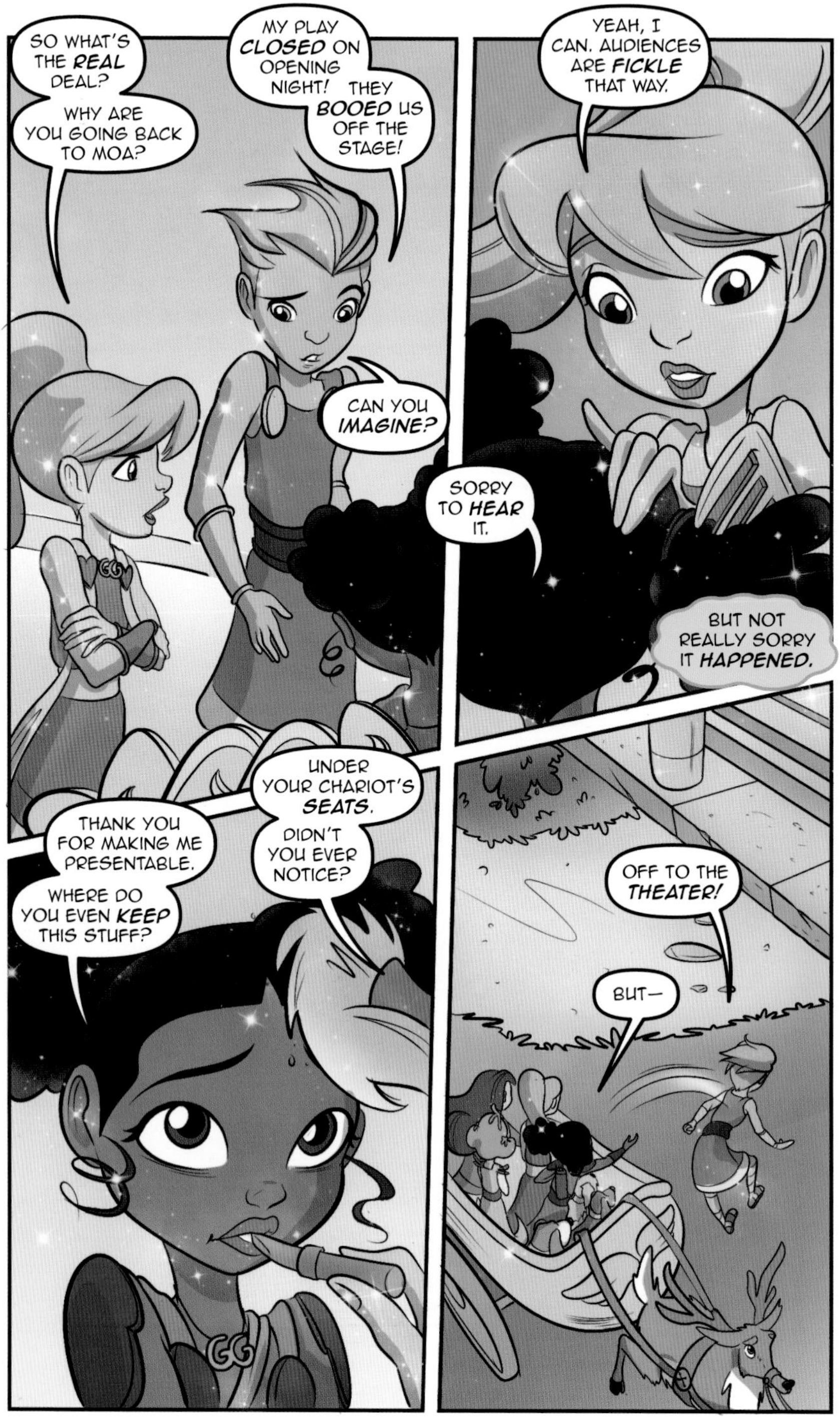
SO WHAT'S THE REAL DEAL?
WHY ARE YOU GOING BACK TO MOA?
MY PLAY CLOSED ON OPENING NIGHT!
THEY BOOED US OFF THE STAGE!
CAN YOU IMAGINE?
YEAH, I CAN. AUDIENCES ARE FICKLE THAT WAY.
SORRY TO HEAR IT.
BUT NOT REALLY SORRY IT HAPPENED.
THANK YOU FOR MAKING ME PRESENTABLE.
WHERE DO YOU EVEN KEEP THIS STUFF?
UNDER YOUR CHARIOT'S SEATS.
DIDN'T YOU EVER NOTICE?
OFF TO THE THEATER!
BUT—

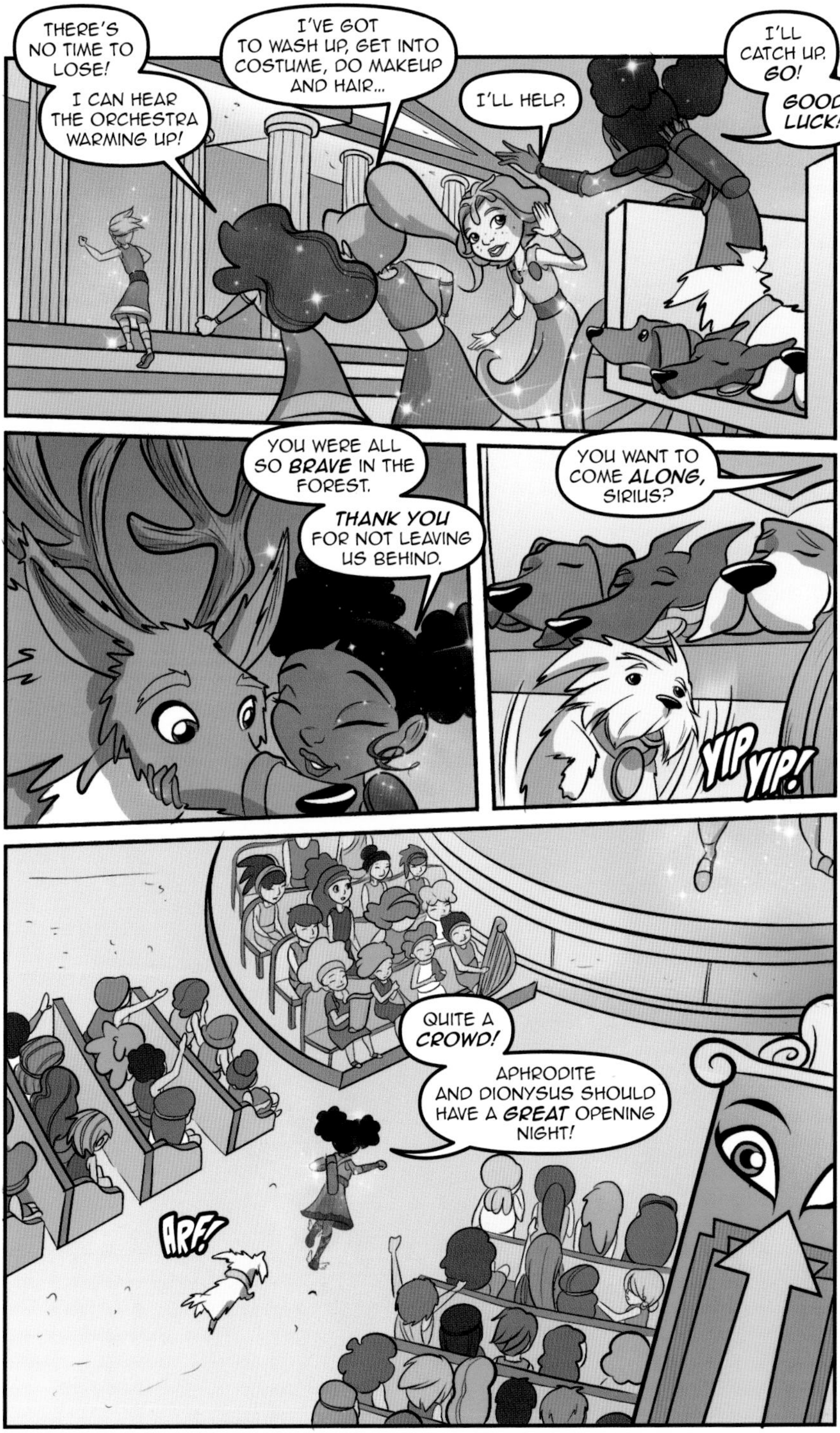
THERE'S NO TIME TO LOSE!
I CAN HEAR THE ORCHESTRA WARMING UP!
I'VE GOT TO WASH UP, GET INTO COSTUME, DO MAKEUP AND HAIR...
I'LL HELP.
I'LL CATCH UP. GO!
GOOD LUCK!
YOU WERE ALL SO BRAVE IN THE FOREST.
THANK YOU FOR NOT LEAVING US BEHIND.
YOU WANT TO COME ALONG, SIRIUS?
YIP YIP!
QUITE A CROWD!
APHRODITE AND DIONYSUS SHOULD HAVE A GREAT OPENING NIGHT!
ARF!

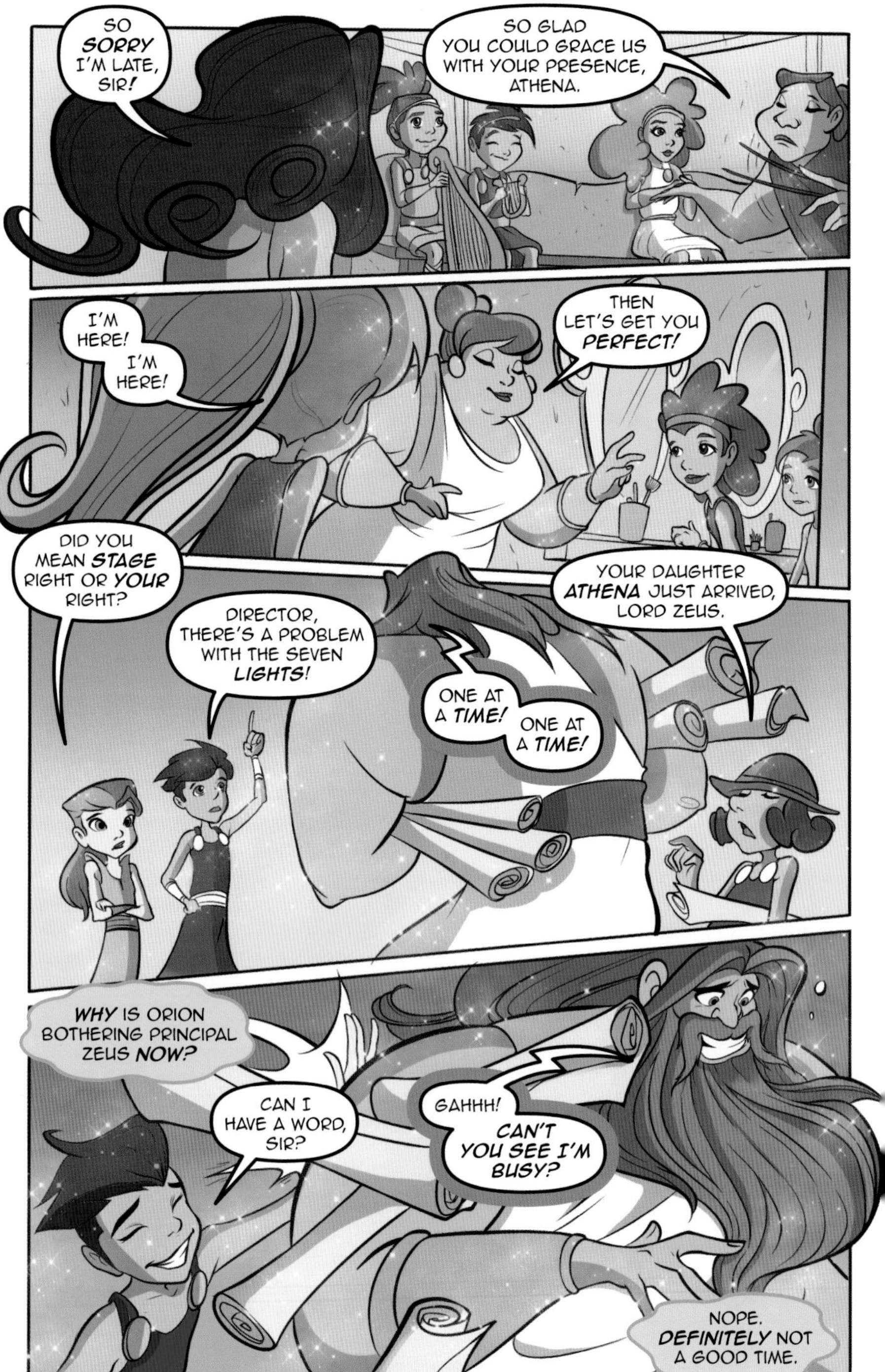
SO SORRY I'M LATE, SIR!
SO GLAD YOU COULD GRACE US WITH YOUR PRESENCE, ATHENA.
I'M HERE! I'M HERE!
THEN LET'S GET YOU PERFECT!
DID YOU MEAN STAGE RIGHT OR YOUR RIGHT?
DIRECTOR, THERE'S A PROBLEM WITH THE SEVEN LIGHTS!
YOUR DAUGHTER ATHENA JUST ARRIVED, LORD ZEUS.
ONE AT A TIME! ONE AT A TIME!
WHY IS ORION BOTHERING PRINCIPAL ZEUS NOW?
CAN I HAVE A WORD, SIR?
GAHHH! CAN'T YOU SEE I'M BUSY?
NOPE. DEFINITELY NOT A GOOD TIME.

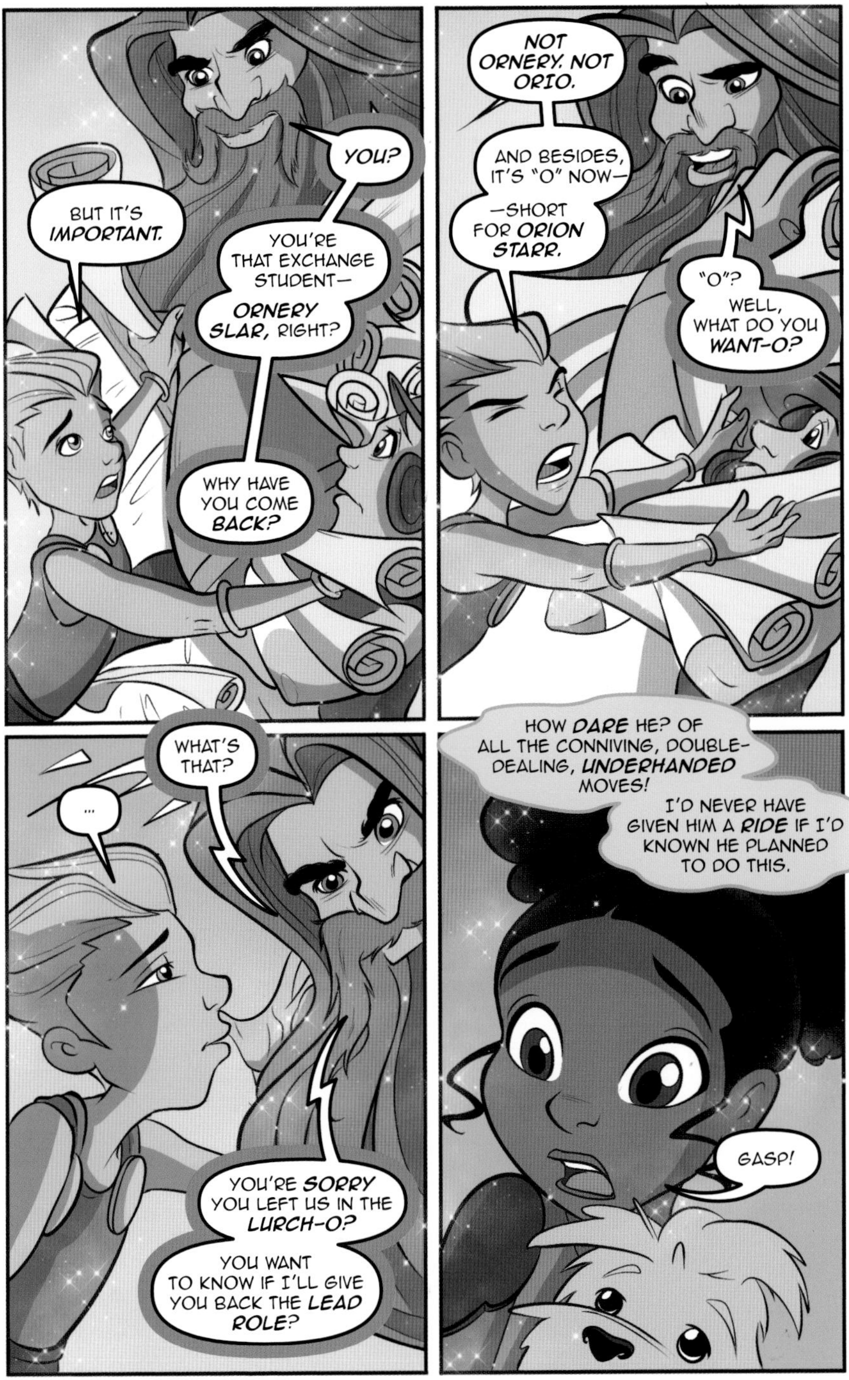

YOU?
BUT IT'S IMPORTANT.
YOU'RE THAT EXCHANGE STUDENT—
ORNERY SLAR, RIGHT?
WHY HAVE YOU COME BACK?
NOT ORNERY. NOT ORIO.
AND BESIDES, IT'S "O" NOW—
—SHORT FOR ORION STARR.
"O"?
WELL, WHAT DO YOU WANT-O?
WHAT'S THAT?
...
YOU'RE SORRY YOU LEFT US IN THE LURCH-O?
YOU WANT TO KNOW IF I'LL GIVE YOU BACK THE LEAD ROLE?
HOW DARE HE? OF ALL THE CONNIVING, DOUBLE-DEALING, UNDERHANDED MOVES!
I'D NEVER HAVE GIVEN HIM A RIDE IF I'D KNOWN HE PLANNED TO DO THIS.
GASP!

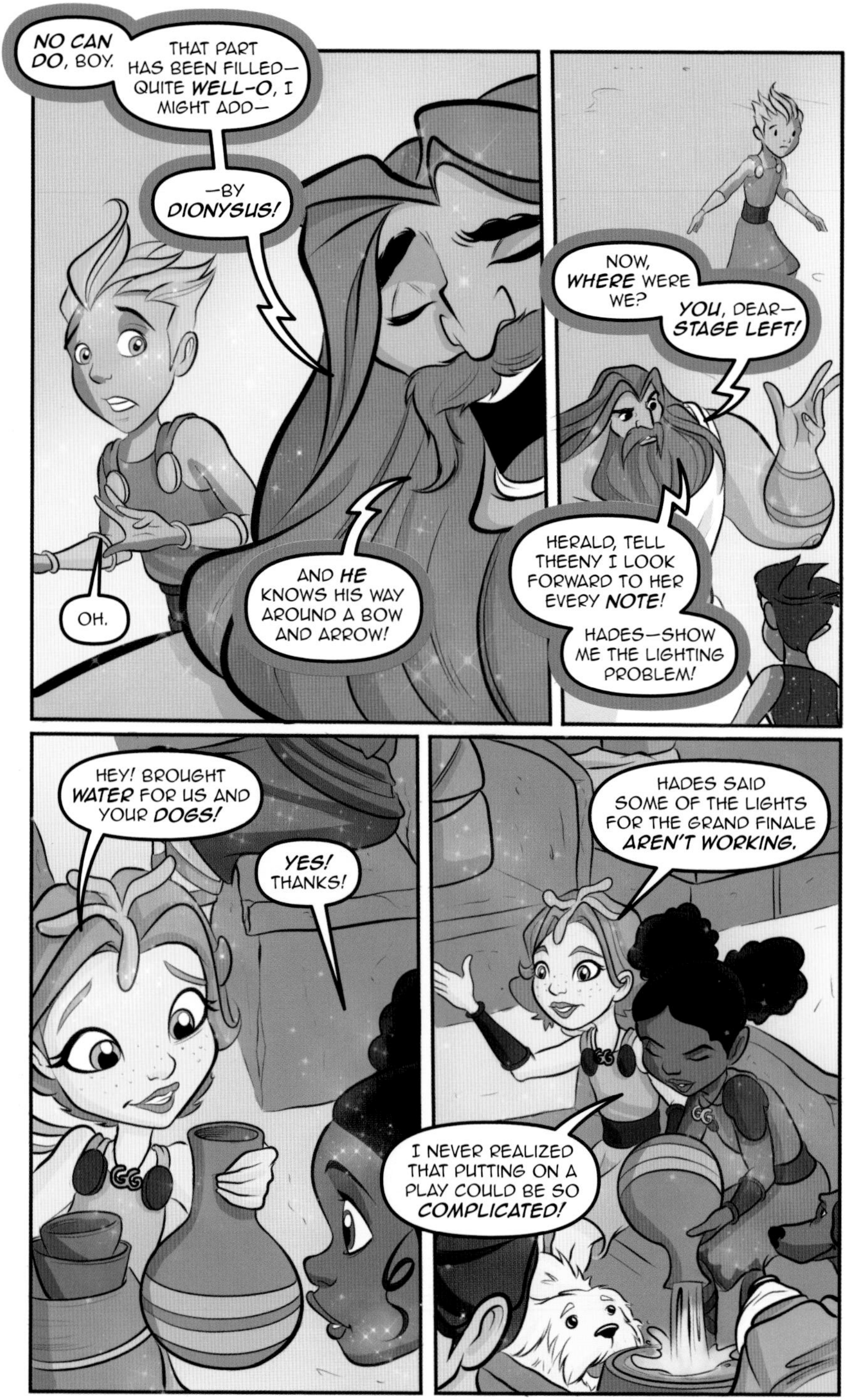
NO CAN DO, BOY.
THAT PART HAS BEEN FILLED— QUITE WELL-O, I MIGHT ADD—
—BY DIONYSUS!
OH.
AND HE KNOWS HIS WAY AROUND A BOW AND ARROW!
NOW, WHERE WERE WE?
YOU, DEAR— STAGE LEFT!
HERALD, TELL THEENY I LOOK FORWARD TO HER EVERY NOTE!
HADES—SHOW ME THE LIGHTING PROBLEM!
HEY! BROUGHT WATER FOR US AND YOUR DOGS!
YES! THANKS!
HADES SAID SOME OF THE LIGHTS FOR THE GRAND FINALE AREN'T WORKING.
I NEVER REALIZED THAT PUTTING ON A PLAY COULD BE SO COMPLICATED!

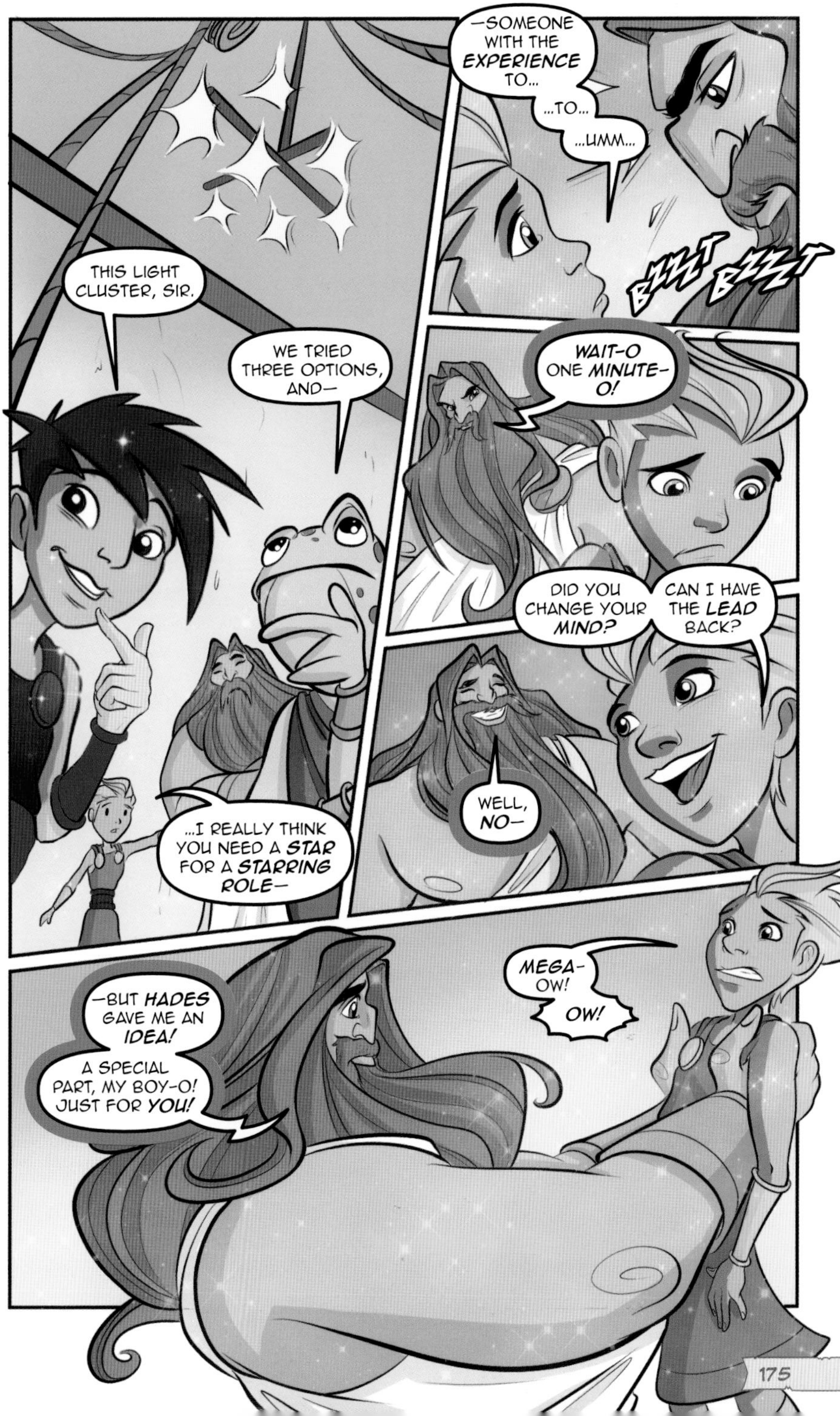
THIS LIGHT CLUSTER, SIR.
WE TRIED THREE OPTIONS, AND—
...I REALLY THINK YOU NEED A STAR FOR A STARRING ROLE—
—SOMEONE WITH THE EXPERIENCE TO...
...TO...
...UMM...
BZZZT BZZZT
WAIT-O ONE MINUTE-O!
DID YOU CHANGE YOUR MIND?
CAN I HAVE THE LEAD BACK?
WELL, NO—
—BUT HADES GAVE ME AN IDEA!
A SPECIAL PART, MY BOY-O! JUST FOR YOU!
MEGA-OW!
OW!

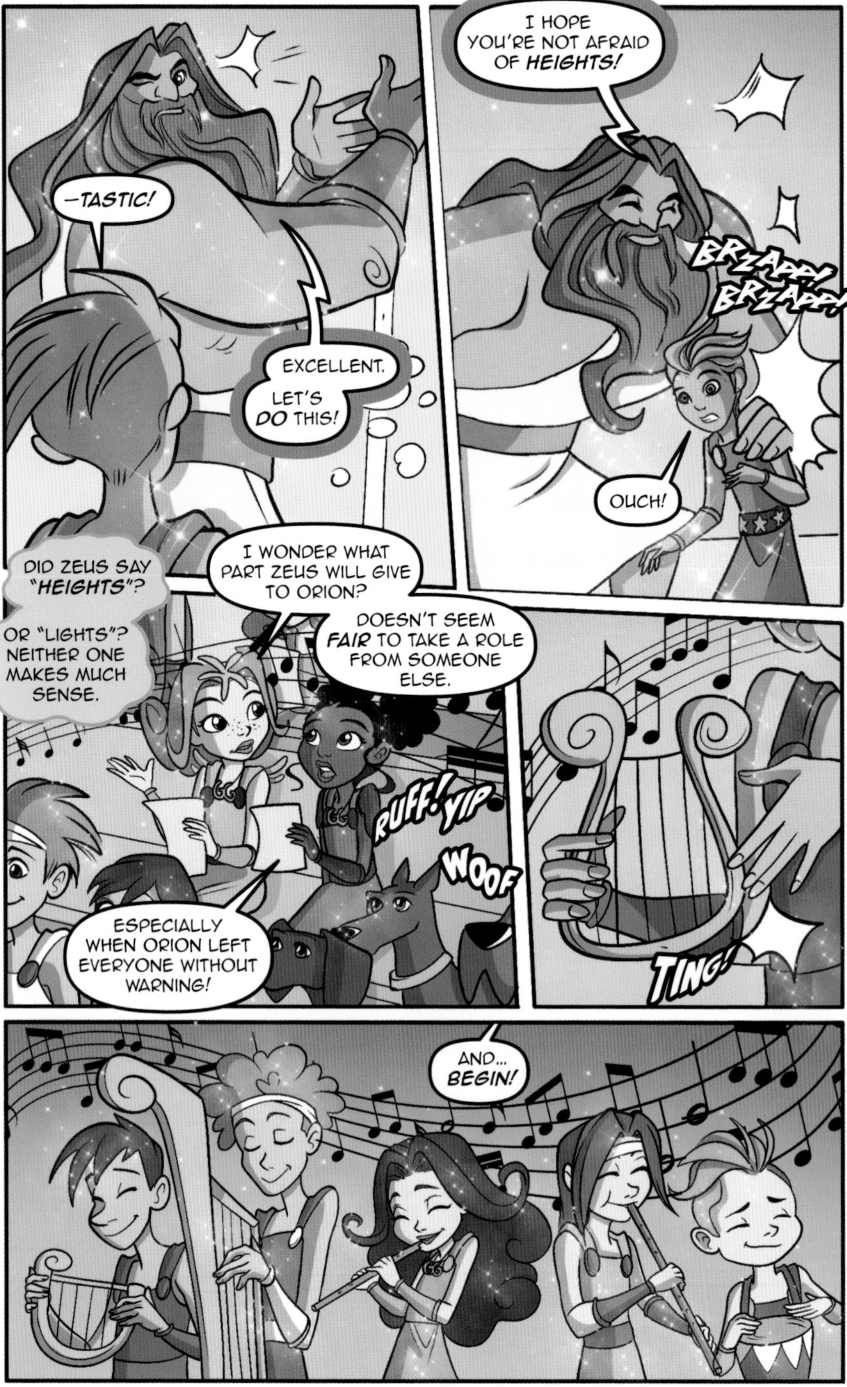
—TASTIC!
EXCELLENT.
LET'S DO THIS!
I HOPE YOU'RE NOT AFRAID OF HEIGHTS!
BRZAPP! BRZAPP!
OUCH!
DID ZEUS SAY "HEIGHTS"?
OR "LIGHTS"? NEITHER ONE MAKES MUCH SENSE.
I WONDER WHAT PART ZEUS WILL GIVE TO ORION?
DOESN'T SEEM FAIR TO TAKE A ROLE FROM SOMEONE ELSE.
RUFF! YIP
WOOF
ESPECIALLY WHEN ORION LEFT EVERYONE WITHOUT WARNING!
TING!
AND... BEGIN!

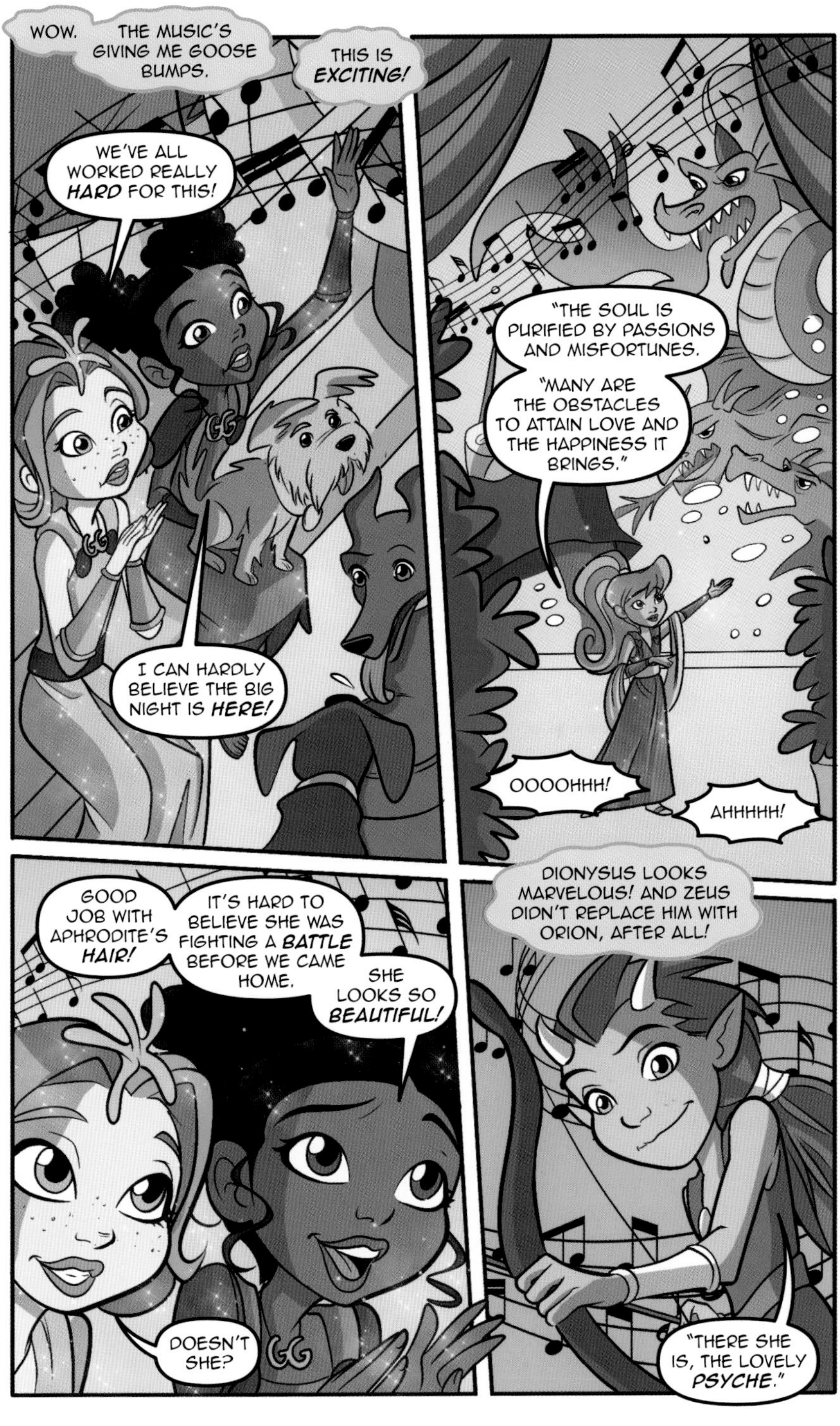
WOW.
THE MUSIC'S GIVING ME GOOSE BUMPS.
THIS IS *EXCITING!*
WE'VE ALL WORKED REALLY *HARD* FOR THIS!
I CAN HARDLY BELIEVE THE BIG NIGHT IS *HERE!*
"THE SOUL IS PURIFIED BY PASSIONS AND MISFORTUNES.
"MANY ARE THE OBSTACLES TO ATTAIN LOVE AND THE HAPPINESS IT BRINGS."
OOOOHHH!
AHHHHH!
GOOD JOB WITH APHRODITE'S *HAIR!*
IT'S HARD TO BELIEVE SHE WAS FIGHTING A *BATTLE* BEFORE WE CAME HOME.
SHE LOOKS SO *BEAUTIFUL!*
DOESN'T SHE?
DIONYSUS LOOKS MARVELOUS! AND ZEUS DIDN'T REPLACE HIM WITH ORION, AFTER ALL!
"THERE SHE IS, THE LOVELY *PSYCHE*."

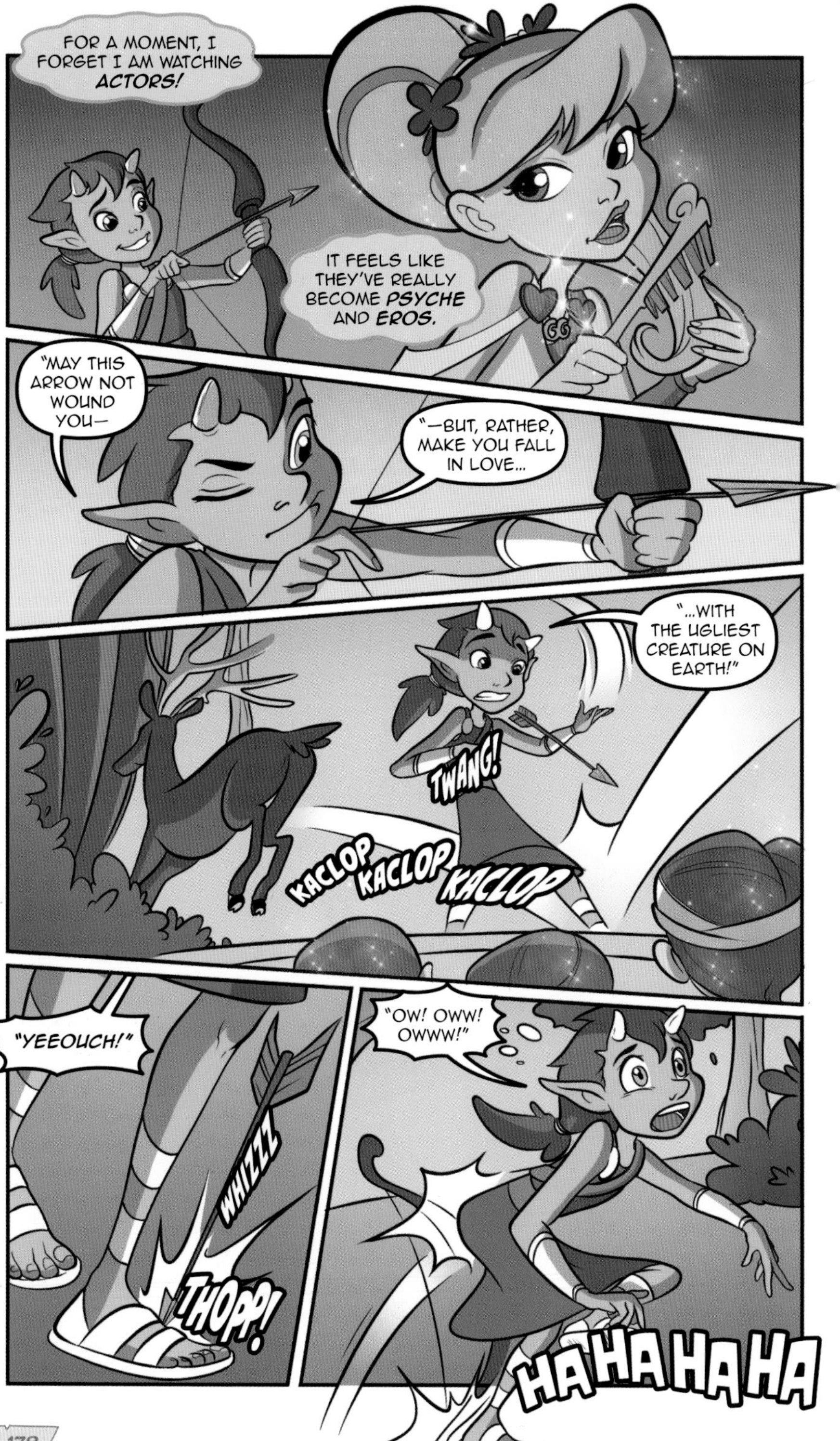
FOR A MOMENT, I FORGET I AM WATCHING *ACTORS!*
IT FEELS LIKE THEY'VE REALLY BECOME *PSYCHE* AND *EROS.*
"MAY THIS ARROW NOT WOUND YOU—
"—BUT, RATHER, MAKE YOU FALL IN LOVE...
"...WITH THE UGLIEST CREATURE ON EARTH!"
TWANG!
KACLOP KACLOP KACLOP
"YEEOUCH!"
WHIZZZ
THOPP!
"OW! OWW! OWWW!"
HA HA HA HA HA

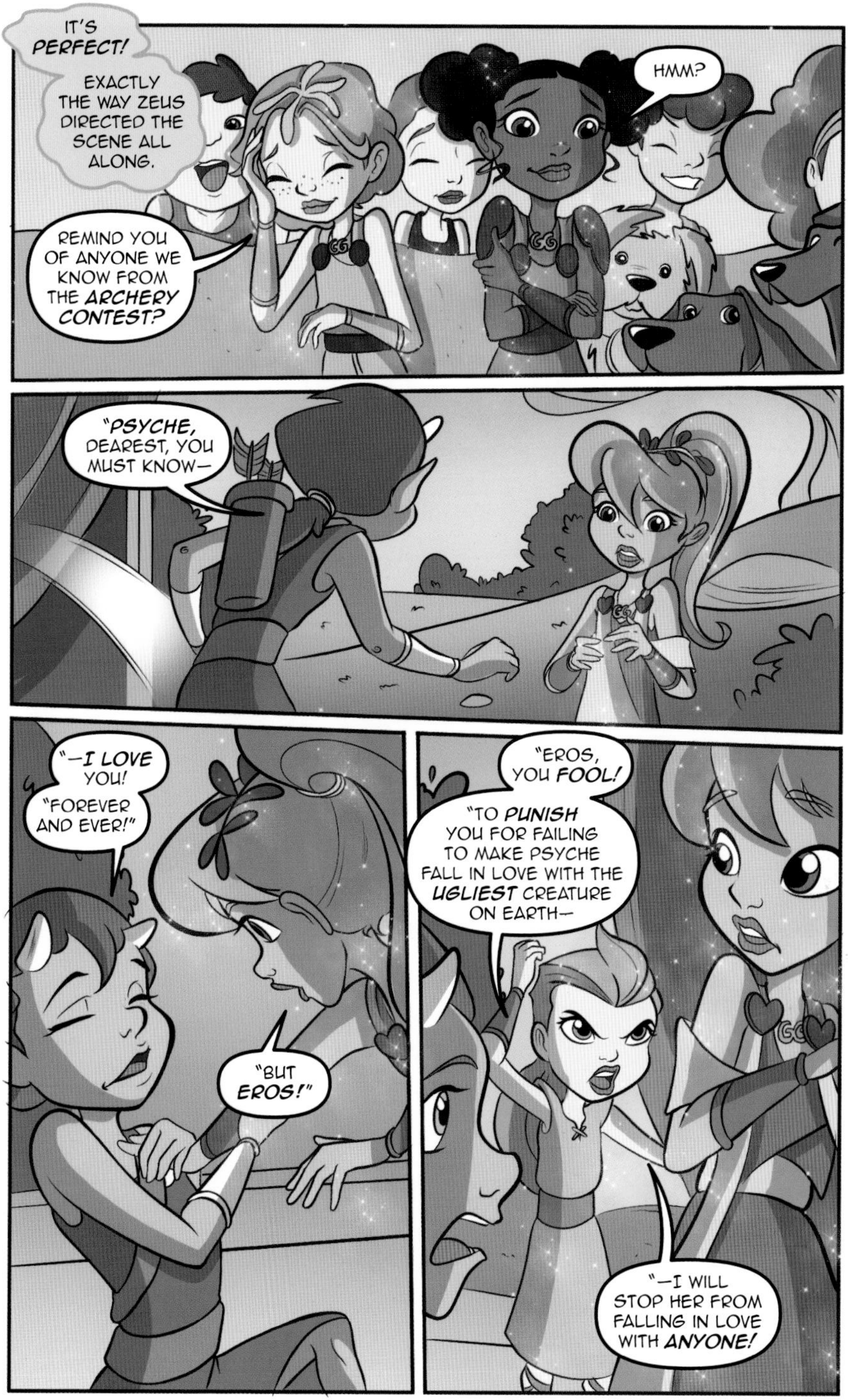
IT'S PERFECT!
EXACTLY THE WAY ZEUS DIRECTED THE SCENE ALL ALONG.
HMM?
REMIND YOU OF ANYONE WE KNOW FROM THE ARCHERY CONTEST?
"PSYCHE, DEAREST, YOU MUST KNOW—
"—I LOVE YOU!
"FOREVER AND EVER!"
"BUT EROS!"
"EROS, YOU FOOL!
"TO PUNISH YOU FOR FAILING TO MAKE PSYCHE FALL IN LOVE WITH THE UGLIEST CREATURE ON EARTH—
"—I WILL STOP HER FROM FALLING IN LOVE WITH ANYONE!

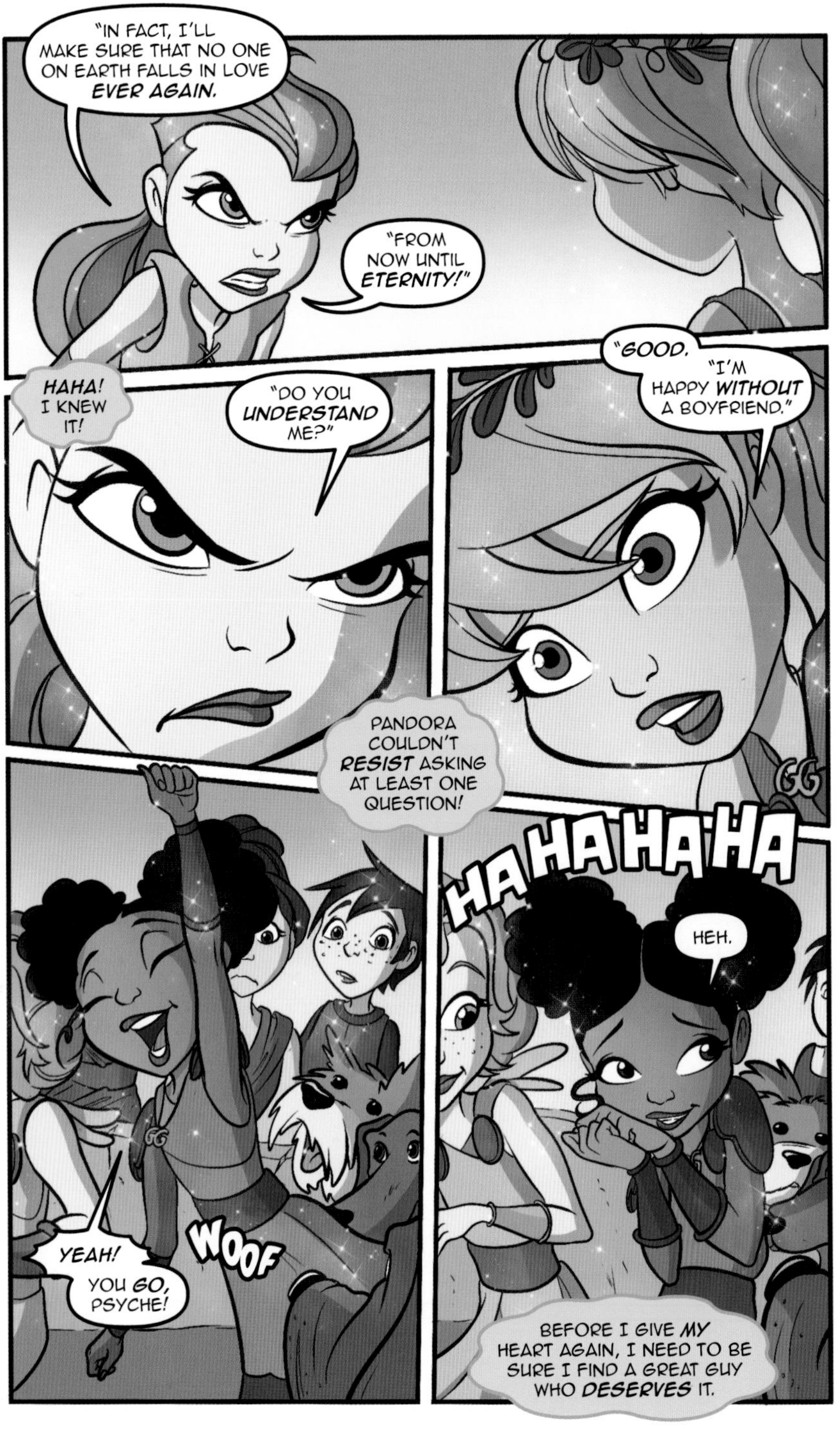
"IN FACT, I'LL MAKE SURE THAT NO ONE ON EARTH FALLS IN LOVE *EVER AGAIN.*
"FROM NOW UNTIL *ETERNITY!*"
HAHA! I KNEW IT!
"DO YOU *UNDERSTAND* ME?"
"*GOOD.*
"I'M HAPPY *WITHOUT* A BOYFRIEND."
PANDORA COULDN'T *RESIST* ASKING AT LEAST ONE QUESTION!
YEAH! YOU *GO,* PSYCHE!
WOOF
HA HA HA HA HA
HEH.
BEFORE I GIVE *MY* HEART AGAIN, I NEED TO BE SURE I FIND A GREAT GUY WHO *DESERVES* IT.

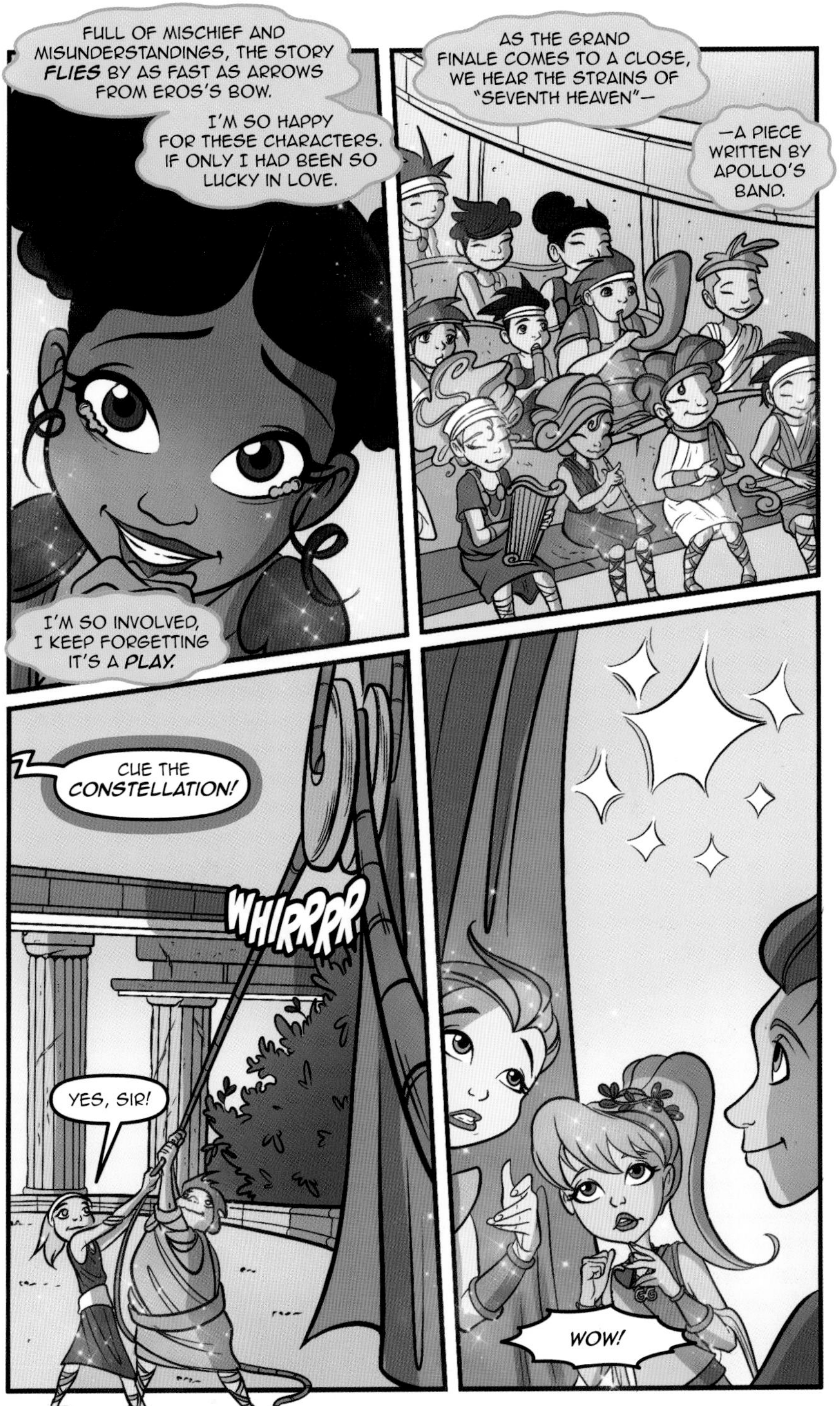

FULL OF MISCHIEF AND MISUNDERSTANDINGS, THE STORY FLIES BY AS FAST AS ARROWS FROM EROS'S BOW.
I'M SO HAPPY FOR THESE CHARACTERS. IF ONLY I HAD BEEN SO LUCKY IN LOVE.
I'M SO INVOLVED, I KEEP FORGETTING IT'S A PLAY.
AS THE GRAND FINALE COMES TO A CLOSE, WE HEAR THE STRAINS OF "SEVENTH HEAVEN"—
—A PIECE WRITTEN BY APOLLO'S BAND.
CUE THE CONSTELLATION!
WHIRRRR
YES, SIR!
WOW!

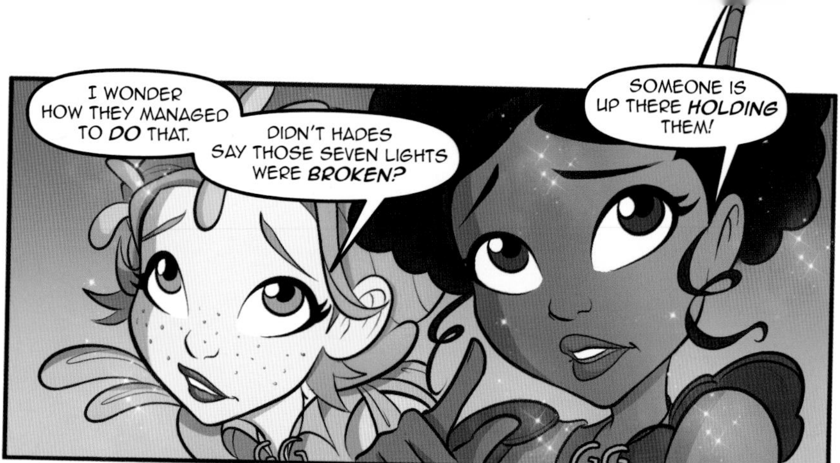
I WONDER HOW THEY MANAGED TO DO THAT.
DIDN'T HADES SAY THOSE SEVEN LIGHTS WERE BROKEN?
SOMEONE IS UP THERE HOLDING THEM!

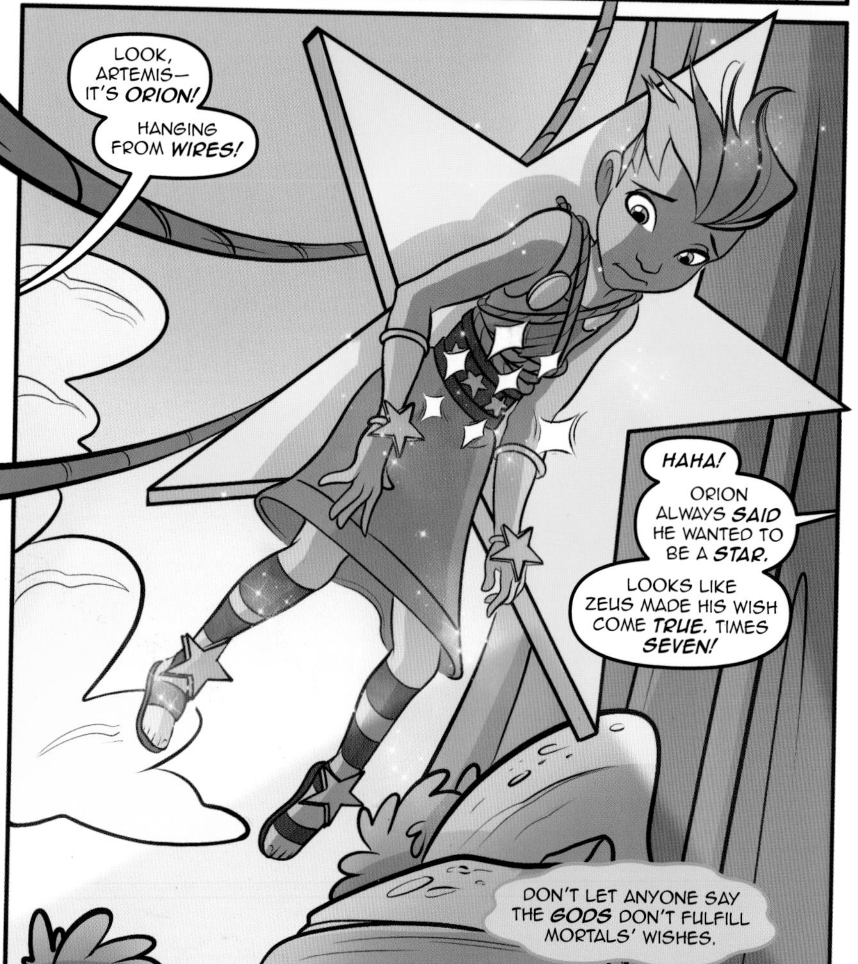
LOOK, ARTEMIS— IT'S ORION!
HANGING FROM WIRES!
HAHA!
ORION ALWAYS SAID HE WANTED TO BE A STAR.
LOOKS LIKE ZEUS MADE HIS WISH COME TRUE. TIMES SEVEN!
DON'T LET ANYONE SAY THE GODS DON'T FULFILL MORTALS' WISHES.

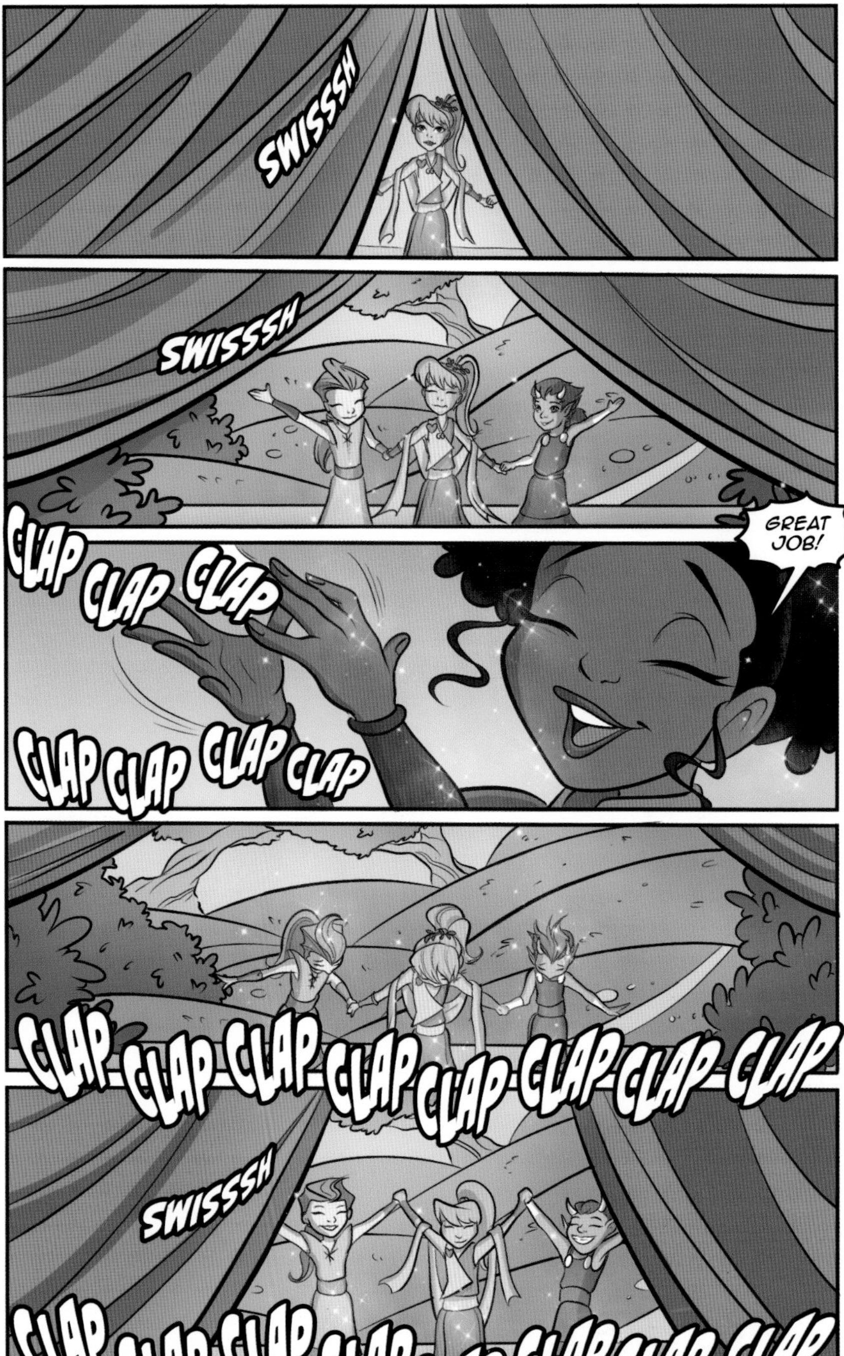
SWISSSH
SWISSSH
CLAP CLAP CLAP
GREAT JOB!
CLAP CLAP CLAP CLAP
CLAP CLAP CLAP CLAP CLAP CLAP CLAP CLAP
SWISSSH
CLAP CLAP CLAP CLAP CLAP CLAP CLAP CLAP

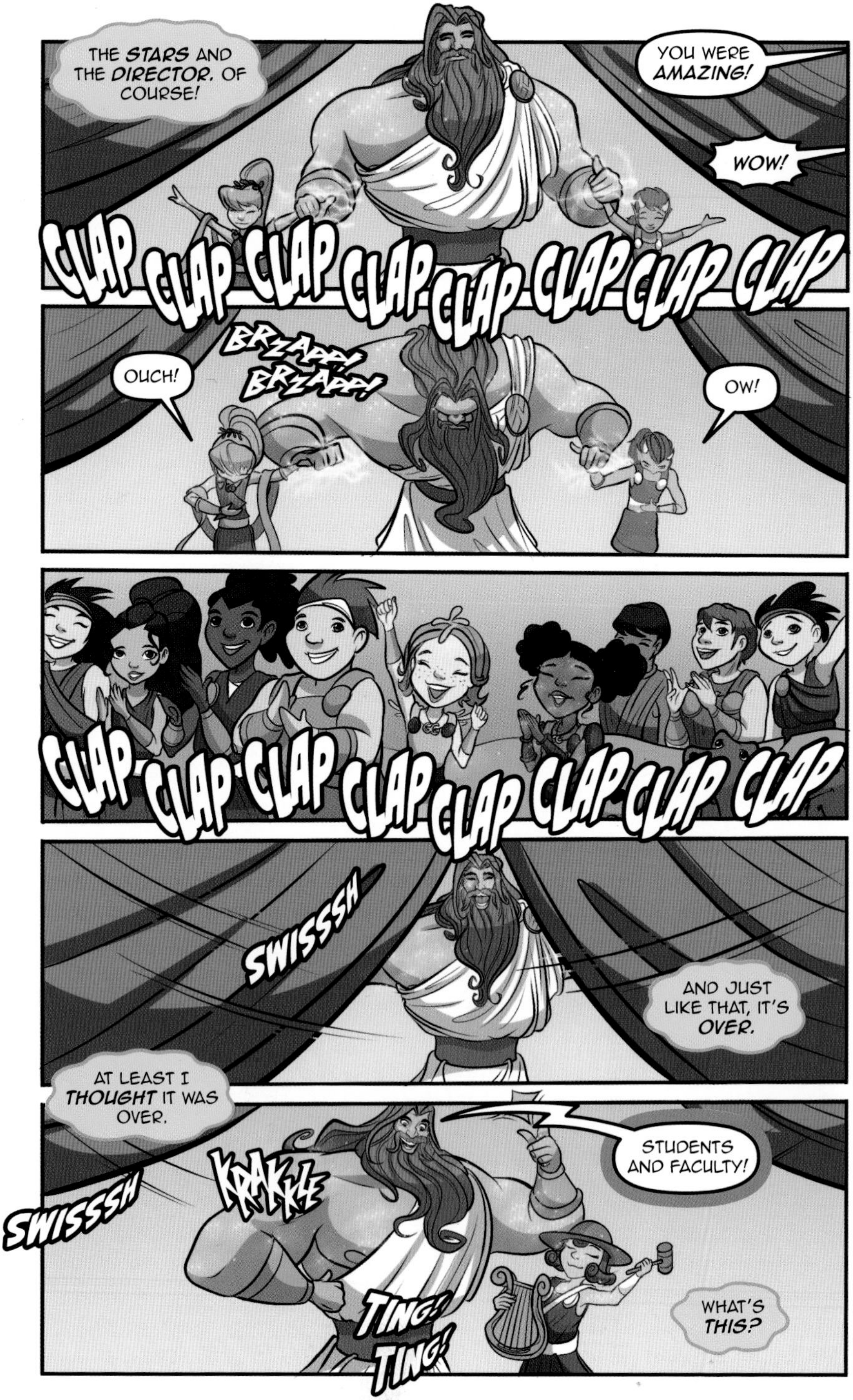
THE STARS AND THE DIRECTOR, OF COURSE!
YOU WERE AMAZING!
WOW!
CLAP CLAP CLAP CLAP CLAP CLAP CLAP CLAP
BRZAPP! BRZAPP!
OUCH!
OW!
CLAP CLAP CLAP CLAP CLAP CLAP CLAP CLAP
SWISSSH
AND JUST LIKE THAT, IT'S OVER.
AT LEAST I THOUGHT IT WAS OVER.
SWISSSH
KRAKKLE
STUDENTS AND FACULTY!
TING! TING!
WHAT'S THIS?

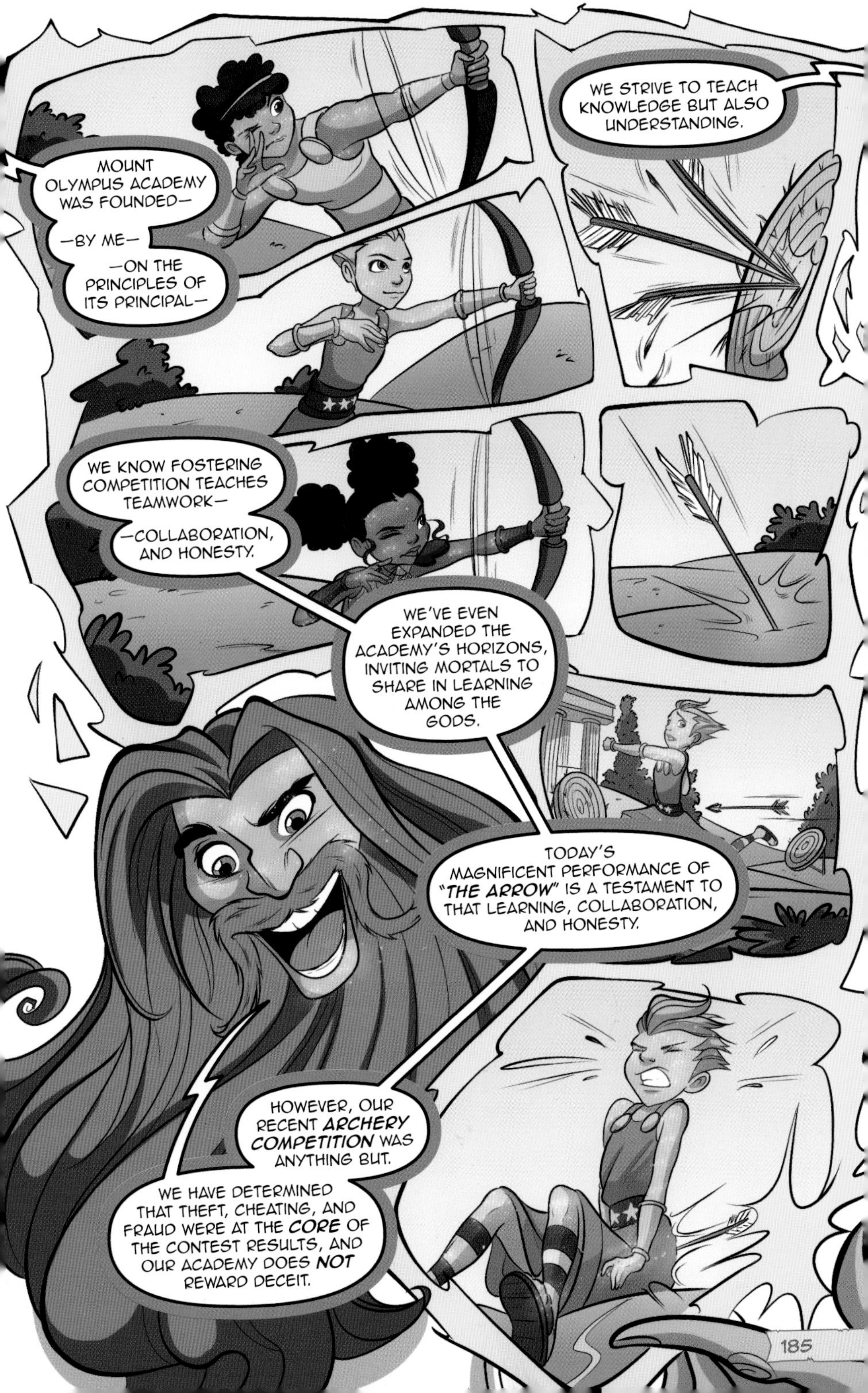
MOUNT OLYMPUS ACADEMY WAS FOUNDED—
—BY ME—
—ON THE PRINCIPLES OF ITS PRINCIPAL—
WE STRIVE TO TEACH KNOWLEDGE BUT ALSO UNDERSTANDING.
WE KNOW FOSTERING COMPETITION TEACHES TEAMWORK—
—COLLABORATION, AND HONESTY.
WE'VE EVEN EXPANDED THE ACADEMY'S HORIZONS, INVITING MORTALS TO SHARE IN LEARNING AMONG THE GODS.
TODAY'S MAGNIFICENT PERFORMANCE OF "THE ARROW" IS A TESTAMENT TO THAT LEARNING, COLLABORATION, AND HONESTY.
HOWEVER, OUR RECENT ARCHERY COMPETITION WAS ANYTHING BUT.
WE HAVE DETERMINED THAT THEFT, CHEATING, AND FRAUD WERE AT THE CORE OF THE CONTEST RESULTS, AND OUR ACADEMY DOES NOT REWARD DECEIT.

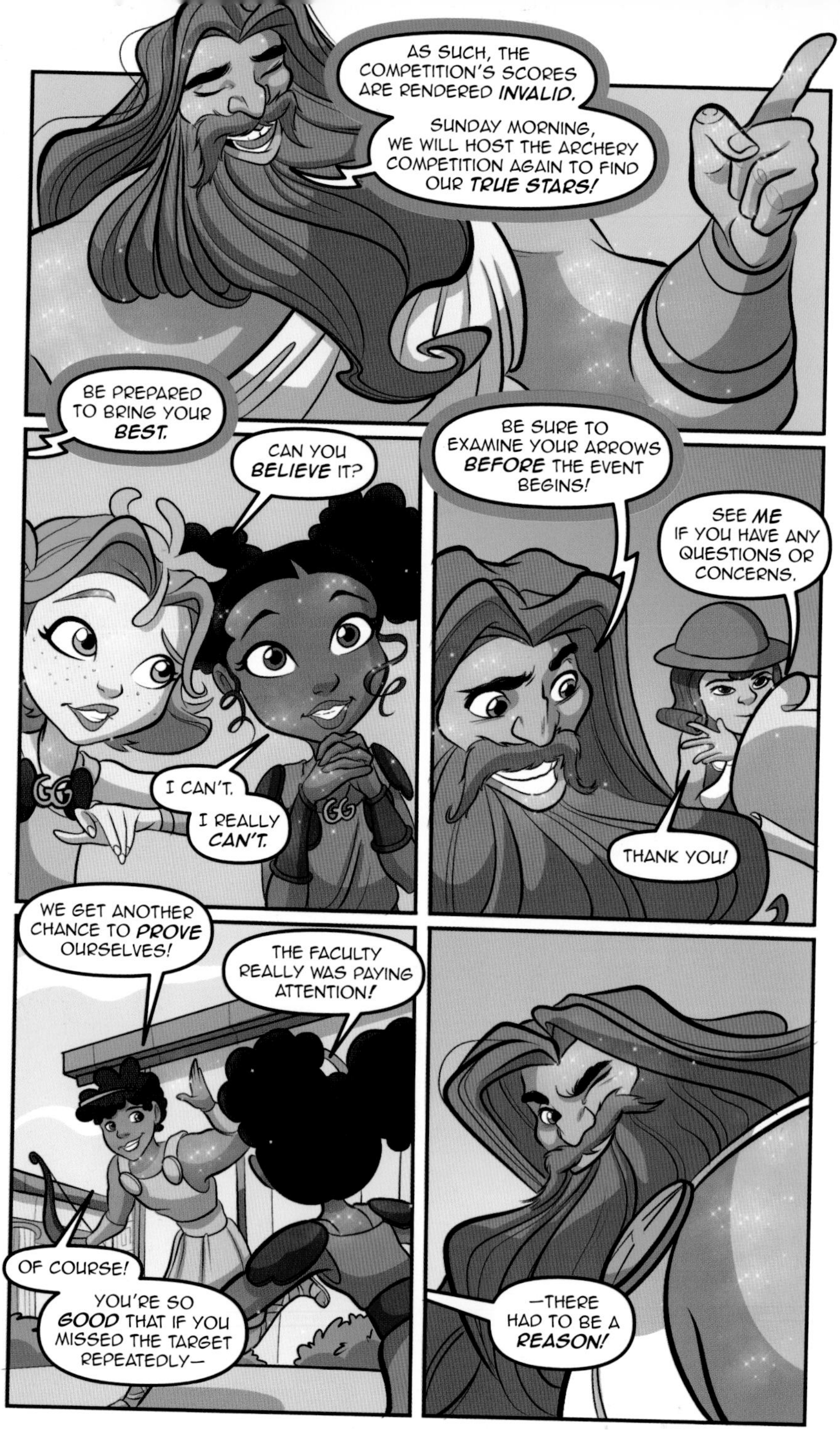
AS SUCH, THE COMPETITION'S SCORES ARE RENDERED **INVALID.**
SUNDAY MORNING, WE WILL HOST THE ARCHERY COMPETITION AGAIN TO FIND OUR **TRUE STARS!**
BE PREPARED TO BRING YOUR **BEST.**
CAN YOU **BELIEVE** IT?
I CAN'T.
I REALLY **CAN'T.**
BE SURE TO EXAMINE YOUR ARROWS **BEFORE** THE EVENT BEGINS!
SEE **ME** IF YOU HAVE ANY QUESTIONS OR CONCERNS.
THANK YOU!
WE GET ANOTHER CHANCE TO **PROVE** OURSELVES!
THE FACULTY REALLY WAS PAYING ATTENTION!
OF COURSE!
YOU'RE SO **GOOD** THAT IF YOU MISSED THE TARGET REPEATEDLY—
—THERE HAD TO BE A **REASON!**

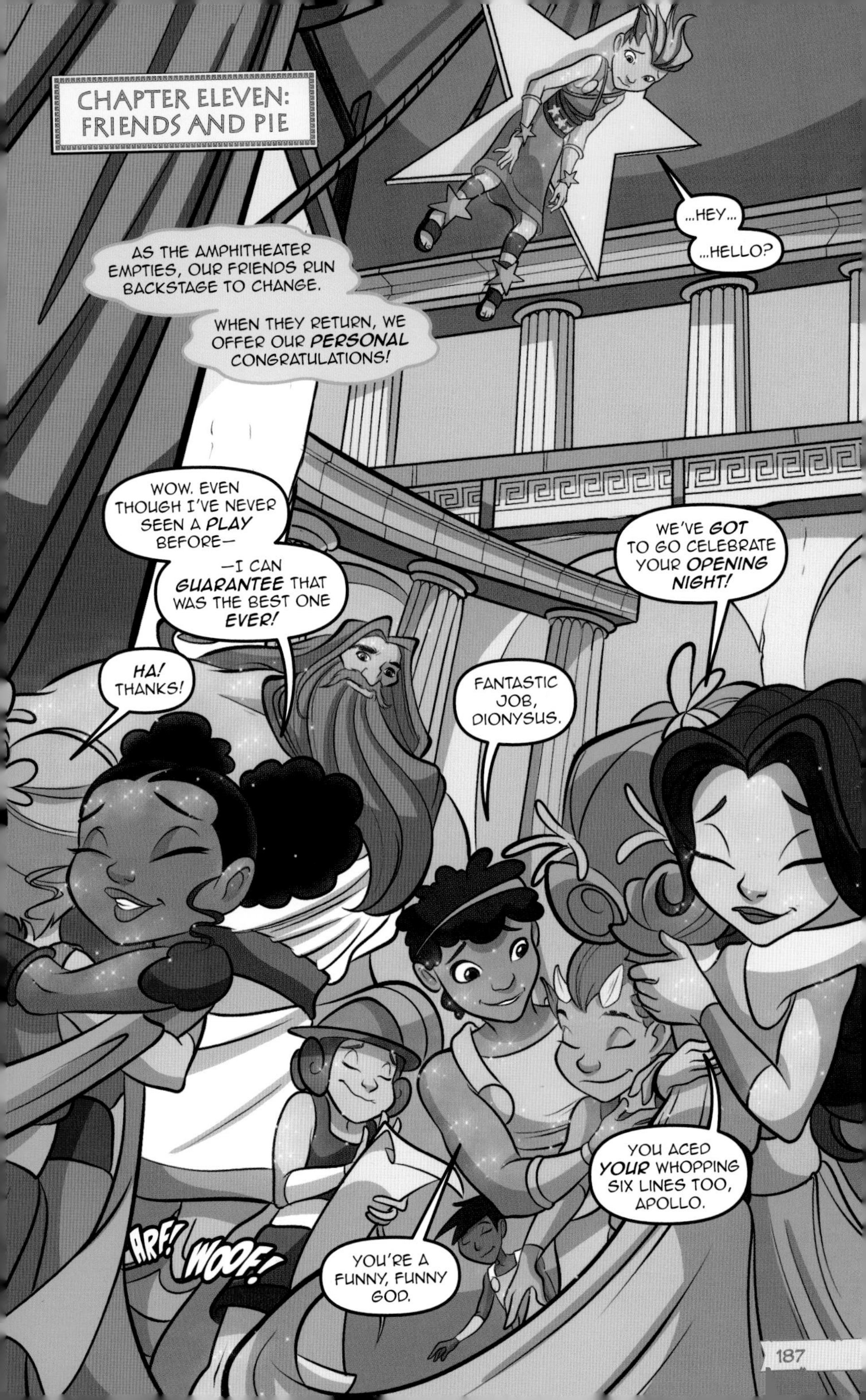
CHAPTER ELEVEN: FRIENDS AND PIE
...HEY...
...HELLO?
AS THE AMPHITHEATER EMPTIES, OUR FRIENDS RUN BACKSTAGE TO CHANGE.
WHEN THEY RETURN, WE OFFER OUR PERSONAL CONGRATULATIONS!
WOW. EVEN THOUGH I'VE NEVER SEEN A PLAY BEFORE—
—I CAN GUARANTEE THAT WAS THE BEST ONE EVER!
WE'VE GOT TO GO CELEBRATE YOUR OPENING NIGHT!
HA! THANKS!
FANTASTIC JOB, DIONYSUS.
YOU ACED YOUR WHOPPING SIX LINES TOO, APOLLO.
ARF! WOOF!
YOU'RE A FUNNY, FUNNY GOD.

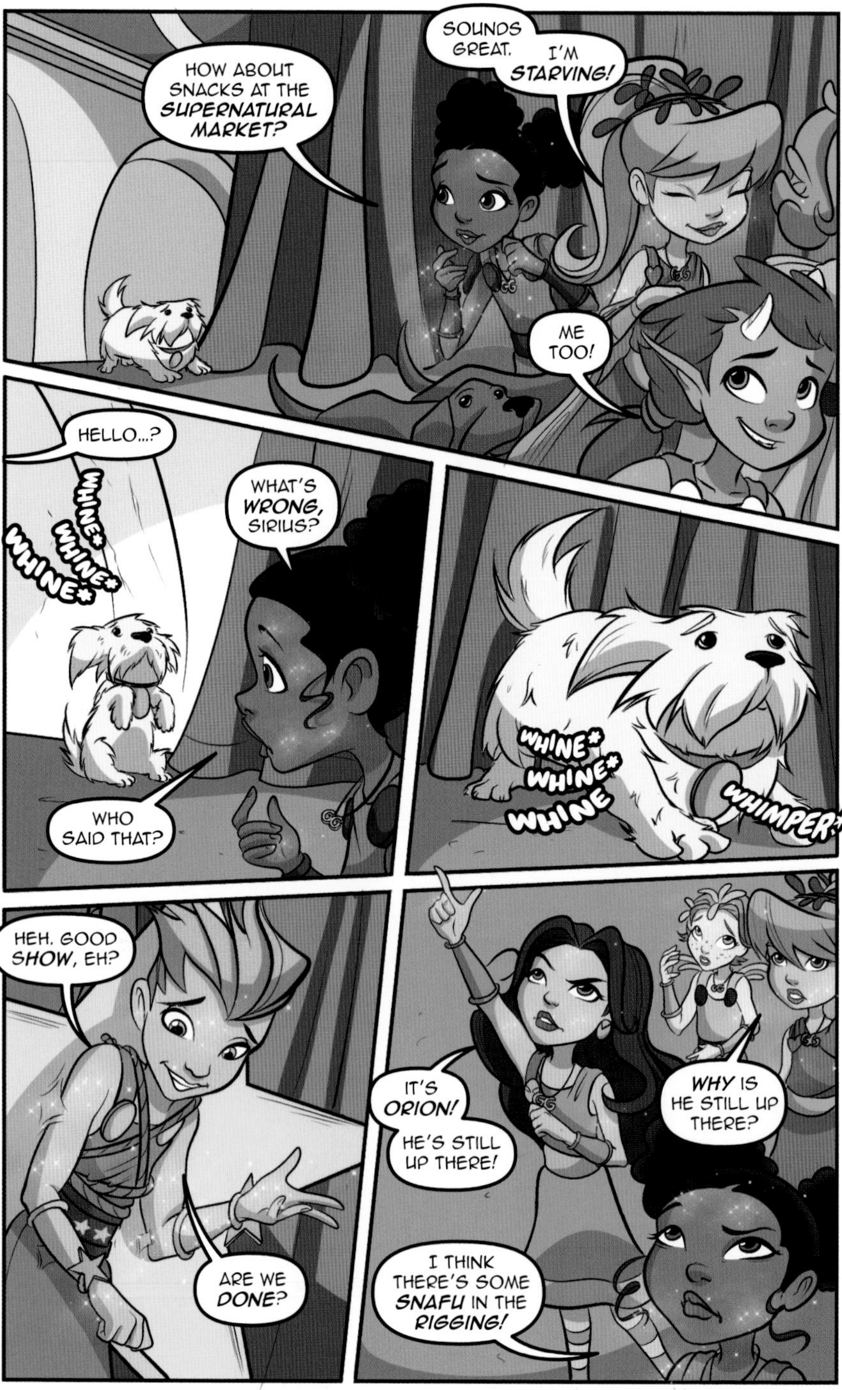
HOW ABOUT SNACKS AT THE SUPERNATURAL MARKET?
SOUNDS GREAT.
I'M STARVING!
ME TOO!
HELLO...?
WHINE* WHINE* WHINE*
WHAT'S WRONG, SIRIUS?
WHO SAID THAT?
WHINE* WHINE* WHINE
WHIMPER*
HEH. GOOD SHOW, EH?
ARE WE DONE?
IT'S ORION!
HE'S STILL UP THERE!
WHY IS HE STILL UP THERE?
I THINK THERE'S SOME SNAFU IN THE RIGGING!

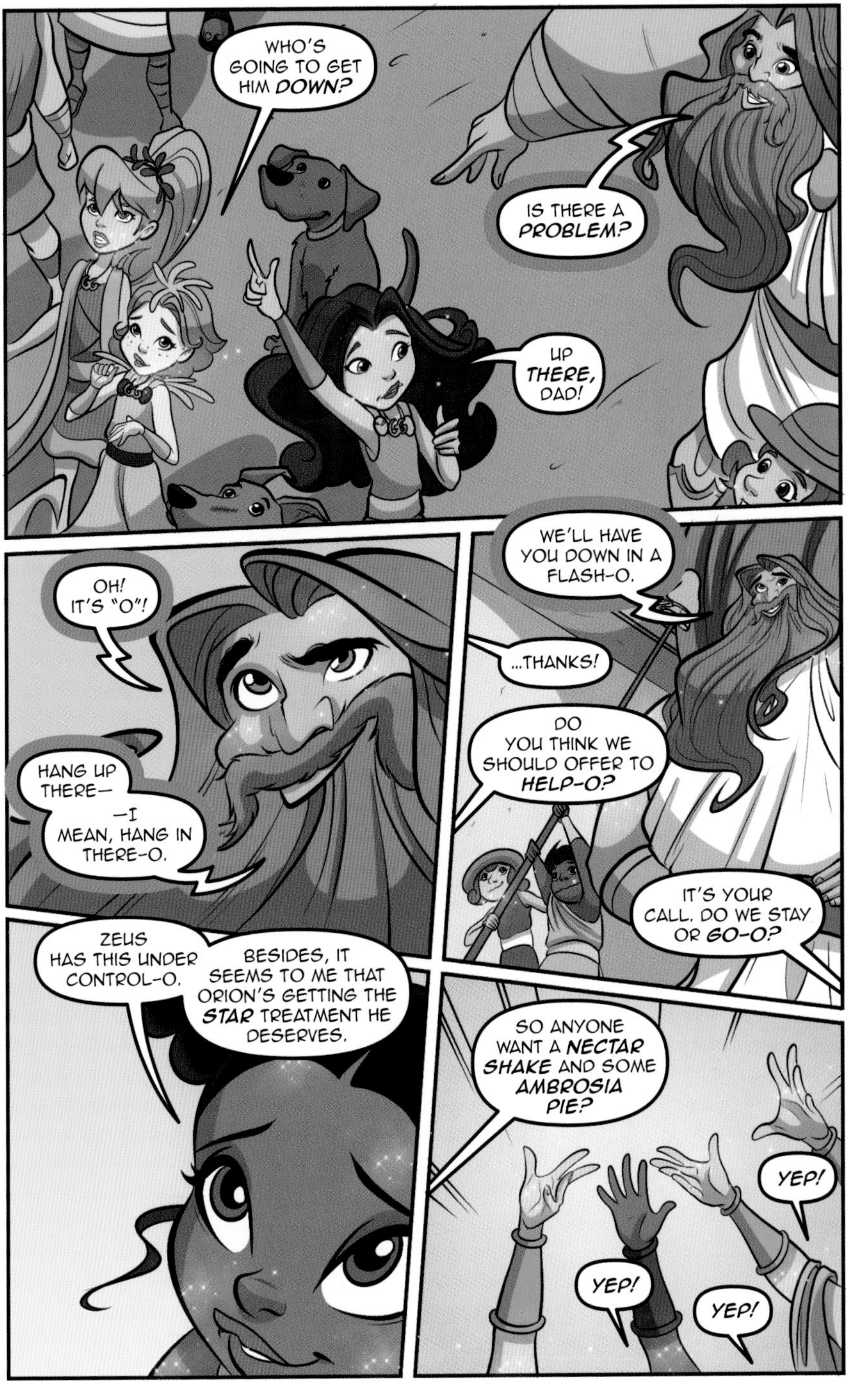
WHO'S GOING TO GET HIM *DOWN?*
IS THERE A *PROBLEM?*
UP *THERE,* DAD!
OH! IT'S "O"!
HANG UP THERE—
—I MEAN, HANG IN THERE-O.
WE'LL HAVE YOU DOWN IN A FLASH-O.
...THANKS!
DO YOU THINK WE SHOULD OFFER TO *HELP-O?*
IT'S YOUR CALL. DO WE STAY OR *GO-O?*
ZEUS HAS THIS UNDER CONTROL-O.
BESIDES, IT SEEMS TO ME THAT ORION'S GETTING THE *STAR* TREATMENT HE DESERVES.
SO ANYONE WANT A *NECTAR SHAKE* AND SOME *AMBROSIA PIE?*
YEP!
YEP!
YEP!

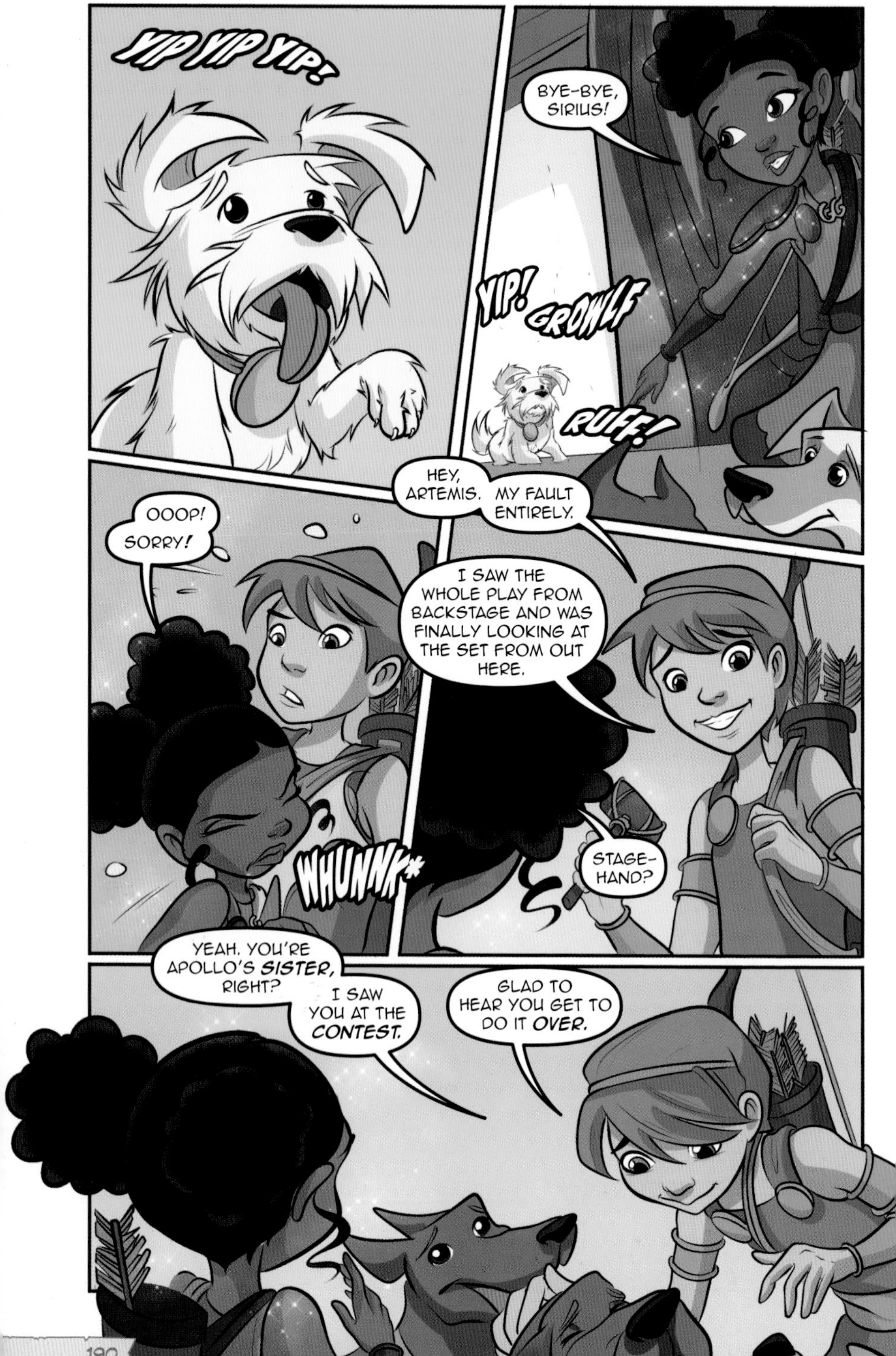
YIP YIP YIP!
BYE-BYE, SIRIUS!
YIP! GROWLF
RUFF!
HEY, ARTEMIS.
MY FAULT ENTIRELY.
OOOP! SORRY!
WHUNNK*
I SAW THE WHOLE PLAY FROM BACKSTAGE AND WAS FINALLY LOOKING AT THE SET FROM OUT HERE.
STAGE-HAND?
YEAH. YOU'RE APOLLO'S SISTER, RIGHT?
I SAW YOU AT THE CONTEST.
GLAD TO HEAR YOU GET TO DO IT OVER.

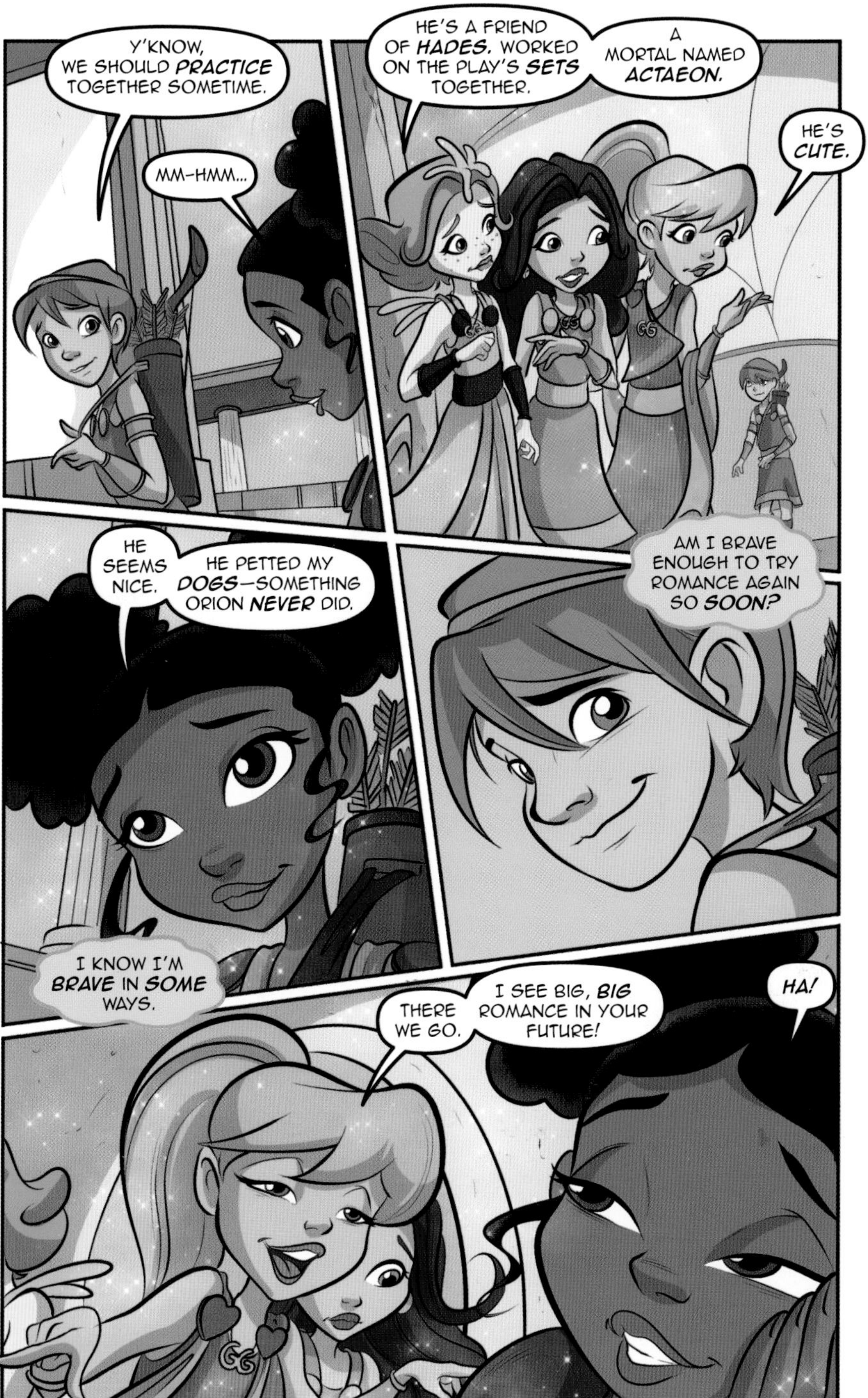
Y'KNOW, WE SHOULD PRACTICE TOGETHER SOMETIME.
MM-HMM...
HE'S A FRIEND OF HADES. WORKED ON THE PLAY'S SETS TOGETHER.
A MORTAL NAMED ACTAEON.
HE'S CUTE.
HE SEEMS NICE.
HE PETTED MY DOGS—SOMETHING ORION NEVER DID.
AM I BRAVE ENOUGH TO TRY ROMANCE AGAIN SO SOON?
I KNOW I'M BRAVE IN SOME WAYS.
THERE WE GO.
I SEE BIG, BIG ROMANCE IN YOUR FUTURE!
HA!

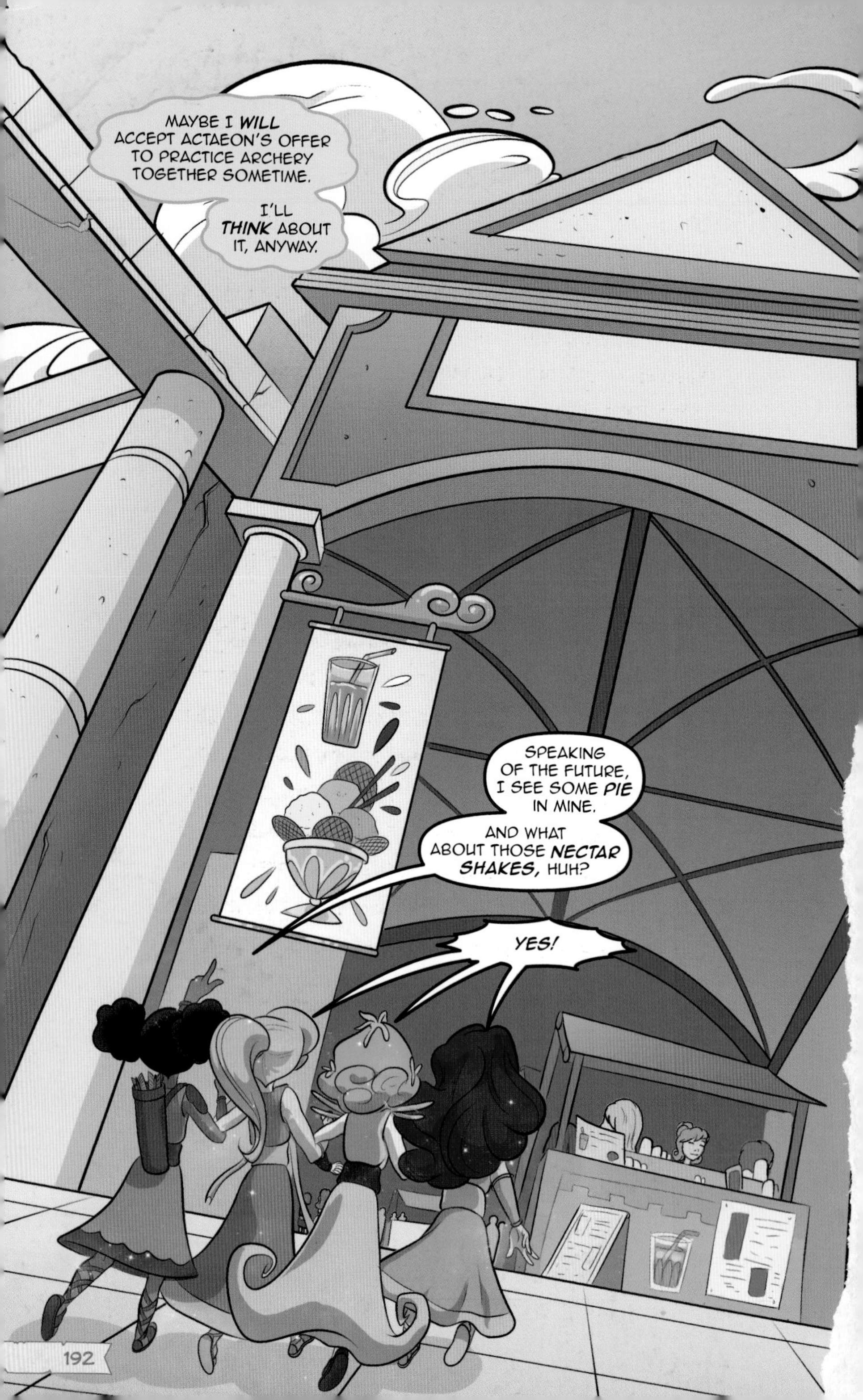
MAYBE I ***WILL*** ACCEPT ACTAEON'S OFFER TO PRACTICE ARCHERY TOGETHER SOMETIME.
I'LL ***THINK*** ABOUT IT, ANYWAY.
SPEAKING OF THE FUTURE, I SEE SOME ***PIE*** IN MINE.
AND WHAT ABOUT THOSE ***NECTAR SHAKES,*** HUH?
YES!